Books by Patricia Johns

THE BISHOP'S DAUGHTER

THURSDAY'S BRIDE

Published by Kensington Publishing Corporation

ks

STILL IN LOVE

"Do you have a stamp for your letter?" Levi asked.

"Not yet."

He pulled open a drawer. "We used to keep them here—Yah. Right here." He pulled out a sheet of stamps and tore one off.

Rosmanda stood up and crossed the kitchen. She took the stamp from his fingers, his warm fingertips brushing against hers, and she froze.

He was so close, and with that shirt open at the neck, his bronzed skin almost glowing in that low kerosene light, she found her breath caught in her throat. Levi didn't touch her, but when she looked up, she found those dark eyes locked on hers, holding her there. He smelled warm and musky, and she sucked in a wavering breath.

Levi raised his hand and touched her chin, his work-roughened thumb moving over her skin and stopping at her bottom lip. That was a gesture from years past—something that felt uncomfortably natural between them even after all these years. . . .

Thursday's Bride

PATRICIA JOHNS

ZEBRA BOOKS
KENSINGTON PUBLISHING CORP.
www.kensingtonbooks.com

To my husband, my biggest supporter.
I love you.

Chapter One

Rosmanda held the plastic bottle firmly between her palms as the brown calf drank hungrily. Milk dribbled from its chin, and it butted the bottle as it slurped back the frothy milk. The cow had delivered triplets—a bovine rarity—but one had died and the cow hadn't allowed the smaller of the surviving calves to drink from her, so it had become a bottle baby, and extra work around the Lapp family farm.

Extra work . . . there was always more to do now. But she liked the quiet out here in the barn, the smell of the hay, the bleat of the goats. It was soothing, and for just a few minutes she could let her mind wander. Afternoons like this, she half expected to hear her husband, Wayne, come into the barn and everything would be back to normal. He'd give her that serious nod of his—the one where she knew the tenderness underneath his reserve. And then she wouldn't have to worry about calves and milking anymore, because the men would take care of the men's work, and she'd head back to the house to help her mother-in-law with the cooking and cleaning, and tend to her twin baby girls. If she shut her eyes, it seemed possible . . .

But Rosmanda didn't have the time to daydream about impossibilities. Wayne was dead and with God now, and she was left here with children to raise and the obligation to help out on her father-in-law's farm.

The calf butted the bottle again as it drank, and Rosmanda was pushed backward a step.

"Hungry, are you?" Rosmanda murmured. "Come on, don't push over the one holding your milk."

The barn door opened behind her, and Rosmanda didn't even bother to turn. It would be her father-in-law, coming to get another load of hay. The calf had emptied the bottle down to foam, and she popped the nipple from its mouth and scratched it behind the ears.

"This one is almost ready for a bottle and a half every feed," Rosmanda said, turning around, but it wasn't Stephen Lapp. She froze, as her gaze landed on the tall, steely-eyed man who'd just walked into the barn, her heart hammering hard in her chest.

"Levi . . ." Her voice sounded breathy in her own ears, not the snap it should have been. "What are you doing here?"

"I'm here to help out my daet," Levi said, coming inside the barn, the door slamming behind him. He was tall, rugged, with broad shoulders and eyes that locked on to her with that intensity he gave to everything that interested him . . . It was like no time had passed, and she hated that—because too much had happened since he'd been here on his father's land.

Stephen had needed an extra man around this farm ever since Wayne died during the first snow. That hard, cold, grief-filled winter had passed with just the three of them working together to keep the farm running, and *now* her brother-in-law showed up?

"Why now?" she asked.

"Daet asked me to come."

"But you knew he was struggling before this," she said.

"You wanted to see me before now?" he countered. "Look, this is complicated. We all know that. I'd offered to come earlier, and Daet had refused. He wanted to give you more time—"

"Me?" She felt that familiar wave of dread. Her father-in-law had struggled on his own because of her? Her position here was precarious enough.

"And maybe he knew I needed a little more time, too." Levi shrugged. "Regardless, he asked me to come now. I came."

Stephen couldn't wait longer than this—with the spring thaw came calves soon enough. He'd need the extra help. And whatever their history together, Levi was their son.

"I know you blame me for what happened to Wayne," Levi said, his voice low. "But it wasn't my fault—"

"No?" she interrupted. "He'd never have been on the side of that highway if it weren't for your antics."

"You can't blame a speeding driver on me," Levi replied. "Yah, he came out to fetch me, but I never asked him to. I was happy leaving the two of you alone. So, stop blaming me for something neither of us could control. If we have to be here together, we might as well get that out of the way."

Rosmanda bit back the words that sprung to her mind—none of them kind. Levi could claim to be innocent when it came to his brother's death, but his public drunkenness had been the reason that Wayne had been called to go collect him, and Wayne *would* go. He was that kind of man—stable, reliable, compassionate. And now, dead because of those very virtues he lived by.

Rosmanda wasn't this snappish person she seemed to be in the moment, and she hated the sound of that spite in her own voice.

God, grant me courage . . . To do what? To face Levi? To forgive him? She'd grieved her husband deeply these last months, and she knew that if Levi had just acted the part of a proper Amish man, she'd still have her husband by her side. But that had been Levi's problem from the start—he was never quite proper enough. Amish men buried their hearts deep and they didn't flash it around when those hearts were broken. Levi should have done the sensible thing and married when Rosmanda chose his brother over him. But he hadn't . . . he'd turned to drinking with the Englishers instead.

As much as her husband's death was on Levi's hands, Levi's downfall just might be on hers. . . .

"So how long are you staying for?" Rosmanda asked. She silently hoped there were some obligation pulling Levi away again. A hired hand around the farm would be easier to bear.

"I'm here for good."

Rosmanda rubbed her hand down her apron and tried to control the emotion that welled up inside of her. And while she might sound angry and hardened, under that protective shell, she was broken, grieving and frightened about her future. She was living with her in-laws for the time being, raising her baby girls and trying not to think too much about what she'd do with herself a few months from now, a year from now . . . Because this arrangement couldn't last. At twenty-five, Rosmanda was young enough to remarry, and her in-laws weren't wealthy enough to allow her to put that off for long. A man would have to take Rosmanda off their hands and provide for her daughters, whether Rosmanda was ready for a new marriage or not. It was simply how things worked.

"You're here for good—" Rosmanda licked her lips and glanced up into Levi's rugged face. If he was staying, did that mean that her in-laws had other plans for her, marriage-wise?

"If I could have just given you some space, I would have," Levi said. "But you've done enough to help out. Your kinner need you, Rosie."

At the mention of her babies, unbidden tears rose up in her eyes. Rosmanda blinked them back.

"Don't call me Rosie," she said, her voice catching. It had been four years since they'd been close enough for nicknames and endearments.

"Sorry. An old habit." Levi scuffed his boot against the cement floor of the barn. "You have nothing to worry about from me. I'm here to help my daet, and that's it."

"Fine. That's clear enough." Rosmanda looked toward the outside door. "If you're taking over here, then I should get back to the house."

"Rosie—" He stopped, pressed his lips together. "Rosmanda," he corrected himself. "I didn't ask anyone to call Wayne that night. I promise you that."

"That's the thing, though," Rosmanda said, suddenly feeling very tired. "You didn't have to. Everyone knew who you belonged to, and Wayne wouldn't have left you outside some bar to sober up. Of course he'd come. You should have known he would."

"So you still blame me," he said woodenly.

"Who else?" Rosmanda shook her head. "We were woken up by the Englisher neighbor at midnight when someone called to fetch you. What was he supposed to do, tell the neighbor thanks for dragging himself out of bed, but Wayne would rather sleep? You were his brother, and of course he'd come for you. All of that ruckus was your fault."

"I didn't ask them to call him!" Levi said, but his voice sounded choked, his earlier calm cracking. "I told them to let me be."

"Abundance has laws against people sleeping in the streets, and you know it," she said. "And why are we even arguing about this? What's done is done."

Levi's face was ashen in the low light of the barn. He pulled his hat off and raked a hand through his sandy blond hair.

"So that's it, then?" Levi said. "I'm supposed to take responsibility for Wayne's death, and we don't get to talk about where Wayne went wrong?"

"Wayne was a good man—" she started.

"He wasn't perfect!" Levi interrupted. "I was his brother, and he moved in and married the girl I'd loved! Everyone talks about how good Wayne was, what a hard worker, how devoted to the faith. But he had no problem betraying me, did he? Isn't there a Bible verse saying you know what kind of person someone is by the fruit they produce? He kept up appearances. That's all I can say about my brother."

"*I* chose!" Rosmanda snapped, her voice echoing in the barn around her. "You didn't quibble over me like some last piece of corn bread! I had a choice between the two of you, and I made it. Don't make this into some brotherly honor system—like you could call dibs on a woman the way you could on a horse. I knew what I needed in life, Levi, and I made my choice!"

Levi fell silent, then nodded. "You did."

And she'd made the right choice. A marriage wasn't about sweet words or a hammering heart. It wasn't about those delicate feelings that couldn't last for the decade upon decade that piled up in a long marriage. It was about an agreement between two people to stand together no matter what, to work side by side and to raise a family. If a woman married a man she could respect, she'd done well. If a man married a woman who was hardworking, he'd be successful.

A fragile emotional connection couldn't last. She'd learned that the hardest way possible back in Morinville when she was at the heart of the biggest scandal to rock that town. Rosmanda wasn't the kind of fool who needed to learn a painful lesson twice.

Levi was back, and Rosmanda would have to deal with him whether she liked it or not. But working together on the Lapp farm didn't change the fact that she was widowed because of Levi's rebellious incompetence. And while she might shut her mouth for the sake of family harmony, she wouldn't forget.

Wayne deserved better than that.

Levi stood back as Rosmanda brushed past him and headed for the barn door. Her long dark hair was rolled up behind her white prayer kapp, a single tendril loose down her neck. She was even thinner than when he last saw her across the barn at one of the rare Sunday services he'd attended before Wayne's death. Amish women tended to stay slim because of their active lifestyle, but after giving birth to the twins, Rosmanda had been pleasantly plump. Levi had liked it—it softened her a little more. But the last few months had taken a toll on her. She was obviously grieving for Wayne deeply, and he wondered how much she was eating.

As if that was even his business. His problem had always been that he'd kept caring, even after he was supposed to step back, but Rosmanda wasn't a woman so easily put aside.

"Rosmanda," he said, his raised voice echoing. She turned back as she reached the door, dark eyes locking on him. Her apron was streaked with dust, and a piece of straw clung to the skirt of her dress.

"What?" She tugged her shawl a little closer around her shoulders.

"Are you okay?" he asked.

"You ask that now?" she demanded. "The last I saw you was at the funeral."

"You had my parents," he countered, but that was a weak argument. "And you blamed me for the accident."

Rosmanda sighed. "I thought I'd be married to Wayne for the rest of my life. And now he's gone. Even the babies miss him—"

"I miss him, too," Levi said, his throat tightening.

"If you missed him you should have done more to keep a relationship with him after our wedding," she said.

"I don't know what he told you—"

"He told me he missed his little brother! He told me that you two used to be close, and he wished you'd just put this silly mess behind you."

"And *you* wanted to see more of me?" he asked with a low laugh. "Really?"

Pink colored her cheeks, and he knew he'd hit on something there. "Whatever was between us was over,

Levi. We were a family, and we should have been able to act like one."

"Like we are now—" Levi spread his hands. "This wonderfully functional family relationship we have going at the moment—"

Rosmanda turned toward the door again, refusing to be goaded. "I'll see you inside for supper."

She pushed outside and the door banged shut behind her, leaving Levi in relative silence. Conversation over, apparently. She'd been his brother's wife, and he'd struggled to see her as only a sister-in-law after that wedding. He knew what it felt like to hold her in his arms, to kiss her, to brush her hair away from her forehead when it came loose from her kapp. . . . He knew how her eyes could sparkle when his lips hovered over hers. And then he had to watch his overly serious brother sit next to her on that buggy seat, reserved and distant. Wayne hadn't loved her like Levi had, but he'd won her anyway.

Levi grabbed a pitchfork and headed for one of the calves' stalls. He'd agreed to come home and help out his daet because they needed him, but this hadn't been his idea. This farm didn't feel like his home anymore—especially after Wayne married Rosmanda and they moved into Levi and Wayne's old bedroom. Amish newlyweds normally moved in with the bride's family, but hers was in another state. He'd done the gracious thing and found a job on another farm. He'd paid for room and board there and stayed clear of his parents' house.

While he had accepted that Wayne had married Rosmanda, he couldn't bring himself to sit around a table with them and wish them any happiness. That would have been the Amish ideal, of course, that brothers could set aside some courting differences and pull together to make a lively, loving extended family that would support the couple as they started their marriage. The Amish life was about community, and in order to maintain a close and effective community, small irritations had to be set aside for the greater good. His daet had expected that of him. Wayne had, too. But Levi wasn't a man who faked the ideals. His brother had betrayed him on a deeper level than anyone else seemed to realize, and Levi hadn't been inclined to forgive him, especially since Wayne didn't seem to think he needed it. Wayne had won—he'd married Rosmanda. Wayne could enjoy his victory, but he couldn't make Levi stand there and watch it, either.

But now Wayne was dead, and Levi had come home. He might defend himself when it came to that buggy accident, but he couldn't help the guilt that plagued him, either. Hard work was normally good medicine for the soul, but today it didn't seem to be helping. Levi had known it would be hard to come home again, but he didn't have much choice. Daet needed help, and Levi was the last son who didn't have a farm and family of his own to take care of. The responsibility was his.

Levi cleaned out the remaining stalls and went to the barn sink to wash up. He pushed open the barn door and headed out in the warm afternoon sunlight. He'd spent the day working with his daet, and he'd avoided going in for lunch because he hadn't been ready to face her yet, but he couldn't do that again. He wouldn't just shrink into a corner. If she didn't like having him around, then maybe she should be the one to avoid him.

As Levi walked away from the barn and toward the house, he left clean stalls behind him, and calves all fed and napping together in one corner. A job well done. Say what they would about his reputation, his drinking, and his un-Amish ways, but he was a good farmer. And he'd been doing his best these last few months to put his life back together again. He'd stopped the drinking, and he'd started attending some Englisher AA meetings in town to help him stay off the booze. He'd been able to attend those weekly meetings with no one noticing when he was working another man's farm, but it would be more difficult here at home with his parents watching him. If he wanted to keep it private, that was. It would also be more difficult to find alcohol, though. God worked in mysterious ways.

Horses grazed in the tender new growth of the west field, and as his eyes ran over the various animals, he spotted a large quarter horse he hadn't noticed before. It was a huge stallion, with a glossy coat and muscles that rippled as it took a slow step forward toward a lush patch of grass. None of the other horses, even the quarter horses, came anywhere near to this brute's size, and Levi headed for the fence, eyeing the animal in silent approval.

Footsteps crunched behind him on the gravel, and he turned to see his daet approaching.

"Supper's waiting," Daet said, coming up beside him.

"That horse," Levi said, not to be diverted. "It's new?"

"New enough," Daet replied. "I bought it last summer. That animal is one beautiful waste of horseflesh."

"A waste? That brute could pull a wagon by himself!" Levi retorted. "He'd even be worth something for breeding . . ."

"If he were trainable," Daet said with a shake of his head. "He's huge and strong, and too bullheaded to break. Your brother tried for months."

"Hmm." Levi eyed the horse for a few moments longer. "Did *you* try?"

"I didn't bother," Daet replied. "You know how good your brother was with the horses. If he couldn't do it—"

"I want to try," Levi said.

Daet pushed his thumbs into the front of his pants and turned. Levi followed, matching his father's pace as they headed back toward the house.

"You?" Daet chuckled and shook his head. "Son, that's one beautiful horse, but the minute anyone comes near it, it goes crazy. It was a complete waste of money. Wayne bought him on a whim from Jacob Eicher just west of here. Jacob said he'd tried and failed to break that horse, and Wayne took it as a challenge. We bought him for almost nothing."

"I want to try," Levi repeated. "I can break him."

"I highly doubt it," Daet said simply. "Don't waste your time. I'll sell him soon enough. He might go for horse-meat, but I'll get some money back."

Levi didn't like the thought of that beautiful creature being destroyed, but he let the subject drop as they headed up the side stairs and took turns kicking the mud off their boots on the boot brush. Then they pushed open the side door and the smell of cooking food met them. His mother's cooking—he'd missed this. No one cooked quite so well as Miriam Lapp did.

The sound of the women's voices filtered out from the kitchen, and Levi glanced toward his father to see him staring at him.

"What's wrong, Daet?" he asked.

"I'm glad you're back, Son," Daet said. "I never liked how things brewed between you and your brother. This was always your home, too, you know."

"There wasn't room for the both of us, Daet."

"There always was."

Mamm and Daet probably didn't know the worst of it between Wayne and Levi. Still, Levi didn't want to talk about it, especially not with the reason for all their conflict standing out there in the kitchen.

"Rosmanda's not so keen to see me," he said, keeping his voice low.

"She'll be fine." The words were sharper than Levi found entirely reassuring.

"She blames me, you know."

His father sighed and looked away.

"You'll have to mend your ways," his daet said at last. "There is a community to consider in every choice you make. It isn't about one man's feelings. It's about holding a community together and doing what you must. Wayne knew that."

His father turned and stepped into the kitchen, leaving Levi alone in the chill of the mudroom. Wayne had known how to protect appearances to the very last. It seemed that even here, his parents thought Wayne had been the injured party in that mess with Rosmanda, and that stung. Because Wayne had convinced Rosmanda to marry him, that let him off the hook? But some men got a reputation that became almost impossible to shed, like Levi had managed. Nothing he did would fix it. He was a drunkard, a ne'er-do-well. He could be counted on for a good time, but not much more than that. Like that horse out there in the field that stood two hand spans taller than any other. That stallion had backed himself into a corner at some point, too.

Levi hung his jacket on a peg and headed into the warmth of the kitchen.

He'd break that horse. Just because his brother had failed at the task didn't make it impossible. Besides, it might give him some welcome distraction when he was finished with his work for the day. Because he sure wouldn't be rushing back to the house for some quality time with his sister-in-law. She made him feel things he didn't want to dredge up again.

Chapter Two

Rosmanda eyed the window as dinnertime approached. The men would come in soon enough, and her stomach felt queasy with worry. Of course, the Lapps wanted a relationship with their youngest son. And of course, they'd want him home to help with the farm. She understood it all quite clearly, but it changed her situation here. She was the widow, the one who couldn't forgive the son they had left. Obviously, his parents had forgiven him, since he was here. And they'd expect her to marry and move on. This winter's comfortable arrangement that allowed her to grieve was over.

Dinner that night was pork roast, potatoes, canned carrots from the year before, and an apple crumble for dessert. Rosmanda worked in silence to get the meal on the table.

"Rosmanda, grab these rolls, would you?" Miriam said, handing a wicker basket over the counter. Rosmanda took it with a tight smile.

"Are you all right?" Miriam asked.

"Yah. Of course." Rosmanda put the rolls next to a large bowl of mashed potatoes just as the side door opened. She could hear the men's boots on the floor in the mudroom, their voices in low conversation, and then Stephen stepped through the door into the kitchen in sock feet.

"It smells good," he said, and glanced over his shoulder. Levi came in behind him. Levi glanced over at Rosmanda, catching her gaze for a moment. He looked away, and hesitated at the table, his hand on the back of a chair.

"Yes—your seat," Stephen said. "It's always been yours."

Actually, that seat had been Rosmanda's, at least after she moved into the house with her husband. She licked her lips. She'd be sitting in Wayne's seat, then. Maybe it was better that way—she'd rather sit there than have Levi in her late husband's chair. That would feel worse. Without a word, she pulled the wooden high chairs to the other side of the table, next to her new seat, and then went to collect her daughters, who were playing with a rattle and a rag doll on the floor beside the staircase.

"Come along, Susanna," she murmured, scooping up the first baby. She tied her into the high chair, and Hannah set up a wail from the floor until Rosmanda went back for her, kissing her chubby cheek and settling her into the other high chair.

It was an awkward meal—different from meals past with her mother- and father-in-law. Stephen talked with Levi about calving, and Miriam interjected here and there to pass her son more food. They had their son with them now, and she could feel those allegiances changing. They had another son to feed, to guide, to dote on. It was all right and good—Rosmanda knew it. She was a mamm herself and could sympathize with how they felt, but it didn't change her own feelings. When she'd sat in front of her food long enough and the babies had eaten their tiny amount of solid food and played with the rest, Rosmanda brought the babies back to their rag rug to play. Then she started filling the sink to wash dishes.

"Rosmanda, come sit," her father-in-law said. "You haven't had your crumble yet."

"I'm just starting the washing up, Daet," she said. "I'm fine. But thank you."

She turned her back on the table, then closed her eyes and exhaled a shaky sigh. From the rug, Hannah and Susanna leaned over to knock the blocks against the hardwood floor where the rug ended and squealed at the sound. Rosmanda loved her girls with all her heart, but she was bone tired tonight.

Why couldn't Levi have stayed away just a little bit longer?

There was good reason why Rosmanda had chosen the stoic Wayne over his brother Levi. She'd only come out to Abundance to stay with her aunt Dina because she'd ruined her chance at a marriage back home in Indiana. Coming to Abundance had been with the shameless goal of finding a husband at the age of twenty-three when she was already considered an old maid and no man in Morinville would have her.

When she was a stupid sixteen-year-old girl, she listened to the sweet words of an engaged young man. Jonathan Yoder had told her everything she wanted to hear, and she'd believed him. He'd even called off his engagement for her, and she'd thought that she'd won a battle and gained her man. Unfortunately, Jonathan, who swore his fiancée felt like a sister to him, had also gotten his fiancée pregnant, so he got married anyway. It seemed like it would all go away, but word got out about Rosmanda's attempt to thwart that wedding, and it flew around Morinville. Rosmanda's image was tarnished beyond repair. Any chance at a marriage had evaporated, and it was her own foolish fault.

So Rosmanda came here to Abundance to stay with her elderly aunt Dina in one last effort to get married. Levi had been the first man she'd met here in Abundance. He was just like Jonathan in one major way—he made her heart flutter and could raise a blush in her cheeks with only a look. It was easy to fall for a man who made her feel that way, but the last time she'd listened to honeyed words from a dangerous rebel, she'd ended up labeled a hussy, and she wasn't making that mistake with her fresh start in Pennsylvania. And Levi was definitely a rebel. He wore his hat askew, looked her in the eye, and grinned as brazenly as any Englisher. Even as a newcomer, she'd heard the stories of Levi's Rumspringa. When Levi's older brother, Wayne, took her aside and suggested that she marry him instead, she was shocked, but her aunt was the one to calm her down. "Wayne is a good man. He's not bad-looking, either, is he? Tall and strong. But he's also serious, where Levi isn't. He's the man you need to repair your reputation, Rosmanda. He's the better choice." So she'd listened to reason, and she'd chosen the more reasonable husband. And she didn't regret that choice, even now.

"Go take care of the babies, dear," Miriam said, putting a stack of plates on the counter beside her. Rosmanda startled out of her reverie and cast the older woman a wan smile.

"Thank you." She pulled her hands from the soapy water and dried them on a towel. It was an escape, and she was grateful for it.

She went to the carpet where the babies were playing and bent down next to them.

"Come along, girls. Time for bed." She always tried to make that sound like a wonderful experience, but it seldom was. With two babies who wanted holding and cuddles, two babies who needed to be fed and put down to sleep, it was Rosmanda's last, exhausting task for the night. Back when Wayne had been alive, he'd always been part of it—cuddling each of his daughters before he passed them over to Rosmanda to be fed and put into their cribs. Without Wayne, the girls refused to be mollified, as if the sheer strength of their grief could call their father back. They seemed to remember him, still. They hadn't forgotten.

At the kitchen table, Levi's and Stephen's voices rumbled low. Rosmanda watched them for a moment, noting the similarity in their features. Levi leaned forward, planting his elbows on the table.

"I can do it," Levi said.

"I don't think you can, and I'm tired of wasting time on it," Stephen replied. "I need you for other things."

"I'll do it after chores." Levi leaned back in his chair, but that granite gaze stayed locked on his father's face.

"Will you, now? And how long will that take? Your competition with your brother—"

"This has nothing to do with that!"

"It has everything to do with it. Wayne was gifted when it came to horse training, and you know it. If you were being rational, you'd see that that horse isn't trainable. Accept it. I didn't ask you to come here to be some hero. I asked you come help me run a farm."

"If it's on my free time, I don't see how you can object to it." Levi pushed himself to his feet.

"Levi, eat your crumble," Miriam said.

"I'm full, Mamm."

Levi headed for the mudroom, and Rosmanda picked up her daughters, one in each arm. It wasn't her business, this battle of wills between father and son.

"Did you have fun with the blocks, yah?" She looked down into her babies' chubby faces, attempting to ignore her father-in-law's irritated finger tapping. That was the men's world, and this was hers—motherhood.

Her daughters were identical, except to Rosmanda. She could tell them apart easily enough. Susanna had a sparkier personality, and she'd get angry faster when things didn't go her way. If there was a baby to feed first, it was Susanna. But Hannah was cuddlier, and she'd nestle into Rosmanda's arms and stay there all day if Rosmanda let her.

Rosmanda accepted two bottles of milk from her mother-in-law, and carried both her babies and the bottles up the stairs to her bedroom. She kicked shut the bedroom door and let out a long sigh. Downstairs, she could make out the soft murmur of her in-laws' voices, and then the bang as the side door shut. She went to the window and looked down to see Levi marching across the grass toward the horse barn. Levi might be back, but all wasn't smooth, apparently.

Rosmanda put her daughters into the middle of the bed. She reached for their nightgowns and fresh cloth diapers. They'd both need a change and a bottle before bed, but this was the start of the process. She missed Wayne most when she was trying to put the girls to bed. He'd had a touch, it seemed. They'd snuggle up on his warm, broad chest and fall right to sleep. With her, it was a bit more of a battle, as if they thought their father was still there somewhere, just refusing to come.

Rosmanda's sister, Sadie, had lost a husband, too. Rosmanda had only been about twelve at the time, and she'd seen her sister cry, sniffling into a handkerchief when she thought she was alone. She'd seen Sadie stare mournfully out of windows, and Rosmanda had understood on a surface level that her sister was sad because her husband had died. How little she'd comprehended the depth of that loss. Losing a husband was like losing a limb. A woman had to learn how to function without him, find ways to support herself without that reassuring presence. She faced the looks of pity the other married women cast her way at church or in town, but they all went home with their husbands at the end of the day.

Rosmanda fed the girls their bottles, snuggled them, rocked them, and sang them the songs she and Wayne used to hum as they put their daughters to sleep, but the girls wouldn't sleep, and every time she lay them in their cribs and tried to leave the room, their wails would start anew. They didn't cry the entire time, but the more tired they got, the closer they came to their final wailing crescendo before they'd slide into exhausted slumber.

Rosmanda kept her bedroom door firmly shut, but even through the barrier, she heard when her mother- and father-in-law went up to bed. They'd be up long before dawn and they needed to rest, yet with crying infants in the next room, Rosmanda had to wonder if they ever regretted their invitation for her to stay after Wayne's death.

No one would sleep until the babies cried themselves out, and Rosmanda paced the bedroom, both babies in her aching arms.

There was a tap on her door. It would be her mother-in-law offering to help as she always did at this point of the evening. The cleanup and preparation for morning would be done downstairs—Miriam having finished it all alone. Rosmanda wanted to be less of a bother to Miriam and Stephen, but the extra help couldn't be refused. Hannah laid her downy head down on Rosmanda's shoulder, breathing in great, shuddering breaths, and Susanna wailed on.

"Come in," Rosmanda said, raising her voice over the baby's cries, and when the door slowly opened, she saw Levi's face in the doorway.

"Levi?" She hadn't heard him come back into the house.

"You okay?" he said.

That was the second time he'd asked her that today, and she was tempted to reply with something curt, but she was exhausted, as were her daughters.

"Not really," she replied, and she felt the tears of frustration rising inside of her.

"Can I help?" he asked.

"Take one!" she said helplessly, and Levi stared at her, wide-eyed, then down at the babies. He put out two hands as if he were catching a greased piglet and plucked the howling Susanna from Rosmanda's arms.

And suddenly, there was silence. Levi awkwardly adjusted the baby up onto his shoulder, and Susanna laid her head down on his shoulder, letting out a shaky sigh.

Miriam came in wearing her nightgown with her graying hair hanging over one shoulder in a long braid. She looked between them, her eyebrows raised.

"I came to see if I could help with the babies," Miriam said. "But it looks like Levi got here first. My goodness . . . Susanna seems to have taken to him, hasn't she?"

"It seems so," Rosmanda said, her throat thickening with emotion.

"It normally takes the two of us a good twenty minutes at this point," Miriam said. "Let me take her, son—"

Yes—that was better. Even if Levi seemed to have the right touch tonight, she'd rather rock her daughters with Miriam as she had every other night. Having Levi here was difficult enough without having him be the answer to her daughter's cries. That was too much.

Miriam put her hands out to take the baby and Levi stood there, looking down at Susanna in his arms, but he didn't hand the baby over and escape as Rosmanda expected him to do. Susanna dropped her tearstained face against his shirt just like she used to do with Wayne, and it gave Rosmanda's heart a squeeze.

Did Susanna think this was her daet, back at long last? There was something very like Wayne in Levi. Their voices were similar. They were both tall and broad. Was that the comfort for Susanna right now—the similarity between her uncle and her father?

"No," Levi said slowly. "I've got this."

Miriam retreated a few steps. "Are you sure?"

Rosmanda sent her mother-in-law a pleading look, but Miriam didn't seem to notice. Her gaze was on her son.

"Yah." Levi nodded. "Go to bed, Mamm. Get some rest. I can do this."

Miriam disappeared from the doorway and for a few beats Rosmanda and Levi stood there in welcome silence, the only sound that of the softly creaking floorboards as Rosmanda swung her weight from side to side as she tried to settle her baby. Her heart pounded in her chest. This wasn't the plan—to have Levi here in her bedroom, or to have him be a help to her at all. But Miriam's bedroom door shut with a decisive click, and Rosmanda felt a fresh wave of misgiving. So much was changing with Levi's return already.

"Your brother used to rock them before bed," Rosmanda said hesitantly. "I think that's what they want. . . ."

"Then let's take them down to the kitchen," Levi said.

For propriety. Of course. She wouldn't exactly invite her brother-in-law into her bedroom, but she would accept his help. For one night only.

She had no other choice.

Levi followed Rosmanda down the narrow staircase to the lantern-lit kitchen, the baby in his arms. He moved slowly, carefully, unsure if he should have just handed his niece over to his mamm, after all. What was he thinking? Except that something had softened inside of him when the baby's cries had gone silent in his arms. He felt— useful. For the moment, the baby seemed to settle into his arms, leaning her plump cheek against his chest.

My niece . . . The realization warmed his heart. He'd seen the babies a couple of times after they were born, but he'd never held them. He'd been doing his best to stay away from Wayne and Rosmanda. They'd been married and happy, and he'd had his own emotional survival to worry about.

"Your brother used to rock them before bed," Rosmanda repeated. "Every night."

She looked down at the infant in her arms as she rocked back and forth, her expression soft. Motherhood had changed Rosmanda. She wasn't the same flirtatious woman he'd first been attracted to. She'd deepened, some- how, maybe even relaxed a little bit.

"Which one do I have?" Levi asked.

"You're holding Susanna," Rosmanda said.

"Yah, right. Mamm said that, right? How do you know?" The babies were in identical white flannel nightgowns.

"A mother always knows," Rosmanda said, looking up skeptically. She eyed him for a moment, and when she seemed satisfied that he wasn't joking with her, she added, "They have very different personalities, and right now, Susanna is just a little bit bigger."

The baby started to whimper again, and Levi tried to imitate the rocking motion that Rosmanda was using. It didn't seem to be helping.

"She's cold," Rosmanda said, and she went to the counter and picked up a folded baby blanket and shook it open before handing it to him. Levi shifted Susanna to one arm latching onto her plump little leg and accepting the blanket with the other. He stood there for a moment, confused.

"Here—" Rosmanda tossed the blanket over the baby with one hand, and he adjusted his grip so that Susanna was covered. She'd made that look easy.

"Thanks," he said as the baby settled again, her whimpers subsiding.

He didn't know why he'd been so bold as to knock on her door tonight. If it weren't for the babies' cries echoing through the house, he would have left her alone and taken himself to bed a few minutes after his parents did the same. And he would have laid there in his bed, ever so aware of the woman in the bedroom across the hall.

Levi was still attracted to her. He couldn't help that. It was a physical reaction that he'd have to get under control, because while Rosmanda might have thought they'd just shared a few kisses when she first arrived in town, he'd opened up. He'd shown her his heart, his fears, his insecurities. He'd been more open and real with her than he'd been with any other human being in his lifetime besides his own mother. Rosmanda had taken a good look at him in all his exposed glory, and chosen his brother instead. Attraction meant nothing in the face of that rejection.

"You wish my mamm were helping you right now," Levi said. He hadn't missed the pleading looks she'd cast in his mother's direction.

Rosmanda pressed her lips together into a thin line. "It's women's work."

"Wayne did it. Are you saying men aren't involved in raising the kinner? That's ridiculous."

"He was their daet. You aren't."

"I'm not pretending to be anything I'm not," he said irritably. "I'm their uncle, and I'm home now. And you're a part of this household. That's all this is."

And for all their mutual resentment, he did seem to be doing something right with the baby, because her eyes were drooping shut.

"I'd prefer it if next time you let your mamm help me," she said.

"Then I will. But, we're family, Rosmanda," he said. "Maybe it would have been easier for us both if you'd fallen for some guy who wasn't my brother, but that's in the past. And you're now my sister-in-law. We're bound together for the rest of our lives. Like it or not."

He absently patted Susanna's diaper, and when he looked down at her, he found the baby sleeping. Did he dare move, would that wake her up?

"If no one ever knew of our history, it would be better," she said softly.

"You didn't do anything wrong," he countered. "What

we felt for each other was honest. And we didn't cross any lines."

Technically, at least.

Rosmanda's cheeks flushed, and she shot him an annoyed look. "I have a reputation to think of, Levi. And if you want me to stop being a burden on your parents, I'll need another husband. So bear that in mind. I won't be here forever, if I can remarry."

"A husband . . ." He tried to keep the bite from his voice.

"A good man, responsible, respectable. Someone who will be kind to my girls and . . . kind to me."

"You know the community will suggest me, right?" he said. She froze, and he shot her a teasing smile. "I didn't say I was suggesting it."

"I'll need a husband," she said firmly. "So don't say anything that will jeopardize that."

In other words, pretty much anyone would do, as long as they weren't him. Levi nodded slowly, looking away from her. He'd known all along that he wasn't enough for her, but it stung to hear that she could put in an order for a husband as short and sweet as the list she'd just made, and he still wouldn't make the cut in her eyes.

"I have to be careful," Rosmanda went on. "You know how it is, Levi. If I were to appear cheap in any way—"

"You aren't cheap, Rosmanda. I can't imagine any man would think so."

In fact, Rosmanda was a hard woman to impress. She was beautiful, smart, sweet, and in the long run, she didn't fall for honeyed words and a cheeky grin. She had expectations that left common Amish men like Levi in the dust.

"It's easier than you think to give people the wrong

idea," she countered. "And that's a lesson I'll be teaching my daughters as soon as they're old enough to understand."

"All right." He wasn't sure how to answer that. The raising of her daughters wasn't his business—not directly at least. "So . . . are you asking me to look around for a husband for you?" He could hear the choked sound in his own voice. Because if that's what she wanted . . .

"No—" Rosmanda stepped back into his line of sight, forcing him to look at her. "I'm not ready to remarry again just yet. I don't *want* to remarry again. But we both know the situation I'm in right now, don't we? Your parents can't afford to keep me forever. It comes down to money, Levi!"

"Money. We're Amish, and we don't prioritize such things," he snapped.

"My father's a bishop. I know that better than anyone, but we do recognize the need for it," she countered. "I need a job, Levi. I'll take care of finding a husband on my own when I'm absolutely forced to. But a job—if I could find a way to make some income . . ."

"So you want me to help you find a job," he said uncertainly.

"Please. As my brother-in-law, and for your parents' sakes. They'd never ask it of me, but you know it wouldn't be refused."

Levi's mind spun. He wasn't good with emotions, but if all Rosmanda wanted was help finding some source of income, that shouldn't be too difficult. Amish women were involved in roadside stands, crafts, quilting . . . An idea snapped into his mind, and he turned his drilling gaze toward Rosmanda.

"What?" she said.

"What about my aunt Ketura? She's been making quilts

and selling them in town. Maybe she'd let you work with her. It seems flexible—just sewing."

A slow smile spread over Rosmanda's face, brightening her appearance. She met his gaze and nodded. "It's perfect. Do you think she'd be willing?"

"I could ask." Aunt Ketura had always had a soft spot for Levi. She'd liked his quick jokes—one of the few people who didn't look at him disapprovingly for his sense of humor.

"It would put off me being forced into some marriage," Rosmanda said, licking her lips. "I'm not ready, Levi. I know I'll need to, but the thought of . . ." She swallowed. "It might give me some time to adjust to the idea, is all. And I could contribute a little money to the family."

Levi could sympathize with that. To go from one husband's house to another—that wouldn't be easy. She'd need to make her choice carefully from the men who courted her. If history was any teacher, then Rosmanda would choose a solemn farmer with a strong reputation around the community. There were worse lives to live.

"I'll talk with my aunt," he conceded.

"Thank you." Both babies were asleep now, and Rosmanda looked toward the stairs. "Would you mind helping me bring the babies up to their cribs?"

Levi glanced back toward the lantern. He'd have to come back for it.

"Yah," he agreed. "Let's get them to bed."

Rosmanda went up the stairs first, and Levi followed. He knew the feel of the stairs by heart, having gone up and down them in the dark countless times during his years growing up here. He even knew which boards creaked, and which didn't. He followed Rosmanda's swaying skirt, and when they got to the top of the stairs, he followed her into her bedroom.

He paused at the door, smelling the soft scent of her soap that lingered in this room. He tiptoed around her bed as she lay Hannah in the crib farthest away, bending over her child for a moment as she did so. He moved to the nearest crib and lay the slumbering baby inside. Susanna moaned, and reached out one chubby arm toward him. Rosmanda's hand brushed past his arm, and she tugged the blanket up over Susanna's shoulder, keeping her fingers against the baby's cheek until she settled once more. Then Rosmanda slowly straightened.

They stood in the darkness; the only light was the faintest glow from the doorway from the lamp downstairs. She was so close, so warm and fragrant. There was something about a woman in the dark—it was all too easy to forget about the consequences come daylight. A burst of memories came flooding back—the feel of her in his arms, the scent of her hair, the way her lips parted ever so slightly before his covered hers. . . .

But that was a long time ago, and he wasn't about to cross any lines. Whatever attraction still simmered inside of him, it would have to stay covered.

Rosmanda put a hand on his bicep, and he froze. Was she thinking of the same thing?

"Out," she whispered.

"Sorry." Of course she wasn't. She hadn't even wanted his help with her babies. He eased out of the room and stood in the hallway as she darkened the doorway.

"Good night, Levi." And the door shut with a soft click before he could reply. It was probably better that way. He was foolish to even let himself remember anything between them. He headed for the stairs and made his way down to the lamp-lit kitchen.

He'd sit in this chair and get his brain back into line.

Rosmanda needed a job, not a distraction from her life in the form of her dead husband's brother. And eventually, she needed an actual husband—he'd have to make his peace with that, too.

Levi sank into the kitchen chair and stared morosely into the lantern. He was home again, with all of the conflicted emotions that came with that. If only he could sweep Rosmanda from his heart for good, all of this would be so much simpler.

Chapter Three

Rosmanda leaned against the closed bedroom door and squeezed her eyes shut. What was with her? She'd been widowed only a matter of months, and she found her body responding in the same way she always had when it came to Levi Lapp. Guilt wormed its way up inside of her. Was she this lonely for a man's touch? Or was she just as immoral as all of Morinville believed she was? Because while she'd told him to leave, staring at him in the darkness, his broad shoulders blocking the only way past her bed, her breath had caught in her throat, and she'd been ever so tempted to just wait a moment and see what he did. . . .

But her good sense overrode that wicked surge inside of her, and she had done the right thing. That had to count for something, didn't it?

Except this tendency of hers to follow those feelings was going to get her into trouble. How often had her sister and mother tried to warn her with common sense? And back then she'd been a mere girl. Now, as a grown woman with daughters of her own, she shouldn't need someone to step in and set her straight. She should be able to see the danger for herself.

And she did! Levi might not be engaged like Jonathan

Yoder had been, but he was still rebellious and direct, and her reaction to him was exactly the same. Anything that was similar to the scandal that irreparably tarnished her reputation back home needed to be avoided. She didn't have the luxury of recovering from that kind of stigma twice.

Feelings came with consequences. Wasn't that the lecture she had stored up for her own daughters? A feeling could sweep a woman right off her feet, but the next day, the next month, there might be a price to pay, and humiliation to endure.

Lord, keep me from temptation . . . she prayed in her heart. And it was an earnest prayer. She'd sensed the danger in Levi years ago, and it hadn't changed. Men who could make her feel like *that*—they needed to be avoided at all costs.

The next morning, Rosmanda woke at four as she always did, but this morning, she didn't need to get up and help in the barn like she had been doing the last few months. Levi would do that; she could stay home with her sleeping babies and start breakfast.

It was almost a guilty luxury at this point. At least when she'd been helping in the barn she'd felt like she was earning her keep. Her mother-in-law didn't actually need her help in the kitchen, although it wouldn't be refused. But if Rosmanda could find a way to bring in a little money, then having her here with the babies wouldn't be such a hardship—she'd be contributing.

"Good morning, dear," Miriam said as Rosmanda came down the stairs, straightening her prayer kapp.

Miriam was at the stove, starting a fire in its dark depths by the light of a lantern. She leaned forward and blew, a little flicker of light growing ever stronger in the belly of the stove.

"Good morning," Rosmanda said with a smile. "I'm sorry about the girls last night."

"Well, babies cry, dear," Miriam replied, putting another log into the stove and then pushing the heavy door shut. She opened the damper with a scrape. "I see that Levi was of help."

What Miriam thought about her time alone with Levi, Rosmanda had no idea, but she felt her cheeks heat anyway.

"They miss their father," she said, hoping against hope that her mother-in-law would understand. "I think that's what it was—they felt something familiar in Levi. Even I'm not enough for them lately, and I hate that. I'm their mamm. I'm supposed to be enough!"

"Rosmanda—" Miriam put a hand on her arm. "The trouble with being a mamm is that the older they get, the more they reach out to others. It's okay. You're doing a good job. You're a good mamm."

Rosmanda couldn't talk about her deeper feelings with her mother-in-law, like how she resented Levi for dragging her husband out that night, or how she wished Levi could just go away and some other nephew or cousin's son could come and help. She wasn't even comfortable telling Miriam that she didn't want Levi's help with the babies. There was some change around here that she was powerless to fight. But last night as she lay in her bed, she'd longed for her home in Morinville more ardently than she ever had before.

Rosmanda and Miriam cooked up some breakfast. They made a sausage and egg casserole, a big bowl of hash brown potatoes, and a pot of oatmeal with sliced apples cooked in. It was a hearty breakfast for hungry men, and Miriam's cheerful humming showed how happy she was to have her younger son to cook for.

"Rosmanda, I'm going to need you to bring some breakfast to Levi this morning," Miriam said. "Stephen will be back to eat, but Levi is determined to break that quarter horse."

"The one Wayne gave up on?"

"Yah, that one."

"He wants to try—" Rosmanda felt anger simmering up inside of her. "I thought Stephen told him not to."

"You know Levi. Sometimes it's better to just let him try."

"If Wayne couldn't do it—"

Miriam shrugged. "I never said he'd succeed, Rosmanda, but he's determined to try, and Stephen doesn't want to turn this into some big issue. We've only just gotten Levi home again."

"Of course," Rosmanda said woodenly.

"He's promised Stephen that he'll do it on his own time, and apparently, he's eager to get started." Miriam smiled hopefully. "Maybe he'll succeed and we can keep that horse after all. He's one big horse—he could pull a plow to Indiana if needed."

Rosmanda covered the bowl of hash browns with a plate to keep the heat in. To Indiana, indeed. Her heart seemed to be flowing in that direction, too. She missed home so much that it hurt.

"Rosmanda, you'll have to make room for Levi to make some contributions around here, too," Miriam said quietly.

"I know," she said. "He helped put Susanna to sleep."

Against her wishes. When she'd much rather have had her mother-in-law helping her.

"I'm not asking you to let him be a daet to your girls. I know that would have been . . . an adjustment to let him help with the babies. But he seemed to really have the touch with them, and—"

And Miriam had been tired. She was a grandmother, not a young mamm anymore. Maybe Rosmanda had been leaning too heavily on her in-laws of late.

"Yah, it went quickly," Rosmanda said. "They were both asleep before long."

Miriam smiled hopefully. "He'll be doing the things that Wayne used to—the men's work, I mean. And that's good. We need it."

How much had her mother-in-law overheard from her conversation with Levi last night? She did a quick mental tally, trying to remember what she'd said.

"It isn't my farm," Rosmanda said quickly. "It isn't my place—"

"I know, and you've always been a wonderful daughter-in-law to us. I'm just saying that we need Levi here, too. Stephen's foot keeps getting worse, and he can't run this place alone with a little extra help from a woman. He needs the muscle of a grown man at his side, and I sense that Levi is . . . I don't know . . . cautious around you."

Cautious? Rosmanda didn't think so. If anything, he took too many liberties, and if his mamm saw caution, it was because he'd already overstepped where she couldn't see. And because of that, Rosmanda was seen as the problem. That was clear enough. Miriam and Stephen had probably discussed this late last night while they lay in their bed—how to fix the problem of Rosmanda. Her stomach sank.

"You won't have trouble from me," she promised quickly.

"Don't begrudge Levi success where Wayne failed," Miriam said quietly. "It isn't a competition. And Stephen doesn't think that Levi will be able to break that horse, either, but it might be a good place for Levi to focus some of that frustration he seems to carry around."

And that was easier said than done, because if it weren't for Levi, Wayne would still be here, and Rosmanda would be a happy, worry-free mother to healthy twins, instead of a widowed daughter-in-law who only seemed to get in the way of the Lapp family dynamics. If it weren't for Levi's willful flaunting of all the rules, refusing to forgive Wayne for marrying Rosmanda, causing tension even when he was working on another farm . . . If it weren't for *Levi*, Rosmanda would still be a *wife*!

Levi stood in the barn, his arms crossed over his chest as he stared at the horse in front of him. The stallion was massive with a glossy mahogany coat and an angry glint in his eye that Levi was inclined to respect.

"How are you, fellow?" Levi said, moving closer to the gate. He shook a pan of oats temptingly, but the horse shuffled backward and laid his ears back. "I'm not going to hurt you." Levi raised a gloved hand toward the horse, and he stepped back again, colliding with the barn wall.

Levi pulled his gloves off. Maybe they were part of the problem. "I've got oats."

He shook the pan again. Behind him the barn door opened, and he glanced back. Rosmanda came inside. She carried a basket in front of her, and her expression was grim. Her complexion looked pale in the dim light of the barn, and she tugged her shawl a little closer around her shoulders—it was a chilly morning, and the sun had only begun to rise.

"Good morning," he said, turning back to the horse.

"I've brought your breakfast," she said. "Where do you want it?"

There was something in her tone, and he turned away from the horse again, eyeing her. "What?"

"Your breakfast," she repeated.

"No, what's the matter?" he said. "Or do you just wake up disliking me afresh every morning?"

She put the basket down on a bench by the door. "I brought your breakfast, Levi. And I have chores waiting for me in the house."

"Ah." He turned back to the horse again and held out the pan of oats. He wanted the oats—Levi could feel the desire building inside this beast. But he also wanted to take a chomp out of Levi's arm, given the chance.

"Your mamm told me that you're trying to train this horse instead of sell it," Rosmanda said, coming farther into the barn. Her voice was quiet, but it carried.

"And that's a problem?" Levi shot her an annoyed look. Was he to be managed by his sister-in-law now? "Is this your horse?"

"No," she admitted. "And your parents are happy to have you try."

"But you aren't," he clarified.

Her mother-in-law had been clear enough inside the house—she wasn't to discourage him.

"How will you do it?" she asked instead.

"First of all, I have to make friends with him." Levi put the pan of oats down. "Wayne used to talk about this horse a lot. He couldn't get the horse's trust. That was the problem. And sometimes, like people, it just comes down to personalities that click together."

She blinked. "When did he tell you about the horse?"

"I saw him from time to time. He'd come by the farm where I was working when he went into town."

"He—" She shook her head. "He didn't tell me that."

"No, I doubt he did," Levi admitted. "He knew how I felt about you, and he was just as happy to keep you and me apart."

"I gave him no reason to think—" Rosmanda started, but Levi waved her off.

"Of course not. It's like with the horse—some things come down to an organic connection. You either have it, or you don't. Wayne may have worried that we had something . . . organic, spontaneous."

The color drained from her face. "My husband wasn't intimidated by you."

"Then why did he insist on seeing me without you?" Levi retorted.

"I don't know . . ." She dropped her gaze, then sighed. "If he was uncomfortable with us being together, it was simple jealousy. Nothing else."

"It doesn't matter. It's over. And he was right—he was the better man for you."

"Yes, he was." Rosmanda drew herself up, and he could see what her marriage with Wayne had given her. As Wayne's wife, she was something a little stronger, a little more self-confident than she'd been as the single girl. She'd achieved a different status that he hadn't yet. She'd been married.

"Then we're agreed on that," Levi said. "The thing we disagree on, is the fact that this horse is trainable, Rosmanda. And I'm going to prove that to you."

"You don't need to prove anything to me," she said.

A smile tugged at his lips. "Maybe I want to."

Her cheeks colored, and she looked away. While he was willing to bend in some ways for Rosmanda out of sympathy for all she'd been through, he wasn't willing to bend now. He was finally home again— where he belonged while the family grieved—and he wasn't going to be pushed into the shadows because of his brother's memory, either. He had to make a place for himself again.

"I have chores in the house," Rosmanda said.

"Yah." He nodded. "I won't keep you."

Rosmanda headed back toward the door, and he turned to the horse. His calm was gone now—and training a horse without some internal peace was next to impossible. That woman had always had a way of rattling him up like gravel in a wagon bed.

Rosmanda didn't see a man when she looked at him. She saw a boy—a ne'er-do-well, a family problem. And having stayed single until his thirtieth birthday, Levi was definitely a family problem. People acted like taking a wife was the safest practice in the world, but it wasn't. A man had to open himself up to a woman, let her see his inner workings, let her see his good days and bad . . . She'd see his failures, whether he wanted her to or not, and then he'd have to come home to her. A woman who looked at a man's bare soul and didn't think he measured up could crush a man over the years. He'd rather be alone than suffer that.

Levi knew what Amish women wanted, and he was no prime example of Amish husband material. He had problems of his own, doubts, a stubborn streak. He had a problematic personal history. And marrying outside of the community wasn't even an option for him. He might not be an ideal Amish man, but he was Amish born and raised. That didn't go away.

The barn door opened again, and Levi glanced back, expecting to see Rosmanda once more. Or maybe hoping . . . But it wasn't. It was his boyhood friend Aaron. They'd drifted apart over the last few years, but Levi didn't exactly blame him. Most people had eased away from him.

"Aaron," Levi said. He hung the bucket of oats on a nail inside the horse's stall and headed in his friend's direction. "How are things? You're the last person I expected to see."

The horse moved forward, dropping his nose into the bucket and crunching on a mouthful of oats. There was time for more training later.

The men shook hands, and Aaron nodded a few times, then said, "Yah, yah. I'm doing well. I heard you'd come back home again."

"For the time being."

Aaron nodded again. "I'm sorry to come by so early, but I wanted to see you before I started work at the shop."

Aaron was a carpenter at a local business, so his days didn't begin quite as early as a farmer's.

Aaron was silent for a beat. "I came to talk to you about something. As a friend."

A friend? Levi hadn't spent any social time with Aaron since Wayne and Rosmanda's wedding. When Levi had started drinking, Aaron had walked away. He may have asked him to stop the drinking and find himself a wife a couple of times, but eventually he'd done what the rest of the community did, and wrote him off.

"So I'm your friend again?" Levi asked curtly.

"You always were," the other man said. "But we went in different directions, didn't we? I was married, you weren't. I was baptized. You weren't." Aaron met his gaze honestly enough. There was a lot meant in those few words. Levi hadn't been willing to be baptized because he wasn't willing to straighten up. And it had cost Levi more than the community's good opinion. It had cost him Aaron's.

"We were on different paths," Aaron added.

"And we aren't anymore?" Levi asked bitterly. "I'm so improved now?"

"I'm on a less-traveled path now, too." Aaron scuffed his boot into the cement floor, then sighed. "It's a delicate matter, I'm afraid."

Levi's curiosity was piqued, and he nodded to the bench where the basket of his breakfast food sat waiting. He opened the basket and looked inside, then tilted it toward Aaron in an offer.

"No, I'm fine, but thank you," Aaron said quickly. "Go ahead."

Levi pulled out a bowl of egg and sausage casserole, and a fork that lay wrapped in a cloth napkin. The food smelled good, and he bowed his head for a silent prayer, then took a bite.

"So tell me what's on your mind," Levi said past a mouthful of sausage.

"There's a woman I've been courting," Aaron said slowly. "A woman I care for a whole lot."

"Ah." Levi nodded. "That's a good thing." Aaron's wife, Lorianne, had passed away in childbirth two years ago, leaving him a young, childless widower. He hadn't shown any interest in remarriage—until now, apparently.

"It's Ketura."

"Ketura who?" Levi asked, racking his brain for a Ketura either of them knew under the age of thirty.

Aaron cast him a wary look. "Your Ketura."

"Our—" Levi shook his head, then burst out laughing. "You had me going there, Aaron! Seriously. Who's the girl?"

Aaron didn't say anything else, just sat in silence. Levi slowly chewed another bite of casserole, then shot his friend a look of shock.

"What?" Levi choked on some food as he swallowed and coughed. "You're serious?"

"I knew it would be . . . difficult," Aaron said. "She told me it would be next to impossible, but I love her."

"My aunt," Levi said. "She's fifty!"

"She's forty-eight," Aaron countered.

"She's eighteen years older than you, Aaron—"

"She's a beautiful woman with a beautiful heart, and I'd be honored if she'd marry me," Aaron said quietly. "Don't insult her. Not in my presence."

"Pointing out some basic math isn't an insult, Aaron. Don't you want kinner? I know it was a terrible blow when Lorianne passed away, and the baby, too . . . but with another wife is another chance at a family."

"It isn't about that. Yah, it was a blow to lose my wife and child all at once. But I'm willing to go without kinner, if it means marrying Ketura."

"You're only thirty. What if you change your mind about that?" Levi pressed.

"I don't want to debate this with you!" Aaron pushed himself to his feet. "Do you know what it's like to love a woman so much that you ache without her? I've found that twice in a lifetime, and that's rare."

Levi glanced toward the door again, and his heart stuttered in his chest. He did know that feeling, and he had ached for years as his brother married and started a family with the woman he'd loved. But emotional anguish wasn't test enough for a marriage, either.

"Aaron, the age difference between you makes this . . . unusual," Levi said delicately. "You know that."

"I do. That's why I need your support."

"*My* support? That means very little in this community," he retorted.

"It's a start. And of all of your family, you I count a personal friend," Aaron said.

"Yah? Still?" Levi eyed Aaron irritably.

"We were once," Aaron said, then he shrugged helplessly. "Levi, I have no one else who might understand me. No one. I thought you might."

"What does my aunt say about this?" Levi asked.

"She says she loves me, too," Aaron said, a smile coming to his face. "And if I could convince just one member of her family that this would be an acceptable match, then she'd have reason to hope."

"Are you engaged?" Levi asked.

"Not yet. She's a practical woman, and she won't be engaged without a date set for the wedding. We can't do that without some support."

Aunt Ketura with a man young enough to be her son . . . It was almost impossible to believe. She'd been married twice now, and her most recent husband was an older man who had passed away of natural causes last year. She'd been eking her way with some crafts and quilts—the family couldn't afford to simply support her outright, and her elderly husband had left her very little.

Was this a marriage of convenience for her? Was this her way to find some financial support? Or was it something deeper?

Levi sighed. "I can't promise my support, Aaron. But

I'll go talk to my aunt. I have other business to discuss with her anyway."

"That's enough for now," Aaron said, and he rose to his feet. "I'd be good to her, Levi. I'd respect her and provide for her."

Did Aaron even know what he was suggesting? Levi wasn't so sure. A woman of forty-eight might look quite attractive still, but she was still old enough to be his mother, and given another five years, no matter how well she'd aged so far, she'd be looking like his mother, too.

"And if you would, mention it to your father," Aaron added.

"That's not a great idea," Levi said with a shake of his head.

"I'm not playing games," Aaron replied. "And I don't want to wait another year before I marry her. I want a wedding this fall, and a life with my bride."

"This fall," Levi said feebly.

"I'm a man in love," Aaron said, with a helpless shrug. "And thank you for going to see her, at least. She'll tell you. You'll see."

In love . . . yes, Levi understood just how agonizing that situation could be. A man in love had his heart bared for all to see. Even if he tried to hide it, people saw, and nothing mattered anymore but that object of his affection.

But marriage—that was a different institution entirely. Not every man in love managed to get his beloved in a wedding apron, or ever would. Because life changed. People changed. Possibilities evaporated. None knew that so well as Levi.

Chapter Four

The next morning, Rosmanda stood at the sink washing up the pans from bread baking. Domed, golden loaves sat on wire racks on the counter, making the whole house fragrant with fresh bread. Her daughters were playing on a worn quilt over by the kitchen chairs, and when she glanced back she noticed Susanna pulling at a chair leg trying to get herself higher. Pudgy hands reached upward, grasping for the back of the chair, and then she plopped back down onto her diapered bottom. Rosmanda watched her for a moment. Hannah didn't seem inclined to try this new feat herself, but her round brown eyes were fixed on her sister in fascination.

Was Susanna close to walking already? The babies were only ten months old, and while they were avid crawlers, Rosmanda hadn't even wrapped her mind around the reality of walking twins. Was it terrible to hope that they'd be crawlers for a good while longer?

Rosmanda turned back to the sink. She wrung out the cloth and wiped down the counter. The clean pans were all in the dish rack, and she pulled the plug in the sink just as the side door opened and her mother-in-law came into the kitchen with an empty laundry basket perched on one hip.

Her graying hair was pulled back perfectly under her crisp white kapp.

"I went to check the mail, and you have a letter," Miriam said, dropping the basket onto the tabletop and handing over the envelope. "Is it from your mother?"

Rosmanda accepted the envelope and looked down at the writing on the front. It wasn't from her mother or sister back in Indiana—she knew their handwriting. And there was no return address on the envelope, either.

"No . . ." Rosmanda said slowly. "I'm not sure who it's from. But thank you."

It was strange to get a letter without a return address on it, but she didn't want to open the letter in front of Miriam. She had little enough privacy these days that a mystery letter felt like a treat.

"The laundry is all on the line," Miriam said, changing the subject. "You need a new dress or two, I think. Yours are getting worn along the hems."

"I'll turn them up again," Rosmanda said.

"They've been turned up enough," Miriam replied. "I don't think we have much choice anymore. You'll need more dresses."

Yes, that was the problem. Rosmanda could feel her drain on her in-laws' home. They'd all been grieving Wayne's death together, but life plodded on, and so did the expenses.

"I've finished the dishes," Rosmanda said. "I was going to start on some shoofly pie."

"Actually . . ." Miriam paused. "There was something I wanted to ask you about. Levi had an idea and he mentioned it to Daet this morning. We think it's a good one."

"Oh?" Had he talked to his parents already? That was good news.

"Stephen's youngest sister, Ketura, has been making

quilts and other crafts that she sells in town," Miriam said. "And she does rather well for herself, all considering. She says that there is quite a market for Amish goods, and a well-made quilt can get a good price. Now, I know that up until now you've been helping Stephen with the farm where you could, but now that Levi is here to take over with that, it will free up some time."

"And let me make some extra money," Rosmanda said. "I'd be glad to start giving some money toward the household."

"Well, it's not about something as crass as money. . . ." Miriam said, color coming to her cheeks, but of course, it was. They all knew it. Everything cost—from formula to cloth and thread for clothes, to canning jars and flour.

"I would really like to make a little bit," Rosmanda said. "And I would like to contribute."

She didn't want to make her mother-in-law feel cheap for agreeing to this. It had been Rosmanda's idea, after all. If she was to stay in this house with her twins, she needed to contribute more than her cooking skills.

"Well, if you'd like to do it, Levi is driving out to Ketura's place this morning. You might as well go with him. He could talk to Ketura for you, since it was his idea."

"That would be very nice," Rosmanda said, a smile coming to her face. "I'll take the babies with me—"

"I could watch my granddaughters for a couple of hours," Miriam said with a shrug. "You shouldn't be too long, I don't think."

"Thank you, Miriam. I do appreciate that. When do we leave?"

"When Levi comes back from chores."

Rosmanda nodded. "I'll go find a clean apron, then."

Rosmanda paused beside her daughters to smooth a hand over their curly heads. Hannah reached for her, while

Susanna grabbed for the chair again. Scooping Hannah up in her arms, she glanced back at Miriam.

"Let Susanna be," Miriam said. "I'll be down here anyway, starting the pies."

Rosmanda smiled her thanks and hoisted Hannah up on her hip. They were getting bigger, chubbier, and so much more active. Hannah leaned her cheek against Rosmanda's shoulder, and Rosmanda leaned over to kiss her forehead.

"How's my girl?" she asked softly, heading up the stairs. Hannah reached for the letter in Rosmanda's hand, and she tucked it under her apron waist instead. "No, that's mine. Come. You can play on my bed while I get changed."

Hannah liked to roll around with the pillows on Rosmanda's bed, so when she got upstairs, she deposited the baby in the center and reached back to untie her apron. She had another ironed apron waiting for her in her closet, and she shook it out and put it on, smoothing her hands over her hips as she checked that it was straight and crisp.

Hannah crawled toward the pillows on the bed, and Rosmanda sank down onto the edge of it and tore open the envelope.

The writing was a little messy, but legible, and she dropped her gaze to the bottom of the page first to see who had written it, and her heart skipped a beat when she saw the name.

Jonathan. She recognized the sweep of his signature. This was Jonathan Yoder—her scandous mistake from Indiana. Her cheeks heated as she remembered her youthful abandon with a much older boy. He'd awoken a part of her that hadn't been ready yet, but she couldn't blame him entirely. She'd been a willing participant.

She'd exchanged a few letters with him after her husband's death, but she hadn't written him back in months.

Dear Rosmanda,

You've told me how deeply you've been grieving your husband, and I keep thinking of you alone out there in Pennsylvania—away from the people who love you. It must be lonesome. And I can sympathize with that. I'm lonesome, too.

Ever since I was manipulated into marrying Mary, I have felt the unfairness of my life. She doesn't understand me, and after five kinner together, whatever affection we used to have seems to have drained away. She is more like a sister in my home than a wife. I married the wrong woman, and it should have been you.

"Manipulated!" she said aloud. Jonathan hadn't been manipulated into marriage. If anything, he'd been the one manipulating two women, claiming to love both, and ultimately impregnating the woman he did marry. Granted, the elders made sure that he married his pregnant fiancée, but that wasn't manipulation—it was the only option.

He'd claimed that Mary was more like a sister back when he was fooling around with Rosmanda, so those words rang rather false. If he'd gotten Mary pregnant, that wasn't the case, was it? And five kinner weren't born from a sibling dynamic.

She read on:

I'm not sure you will want to see me after all these years, but I can hope. I'm coming to Abundance to see you—to make sure you're okay . . . to ask you in person if you love me still. After your letters, I've started to hope that you might. Or that you could love me again. I

*know that marriage before God is for life, and
that you are now free, and I am not . . . but is
there no mercy for a man who made a terrible
mistake? Is there no second chance at
happiness?*

*I will be there soon. There must be a way for us.
Don't answer this letter. It will only make Mary
suspicious. Wait for me.*

> *Your own,*
> *Jonathan*

The blood emptied out of Rosmanda's head and she felt
like the room was tipping for a moment. He was coming
here—to Abundance? She sucked in a breath and scanned
the words again—she wasn't to answer him lest his wife
get suspicious . . . *and he was coming.*

"You idiot . . ." she breathed. She wasn't sure if she
was referring to Jonathan or to herself. She never should
have written him back when he wrote to her the first time.
She never should have shown him any bit of her grief. She
should have seen what he was up to—again!

This man had already ruined her chances at a marriage
in her home community of Morinville, and he was coming
to her new home—the place where she'd managed to
maintain a reputation of being a good, honorable wife and
mother—and he was going to expose her.

Her heart hammered in her chest, and she licked her
dry lips, wondering if there was anything she could do to
stop him. But she couldn't think of anything. Mary might
think Rosmanda was trying to meddle in their marriage
if she wrote to her . . . And did she dare write to her daet
and ask him to intervene? Her father was the bishop in

Morinville, and he might be able to help. If she wrote him right away, it was possible that he'd get it in time.

Hold Jonathan back, Lord, she prayed earnestly. *Stop him. Don't let him come and ruin everything I've worked for!*

Because if Rosmanda was to find another good, decent husband to help her raise her daughters, to give her more kinner and to give her an honest place in the Amish community, then her secret must stay deeply buried.

Hannah crawled back over the quilt in Rosmanda's direction, drool dripping down her chin from her gummy little smile. Rosmanda scooped her daughter up into her arms and held her tight as her mind spun. This didn't only affect her, it would affect her daughters, too. Their reputations could be sullied by her past sins, if they came to light.

What exactly did Jonathan Yoder want from her? And what would it take to buy his silence about their history? She'd write to her father today and send it off. May the angels speed its arrival at her parents' farm. Because from what she could tell, this was her only hope.

Downstairs, she heard the door bang shut and the murmur of voices came through the floorboards. Levi was back in from chores, and that meant she'd be expected to leave soon. She looked around the room and spotted the matches next to the kerosene lamp on her dresser. She kissed Hannah's cheek and put her onto the floor, then grabbed a match and struck it.

The letter caught fire in a whoosh, and it flared up, then crinkled down into an ashy crumple. She dropped it into the empty garbage can and let it burn out.

Maybe Jonathan wouldn't come. Maybe God would answer her prayers and keep him at home with Mary and their children. Maybe he'd realize before he left Morinville that Mary was the woman for him, and he'd leave Rosmanda alone.

But there was no time to write a letter home this minute.

"Rosmanda?" Miriam's voice came up the staircase. "Are you ready?"

Rosmanda rubbed her hands over her face, then pushed the garbage can back into the corner. She'd kept her secret all these years, and she'd continue to keep it until she was forced to do otherwise.

There was still a chance that God would have mercy on her and would keep Jonathan Yoder far from her. She'd paid the price for her sin. She'd done her penance. She'd changed her ways and found a good, solemn, Amish husband. She was a woman now, no longer a naïve girl. While Jonathan was pining for second chances at happiness, all she wanted was a second chance at respectability.

"Come now, Hannah," Rosmanda said, picking up her daughter from where she sat at her feet and pasting a smile onto her face. "Let's go down to Mammi."

Levi eyed his mother. "She's coming with me?"

His heart sped up, and he glanced toward the stairs. The last time he'd spent some time alone with Rosmanda, he'd flirted with her. He told himself it had been habit, but it wasn't just that. There was something about her that made him want to prove himself to her—to train that horse to make her look at him with some respect in her eyes.

Would that even be enough to gain her respect? Probably not. But he wanted to do it, all the same.

"It only makes sense," Miriam said. "Doesn't it? You

suggested she work with Ketura, and she seems to like the idea, too. Then Ketura and Rosmanda need to talk."

Levi had other things to discuss with Ketura like the fact that Aaron was in love with her. Did his aunt feel the same way, or had she been trying to put the younger man off with a bit of kindness and Aaron hadn't taken the hint? Levi wasn't sure, but he needed Ketura's side of the story before he could do anything on Aaron's behalf, and he wasn't ready to bring this up to his parents just yet.

"Sure, Mamm," he said.

Rosmanda had asked for this favor, and he owed her. The tension in his chest came back at the thought of that obligation. He wouldn't take responsibility for his brother's death—not when it was an Englisher drunk driver—but he hadn't been the man he should have been, either, these last years. He'd been drinking and hanging out in Englisher bars when he wasn't working the Peachy farm. He'd been drowning his own sorrows and caring little about how that made his family look. They certainly hadn't cared what Wayne's betrayal had done to him, had they? A wedding didn't just smooth things over for the guy who got tilled under. But he'd been acting like a rebellious fool, and for that, he hadn't forgiven himself. He should have hidden things better—covered it over with Amish stoicism.

So maybe if he could help Rosmanda to move her life forward it would lighten the resentment that stewed in her dark eyes. Facing his own self-recriminations was hard enough. He didn't need to add hers.

"Oh, and bring these baked goods, would you?" Mamm said, lifting a cloth-covered basket. It smelled of fresh bread, and when he peeked in the side, he saw an array of buns and cookies, with a plastic-covered shoofly pie balanced on top.

"Yah, sure," he said with a nod. Ketura and her late husband's brother and his wife would enjoy some extra food. Ketura hadn't been left much upon her husband's death, and her refusal to remarry so far wasn't making her life easy.

Rosmanda came downstairs, one of her daughters in her arms. She looked tired, a little pale, but poised all the same. She kissed the baby's plump cheek, then handed her over to Levi's mamm.

"I'll be back," she said, smiling down into the baby's face, and then she turned and picked up the other baby, who had been playing on a blanket next to the table. "Be good, Susanna. I'll be back."

She kissed Susanna, too, and then reached up to check her kapp with the tips of her fingers. She looked younger with all the weight she'd lost—more fragile. Rosmanda was so proper that it irritated him sometimes. Never a misstep. She was a widow and mother, and there wasn't a stain upon her apron or a hair out of place. He'd seen a more playful side to her once upon a time—but seeing her like this made the memory seem more like something he'd made up than actual fact. She pulled a woolen shawl around her slender shoulders, then looked back at Mamm.

"Thank you for watching them," Rosmanda said. "I'll try not to take too long."

"Never mind that," Mamm replied with a smile. "They'll be fine with me."

When Rosmanda turned toward the door, Mamm shot Levi a warning look. His mother had told him he was to get along with his sister-in-law, and he knew what Mamm wanted—a harmonious family for all to see. But Rosmanda wasn't the only one to resent him. Mamm might not blame him for Wayne's death, but she did blame him for the family discord of recent years. It had been Levi's responsibility to step back emotionally and find it in his heart to wish Wayne and Rosmanda well. And he hadn't been able to do it.

Levi opened the door and held it while Rosmanda joined him outside. Then he headed over to the buggy barn. Rosmanda kept up with him, but she didn't say anything. He put the basket of baked goods into the back of the buggy, and when he headed into the stable to get the horses, she stayed outside.

He paused, looking out at her through the window. She stood with her head down, her gaze locked on something at her feet. She was rigid—her spine straight and her shoulders back. She looked strained, worried, even. But even the chilly wind couldn't move a tendril of hair free from her kapp.

"So bloody proper . . ." he muttered.

The curse was a habit, picked up in bars, but he liked it. It vented his frustration. Just once, he'd like to see her slip up—come out with a colorful curse, or slap someone straight across the face. Just once, he wanted to see her step down to a human level, and maybe that was why he enjoyed fighting with her so much. When she was mad, that careful veneer of hers that she'd polished up these last years slipped aside, and it was satisfying to see.

But no one else had seen that passionate side to Rosmanda. She was a good woman, a wife who had done well. And he was still the rebellious clod who embarrassed his family.

When Levi came outside with the horses, Rosmanda stood back, watching him as he got the horses saddled and ready to hitch up to the wagon.

"You don't want to bring me along," she said, breaking the silence between them for the first time.

"No, I don't," he admitted as he pulled the breast strap over the head of the first horse. He secured the strap and reached for the traces. His fingers knew the work.

"This is for your mamm and daet," she said.

"Yah. I got that."

Rosmanda sighed and grabbed the other breast strap off its hook on the wall and headed for the other horse.

"You don't have to do that," he said briskly.

"I'm not some helpless woman," she said with a shake of her head. "I'm trying to contribute."

"Yah. So am I," he shot back.

Rosmanda worked on harnessing the other horse, and he could see the white of her kapp over the horse's back as she worked. Levi attached the shaft from the buggy, and then headed around the horses' heads to the other side. He lifted the shaft for her and held it in place while she did the buckles. Her fingers trembled as she worked, and he eyed her uncertainly.

"You okay?" he asked.

"Yes, I'm fine."

"You don't seem fine. Have you eaten?"

"What is it to you if I've eaten?" A mist rose in her eyes, and she blinked it back. "Never mind. Yes, I've eaten." She turned and fixed him with that dark stare of hers. "We need a truce."

"What, an agreement to act like a civil family?" he asked with a short laugh.

"Yah." Pink tinged her cheeks. "It would be good for both of us. We don't need to draw any unnecessary attention toward ourselves. I haven't been easy on you, I know. And you haven't been easy on me—"

"Me?" he retorted. "I haven't done anything to you!

I'm trying to help my daet, and you're angry that I'm here. I think I'm clear on how things stand."

"You keep mentioning . . ." She swallowed. "When I first came to Abundance, I didn't behave like a proper young lady."

"You kissed me." A roguish grin spread over his face. "Repeatedly. And you liked it."

"That." Her expression darkened. "I'm not that woman anymore, Levi."

"I'm not exactly offering to rekindle things," he retorted.

"If you'll stop bringing it up and just let it . . . die . . . then I'll do my best to let things go about Wayne."

Her voice was tight, and he could tell that letting things go would be no easy feat for her. But those memories that wounded her, meant something more to him.

"Remembering your relationship with me is embarrassing," he said.

"It wasn't a relationship," she said curtly.

"Then what was it?" he asked, shaking his head. "I brought you home from singing, we'd go driving together, we'd do all that kissing you hate talking about . . ."

"We weren't courting—officially." She licked her lips. "And it was a long time ago. I'm not that young woman anymore. I've been married, I'm a mamm, and I'll carry on with the dignity of a proper woman. It's mean of you to keep bringing it up."

"Right."

She didn't say anything else, but she was watching him. He sighed.

"And you'll stop blaming me for Wayne's death, then?"

"I'll—" She paused. "I'll never speak of it."

But she wouldn't actually stop blaming him. He smiled bitterly. She was nothing if not honest. "The Bible talks about people keeping up appearances that don't match what goes on inside. Something about whitewashed tombs, I believe."

She didn't take the bait. "I won't be meddling with what's going on inside of you, either, but we both want fresh starts here, I think. I want to forget about my earlier mistakes . . . as do you."

And Levi had been her mistake. That was abundantly clear. He felt the stab of those words, but he couldn't pass up her offer here. She was willing to make things more comfortable for them both, and since they didn't have much choice but to deal with each other, he'd be a fool to pass this up.

"And we'll . . . act like friends, then?" he asked.

"We'll act like friends," she agreed. "We'll . . . be nice and civil and act the way people expect family members to act toward each other."

They'd act a part. She was right, it would make things easier for both of them. Except it wasn't really acting for him. He did care about her. He did want to help. Apparently, it was more difficult on her side.

"Fine," he said curtly, and he led the horses forward, the buggy rolling smoothly behind as he brought it through the covered shelter and out into the sunlight. Rosmanda waited until he brought the buggy to a stop before she approached it again.

"Thank you, Levi," she said, and just for a split second he saw the old Rosmanda in her eyes—the hesitant young woman with a heart longing to be filled.

Levi held out his hand and she took it just long enough to get up into the buggy, and then she tugged her fingers free of his grip. He looked up to see his mother looking out the screen door with a baby on each hip. She met his gaze, her expression serious.

Mamm was nervous about sending them off together, it would seem, and he wasn't sure he blamed her. This family was far from the Amish ideal. He met his mother's gaze for a moment, then Levi pulled his attention back to the buggy.

"What are we supposed to talk about, then?" he asked as he hoisted himself up onto the seat next to her.

"I don't know," she said.

Before Wayne swooped in that one night and drove her home from singing instead of Levi, Rosmanda and Levi had found plenty to talk about. She'd been funny with a quick sense of humor and a way of noticing details that he'd admired. She'd liked to hear his funny stories about his family and his overly serious brother—until she'd married that overly serious brother and whatever had been brewing between them stopped dead.

"We used to be able to talk to each other," he said. "And I don't mean to bring up any past unpleasant memories for you, but we'd almost counted as friends." She'd almost counted as a whole lot more than a friend. "Maybe we could . . . pretend that we're friends, after all," he suggested. "I don't see how that would tarnish my reputation too badly."

She shot him a sharp look and he grinned in return. "I mean, a man has to think of how these things look, but . . ."

"So funny," she muttered.

"It shouldn't be too miserable," he said. "I'm actually quite nice. Given the chance."

She eyed him for a moment.

"To make this easier on everyone, I agree that we should get along," she said.

Exactly how hard would this be for her? She made it sound like punishment. And a small, petty part of him wouldn't mind driving her a little crazy with friendliness.

She didn't want to talk about the bigger issues? Fine with him. There were a few things he'd rather not face right now, anyway.

Levi flicked the reins and Rosmanda turned toward the house and waved at her daughters as the buggy rattled forward over the gravel drive. She leaned forward to see them as the horses plodded on, and then she leaned back in the seat with a sigh.

Rosmanda was a widow and a mamm, and she'd always been a step above the likes of him. He was the kind of man who couldn't put his heart aside for the greater good—a general disappointment to the Amish at large. And she'd been the reason he drank.

But it was time to stop this, and grow up. He couldn't keep ruining his own life because of a woman. Even *this* woman.

Chapter Five

Rosmanda adjusted herself on the wooden seat and turned her attention toward the passing fields, but her mind was still on that letter. She'd burned it, so until Jonathan showed up—if he even did—her secret was safe.

Would he come? That was the question that hammered in her chest. Had he meant it, or was that letter the result of a maudlin moment after a fight with his wife?

It would ruin her if her past with Jonathan ever got out. She'd already decided to write to her daet so that he could visit Jonathan and Mary and fix things before they got out of hand. Jonathan had five children . . . why would he leave them? A few years ago, she might have been flattered that she was such a draw for that man, that he'd abandon everything to be with her, but after a marriage of her own, she no longer found it flattering. The truth of the matter was, Jonathan was a coward. He wasn't drawn to her—he was drawn to any exit that might provide a few creature comforts. And he seemed to think she could be counted on for that.

She swallowed down the rising bile. She'd thought she was rid of Jonathan when he got married and she moved away. She'd *hoped* she was rid of him. . . .

The thought put a bitter taste in her mouth. A letter to her daet was the only solution she could think of so far. That, and to try to come to some sort of agreement with Levi so that her short lapse in judgment with him could be buried as deeply as possible, too. She was no longer that woman, and there were two men who needed to know it.

Her stomach roiled as the wheels rattled over a bump in the road, and she reached forward to steady herself.

"You look sick," Levi said.

Rosmanda swallowed back the rising bile again. "I feel sick."

Levi reined in the horses, and he looked over at her uncertainly. "Should we turn back?"

"No. It's just the motion."

Rosmanda moved toward the side of the buggy and eased down to the ground. She felt better with solid earth under her feet, and she sucked in a breath of crisp air. Her legs were trembling, and she halfway wished she could just vomit and get it over with, but the human body didn't work that way. She inhaled a shaky breath as her stomach calmed.

"Rosie—"

"Don't call me Rosie. . . ." But she didn't have the strength to snap at him. The words came out in a breath instead, and she closed her eyes, trying to soothe the queasiness in her stomach.

"Rosmanda, then," he said. "Are you okay? I mean, really. I know there isn't a lot of love lost between us, but I do care."

Rosmanda looked up at him. He sat in the buggy still, the reins loose in his hands. He looked so broad and strong, so comforting. Or he would if he were any other man. But that had always been her problem—turning to the wrong men to mend her broken heart. And Levi was most definitely the wrong man.

"I'm tired, and the motion got to me," she said.

"Is this new?" He eyed her uncertainly.

Yah, it was new. It came with the knowledge that her carefully re-created life was about to be ripped out from under her because of one cowardly man who couldn't face his family responsibilities. That was what made her stomach feel sick, but she had to get this under control. She had to keep moving, because there was still hope that this scare was just that—a scare.

She took a few more deep breaths. Her stomach had settled.

"I'm better now." Rosmanda took hold of the buggy and hoisted herself back up. Levi's dark gaze stayed pinned on her while she got herself settled again.

"Yah? You sure?"

She forced a smile. "Positive. We'd better get moving."

Levi flicked the reins and the horses started forward again. Her stomach behaved this time, and she kept her eyes firmly fixed on the horizon ahead of them. The road was empty, and it was possible to believe that there was no one for miles around, but that was only a trick of the imagination. Anyone could come over the hill ahead at any moment. Anyone could come up from behind them. Anyone could see something and jump to a conclusion. Reputations mattered because they were the difference between a respectable life in the community and being branded as "the wrong kind of woman," who was treated like a threat to every home around. Amish women protected their marriages. Fiercely. If the women rejected her, she'd be as good as shunned.

"Does Ketura still live with her brother-in-law?" Rosmanda asked.

"Yah. Josiah and Anna are getting on in age, though. So Ketura's doing more of the housework for them, and keeping up with her sewing in the evenings."

Rosmanda had never been out to see Ketura, since Ketura always came to them at family functions and was sent home with baking and leftovers from the meal. The fact that she always left laden down with food suggested a certain amount of pity from the family—perhaps just the fact that she was a widow. It was highly possible that Rosmanda should prepare herself for the same treatment.

"Are you going into town?" Rosmanda asked, turning toward Levi.

"Now?"

"No—later, I mean. Tonight, or tomorrow, perhaps. Are you going into town? Will you pass a mailbox?"

"Yah, I could pass a mailbox tomorrow, I suppose." He shot her a curious look. "Why?"

"I need to write a letter to my father," she replied, and her voice trembled at the mention of her daet. "And I want to mail it as soon as possible. And with the babies at home, it's hard for me to just get away to run an errand."

"Ah." He flicked the reins and the horses trotted a little faster. "Sure. There's the mailbox at that corner store. I can pass there for you after chores."

"Thank you. It would mean a lot to me."

"That's what friends do, right?" he asked, but when she looked over at him, he was staring straight ahead, a solemn look on his face.

Maybe it was just for appearances, but right now appearances mattered a great deal. Tomorrow morning would have to be soon enough for her letter to be sent. It would take another two days for the letter to get to her parents' farm, if nothing went wrong en route. And hopefully, Jonathan wouldn't be able to get away from Morinville quite so easily.

Ketura lived with her late husband's brother Josiah and his wife, Anna, an elderly couple living on an acreage just outside of the town of Abundance. As the buggy rattled up the drive, a curtain moved, and then the front door opened revealing a bent old woman whose white hair was almost the same color as her kapp.

The yard was a little overgrown, and an elderly man appeared around the corner, a pitchfork in one hand and a wool knit sweater thrown over his Amish clothing. It wasn't until Levi had reined in the horses and they'd gotten out of the buggy that Ketura appeared at the side door, her apron stained from cooking and a tendril of graying hair loose about her face. If it weren't for her graying hair, Ketura could pass for a woman in her mid-thirties. She had a slim figure and an easy smile.

"Oh!" Ketura said. "What a nice surprise!"

Levi reined in the horses next to the house, and Rosmanda got down.

"I'm such a mess," Ketura went on. "I'd rush off to clean myself up, but you've seen the worst of it now. I'm making a leftover meat pie, if you're interested."

Levi started to unhitch the horses. Josiah headed off in that direction to lend a hand, so Rosmanda wouldn't be needed. She pulled the basket from the back of the buggy, wielding its awkward weight more cautiously than Levi had needed to do. She turned back toward Ketura and followed her into the house.

"For you," Rosmanda said, handing over the basket.

"Really?" A smile broke over Ketura's face. "This is very kind of you all. It never goes to waste, I can tell you that. And Josiah does love Miriam's shoofly pie. Anna gets a little jealous, I think."

"I get jealous now?" Anna said, coming back into the kitchen, but there was a twinkle in her eye.

"Just a little bit," Ketura said, and Rosmanda laughed.

"Then we should cut it now," Rosmanda said. "And Anna should have the first piece."

"Oh, I shouldn't . . ." But Anna peeked under the cloth and pulled the pie out with knobby, weathered hands. "It does look good, though . . ."

This house had been an Englisher house once upon a time, because there was a tall electricity pole outside, the wires cut off and coiled up. The inside of the house had that latent Englisher feel, too, with electrical plugs along the walls and above the countertops.

"So, how is everyone?" Ketura asked, reaching for some plates in the cupboard.

"Oh, fine . . . fine . . ." Rosmanda attempted to sound cheery. "My daughters are crawling and even starting to pull up on furniture."

"Already?" Ketura nodded. "They'll be walking soon."

"I hope not too soon," Rosmanda said and Anna laughed at that.

Rosmanda helped in cutting and serving pie and Ketura put the baked goods away in another cabinet. She folded the cloth and put it into the basket—neatly ready for Rosmanda and Levi to take away with them.

"And you?" Ketura asked, fixing Rosmanda with a frank look. "How are you getting on?"

The question was so pointed that it took Rosmanda by

surprise. She licked her lips, then shrugged. "As well as I can, I suppose."

"Yah. I understand that." Ketura smiled gently. "It's hard to lose a husband."

Ketura had lost two, so she truly did understand that hole in a woman's heart.

"I actually wanted to . . ." Rosmanda stopped, unsure if she should bring this up so early. Perhaps it was better to let Levi broach the subject. But Ketura seemed so friendly, and she seemed to care.

"Yah?" Ketura pressed. "You wanted to . . ."

"I wanted to ask you to show me how to do what you do," Rosmanda said. "How to make some money off your quilts and things. Because I need to contribute to our household with a little extra money—I know it's crass to even speak of, but I'm not needed as much around the house, and I have my girls, but I need to do something more."

Ketura set some forks on the table, passing one to Anna first, and then to Rosmanda. She set two more places for the men, but she didn't touch the piece of pie in front of her. Had Rosmanda gone too far?

"It isn't easy," Ketura said at last. "It's hard work. You've got to be able to sew fast if you're going to make it worthwhile. And there are enough Amish log patterns and basic block quilts at the markets in Abundance that you won't get a high price for those. What can you sew?"

"I've been working on a quilt this winter," Rosmanda said. "It's just a rag quilt of leftovers, but I've chosen the colors so that they look like a tree in autumn—yellows and reds and orange."

It was a grieving quilt of sorts . . . the work she pored over when her heart ached so deeply that she thought it might truly break. It was a tree in autumn because it reminded her of her autumn wedding . . . that day that she began her life as a wife to a good man. It was a personal quilt . . . but she recognized that it was also quite good.

Ketura shot Rosmanda a direct look. "Yah? And how is your stitching?"

"I've always been good with a needle," Rosmanda said.

"And if you were asked to finish that quilt in a fortnight, could you do it?"

Rosmanda paused. "I suppose. If I stayed up late and sewed in the spaces during the day. Why do you ask?"

"Because customers will ask for a quilt made specially for them, but Englishers aren't patient people. They make an order and they want results. If you can finish a quilt quickly enough, they'll pay top dollar for it. But that means working hard on your part."

"I wouldn't know how to find a customer," Rosmanda said.

"Right." Ketura nodded. "You want to work with me, don't you?"

Rosmanda felt the heat in her cheeks. She was asking a lot, and she knew it. Ketura had a business of her own, and she had her own customers.

"I can sew well," Rosmanda said. "And I'll work hard. The thing is, Ketura, I'm not ready to remarry just yet. I know I'll have to, but I want some time first. I need to grieve . . . to be sure of my next husband."

"I can understand that," Ketura agreed.

"If it's asking too much, you can tell me that," Rosmanda said.

"You're family, Rosmanda," the older woman replied. "I'll tell you what. Finish your quilt, and then I'll see what you can do. If all goes well, perhaps we can sort out a financial arrangement that works for both of us."

The side door opened and the men came inside. Anna stood up to welcome them, and Ketura leaned closer.

"You should think twice about taking this path," she murmured, her voice low. "It's hard work. And I only manage it because I live in a little room off the side of the kitchen here. If I wanted more than this, I couldn't afford it. Do you understand?"

Rosmanda stared at Ketura, her breath bated. Ketura's expression was grim, the lines around her mouth deepening.

"A husband will give you a home and pay those bills, Rosmanda," Ketura went on in a whisper. "Think of that."

But that home would be his, and Rosmanda wasn't quite so eager to fall under another man's dominion. Girls dreamed of marriage with wistful smiles on their faces, but grown women considered these things more pragmatically.

"I'm not ready to marry," Rosmanda whispered back. "And I need to make some money."

"Then finish your quilt. At least you'll know how fast you can sew."

Ketura stood up and went around the table to greet Levi with a handshake and a smile. Everyone said their hellos all over again, and the health and well-being of all the family members was asked about individually, but Rosmanda's mind wasn't on the pleasantries.

A husband was a safety net in many ways, but he could also be a woman's demise. Rosmanda knew that well enough, because she'd seen a good woman tie herself to a coward. Jonathan's wife, Mary, now faced a lifetime of consequences for one ill-considered choice in husband.

In fact, that very husband may already be on his way to Abundance, abandoning Mary and the five children he'd fathered with her.

Rosmanda could not let that kind of dismal future befall her. If it could happen to Mary, it could happen to anyone.

Levi smiled at old Anna and sank into the seat she gestured toward. A slice of shoofly pie waited for him on the table, next to Josiah's seat. Levi waited until the old man lowered himself into his chair before he sat down next to him. Josiah made a little sound of happiness as he pressed a trembling fork into the caramel-colored filling.

"Is there anything I can help you with today?" Levi asked, then he glanced around the kitchen, looking for a clue to what needed doing. "I could fill the wood box for you. Or get the eggs."

This old couple really should move in with their children soon, but they'd wanted to keep their independence. When Josiah's brother passed on, Ketura's staying here seemed to resolve that issue for the time being—she got a home to live in, and they got the help they needed. But how long this solution would remain viable was anyone's guess.

"The eggs? The last of the chickens stopped laying," Josiah replied. "So we ate them this winter. The chicken house is empty. But that's okay, because my daughter brings us eggs from her farm—they have too many."

"That's good of them," Levi said. "What about wood for the stove?"

"There's lots at the side of the house," Josiah said.

"But there must be something I can help with. I'll muck out your stables, maybe."

"Oh, no need to worry about all that," Josiah said, lifting the fork to his lips. "That King boy comes by . . . Aaron. You know him, right?"

Levi paused for a beat, glancing in Ketura's direction. His aunt's cheeks pinked and she wouldn't meet his gaze. Yes, that "King boy" would be coming by here quite often, wouldn't he? And being the decent sort of man he was, Aaron would be helping out old Josiah.

"Yah, I've known Aaron since our school days," Levi said.

"A good boy," Josiah said with a nod. "He comes by a few times a week after he's done his chores at his daet's farm. He helps with the stables, fixes things that break . . . Between my grandsons and that King boy, we're well taken care of."

"Not a boy, Josiah," Anna interrupted. "He was married to that sweet young thing—Lorianne. So he's a grown man, now. And high time he was married again, if you ask me."

"Oh, well, you all look like children to me," Josiah said with a short laugh, and he put the fork into his mouth closing papery lips over the tines. He pulled it free and chewed slowly. "Mmm. Good pie."

Levi glanced toward his aunt again, and she smiled tightly, then rose to her feet, moving toward the sink. He watched her retreat.

"Ketura takes good care of Aaron after he helps us out, too," Anna added. "She always makes him a nice meal and makes sure it's hot. And there's always some baking waiting for him, too. Don't know what I'd do without Ketura. I certainly couldn't keep that young man fed the way she does. I'm too slow these days. She keeps this kitchen humming."

"Speaking of Aaron marrying again," Josiah said, wiping a crumb from his chin. "Rosmanda—you could do worse. He's a hardworking young man and he's about your age, I believe. And he knows the pain you've been through in losing your dear husband. There's much to be said for that kind of shared experience."

A shared experience, perhaps, but Levi couldn't help the surge of annoyance that rose up inside of him, and he couldn't explain exactly why. Rosmanda didn't answer, dropping her gaze instead.

"Wouldn't you say, Ketura?" Josiah asked, raising his voice. "That was what brought you and Matti together, wasn't it? You'd both lost someone, and it was good for both of your hearts to come together."

Ketura's face paled, and she licked her lips. Methuselah had been Josiah's younger brother, younger than Josiah by ten years.

"Josiah's quite the matchmaker," Ketura said with a low laugh. "He sees weddings everywhere."

"The right marriage is a blessing," Josiah said sagely. "I've lived these ninety-three years because of Anna there. She's the one who breathes life into me. Marrying her was the best thing I ever did. And was she ever pretty in that wedding apron . . ." He chuckled, pushing his fork into his pie once more. "I'd go on for another ninety-three if I thought I could live them all with her."

Anna smiled over at her husband and shook her head teasingly. "He says this with another woman's pie on his plate."

Levi laughed at that, and when he glanced toward Rosmanda he noticed that her expression was worried and distanced again, the joke having missed her entirely. Her hands on the tabletop were balled up into fists and when her gaze flickered in his direction and she found him scrutinizing her, she pulled her hands down into her lap.

"Ketura, let me help you clean," Rosmanda said, and she started to rise.

She didn't need to be put to work just now . . . besides, he'd come to talk with his aunt privately. Levi pushed back his chair and stood up before Rosmanda could stand.

"No, let me," Levi said quickly. "I was hoping to talk to my aunt, anyway."

Rosmanda sank back into her chair, and Levi gathered up his plate. Rosmanda smiled wanly and leaned toward Josiah as he turned his conversation toward her and Levi headed toward the sink where Ketura stood.

"Is she okay?" Ketura asked softly, glancing in Rosmanda's direction.

Rosmanda was listening to something Josiah was saying, nodding politely, but the spark had gone out of her eye. Was it just her anger toward him that brought it back these days?

"I'm not sure," Levi replied. "I've only been back for a few days."

"Yah." Ketura sighed. "She's lost her husband, though. I know what that's like."

Was that what Levi was seeing, the worry and sadness tugging at her—was it grief? He could understand that, because he was mourning the loss of his brother, too. To be home again without his brother here . . . to be tramping over those familiar fields without Wayne to nag him about how he lived his life, or to joke about their daet's way of doing things—it felt hollow. He missed Wayne, even the most irritating parts of his stoic personality.

"Just keep an eye on her," Ketura said quietly. "She's trying to be strong, but she's afraid of the future."

"Aren't we all," Levi murmured.

"Women more than men," Ketura said, casting him a sharp look. "At least you have control over yours."

"Did she say something to you?" Levi asked.

"If she did, would it be your business?" His aunt raised an eyebrow, and he felt the heat in his own face now. Ketura was right. Whatever passed between them wasn't for him to worry over.

"Maybe you'd be a better one to keep an eye on her," Levi murmured.

"She's in your home," Ketura said with a shake of her head. "There is no shifting that responsibility. When you lose a spouse, it cuts away a part of your heart. But it's more than that. She's got to find a way to make an income. She'll have to find a new husband, too, and she won't have much choice—just the ones who step forward. If there is more than one. She's afraid, as well she should be. Life as a widow isn't easy."

It wouldn't be, and somehow, the thought of sending Rosmanda off to marry some man just for the financial support was an ugly one. She'd stay with them as long as she needed. She might drive him crazy, but he'd take care of his own.

"It isn't easy for you, either," he said. "Is it?"

"No." Ketura shook her head. "It isn't. But sometimes scraping together a little income is preferable to the men who offer me marriage."

He stepped closer and lowered his voice. "Aaron King came by to see me," he said. "Is he one of the men you'd rather avoid, then?"

Ketura's cheeks pinked again, and she pressed her lips together into a firm line.

"He says he loves you," Levi went on. "He says he wants to marry you. He was very clear about that. Is he bothering you?"

Ketura's gaze met Levi's for a moment, then she sighed. "I don't think marrying him is even possible."

"But is he bothering you?" Levi pressed. "Has he been harassing you? Because I can speak to him and tell him to leave you alone. I mean, it's silly to think of a young man like him proposing to a woman your age—"

"It's not silly," she interrupted him, and her eyes snapped in irritation. "It's embarrassing, and a little humiliating, but it's not silly. He and I have been getting to know each other, and I know there is a huge age difference between us, but he's got an old way about him. And he listens . . ." Tears misted her eyes. "And I may have allowed myself to feel things I shouldn't."

Levi stared at her, processing her words slowly. "So . . . you return his feelings?"

"I do." She shrugged weakly. "It isn't smart, mind you. And I know we have no future, but he isn't bothering me or overstepping. If I wanted him to go away, I could take care of that myself."

Levi was silent for a moment, his mind chewing over this new turn of events. So Aaron wasn't completely off base here . . . There'd been something developing between them, and Aaron wanted to make an honest woman of Ketura.

"You're old enough to be his mother," Levi said after a couple of beats of silence.

"Except I have no children," she said. "So it doesn't feel that way to me."

"What about him, though?" Levi angled his body so that he was shielded from view from the others at the table. "What if he wants children?"

"I couldn't provide them."

"And what would people say?" he pressed. "If you were to announce your engagement at church . . . What would the reaction be?"

He could only imagine the shock and gossip that would whip through the community. It would be the topic of conversation in every house.

"They'd say about the same as what you're saying right now," she said, and he saw the hurt in her gaze then.

"I'm sorry, Auntie," he said quietly. "It isn't my business, but he asked me to speak to my daet about you two getting married, and I couldn't do that for him without talking to you first."

He saw tears mist her eyes, and she pressed her wobbling lips together, holding back the emotion.

"Do you want—" He swallowed. "If you could, *would* you marry him?"

Ketura turned her pain-filled gaze toward him. "It isn't about what we want, is it?"

"It might be."

"I love him," she breathed. "He's kind and sweet, and he has a strength about him that I can't deny . . . I don't know what to say. I've fallen in love with him, but I don't want to drag him through some embarrassing, public humiliation, either. His feelings might change. I wouldn't blame him for coming to his senses."

"Maybe your feelings will change, too," Levi said hopefully.

"No, not mine." She shook her head. "But I could go

on with a broken heart. I've done it before, and I can do it again."

"Do you want me to speak to my daet about this, then?" Levi asked cautiously.

"Only if you can ensure that it will stay a secret," she said earnestly. "I don't want either of us to be embarrassed."

Levi nodded quickly. "I can promise you that. I'll talk to Daet privately, and I'll make sure he knows your wishes."

Ketura sucked in a deep breath and gave him a quick nod. "You always were my favorite nephew. Thank you, Levi."

Her favorite . . . she said that to all her nephews and nieces. And it brought him back to his younger years when he was a kid and Aunt Ketura was the fun-loving aunt who would hike up her skirts and run races with the kids outside on the lawn.

And now she was in love with a man his age . . .

It didn't sit right with him, and he wasn't going to pretend that it did. But he also didn't want to hurt his aunt. She'd had her share of loss in her life. She'd married older farmers twice, and both had died, leaving her very little. She'd never had kinner of her own, and after two marriages, it would seem that hope for her own babies had passed. So if she loved a man now, who was he to take it away from her?

Levi licked his lips and glanced back toward the table where Rosmanda sat.

"She's a better match for Aaron," Ketura said bitterly. "Josiah is right about that."

"Does Josiah know about you and Aaron?" Levi asked.

Ketura shook her head. "We've kept it a secret."

"Josiah's not right," Levi said, his voice low. "He's all wrong for Rosmanda. A dead spouse isn't enough."

Rosmanda would marry again—it was only a matter of time—but God willing, it wouldn't be to one of his friends. He'd been forced to wish her well with his brother. He wouldn't have the strength to wish her well with Aaron, too.

"Oh, I hear a buggy—" Anna slowly rose from her seat and shuffled around it, moving toward the side door.

"It's him," Ketura whispered.

"Yah?"

Ketura smiled then, a sweet smile that made the years drop away, and she reached for another plate and fork—for Aaron, presumably.

It was time for Levi and Rosmanda to go home.

Chapter Six

Rosmanda sat at the kitchen table that night, a kerosene lamp burning next to her. The night was silent, the only sound was the distant snores of her father-in-law that filtered through the floorboards. She pulled her shawl closer around her—the nights still dropping down to near freezing this early in the spring. Upstairs her daughters were fast asleep in their cribs, at long last. It had taken some time to get them settled, but her mother-in-law had helped her with the rocking, and all that time, Rosmanda had been silently composing the letter she would write to her daet. When the babies were finally sleeping and Miriam had gone to bed with Stephen, Rosmanda had crept back downstairs with paper and pen in hand.

She normally wrote to her mother, not her daet. She knew that the letters she wrote were read by both her parents, but writing directly to her father felt strange. And perhaps this should feel a little strange, because it was no ordinary letter. It was a plea for help.

Daet was a kind father—loving and wanting only the best for his children—but he had high expectations, too. He knew all about the original situation—all of Morinville did—but he'd also been clear with her before she got into the van that would take her to Aunt Dina's house:

You have a second chance, Rosmanda. I cannot stop life's consequences from hitting you. Be careful in everything you do. You have seen how quickly a reputation is ruined. Don't squander this. God forgives, but consequences follow regardless of our soul's condition. I'll pray for you, but watch your steps, my girl. And may you find a godly husband.

He'd said that standing in the drive as they waited on the van to come and pick her up. And when it did at last arrive, her own dear daet with his cautious movements and heavy breathing from his heart condition picked up her bags one at a time and loaded them into the back of the vehicle.

When Daet read her letter this time, he may very well tell her that this was the kind of consequence he'd foreseen coming. Maybe in her naivety, she'd missed out on the possibility of Jonathan coming to Abundance to break open her secret, but if anyone could put a stop to Jonathan Yoder, it would be her father, the Morinville Amish bishop. If anyone could talk some sense into that man and give his marriage a second chance it was Daet. If he was feeling well enough these days to do the rushing this would require.

A lump of worry settled into her stomach, and Rosmanda smoothed her hand over the sheet of paper and began to write in her careful, tight handwriting:

Dear Daet,

I need your help. I got a letter from Jonathan Yoder the other day. I burned it. Now that I think of it, I shouldn't have—I should have kept it so I could send it to you and you'd see exactly what he said. But I didn't. I panicked. I didn't want to take a chance of anyone finding it.

Jonathan claims to be unhappy in his marriage. He says he's coming here, to Abundance, to find me and ask me if there is any hope of a future between us. I don't know how he expects that to be a possibility, seeing as he's married with kinner of his own, but he seems to think that I still have feelings for him.

You have to believe me, Daet, that I don't know where he got that idea from. He wrote to me when Wayne died, and we corresponded for a handful of letters, but I was in no way flirting with him. I've lived my life here with dignity and purity. I don't understand why he'd think I was the solution to his marital unhappiness, but if he comes to Abundance, he'll ruin everything I've worked for! Everything.

No one knows about him, or the scandal that made me unmarriageable there. This was a fresh start, a truly clean sheet. And if he tells them what I did, I'll be equally unmarriageable here. I have my daughters to worry about, and a future of my own. And I'm not that same stupid girl—not that it will matter.

So please, Daet, go talk to him right away— stop him from leaving his wife! I can't think of anything else I can do but to ask for your help.

The girls are doing well—they're healthy and happy. Everyone here is fine, except for me. I'm a wreck, and I can't tell anyone why.

Help me, Daet.

> *Your daughter,*
> *Rosmanda*

She read it over once more, and when she was satisfied that she'd given all the information that she could, she folded it twice and slid it into an envelope she had waiting. She wrote her parents' address on the front, her own in the corner, and she licked the glue and firmly sealed it shut.

Lord, speed this letter to my daet, she prayed. *And let him catch Jonathan before he leaves . . .*

Consequences might come, regardless of the state of one's soul, but if God could hold it back this once, she would never step out of line again. She'd find a good, solemn husband, and she'd serve him diligently for the rest of her days. She'd never raise her voice. She'd never question him or disobey his orders. She'd be a compliant and sweet wife no matter what came her way . . . if only she could avoid Jonathan's threatened arrival.

The top stair creaked, and Rosmanda startled out of her own thoughts and looked up to see Levi coming down the staircase. She sucked in a deep breath, hoping she looked normal and relaxed as if she spent many an evening staying up too late. His feet were bare, and while he wore a pair of work pants, his shirt was unbuttoned. He glanced in her direction but didn't move to close his shirt. Instead he headed straight to the kitchen and opened a cupboard.

"You're up?" he said.

"Yah," she replied. "I was writing that letter to my daet."

"It's done then?" He pulled a platter of cinnamon buns down from the cupboard and took down a plate.

"It's done." She nodded quickly. "If you'll mail it—"

"Do you have a stamp?"

"Not yet."

He pulled open a drawer. "We used to keep them here—Yah. Right here." He pulled out a sheet of stamps and tore one off.

Rosmanda stood up and crossed the kitchen. She took

the stamp from his fingers, his warm fingertips brushing against hers, and she froze.

He was so close, and with that shirt open at the neck, his bronzed skin almost glowing in that low kerosene light, she found her breath caught in her throat. Levi didn't touch her, but when she looked up, she found those dark eyes locked on hers, holding her there. He smelled warm and musky, and she sucked in a wavering breath.

Levi raised his hand and touched her chin, his work-roughened thumb moving over her skin and stopping at her bottom lip. That was a gesture from years past—something that felt uncomfortably natural between them even after all these years. She took a step back, and he dropped his hand.

"What's the emergency?" he asked, his voice low. "At home, I mean. What happened? Is your daet okay?"

"Daet is fine," she said, and her voice sounded foreign in her own ears. She was trying to sound normal, unfazed by his touch, but it wasn't working.

He nodded slowly. "Then what has you on tenterhooks like this? Or do I just make you that uncomfortable?"

Her gaze moved over his chest—strong and well-muscled. She shrugged weakly. "Your buttons, Levi . . ."

"Oh." He smiled ruefully and did up a few of the buttons, slowly and without looking at them. His gaze moved over her face as if he were trying to figure her out.

"The letter—the bigger issue—it's not you, Levi," she said.

"Good . . ." He turned to the cinnamon buns, cut out a pastry, and dropped it onto the plate. "That's something. Ketura said you're worried about another marriage."

"Every woman worries," she hedged. "I can't stay here

forever. I'll have to find another husband. I told you that already."

"You won't be chased out, you know. I'm here to help my daet now, and I know it's been hard, but—"

"It isn't that. It's my problem. You don't need to bother with it. I just need to send this letter." The last thing she needed was her brother-in-law to try to help her . . . this brother-in-law who made her body respond to him in the most dangerous of ways. She needed privacy over this— utter secrecy. And she needed Jonathan to stay with his wife where he belonged. That was all. Rosmanda met his gaze. "Please."

"All right." Levi tore off a piece of the cinnamon bun and popped it into his mouth.

"How come you're up?" she asked.

"Couldn't sleep."

He pushed the plate toward her, and Rosmanda hesitated for a moment, then she tore off a piece of her own. It was sticky and sweet, and she licked her fingers. Outside, the wind whistled as it swept around the house, and it felt secure and safe inside.

"Do you have worries of your own?" she asked.

"You could say that. There was a time when I would have drowned that in alcohol, you know."

"I know."

"I'm not doing that now. So instead of getting some booze—" He held up another strip of cinnamon bun.

"You're eating your worries away?" She smiled faintly.

"I don't know. I heard you down here. I . . . came down for the company." He took another bite and regarded her thoughtfully. "I know we agreed to pretend to be friends, but there was a time when I honestly considered you one."

Back when she was new to Abundance and rather

lonely spending all of her time with her elderly aunt . . .
Rosmanda remembered him too well from those days.
He'd been funny and warm, and he'd woken her up inside
in a way that turned off her brain. And looking at him with
his half-done-up shirt, and those warm brown eyes
moving over her face . . . She licked her lips and dropped
her gaze.

"Then why the four years of distance?" she asked.

"Because we were more than friends, and you know
it," he said. "That didn't just go away for me like it did
for you."

Rosmanda swallowed. "You didn't even try."

"I tried." His voice was low and husky, and he took
another bite of the cinnamon bun.

"We couldn't stay that way," she countered. "We
couldn't stay close—even in friendship. How would that
have worked?"

"No, I agree, it couldn't keep going," Levi said. "But I
had good reason to keep my distance. Besides, Wayne
wouldn't let me near you. There was something between
you and me that Wayne couldn't compete with."

"Like what?" she breathed.

He met her gaze and a small smile quirked up one side
of his mouth. "Whatever it was that sparked between us.
You either have it, or you don't."

Did he know more than she thought about her marriage? Wayne wouldn't have told his brother anything that
intimate, would he?

"That was a long time ago," she said. "I don't feel that
way anymore." It was a lie told while staring at his broad,
muscled chest, still visible above those two buttons.

"I'm just saying that my issues with my brother are my
own. If I'm still angry with him, then that's my business."

She held her breath, waiting for him to say more, but he didn't. Instead, he turned his attention to the cinnamon bun on his plate, tearing off another soft segment and rolling it up between his fingers.

While Wayne had been the better man in almost every way—more pious, more respected in the community, a harder worker—he hadn't awoken that part of her, and she'd often felt guilty about it. He'd been her husband! He'd been the man with every right to her, body and soul. But while she'd imagined having a passionate and exciting nighttime relationship with her husband after a hard day of work, they'd never quite ignited that spark. Obviously, they were man and wife in every sense, and their connection had been tender, but she'd stupidly assumed that those passionate feelings would come easily with him. They hadn't.

And she would have lived without the spontaneous draw toward each other. She'd been doing so for long enough, hadn't she? He was kind. He was funny, too, with his dry humor. And it wasn't like they hadn't loved each other, because they had. But it had been different . . . and Rosmanda had come to a realization during her marriage that had never dawned on her before:

Good husbands didn't necessarily awaken anything so passionate in their wives. But their honesty and faithfulness were worth more. A good husband and father could be counted on to be there when things got hard, when his wife needed him. The scoundrels of the world— the Jonathans and the Levis—could awaken her body without much effort at all, but they couldn't be trusted, and what use was that? A marriage was for a lifetime, and whatever attraction she felt for an unworthy man would be snuffed out when he let her down in the more practical ways. Besides, her marriage wasn't only about her now. Her next marriage would be both an example and place of safety for Hannah and Susanna, too.

So yes, she could have done without that sensual spark and passion and been grateful for her good, honest husband. And she'd do so again, if God was kind enough to bring her another man as good as Wayne had been. Because in her experience, the spark lay with the unreliable, dangerous, interesting men . . . and they made terrible husbands. Just ask Mary Yoder.

"Have the rest—" Levi held the last coil of cinnamon bun out to her—the softest part in the center that had been drenched in butter, cinnamon, and sugar. She shook her head.

"Oh, come on." That same tempting smile turned up the corners of his lips. "It's the best part. You know you want it."

And she did. She wanted it so much that she could already taste it, but she wouldn't give in to temptation again. Wanting something wasn't enough.

"No, thank you," she said, and she held out the letter toward him. "Would you take this now? That way I won't have to find you later to give it to you. It might make things easier."

"Yah." He took the letter from her fingers and gave a quick nod. "Sure."

"And let me know when you mail it—so I stop worrying—would you?" she said.

"Yah. You can count on me for that."

The beguiling look had left his gaze and he eyed her with a slightly perplexed expression. Rosmanda didn't have it in her to try to explain. It wasn't his fault that she had such terrible attraction to the wrong kind of men. And she'd never let him know it. She moved toward the staircase.

"I'd better get some sleep," she said. "The morning won't come any later."

And she'd better get some space between herself and Levi Lapp. He'd always had a way of tempting her into more than was good for her, and he still seemed to have that ability.

"Good night, Rosie." His voice was low and warm, and she looked back at him over her shoulder. *Rosie.* He shouldn't call her that. But they were feigning some sort of friendship, weren't they? He popped the last of the cinnamon bun into his mouth, and she turned away.

"Good night," she said, and moved up the stairs toward her bedroom where her babies were sleeping. Her children—the ones who would have to pay for her indiscretions for the rest of their lives. Her good reputation was the shield that would protect her daughters, and she'd best not toy with something as powerful as attraction.

She knew how that went. Rosmanda wasn't the naïve, lonely girl anymore.

The next morning, Levi held the bottle of milk as the calf hungrily drank. Rosmanda had been feeding this calf when he saw her for the first time when he came back to his parents' farm, and the little calf had already grown. She'd been right—the calf was downing more milk at each feeding now, and was almost ready to be fed from a bucket.

Stephen worked in the stall next to him, shoveling soiled hay into a wheelbarrow. His shovel scraped against the cement floor, then clanged as he knocked it against the wheelbarrow in a steady rhythm.

Levi's mind wasn't on the calf, or on his father working next to him . . . he'd been kicking himself all morning for having gone downstairs the night before. He shouldn't have done it. He'd known she was down there. He'd been laying in his bed, unable to sleep, when he heard her footsteps creaking down the hallway. He'd stayed in his room, waiting to hear her come back up, but she hadn't, and after a while, he pulled on his pants and a shirt, and headed on down to see what she was up to.

He'd pretended he was hungry, but that was a stupid stunt. He'd been going down to see the woman who resented him and had to pretend to even be his friend. And looking at her with those pale cheeks and liquid brown eyes, he'd been thinking about doing things that he had no right to. Those lips weren't his to kiss. And she wasn't exactly going to fall into his arms . . .

And yet he hadn't just been thinking about how tempted he was by living under the same roof as Rosmanda, even though he was. He'd been thinking about what Ketura had said, how worried Rosmanda was about her future. It had felt like Rosmanda wielded all the power—two brothers vying for her attention—but she wasn't the one with the power anymore. She was now a widowed mother of infant twins, and she was scared. He'd seen it in her eyes. And the thought of Rosmanda afraid made him want to go stomping in to fix things. It was a testosterone-fueled reaction, and he knew it. Every instinct he had with her seemed to be fueled from the same source. There was something about her—her femininity, her spunkiness, the way she pursed her lips just slightly when she met his gaze—that made him want to prove just how much of a man he was to her. Stupid as that might be.

The calf's drinking had slowed, but there was a little bit of milk left in the bottle, and Levi gave it a jiggle to encourage the animal to finish it off. Stephen straightened his back and stretched, then leaned his shovel against the side of the stall.

"Daet, there's something I needed to talk to you about," Levi said, letting himself out of the calf's stall.

"Yah?" Stephen bent down and lifted the wheelbarrow, rolling it out of the freshly emptied stall. "What's that?"

"Ketura."

"Oh?" Stephen put the wheelbarrow down again and straightened. "What about my sister?"

"She . . . and a certain man . . . have asked that I bring up the subject of her remarrying," Levi said.

"A third marriage? Well, I don't see why not. She's not fifty yet. There's lots of life left in her. Who is the man?"

Levi hesitated, then sighed. "Aaron King."

His father eyed him for a moment, then a smile turned up his lips. "Yah. I'm sure. You had me going there for a minute—"

"No, it's not a joke." Levi shrugged helplessly. "It's true. Aaron came to see me about it the other day. He said he loved her and he wanted to marry her. I wasn't sure if Ketura even knew of his intentions. So I went there yesterday, and I talked to her myself. And . . . it's true. They're in love with each other, she says."

"And she wants to marry that boy?" Daet breathed.

"Technically a man," Levi added feebly. "He's a widower."

"Right. A widower no older than you!"

"I know." Levi watched his daet, waiting while all of

this settled into his mind. Stephen nodded several times, then shot Levi an incredulous look.

"She's old enough to be his mamm!"

"I said the same thing. She says that since she has no children of her own, that it doesn't feel that way to her," Levi said.

"So you're in support of this?" Stephen asked.

"Now, support is a strong word," Levi said, shaking his head. "I love my aunt and I want her to be happy. That's where I stand. I don't know what's right here. I said I'd mention it to you. That's it."

Stephen bent and picked up the wheelbarrow again, wheeling it away toward the side door. It banged shut after him, and Levi picked up the shovel and opened the next stall. The door opened again, and Stephen came back in with the wheelbarrow.

"Happiness—what is it?" his father barked. "I want my sister to be happy, too, but how does one even measure that?"

Levi looked back at Stephen but didn't answer.

"Is getting your way happiness?" Stephen went on. "Is selfish gratification happiness?"

"Aaron arrived at Josiah's place just as we were leaving," Levi said. "And she . . . I don't know. She lit up."

"Lit up?" Stephen repeated the words slowly.

Levi shrugged.

"Is happiness in the moment worth a lifetime of regret?" Stephen asked. "Because my sister is a beautiful woman, but her childbearing years are behind her. And while she looks quite young now, that won't last long. What happens when she looks like his mother? Will Aaron be satisfied then? Will Ketura regret a hasty marriage when her husband is no longer attracted to her?"

His father had a point. Whatever a couple felt in the moment, did not necessarily turn into happiness for a lifetime. He'd be wise to keep that in mind, too.

"The community would have a hard time accepting this, too," Levi said.

"There is wisdom in a community," Stephen replied. "Those who are older than you and more experienced have a better idea of how life unrolls."

And yet, Ketura had been married twice, had buried both her husbands, and was no spring chicken anymore. She had a very good idea of how life unrolled.

"What will Aaron's family think of this, I wonder?" Levi said, knocking a shovelful into the barrow.

"If he's coming to you, then he isn't asking them," Stephen replied. "These are the hesitant first steps, seeing if there can be any support. If his family were on board, his father would have been the one coming to me."

"There are marriages that go against public opinion, you know," Levi said.

"Yah. And if this one goes through, it would go completely against public opinion. It's more realistic for Aaron to look for a woman his own age, maybe a woman who has lost a husband. Rosmanda will need to find another husband one of these days. . . ."

Levi looked up at his father, and the older man smiled ruefully.

"You don't like that," Stephen said.

"No, not a lot," Levi replied. "She'll marry again, I know, but not Aaron. He's not the right match."

"Says who?" his father retorted. "She needs a husband and those girls need a new daet."

"He's not asking for Rosmanda, is he?" Levi retorted.

"Are you asking for her?" his father asked pointedly.

Rosmanda—the woman whose very presence in his home was proving to be a dangerous distraction . . . He'd never quite gotten her out of his system. Did he want to marry her—claim her as his?

Levi sighed. "No."

"Then who are you to stand in her way?"

"We weren't talking about Rosmanda. This was about Ketura," Levi said, irritated. He straightened and turned back toward his daet.

"Yah," Stephen replied. "But I'm more concerned about you now, Levi. You've really been straightening yourself out. And I'm glad to see it. You're home again and working with me . . . And you're old enough to find a wife."

A wife. He was a red-blooded man, after all, and he knew all the comforts he was missing out on, but just any woman in an apron in his kitchen wasn't enough.

"One step at a time, Daet."

"You and Rosmanda had something between you once," his father pointed out.

"It's in the past."

"Yah, but things change. She's here, and so are you—"

"Daet, Rosmanda blames me for Wayne's death."

His father sighed. "She won't forever."

"Won't she?" he retorted. "Maybe I blame myself. Wayne was trying to look out for me, and it wasn't just because I was his brother. It was because he felt like he owed me after what he did."

"This isn't about Wayne," his father replied. "Your brother is with God. We have to trust that God knew what He was doing when He took him." His father's eyes misted, and the older man dropped his gaze. He sucked in a breath, seeming to rally his self-control once more. "Levi, Rosmanda will need support."

"And I'm willing to provide for her. She can stay here with us, can't she? There is no pressure for her to leave."

"She'll need a husband, Levi. There is more to life than food and work. You should know that."

Was his daet going to give him a lecture about the satisfaction of physical needs? He certainly hoped not.

"Rosmanda made her choice between us," Levi replied. "She knew what she needed and what she wanted, and it wasn't me."

"Are you holding a grudge, Son?" his father asked. The disapproval of such a thing was between the lines. Forgiveness was the only way forward for any close-knit community. And maybe Levi was holding a bit of a grudge. But it went deeper than that. Wayne had betrayed Levi by moving in on the girl he'd been in love with, but Rosmanda had betrayed him, too . . . even more deeply.

"Daet, that woman knew me. It was no idle flirtation on my part. I opened up. I showed her who I was, what I wanted out of life, what scared me. She *knew* me, Daet!"

"And she chose your brother." Stephen sighed. "Yah, I get that."

"And I can't say that I've improved a whole lot over the last five years," Levi added. He hoisted another shovelful of hay and dumped it into the wheelbarrow. "I'm not a new man! If anything, I proved just how low I could go. So I don't need a woman who saw me at my best and figured I wasn't good enough."

He didn't need a woman who had held his heart in

her hands, and then tossed it aside for his brother, of all people.

"So what kind of girl are you going to marry, then?" his father asked. "Because you'd best be thinking about it. If Rosmanda isn't for you, that's fine. But you've got to find someone."

Someone. A woman in an apron waiting for him at the end of the day. But the face was still blurred. He couldn't put a woman he knew into that role, somehow.

"I don't know," Levi admitted. "I guess I need a woman who can see me for who I am and see the best in me. I need her to know the worst and still feel safe in my arms."

His father nodded a couple of times, then pursed his lips in thought. Levi shoveled for another minute or two, the only sound between them the clank of the shovel knocking against the side of the wheelbarrow. He was waiting for his father to say something—to set him straight, so to speak. When Levi had finished with that stall, he straightened.

"Well?" Levi asked testily. "You have nothing to say about that?"

Stephen shrugged. "It might be better to find a girl who doesn't know about your past at all. And then keep it that way."

Stephen wheeled the barrow out of the stall and down the aisle toward the side door once more. Levi watched him go, trying to put a cap on his own anger.

Levi wasn't mad at his daet—Stephen hadn't done anything to him. He wasn't even angry with his dead brother, although his feelings for his brother were complicated. He was furious with himself, because he didn't blame Rosmanda for the choice she'd made. He hadn't been good enough back then, and he wasn't good enough now. But she wasn't the only one who'd have to marry sooner than later. There was no way around it. And when he saw a woman in his kitchen, the wife to share his life and his bed, it wouldn't be Rosmanda.

It couldn't be. And that fact stung.

Chapter Seven

Rosmanda reached into her bag of scraps and pulled out a rust-colored cloth. She took her shears and cut a piece off, and then measured it against her patchwork quilt. She folded down an edge and eyed it for a moment, then stood up and went to the stove where an iron stayed hot. She used an oven mitt to bring the iron to the board and put the heavy metal over the cloth fragment, pressing down the fold. It would do. She returned the iron to the stove and went back to her seat at the table.

"No, don't touch," Rosmanda said, looking down at Susanna, who had clutched at a handful of fabric that fell off the table. Rosmanda picked it back up, getting all of her project clear of curious little fingers. "That's for Mamm. You play with your blocks."

Susanna and Hannah sat on a quilt on the floor, their colored blocks spread out around them. For the moment, they were satisfied on the floor, and Rosmanda had to make use of this time. She turned back to her work and ran her fingers over the patches of orange, gold, and red that she'd already sewn into place over the last few months, and each piece was attached to a memory. She'd started the quilt in memory of Wayne, but it had become so much more than that as she sewed. Every patch contained a prayer—the deep kind of prayer that sank down into her very soul. Grief had a way of laying bare everything else around it.

Rosmanda threaded her needle with the crimson thread she'd been using for this quilt, and she tied a knot at the end. So far, this quilt had been an act of love, but it was going to have to change form. She'd need to finish it up so that she could sell it. It would lay on someone else's bed—an Englisher bed, no doubt. And no one would understand the heart that had gone into every piece.

No one would think of Wayne, of Hannah and Susanna, of her daet back home in Indiana, or of her mamm who wrote letters every month. No one would look at those patches and remember the prayers she'd silently said while she'd stitched them.

Even Levi had been a part of that quilt—an angry part, mind you. She'd hated him because it was easier to unload her rage on her rebel brother-in-law than it was to face her more complicated feelings for him . . . and to face her own regrets.

Wayne had gone behind her back to visit his brother—why? Levi was right. It was because he hadn't trusted them together—that spark, whatever it was that she'd shared with Levi, hadn't sprung up between her and Wayne, and she had never reassured Wayne. She'd never once told him that she didn't need that to be happy—that she only needed him. She hadn't thought she needed to say it, because she thought whatever she'd had with Levi was safely hidden away.

She'd been wrong. So wrong, and Levi's confession that Wayne had gone to visit him secretly had been weighing on her. Wayne—sweet, honest, noble Wayne had kept secrets.

She should have known.

Even now, it was easier to stay angry than to face that. But Levi hadn't changed over the years—not really. And that wasn't a good thing. He was still handsome and roguish. His dark gaze could still start a blush all the way down in her toes, and he was no safer than he'd ever been. And he was here—sleeping under this roof and eating the food she cooked each morning. He reminded her of earlier years before she had the worries of a married woman and a mamm. He reminded her of the days when she thought she'd fall in love and then get married—the order being of some importance.

She'd had an aunt once who laughed at her when she said she'd fall in love and then marry a man.

"Will you now?" she'd chortled. "A boy will choose you, and if you're foolish enough to fall in love with one before he's chosen you, then you're likely as not to have your heart broken when he chooses another girl. You'll take your pick from the ones who offer themselves . . . if there is even more than one. And you'll be grateful for it."

Her aunt had seemed so brittle and heartless back in her girlhood, but Rosmanda could see the wisdom in her words now. She'd fallen for Levi, but he wouldn't have made a good husband, and she knew it. She hadn't been in love with Wayne when she married him, but she'd respected him a great deal, and she'd been truly grateful that he'd offered himself to her. But love?

What was love anyway? It was a broken heart when that husband died in an accident. It was a torn and aching body when she gave birth to her twins. It was a heart filled with memories and a quilt dedicated to those memories of a life together cut short.

Had she loved her husband after all? It would seem she had.

Outside, there was the rattle of a buggy, and Miriam went to the window.

"Who is it?" Rosmanda asked.

"It's Ketura," Miriam said. "Stephen is out there. He'll help her unhitch."

Rosmanda didn't look up as she began stitching the piece into place, her needle flashing in the midmorning light. She pulled it out of the fabric, the thread sliding through until it tugged tight. Then she pushed the needle in again and caught the fabric in two stitches at once.

"It's nice of her to show you how to make a bit of a business," Miriam added.

"Yah, it is," Rosmanda agreed. "I'm grateful for it. I'll work hard."

"You've been working on that quilt for months, though," Miriam said.

Rosmanda had a part of her quilt in a smaller frame so that she could keep the section she was working on nice and flat, but the rest of it lay in a rumpled heap on the table beside her.

"I had no rush to finish it then," Rosmanda replied. "I do now. It'll be done in a week."

Miriam didn't answer. She likely didn't believe that Rosmanda would be able to come through on that promise, but Rosmanda was determined.

This quilt might be full of memories, but her daughters had needs in the here and now.

There was a knock at the door, and Ketura opened it and came inside without waiting for anyone to open it.

"Hello!" she called.

"Come on in, Ketura," Miriam called back. "I'm just getting the tea on."

Ketura came into the room, unwrapping her shawl as she entered the warm kitchen. She spotted Rosmanda's quilt and immediately crossed the room, folding her shawl over her arms as she approached.

"Can I see it?" she asked, but she paused when she saw the twins on the floor. She bent down and scooped up Hannah, then turned her attention to the first layer of quilt that was nearly finished. She lifted the folds of fabric, smoothing her fingers over the stitches, and when Hannah reached for the fabric, too, Ketura lay it out flat so she could see the pattern better and took a step back.

For a moment, Ketura was silent, and she pursed her lips, looking at the quilt from one angle and then another. Miriam dropped a tea bag into the pot, and then froze, watching Ketura, too.

"Well?" Rosmanda broke the silence.

"This is good." Ketura tapped the tabletop through the fabric. "This is more than good . . . Rosmanda, this is art."

Rosmanda felt some warmth in her cheeks, and when Susanna started to crawl off the blanket, she secured her needle into the fabric, and stood up to fetch her daughter.

"But will it sell?" Rosmanda asked as she picked up her daughter and kissed her plump cheek.

"Yah, it'll sell," Ketura replied. "For the right customer, this could go for several thousand dollars."

Rosmanda gaped at her. "Several *thousand*?"

"For the right customer." Ketura nodded. "We need to be able to offer pieces at a few different price points. Some of the tourists can't afford much, but they want a keepsake from their trip. Others are willing to spend a bit more for a quality Amish quilt to use at home. And then there are the rare few who come looking for something truly extraordinary, and they are willing to pay . . . They don't come every day, mind you, but if you have something like this on display when they do—"

"People will think I'm high on myself if they see a price like that," Rosmanda said.

"You don't put a price on it," Ketura said with a shake of her head. "In fact, you say that it's personal and it isn't for sale. There is something about a story behind a piece, it raises the value for them."

"It is personal," Rosmanda replied. "It's a mourning quilt, of sorts. I started it when Wayne died. It . . . helped me think."

Ketura's expression softened. "Are you willing to sell it? Really?"

"Yah. I have to start somewhere, don't I?"

"Then that will be perfect. We'll call it a mourning quilt, and it will be for display only. Until the right customer comes."

Rosmanda nodded, and a lump rose in her throat. It wasn't even finished, and it already felt so final. Everything changing, slipping out of her fingers.

"You could make some smaller pieces in fall colors," Miriam suggested. "Maybe potholders or lap quilts, and with somber enough colors, they could be mourning pieces, too. If that's . . . something that sells."

Ketura looked over at Miriam with raised eyebrows. "That's a good idea. I could work on some smaller pieces, myself. I have enough heartbreak to pour into them."

"Don't we all," Miriam murmured with a smile. "At least it's worth something to someone."

Mourning pieces. Heartbreak in stitches . . . Funny the sorts of things that people would pay for. But if it was worth that much money to the Englishers, then the things that broke her heart could at least pay for her future.

"We should work together one of these days. Are you free on Wednesday?"

Rosmanda looked up at Miriam.

"I'd be happy to babysit," Miriam said with a smile. "You two should focus on this. I have a good feeling about it."

It would seem that Rosmanda was part of the business now.

Levi hoisted his bag of tools a little higher on his shoulder. He'd been out fixing a hole in the fence, and as he walked across the field toward the house, clouds rolled in, covering the sun and dropping the temperature. The clouds were low and heavy, and he could smell the moisture in the air.

The cows were grazing, their calves next to them. It looked like they had another three or four new calves today—tiny, wobbly legged creatures. They were all cleaned off, though, and two were nursing from their mothers, so there was no worry. He'd mention them to his daet, all the same. The herd was growing—that was a good thing.

Levi hadn't slept well last night. He'd been kicking himself for going downstairs to see Rosmanda. What had he even been thinking? Getting alone with her had been a bad idea from the start. There was something about that woman that woke up the man in him still, and all he'd been able to think about in that kitchen was pulling her into his arms and kissing her. She'd been so close, so fragrant, and when she'd looked up into his eyes, it was like all the years evaporated and it was just him and Rosie again, when his heart belonged to her and every day was another challenge to find a way to see her. . . .

Except now, she was living in the same house. She was sleeping in the bedroom across the hall, and he could hear her soft footfalls, her voice filtering through the walls as she talked to her daughters. Now, seeing her alone was far too easy, and the new challenge was to keep his attraction in check.

Which he hadn't done last night.

The wind picked up, and he walked a little faster, heading toward the chicken house. The door tended to stick and took a solid shoulder to bang open in wet weather. He might as well fix it today while he had his tools out with him.

The first drops of rain pattered down in icy spit, and he hunched his shoulders against the cold. The chicken house door was ajar, which meant his mamm was probably collecting the eggs. He paused, looking inside, but instead of his mother, he spotted Rosmanda with a white plastic bucket, reaching under the fluffy body of an annoyed hen to retrieve an egg. Her shawl hung off of one shoulder. He could see the line of her collarbone through her pale skin, and her wrists looked more fragile than they should. He froze, watching her. She didn't hear him at the door, and she stood on her tiptoes and reached up onto a beam, pulling an egg down from there. There was a sneaky hen, apparently.

He watched her for a moment. He should leave—the door could be fixed later. He'd already proven to himself exactly how much self-control he had around this woman . . . And he was about to back away when Rosmanda turned toward the door and startled when she saw him. Pink suffused her cheeks.

"I didn't hear you," she said, and she tugged her shawl up over her shoulder again.

"I came to fix the door," he said.

"Yah, it sticks." She licked her lips, and he found himself looking at those pink lips a little longer than necessary. He cleared his throat.

"Is Ketura still here?" he asked after a beat of silence.

"She left a few minutes ago," Rosmanda replied.

Right. He'd meant to tell his aunt that he'd mentioned Aaron to his father, but he wasn't even sure what he'd tell her. His father seemed to like the idea even less than he did. It was probably best to put it off a little, anyway.

"She has some ideas on how to sell my quilt," Rosmanda added. "It's the one I started sewing when Wayne died, and . . . apparently, it's good."

"I don't doubt it," he replied. "You sure you're willing to sell it?"

"I don't have much choice."

"You always have a choice," he retorted. "I don't know what you think, but I'll never push you out of this home—"

"I need to make something new. It's time."

Was she talking about quilting, or her life as a whole? He wasn't sure why that felt ominous to him. Whatever they had here between them was uncomfortable at best, but he didn't want to sweep it away, either. Sometimes the painful familiar was easier to bear than the unknown.

He stepped inside and dropped his tools to the floor with a thunk. The chickens fluttered a little, then resettled again. He might as well fix the door now. There wasn't going to be a graceful escape. Rosmanda stood with one hand holding her shawl together, and his gaze was drawn to that slim wrist. Before he could think better of it, he reached out and ran the back of his finger over her soft, warm skin.

"You need to eat more, Rosie . . ." he murmured.

She smiled faintly. "I try. I have babies to chase."

"Yah, well . . . try harder," he said with a small smile of his own. "Eat cinnamon rolls at night. It's bound to plump you up a bit."

She rolled her eyes. "I'm fine."

But she wasn't fine. Ketura had told him that much, and looking at her now, how much weight she'd lost even after giving birth . . . He wasn't okay, either. They were both grieving. They'd both lost Wayne.

"I dreamed about my brother last night," Levi said quietly. "It was like he was there—"

Levi shouldn't be saying so much, and he clamped his mouth shut. Hadn't they agreed not to talk about this stuff?

"I'll just work on the door," he said. "I don't need to get into it."

He needed to focus on the stuff he could actually fix, right? And he could pretend he hadn't said anything.

"It wasn't your fault . . ."

Her words were so soft that he almost didn't hear them over the creak of the hinges, and he stopped. He slowly raised his gaze. She wasn't looking at him, her gaze trained on a hen that was ruffling herself back up on a nest. Rosmanda's lips were pressed together, and she clutched the bucket in a white-knuckled grip.

"What?" he said feebly.

"It wasn't your fault, Levi." Tears welled in her eyes and she swallowed hard. "He used to visit you—without telling me. That is rather telling, I think. I've been blaming you for months, but if Wayne was going to see you, keeping me away . . . You two needed each other, and I was the one standing between you. If I had reassured him more, maybe he wouldn't have been so intimidated by what we had. Maybe he'd have had you come home, and you wouldn't have felt so . . . so . . ." She shrugged weakly.

"Abandoned," he said hollowly.

"I'm sorry," she breathed.

"It wasn't your fault, either," he said quietly. "I made

some bad choices, and those are on me. Not Wayne. Not you."

"I still wonder if I could have made things easier on both of you."

"It was between us men," Levi said. "You wouldn't understand that. He crossed a line when he courted you. It wasn't that you married him, it was how he went about it. And he knew that. He hadn't apologized for it, and I hadn't forgiven him. It wasn't your fault, either, Rosmanda."

"Then who do we blame?" she whispered. "Who do we hate?"

Levi shook his head. "No one, Rosie."

"Because Christians don't hate—" Her words caught in her throat.

"Because humans don't hold the key between life and death," he said.

He didn't even have control over his own heart, it seemed. Because looking at her with that bucket of eggs clutched in one hand, her round dark eyes fixed on him pleadingly, he could feel his options slipping away.

Levi stepped closer, taking the bucket from her grip and setting it aside. He caught her freed hand in his and lifted it, his gaze moving over those slim fingers, the narrow wrist . . . He pressed his lips to her fingertips. A tear escaped her lids and trickled down her cheek, and before he could stop himself, he pulled her closer and dipped his head down, caught those pink lips with his.

She hesitated for a moment, and then when he was about to pull back—uncertain if he'd gone too far—she sank against him, her frail frame resting against his chest in a way that sped his heart up to a gallop. He wrapped his arms around her, tugging her closer still, and as his lips moved over hers, he felt a wave of relief crash over him.

It was a kiss that had been waiting for five years—a

kiss that had been lingering in his dreams and in his grief. Her mouth tasted sweet, and as he splayed his fingers over the small of her back, the blood rushed to his head like an explosion. She moved against him, pushing against his chest so that he could feel her heartbeat pattering next to his. Her hands pressed against his muscled torso—a movement both innocent and subtly suggestive. He wanted this kiss, and more.

She pulled back and he loosened his hold on her, letting out a wavering breath.

Neither of them said anything, but when he opened his eyes, he found her looking at him with mild panic in her pale face. Her hands were still hot against his body, but now she pushed him away and he dropped his arms. What had he just done?

"I'm sorry . . ." he whispered hoarsely. Suddenly, he wasn't feeling the relief of holding her again; he was remembering all the reasons she was wrong for him. Rosmanda had always been the innocent one, and he'd been more experienced than she'd been—physically, at least. Falling in love with her had been completely unfamiliar territory, and he wasn't willing to fall in love with her again. But *she* was the more experienced of them now, he realized in a rush. She was no longer the innocent girl to be taught. She'd been married, after all—she was a woman in every way—and he was the unmarried "boy."

"We can't do that . . ." she breathed.

"I know." He picked up the bucket of eggs and handed it to her once more. She took it from his grasp, her soft fingers brushing against his.

Every logical reason pointed to keeping himself away from her, but after feeling her fingers brush against his, it took every ounce of self-restraint to keep himself from pulling her back into his arms all over again. Instead he clenched his teeth together and nodded toward the door.

"I'll finish up in here," he said gruffly.

Rosmanda brushed past him, and he turned to watch her go. His hands felt empty and awkward at his sides. She looked back as she reached the door, her lips parted. Whatever had sparked between them five years ago, this was something entirely different. She was no longer the innocent girl looking back at him. She was the woman who knew what she needed.

Not him. He read it in her face. Whatever he seemed to awaken inside of her wasn't the kind of thing that could last. He needed a fresh start as much as she did, and neither of them would find that in each other's arms.

Chapter Eight

Levi stood in the barn doorway next to his daet, looking at the massive stallion standing in the rain. He didn't seem to mind the weather. If he did, he could come under the shelter with the other horses, but the big brute stood at the far side of the corral, muscles trembling from time to time when the rain gusted sideways. Resolute.

Levi had been forging a bond with that beast, albeit a slow one. He'd taken to calling him Donkey, which had started out as a joke because of his stubbornness, but it seemed to suit him, and he'd look over now when Levi called him by his new name. But it wasn't just an acknowledgment of a name. Donkey had started to perk up when Levi came in with oats for him, and Levi could now pet him while he ate.

"Donkey!" he called. "Oats!"

He shook the bucket, but Donkey looked away. The other horses immediately perked up and ambled in his direction hopefully.

"Come on, Donkey." He reached into his pocket and pulled out a carrot. "How about this, boy?"

Donkey looked with some new interest at the carrot, but still didn't make a move in their direction. Another horse stretched forward with reaching lips, and Levi fed the carrot to that horse instead. The rain continued to fall, puddles forming by the fence posts.

"Maybe it's because I'm here," Stephen said.

"Yah. But not necessarily," Levi said, wiping off his hand. "I'm still working on him."

Proving Wayne wrong seemed less important somehow. He'd wanted to prove himself just as able as his brother, but that kiss had changed things a bit. It left him guilty. Wayne had betrayed him, but kissing Rosmanda now felt . . . like Levi was crossing lines, too. Maybe it was time to call it even and end this competition with a ghost and let his ravaged conscience rest. Whatever their competition in life, it was over now, and Levi didn't seem to be a whole lot better than his brother had been when it came to Rosmanda.

"Come on, Donkey," he called.

The stallion looked back at him, but still didn't move.

"He knows his name, it seems," Stephen said.

"Yah, he does. He's coming along—he's gentler now."

Stephen nodded slowly. "Well, let's get inside and warm up before supper. I don't know about you, but I'm hungry."

Right—Levi sighed. He was getting hungry, too, but the thought of facing Rosmanda curbed his appetite somewhat. He couldn't sit across from her at the table and pretend he hadn't pulled her into his arms mere hours ago. Was it a mistake? Oh, absolutely. But he'd meant it. And kissing her had been more of a relief than he'd even imagined, because that kiss hadn't been some one-sided fumble. She'd kissed him back.

And he had no idea what that meant. To her. To him . . .

"I figured I'd go into town," Levi said, stepping back

away from the door. "I can order the fencing while I'm there, and get something to eat at the diner."

"It's a waste of money when dinner is ready in the house," Stephen said, squinting at Levi. "And it's raining. Not great driving weather on those roads."

"We need to order the fencing anyway," Levi replied. "And I've got some money to buy myself some dinner."

Levi's father shrugged. "It's up to you. I still think it's a waste when you have a perfectly good dinner here at home. Your mamm is making a pork roast."

It would be a good meal—one of his favorites—and he was still enjoying being back with his mamm's meals, but this wasn't about how good the cooking would be.

"I'll be back in time for chores after dinner," Levi said.

His father shrugged in reply. "Drive carefully. You know how the Englishers are in this weather."

Levi met his father's eye, then nodded. They'd already experienced the worst in that, and he knew his daet was thinking about Wayne.

"Yah," Levi said. "I'll take care."

"Pick up some rat poison while you're at it," his father added. "And some new ear tags. We're getting low."

"Sure. I'll do that."

"Tell Hans I'll pay up next week."

"I'll tell him."

Stephen headed back to the house, and Levi hitched up two draft horses to his buggy. It was better this way. He'd been so determined to take care of Rosmanda and do right by her in her time of need, and he wasn't doing that right now. He was crossing lines, doing things he knew he shouldn't. Whatever he felt for her wasn't her problem, and giving her a break from him was the best gift he could give her right now.

Levi set out for town. The rain let up a little as the horses plodded along. It felt better to be putting some space between himself and Rosmanda, and he breathed a little easier. He'd known that coming home would have its challenges, but he hadn't expected this one. There'd been some safety in her resentment of him. Maybe he shouldn't have tried so hard to dispel it.

Lord, take away whatever it is I'm feeling for her, he prayed silently. *I'm the problem—not her. That was on me.*

Levi felt somewhat scuffed and tarnished next to her. He was the messed up one—the recovering alcoholic with the secret meetings in town, the one who struggled with his faith, the one who crossed lines that shouldn't be crossed. While he might feel things for her he had no right to, he was very aware that she was a step above the likes of him.

And he'd seen that again in the way she'd looked at him after she'd given in to her baser self and kissed him back just as passionately—that mild panic. He was dangerous, rebellious, a proven risk. And she was so achingly, sweetly good that he felt like an even bigger problem in contrast to her. And maybe that was what made her feel so irresistible all these years—how proper she was, how unsullied. If he cared for her at all, he'd leave her alone.

When Levi got into town, he parked his buggy in an Amish-friendly parking lot downtown. Everything was walkable from that parking lot, and he left his horses hitched up, but underneath a tarp covering erected to protect the animals from the weather. He put a feedbag onto the muzzles of both horses, and headed across the street to Groutman's, the Englisher farm and ranch supply store.

A few Amish men loitered by the door, having stepped inside to avoid the rain, and Levi nodded to them as he came inside. Some Englishers were talking over the benefits of a new porch swing rather loudly from across the store, and the owner, Hans Groutman, was at the front window, taping a sign up advertising for an upcoming sale on gopher traps. In a rural community, the farm and ranch supply shop was the hub.

"Oh, speaking of Levi Lapp, here he is," Mark Graber said, raising his voice and waving Levi back toward the door.

Levi looked over at the men who were chatting—he knew them all, but one. A young man about his own age with a sparse but married beard. He was tall, lanky, and had a friendly look about him.

"Yah?" Levi asked, coming over.

"This young fellow here—" Mark said. "His name is Jonathan Yoder. He's come from Indiana."

"Morinville," Jonathan added.

"Yah?" Levi hesitated. That was Rosmanda's home-town where her mamm and daet lived. Her brothers and sister were out there, too. She had a whole heap of family. But he'd never heard of this fellow before.

"I'm looking for a family friend," Jonathan said. "Her name is Rosmanda Lapp."

"She's my sister-in-law," Levi replied.

"God must be looking down on me," Jonathan said with a relieved grin. "I came out on a bus, and I've been asking around, but this is downright providential."

"And you are . . ." Levi prompted.

"Jonathan Yoder," he repeated. "Family friend, like I said. I heard about her husband's passing—your brother?"

"Yah."

"My condolences."

"Thank you." Levi nodded.

"Anyways, I heard about your brother's passing, and

we like to take care of our own in Morinville. I came out to see her—make sure she's okay."

"And your wife?" Levi asked, glancing around. How many of them had come out?

"At home with the kinner." Jonathan smiled meekly. "It's just me. But she sends her best, especially at this difficult time."

So Rosmanda's people were reaching out—albeit a little late. It wasn't surprising—it was a relief, actually. She'd come out here and never looked back—something that suited the Lapp family just fine since there weren't any complications for Wayne. It was nice to know that there were people who worried, though, who wanted to help her. She deserved that.

"Rosmanda lives with me—my family, that is," Levi said. "If you'd like to come back with me once I'm finished here, I can bring you along. There's an extra room for tonight, and lots of good food."

"Yah. Thank you." Jonathan nodded eagerly.

They moved away from the other men.

"How come you didn't write?" Levi asked. "I mean, before coming out. We could have prepared better."

"I did." Jonathan shrugged. "I never heard back. We . . . worried. I guess. I know you're thinking that maybe she wasn't keen on the visit if she didn't reply, but we were all such good friends once upon a time, it's hard to imagine that changing so much. We were in the same youth group."

"Before you all got married," Levi said.

"Yah, well . . . life does move on." Jonathan smiled. "How is she? Is she doing all right?"

"As well as can be expected," Levi said, and his mind went back to those slim wrists, the pale skin. She'd be a shadow of the girl they remembered. "The grief has been hard for her, I have to say."

"It would be." The other man nodded sympathetically.

"Did her father send you?" Levi asked. Something here wasn't quite adding up.

"No, no . . . Not this time. He's not well lately, and it isn't right to burden him."

It didn't seem like checking on his daughter would be a burden, and that struck Levi as slightly strange . . . but how sick was Benjamin Graber? Mark Graber was of no relation to the Indiana Grabers, so he couldn't give any insight, either.

"How is he doing? Is he worse than he was?" Levi asked, lowering his voice.

"No worse than usual lately, but he doesn't have a lot of strength," Jonathan replied. "We love our bishop in Morinville, and we're grateful for him as long as the Lord allows him to serve us."

"Yah, yah . . ." Levi nodded. That didn't tell him much, and he found himself feeling protective of Rosmanda right now.

"If there's bad news," Levi began. "It might be better to break it gently. It's been a rough time for her, and—"

"No, no bad news," Jonathan said with a quick smile. "I promise you that. Just friends who care."

"That's good." Levi nodded quickly. "Well, let me place my order here with Hans, and then I'll take you back with me. I'd meant to eat here in town, but it seems like you're pretty eager to see her, so—"

Jonathan pulled off his wet hat and shook it, then replaced it on his head. "Yah, it's been a long day of travel. It would be nice to see her sooner rather than later. I'd feel better, at least."

"And you might feel better to get in front of a wood stove and dry out," Levi said.

A smile broke over Jonathan's face. "Sure would."

Was this man checking up on *them*, maybe? Making sure they were treating Rosmanda well? Had some rumors traveled back? Rosmanda was thin these days—had some mutual friend seen her and grown concerned? A married man didn't just show up from her hometown without his wife asking to see a widow with no other reason than to say hello. It wouldn't be proper.

Levi nodded. "Yah, we'd be happy to have you. It's nice to see some of her people. Let me just place my order, then."

"Yah, of course. I'll just wait for you. Thank you, though. I'm glad to have found you like this."

Jonathan had an easy smile and a friendly way about him, but Levi still felt a pang of uncertainty about the man. Maybe there was nothing wrong with this Jonathan Yoder at all, and he was feeling something as common as jealousy. Was it that another man might have claim to her in some way, even in the most casual sense, and that bothered him? He couldn't be that kind of man. He wouldn't be. Who was Levi to stand between Rosmanda and her friends from home? He'd bring her friend home and then step back. And at the very least, there would be one more person in the room to be a buffer between them.

Levi had to get things back to normal. It was one kiss. Hopefully, that was forgivable. because he couldn't be the reason that Rosmanda lost any more peace of mind.

Miriam had planned a large supper that night, and Rosmanda had helped to get it all cooked and laid out on the table in time for Stephen to come inside alone. Rosmanda listened with breath bated for that second thud of boots, but it didn't come.

"Levi has gone into town," Stephen said. "It will be just us."

She'd done it again . . . She'd followed that pounding of her heart, the rushing of her blood, and her mind had turned off, leaving her at the mercy of whatever it was she felt for Levi. All over again. She looked away, hoping that her feelings weren't written all over her face.

"In this weather?" Miriam asked.

"He wanted to order the fencing," Stephen said. "Miriam, he's used to living on his own. It's nice to have him home again, but he's going to want a bit more freedom. He's a grown man, after all."

"I know. Of course." Miriam forced a smile, but Rosmanda knew that this meal had been special—Miriam had made her son's favorite. And Levi hadn't come back to dinner because of that kiss.

Rosmanda uncovered a bowl of rolls and took her seat at the table between her daughters' high chairs. She waited while Stephen and Miriam got settled, and for a moment it felt like old times—their sad winter of grief shared together without the complication of Levi's presence.

"Let's bow our heads for grace," Stephen said, and Rosmanda bowed.

Rosmanda ate in silence while Stephen and Miriam chatted about that stallion that Levi had named Donkey, the calves being born, and whether or not they should buy a few more hens for the coop. Susanna and Hannah got their fingers messy with mashed potatoes, and Rosmanda choked back as much of the meal as she could, which didn't turn out to be much. Her mind wasn't on the delicious food, it was on that kiss.

Her in-laws ate at a leisurely pace, and Rosmanda attempted to get her daughters to eat some mashed potatoes and gravy, but most of it ended up on their faces and smeared across their bibs. They'd have their bottles later. They were still young for solid food, although some playing in their plates was the beginning of the process.

"I'm worried about Levi," Miriam said, and Rosmanda's attention returned to the conversation.

"He's fine," Stephen replied.

"Is he?" Miriam shook her head. "He won't talk about the accident. I tried to talk with him earlier, and . . . Shouldn't he talk about it?"

"Maybe he'd rather not," Stephen said. "Not all men want to talk."

Miriam sighed. "We should have tried harder to have him spend more time at home. I know he and Wayne were at odds, but we should have done more as their parents to mend fences."

Rosmanda dropped her gaze. She should have done more as Wayne's wife, for that matter.

"I'll clean up," Rosmanda said, rising, but as she did, she heard the rattle of a buggy pulling past the house.

"Rosmanda," Miriam said gently. "There is no rush. You need to eat. For your girls, at the very least. You need your strength. If they get fussy, I'll take care of them. But I'm asking you to sit here and eat a meal."

"Yah, and eat a piece of pie afterward," Stephen added sternly. She looked down the table at her father-in-law, and his expression softened. "Or two pieces. It'll do you good. Get some meat on your bones."

Miriam got up and looked out the window. "Yah, that's Levi back. It's early. I thought he'd said he'd eat out?"

"Maybe he changed his mind," Stephen replied.

Miriam brightened. "Well, we certainly have food."

So he'd come back . . . Rosmanda found her heart speeding up a little bit at the prospect. It had been good of him to go away for the day—it showed that he knew just how big of a mistake that kiss had been—but she still wanted to see him.

Was that her moral weakness shining through? Or just her natural inclination toward the wrong kind of men? Her husband had been dead for half a year, and she was already having the same problems. She didn't want to be this woman who allowed herself to get stirred up over a man she knew was wrong for her. She wanted to have strength and fortitude. She wanted her mind to be stronger than her desires. She had to be an example of the kind of woman she wanted her own daughters to be . . . wise, strong, good.

Whatever attraction she was feeling with Levi didn't fit in with that. Maybe the others were right, and she'd be safest married off again.

Hannah and Susanna started to squirm in their seats, and Rosmanda took another big bite to finish off her plate of food and turned toward her babies. Miriam always offered to do more, but Rosmanda knew just how tired her mother-in-law was, especially when she gratefully allowed Levi to help out in her place so that she could get some rest. No, the offer was meant in kindness, but Rosmanda couldn't continue being a burden on these people.

Rosmanda chewed as she went to get a cloth to wipe off those potato-covered hands, and as she turned back toward the table with the wet cloth, the side door opened and Levi came inside. She felt some heat in her cheeks, and she swallowed quickly—too quickly, because it felt like a lump moving down her chest. Levi smiled at his parents, and then his gaze landed on her for a couple of beats. He didn't say anything, and she dropped her gaze, moving to wipe her daughters' fingers.

"You're back," Miriam said with a smile. "Just in time. Everything is still on the table."

"Yah, it smells great," Levi said. The door shut behind him, and Rosmanda could see the form of another man behind him in the mudroom. A friend? "I brought someone home, Mamm."

"There's plenty of food," Miriam said.

Rosmanda put her attention into wiping her daughters' chubby faces, and when she glanced up, Levi's friend stepped past him and into the kitchen, and for a heartbeat, she didn't recognize him with the beard. But then her heart hammered to a stop, and the kitchen tilted and spun.

"I'm . . . a friend from Morinville," Jonathan said, reaching out to shake Stephen's hand.

"I'm Stephen Lapp—Morinville, you say? Rosmanda's town?"

"Yah." He turned toward Rosmanda and shot her an easy smile. "How are you? Sorry to surprise you like that. Do you need to sit down? You look a little pale."

She did, in fact, need to sit, and Rosmanda sank into the chair next to her daughters. She sucked in a stabilizing breath as her mind spun to catch up.

"How did you find me?" she asked weakly.

"It's the funniest story," Jonathan said, and he chuckled in preparation for it. "I wrote you that letter, and I didn't hear back. We were worried, you know. It had been so long since we saw you. Anyway, I took a bus out to Abundance, and the first place I started asking around for you, Levi here walked right in and said you lived with his family."

"That sounds like providence to me," Stephen said.

"That's just what I said!" Jonathan smiled again. "And I'm glad to see you, Rosmanda. You look well."

That wasn't true. She didn't look well, and she knew it. But he was lying in more than that. His easy smile, his talk of providence . . . he wasn't acting like a man who'd just abandoned his family.

"Did you get his letter?" Miriam asked, turning toward Rosmanda. "Was that the one that came the other day?"

She smiled weakly. "Yes, but I didn't answer because a visit wouldn't have been convenient—"

"It's no bother," Miriam said. "Rosmanda, really. Your friends are our friends. If you'd only told me, we could have made plans."

Jonathan wasn't her friend in the strictest sense, and she'd made a mistake in communicating with him at all. Rosmanda looked at him hesitantly.

"Sit down and have something to eat," Miriam said. "Both of you! You must be frozen from that rain tonight, and there is plenty of roast left."

For the next few minutes Rosmanda cleaned her daughters' places at the table, and then scooped them up in her arms, holding them close. She felt the threat in the room as palpably as if it were a snake winding around her ankles. She wanted her babies as far from this man as possible, and yet she was terrified to leave the room, unsure of what he'd say.

In the letter he'd said he was coming to declare his feelings for her—had he changed his mind?

"Rosmanda—"

She startled and found her mother-in-law at her side.

"Dear, are you all right?" Miriam asked.

"Yes," Rosmanda said, forcing some brightness to her tone. "Surprised is all."

"Let me get the girls washed up and start their bottles," Miriam said. "Your friend has come a long way to see you, and I suspect he wants to be able to report back to your daet that you're doing well. Spend a little time with him. He seems like a decent, married man who is very likely helping your father to find out how you are."

Jonathan might be married, but he wasn't decent, and Rosmanda could say nothing without giving herself away.

"Come to Mammi, little one," Miriam said, holding her arms out for the girls. Susanna reached back, but Hannah clung to Rosmanda's dress.

Miriam took Susanna in her arms, shifted her to one hip, and held out her other arm expectantly. Handing her babies over to let their grandmother help—it was the most reasonable thing in the world, but nothing tonight was reasonable. And her mother-in-law was right, albeit more right than she realized. Rosmanda needed to deal with Jonathan herself, and head-on. She needed to get rid of him before he did any damage to her reputation.

"Go to Mammi, Hannah," Rosmanda said, kissing her daughter's cheek. "Mamm will come soon to cuddle you, okay? Go with Mammi."

Rosmanda unlatched Hannah's grip, and as the baby started to wail, Miriam whisked them both up the stairs. Hannah's cries subsided after a moment or two, and Miriam's cheerful voice filtered down the stairs toward them. Her daughters were fine. Rosmanda steeled herself and turned toward the table where the men were talking amongst themselves.

"How long have you been married?" Stephen asked.

"Nine years now," Jonathan said.

"He's married to my older sister's best friend," Rosmanda cut in. "Her name is Mary, and she's a good woman."

Jonathan paused, eyeing her for a moment. Stephen shot Rosmanda a look of surprise.

"Rosmanda. The man was talking," her father-in-law remonstrated.

Rosmanda pinched her lips shut. Yes, when the men spoke, the women stayed silent. What happened when the men lied?

"Rosmanda is right," Jonathan said. "We all knew each other . . . rather well."

Rosmanda picked up some empty plates and began to stack them at one end of the table.

"But I want to know about Rosmanda," Jonathan said, turning toward her. "Your daughters are very sweet."

"Thank you." She reached for Levi's plate this time, and when she looked up, she found his dark gaze locked on her face. But unlike his father, he wasn't judging her tartness. He looked perplexed, and a little worried, and as she reached for the plate, his finger brushed against hers.

Rosmanda was tired of playing this game already. She didn't want Jonathan under this roof tonight, and it would have to be his choice to leave, because her in-laws would hospitably host him otherwise.

"Jonathan, I assume that you want to speak with me about something," Rosmanda said, wiping her hands on a cloth. "After coming all this way to see me . . ."

"I do, actually." Jonathan glanced toward Stephen.

"Why don't you go talk in the sitting room?" Stephen suggested.

Rosmanda shot her father-in-law a grateful smile, hoping to set everyone's minds at ease.

"Thank you, Daet," she said. "Jonathan, shall we?"

She was taking control of the situation in a rather unfeminine way, but she wasn't looking to impress Jonathan on her femininity. She wanted to chase him out. But all the same, she waited for him to go ahead of her into the sitting room, and she followed him at a polite distance. She'd find some way to explain herself to her father-in-law later, but she had to face the threat first.

"Daet, do you want some tea?" Levi asked, and Rosmanda glanced at Levi catching that same cautious, perplexed gaze following her.

Rosmanda didn't hear her father-in-law's response as she entered the sitting room. Jonathan stood on the opposite side, as far from the kitchen as he could get. Good—she didn't want their conversation overheard, either.

"I got your letter," Rosmanda said softly. "And the answer is no."

"Rosie—" He reached for her, and she slapped his hand away. He recoiled, eyeing her with a mixture of anger and surprise.

"Don't touch me," she hissed. "You are married, Jonathan. What do you expect? You have five kinner! You have a life. I don't know why you'd even come to me . . ."

"Rosmanda," he said, but his tone was more cautious this time. "What we felt—it was real."

"You married her, Jonathan."

"I was forced—"

"You got her pregnant!" She lowered her voice to a whisper. "You lied to me! You told me that your engagement was a little too pure, that you felt more like a fond brother than anything else. But she was pregnant before you got married, and you know how that happened."

Jonathan chewed the side of his cheek. "She should have stopped me."

"Yah? Like I'm doing now?" Rosmanda stepped closer so that she could keep her voice low. "You need to leave."

"Not yet," he replied. "I've surprised you. You're upset. But if I can't tell you how I feel about you, at least, I think I'll go crazy."

"I don't want you here. You came for me, and I'm not interested. Get out." It seemed simple enough to her. He'd asked in his letter if she loved him still, and this was her answer.

"No." He cocked his head to one side, and his eyes narrowed. "I didn't come all the way out here for a five-minute conversation, and to be sent home. I came a long way for you. I deserve a proper conversation at least."

She shook her head. "And what kind of future do you envision, Jonathan? Because you're a married man with kinner. Are you actually planning on leaving them?"

"We could go to another community," he said with a wistful smile. "We'll change our names. We'll call ourselves Nathaniel and Patience Lantz. We'll start over. No one will know we aren't already married."

"No! God would! And I certainly would." This time, she couldn't keep her voice down and the words rang out through the room.

"Shh . . ." Jonathan hissed and he crossed the room, catching her by the arm. "Rosie, I don't even know what I'm saying. I know that's not really possible. I do. It's just . . . I can't go on pretending that everything is fine, either. I can't pretend I don't love you. I adore you. I have for years. I should have married you when I had the chance—"

He went on in that manner, but Rosmanda had tuned him out. She stood there, her arm in his grip. What was he asking of her—to be his mistress? To run away with him? Or was he just taking a little vacation from family life to indulge some emotional excess?

"What about the love we used to share?" Jonathan asked, shaking his head. "We didn't care what the community wanted. We didn't care if we went against all their expectations . . . You loved me then, and you won me!"

"No, I didn't," she said, her voice shaking. "You married Mary."

"What about our happiness, Rosmanda?" he pleaded. He dropped her arm, though, and she rubbed the spot where his fingers had dug into her flesh.

"What about it?" she asked numbly.

"We do the right thing at all cost, and for what? To please the community? To please the church? What about *us*? What about what makes us happy? A lifetime is a long time, Rosie. I'm realizing that. I know who I love, and I know who I want to be with. I don't have the answers, but I know what I feel."

"Jonathan, stop that nonsense," she said quietly, trying to keep her voice controlled.

"Do you think God wants us to deny our love? For people? For the opinions of others? Are we supposed to obey men or God?"

Jonathan was twisting Scripture now, and Rosmanda crossed her arms protectively over her middle. There was a time when she'd swooned for words like those, feeling some sort of rebellious freedom, but not anymore. Not only had she gotten over those naïve feelings for Jonathan, but she'd seen the error of her ways. Jonathan hadn't had to pay like she had . . . if she hadn't left town and gone as far away as possible, she'd still be unmarried and childless. And he'd still have his wife and five children.

"There is no love," she said. "I don't know what you're feeling, but I don't love you anymore. And I'm not that woman who was willing to break up another couple anymore, either. I have done things that I truly regret now, but I got my new start here in Abundance, and what you're suggesting is repugnant and wrong. You think God is in this? You're fooling yourself."

Jonathan fell silent. What was he hoping to do? The longer he stayed here, the more questions would be asked. And when people started asking questions of the right people, stories emerged. Her life here could be over just as quickly as hers had ended in Morinville.

"You need to leave," she said quietly. "*Please*."

She had run out of ammunition, and she'd resorted to pleading.

God, help me . . .

This was desperation.

Chapter Nine

Levi stood at the doorway to the sitting room, watching Rosmanda and Jonathan. They stood by the window, only a few inches between them. Rosmanda's spine was rigid and she had her arms crossed over the front of her. Jonathan leaned in, his words too quiet for Levi to hear.

He'd fully intended to give Rosmanda her privacy, but after his daet had gone out to the outhouse, Rosmanda had shouted out a "No" that made his hair stand on end. So now he stood here at the door, watching them.

Rosmanda didn't seem to be in any danger—except that closeness between them gave him pause. She didn't back away. She didn't sit across the room from him as would be proper. She stood there in the center of the room, arms crossed and barely inches away from this man.

Jonathan's gaze flickered up, and he froze for a moment when he saw Levi standing there. Rosmanda turned then, too, and she stared at him with those wide, dark eyes, and her cheeks ashen.

Was that fear? But of what? Something was wrong.

"Everything okay?" Levi asked, his voice low.

"Yah. Thank you," Jonathan said, a smile coming to his lips. "I was hoping for a cup of tea, actually—"

"Rosie?" Levi said, meeting her gaze. "Are *you* okay?"

"No," she whispered. "I'm not."

Levi's hands closed into involuntary fists, and his gaze moved between them. What was happening here? Had there been some bad news about her daet, after all? He'd told Jonathan that she'd need some warning—some tea, even. A seat . . .

"Is your daet okay?" he asked.

"My daet?" She looked confused, then shook her head. "I think so. Yah."

So it wasn't that.

"Jonathan, you can feel free to serve yourself a mug of tea out in the kitchen," Levi said. "Mamm will be down soon to get you some pie, I'm sure. I just need to talk to my sister-in-law for a minute."

Jonathan looked pleadingly at Rosmanda, but she looked resolutely at a point to her left. Whatever they'd been talking about in hushed tones, it had left Rosmanda visibly shaken.

"I hope I didn't upset her—" Jonathan said with a wince, sharing a friendly look with Levi. As if they were buddies, on the same team. Levi wasn't so sure that they were, though.

"I'll just be a minute," Levi said.

Jonathan headed out of the room, and Rosmanda slowly lifted her gaze to meet his.

"What happened?" Levi asked, crossing those last few feet between them. "You look like you've seen a wolf."

"You have to get him out of here." Rosmanda's voice trembled. "Please, Levi. Get him out!"

"Why?" Levi shook his head. "I thought he was a friend from your town—"

"He is." She shook her head. "He was . . . I don't know how to explain this quickly, but Levi, you have to trust me on this. He can't stay here tonight. You have to get him out!"

"I can't just throw him out," Levi said with a short laugh.

"Why not?" She shook her head.

"What reason do I have?" He caught Rosmanda's hand, and she squeezed his fingers back.

"You have *me* asking you—begging you—to get him out of here and not let him back. I'll explain later. I promise. But right now—"

Levi heard the front door open and Daet came back inside from the outhouse. They both looked toward the door, and Rosmanda squeezed his hand again.

"Please, Levi. Trust me on this. That man can't stay under this roof without my reputation being forever damaged."

The low murmur of male voices came from the kitchen, and Levi met her gaze. She was scared, that much was certain.

"Who is he?" Levi whispered.

"Jonathan Yoder." Her lips turned down in distaste, but she didn't explain further. Levi looked toward the kitchen, his mind spinning. He could go in there and demand explanations from the man, or he could do as Rosmanda was pleading with him to do, and he could bring Jonathan back to town. "He wrote me a letter saying he wants to leave his wife for me. And now he's here—"

Her words hit him like a punch to the gut. "He wants—" Levi blinked. "What?"

"It's true." Her lips quivered. "Levi, get him out! Please!"

Yah—there was no way around that, but he couldn't just go out there and throw a man from his father's house, either. He'd find a way.

"Leave it to me," Levi said, and he turned and strode back into the kitchen, leaving Rosmanda in the sitting room alone. Miriam was back downstairs, and she handed Jonathan a plate of pie that he accepted with an easy smile.

Jonathan sat at the table, the dirty plates piled on one end still. A mug of steaming tea sat in front of him and he picked up a fork to take a bite. He looked comfortably settled in for the evening.

"Where is Rosmanda?" Miriam asked. "The babies are in bed now. They went down without a fuss tonight."

"Jonathan, let's talk," Levi said with a chilly smile. "Shall we?"

Jonathan froze. "Uh—"

"What's this?" Stephen asked as he sat back down at his place at the table. Miriam brought him a plate of pie, too, and he accepted it, his gaze locked warily on Levi.

"Just . . . something between us," Levi replied. "You and me, Jonathan. Let's walk a little bit."

Jonathan rose to his feet, hesitating slightly when he saw the look on Levi's face.

"Levi," Stephen said, irritated. "What's going on?"

"Nothing I can't straighten out," Levi replied. "Jonathan—*now*."

Jonathan laughed uncomfortably. "Whatever it is, I'm sure we'll sort it out."

Levi waited for him at the door, and when he passed into the mudroom, Levi picked up his suitcase and marched outside in the evening chill. Jonathan followed him, eyeing his suitcase.

"Walk," Levi said brusquely, and he headed toward the stable.

"If you're planning on fighting me—" Jonathan started.

"I'm not fighting you," Levi said, turning back. "It

wouldn't be a fight, my friend. Trust me on that. I'm used to bar brawls—the dirty kind. So I don't suggest you try anything, either. I'm taking you back to town."

"Now?" Jonathan looked up at the darkening sky. "It's late."

"It is," Levi agreed. "And you're leaving."

"I don't know what Rosmanda said to you," Jonathan said with a short laugh. "But there must have been some confusion."

"She said you want to leave your wife for her," Levi said, looking back at the other man with one raised eyebrow.

Jonathan rubbed a hand over his beard, then laughed, a beat too late. "She mustn't have understood me. I'm not leaving my wife."

Levi eyed the other man for a moment. Maybe he was telling the truth. Maybe he had no intention of leaving his wife, but he most certainly wanted something from Rosmanda. She wasn't the hysterical type. If anything, she was level-headed to a fault.

"Don't call her a liar," Levi said curtly, but even as the words came out of his mouth, he wondered what else there was to this story. A man didn't arrive in a strange town asking a woman to run away with him without any encouragement at all . . . did he? How much had Rosmanda held back?

He'd seen her frightened, and he wanted to protect her. But as the chilly spring air did its work on his brain, freeing up his thoughts and slowing him into a regular rhythm once more, he couldn't help but see the holes in his understanding of what happened tonight.

This young man came looking for her, and Levi had trustingly brought him home. But there was more to this than Levi was going to understand fully before he was through tonight.

"Help me hitch up," Levi said. "If you stay tonight, I'll be fetching the bishop to deal with you directly. So I suggest you come with me and I'll drop you off at the bus station."

Jonathan didn't say anything else, but he did lend a hand in hitching up the horses. He tossed his suitcase into the back of the buggy, and when all was secure, both men got inside.

"I haven't done anything wrong," Jonathan said.

Levi flicked the reins and they lurched forward. He heard the side door open, but he didn't even look over to see his confused parents stare at them leaving. They'd want an explanation, and he didn't have all the information yet. He was doing this for Rosmanda—that was it.

They rode in silence for several minutes as they left the farm property and headed out onto the open road.

"You've judged me," Jonathan said, breaking the silence.

"Yah," Levi agreed. "I have."

"Rosmanda and I used to mean a great deal to each other, you know," Jonathan said.

There was a lot that Levi didn't know about Rosmanda's past. She didn't like to speak about it. He'd assumed it was the humiliation of being passed over in the marriage market, but of course, there might have been some "near marriages."

"That happens," Levi said gruffly.

"I'm not some lecherous animal trying to ruin a good woman," Jonathan said with a sigh. "I'm not. I know you don't believe that right now, but you could be in my shoes just as easily. Do you know what it's like to marry the wrong woman?"

"Obviously not," Levi said.

"Yah, you're still single. But you could do it. You could find a good girl from a nice family and start taking her home from singing. And there might be no good reason to stop. Maybe your fathers do business together, and everyone is so happy that you're courting this girl. And you think everything is fine until this other girl starts making eyes at you. She tells you that if only she were older, she'd like to go around with a man like you. She asks you to kiss her, just once, so she can see what it's like. . . ."

Rosmanda? This didn't sound like her at all. She'd gone after a man who was already courting another girl?

"You're saying Rosmanda did this?" he asked.

"And more. She woke me right up. If I had a choice between the prim and proper Mary or Rosmanda, I wanted Rosmanda."

"Then you could have broken it off with the first one," Levi said.

"Yah. And I did. We were about to announce the engagement in service, and I told Mary I couldn't go through with it. The problem was, I'm a man with a man's appetite. And before Rosmanda cast a glance at me, I thought I was going to marry Mary, and just once, Mary and I went too far. Once. It wasn't a beautiful event. It didn't leave me feeling bonded to this woman. It left me feeling rather empty and guilty for my mistake. I thought that was because it was outside of wedlock, and that once we were married it would be satisfying."

"And she got pregnant?" Levi concluded.

"Yah. She got pregnant. So that wedding was going through, or I was going to be shunned."

"Look, I can sympathize with missing out on the girl

you love," Levi said. "I really can. But you make the best of it. You had a wife. A child."

"They tell you that if you find a good mother with good daughters, any girl you choose will do," Jonathan replied. "They tell you that when you settle down with a wife who loves you, that it all comes together. That you find peace, contentment, happiness. It wasn't like that for us."

Levi didn't answer. He didn't know what to say. There was a woman somewhere in Morinville waiting for her husband to come home. Blissfully married or not, that woman would be beside herself with worry. And Jonathan had come out here after the woman who had almost succeeded in breaking up his engagement?

Rosmanda . . . It was so hard to imagine her in that position. Had she really been that callous and coy? Or was this man lying? He hoped that Jonathan was a very competent liar, because if he wasn't, then Rosmanda was.

"It isn't just the arguing," Jonathan went on. "A man can learn to avoid that by just shutting his mouth. And it isn't like Mary goes out of her way to pick fights with me. It's the loneliness. We sit at the same table, and there is no connection between us. Not like I had with Rosmanda. It never came. We live our life, we raise our children, we do our work. But I've spent the last nine years feeling utterly alone."

"Does your wife know where you are?" Levi asked.

"No."

"Do you care how she feels right now?"

Jonathan sighed. "Of course. I don't want to hurt her. I don't want to hurt our children. I want to love her like I should, but I can't. I've spent nine years trying and failing."

"So why are you here?" Levi asked.

"I don't know . . ." Jonathan shook his head. "I

shouldn't be. I know that. But I can't just go back, either. I can't do it . . ."

"Maybe the elders can help you reconcile with your wife."

"If only it were that easy. Mary will take me back. It isn't about that. She's a good Amish woman. She married me for life, and we have five children together. And I'm not a monster. I love my children. It's . . . I don't know. I hadn't realized how deeply unhappy I was until I got on that bus."

There was the right thing to do, and then there was living with it. Levi understood that experience rather well. His brother had married the woman he loved, and Levi had been forced to accept it. What else could he do? But that didn't make it easy, and it didn't get any easier over time. When Levi had fallen in love with Rosmanda, it had been more permanent than he'd imagined. If he could have stopped loving her, he would have. It was why he'd turned to drinking, and why he hadn't courted another girl. He could definitely understand how loving another woman could hold a man back, but this man beside him was a married father.

"Just because you love a woman doesn't mean she's good for you," Levi said. "Chasing her will ruin your life. You'll lose everything—your wife's love, your children's respect, your community's good opinion of you—"

And Rosmanda wasn't good for Levi, either. Levi would do well to find a nice girl and settle down, except that he was afraid that settling down with another woman wouldn't fix his problem. Much like Jonathan. But even so, Levi wouldn't become like Jonathan. He wouldn't be unfaithful.

"I know," Jonathan said softly.

"Why did you come?" Levi asked. "It's been nine years. Why now?"

"Didn't you know?" Jonathan raised an eyebrow. "She and I have been writing to each other for months."

No, he hadn't known. But it did explain why a man would expect a welcome.

"Months?" he asked feebly.

"Yah. I wrote when I heard of her husband's death. And she wrote back. She's been the one bright spot in my days. I looked forward to her letters like food for the starving."

It was a poetic turn of phrase, and that uneasy feeling in his gut stretched into something deeper—something closer to heartbreak.

She'd been writing to him for months. . . .

"Go home," Levi said at last. "Go back to your wife. Hold your kinner. If you push this too far, you'll lose not only your family, but you'll get yourself shunned, too."

The very thought of a shunning was enough to send shivers down Levi's spine. To be shunned was to lose everything a man held dear, everything familiar.

"I can't," Jonathan said quietly. "It would be easier for me to lie to you, so please accept my honesty with the respect that is intended. I won't get on a bus tonight, or tomorrow, or the next day. I'm staying here until I've had my chance to talk to her properly."

And the words were said so meekly, but Levi could hear the threat underneath them. Jonathan wasn't leaving, and he wouldn't be pushed out of town. He wanted something from Rosmanda, whether she was willing to give it or not.

"She doesn't want to see you," Levi warned.

"I know."

"And I'm not letting you near her unless she wants to see you," Levi added.

"Understood." Jonathan smiled weakly. "I'm not leaving. Drop me off at the hotel, if you could be so kind."

Right. Levi wasn't feeling particularly kind tonight. And while Jonathan knew how to talk, how to defend himself, how to find some empathy in the breast of complete strangers, he couldn't undo the look on Rosmanda's face while she begged for Levi to get rid of him. She wasn't the woman Levi had always thought she was, but he wouldn't leave her to the wolves, either.

"I'm dropping you off at the bus station," Levi said curtly. "What you do from there is your business."

Jonathan didn't answer, and Levi drove on.

"What happened?" Miriam asked. "Where did he go?"

Rosmanda's mother-in-law stood at the bottom of the stairs holding a baby on each hip. They'd woken up again, not quite so easy to put to bed tonight as they had seemed.

"I'll put my girls to bed," Rosmanda said, coming forward to collect her babies. Hannah reached for Rosmanda with a plaintive cry, and even Susanna seemed rather eager to get back into her mother's arms.

"Wait." Stephen's voice was quiet, but it held authority.

Rosmanda adjusted the babies in her grasp and turned back.

"Yah, Daet?" she said weakly.

"Your father's friend came from your town to see you for a reason—"

"Not my father's friend," she interjected.

"Then who is he?" Stephen demanded.

"Like he said, he knew me when I was young. That's all."

"And why did Levi take his bag and drive him out of here?" Stephen demanded. "He was set to stay the night under this roof, and after a talk with you, Levi is herding him out of here like a rat."

A good image—Jonathan was just that. Rosmanda licked her lips. "He knew I was widowed . . . and single."

"He's a married man, Rosmanda," Miriam said with a shake of her head. "He's not here courting you."

"No, of course not," Rosmanda said bitterly. "All the same, I felt it was best he go back to his wife. I have my own reputation to worry about."

"At this time of night?" Miriam asked. "He wasn't even dry yet from the rain, and you thought it best he return to his wife? I'm sure his wife would like to get him back without pneumonia!"

Rosmanda couldn't tell them what Jonathan was really after, and as much as she could say made her look like a selfish idiot.

"You should go after him, Stephen," Miriam said. "Rosmanda has been under a lot of pressure. She should rest, and we need to fix this."

Rosmanda's heart sped up in her chest, and when her gaze flickered toward her father-in-law, she saw him scrutinizing her, her brows furrowed.

"No," he said slowly. "Levi took him back to town. We'll let that be."

She didn't dare thank her father-in-law for that, but she had to wonder what he'd read in her face that changed his mind. He pushed himself to his feet.

"I'm going to spend some time in prayer in the sitting room," Stephen said. "Don't disturb me."

Rosmanda looked over at her mother-in-law, wondering if Miriam would let this go, or demand more of an explanation. Miriam looked at the table filled with dishes and heaved a sigh.

"Go put the babies to bed," Miriam said. "I'll get the bottles for you."

Rosmanda carried her babies upstairs, her mind in turmoil. She might have escaped tonight—she could only pray that she'd managed it—but Levi was in a buggy with Jonathan right now, and she had no idea what Jonathan was telling him.

Rosmanda got her daughters to sleep that night without too much trouble, and once they were both sleeping, she gathered up the empty baby bottles and carried them downstairs.

"I can finish cleaning, Miriam," Rosmanda said.

Miriam stood at the sink, and she glanced over her shoulder in Rosmanda's direction.

"What happened, Rosmanda?" her mother-in-law asked softly. "Between us. As women. What did he want from you?"

"I don't know," she said softly. "But he wanted more familiarity than his wife would have liked, I can assure you. He and I are no longer friends. This will be a scandal if he stays. I know it."

Miriam pulled her hands from the water and dried them on a towel.

"All right," she said. "I'll let it go, then."

"Thank you, Mamm." Rosmanda smiled gratefully. "Go on up to bed. I'm going to be awake anyway, so I might as well keep my hands busy."

"Thank you, Rosmanda. Are you sure you're all right?"

"Yah. I'm all right." And she realized in a rush that she really was, and she managed a more natural smile.

"Good night," Miriam said, and she passed Rosmanda and headed for the stairs.

* * *

After the kitchen was clean, Rosmanda pulled out her quilt and tried to settle into work, but it was hard to focus. Stephen went up to bed shortly after his wife, and Rosmanda was left in the chilly quiet of a spring evening. Had she done it—had she escaped unscathed with her reputation intact?

Her in-laws seemed willing to accept this based on what they knew of her. And if this could go no further, she might be safe. If Jonathan went home now, perhaps he could tell Mary some story that wouldn't include her in it, and this could all pass by like a rock under a buggy wheel.

She lined up her next patch of color and pushed the needle into the fabric. Life was safer when she was married to Wayne, but it hadn't been easy, either. She'd done her best to please her husband, but she could sense that she'd been a disappointment to him, too. He might not have awakened any passion inside of her, but it went both ways. She couldn't give him what he craved, either.

Years ago, Rosmanda's sister Sadie had married an older man named Mervin Hochstetler. And Rosmanda had wondered why her beautiful sister would throw herself away on a man like that. He'd been nice enough, but quite old and gruff. While Rosmanda had only been a girl at the time, she'd noticed her sister's marital unhappiness. Mervin didn't make Sadie's heart sing. And seeing her sister's sparkle dwindle down to nothing had been part of what had driven Rosmanda toward that feeling of passion and excitement with Jonathan. She didn't want to lose herself in a humdrum marriage.

Wayne wasn't old and gruff like Mervin, but there hadn't been that spark of desire between them, either. At least not at the same time, it seemed. And she'd told herself that the mutual simmer between her and Jonathan had been because they were young. And then when she felt it again, except stronger, with Levi, it had frightened her. That kind of passion could be dangerous, too, and she didn't dare risk her future on it, especially after Aunt Dina had warned her about Levi.

And Jonathan's arrival had only solidified that point. Whatever allure Jonathan used to have as an older, more worldly-wise man had evaporated and now all she saw was a man willing to be unfaithful to his wife, and she wasn't willing to be partner to it. Would anyone care what she wanted? Or would Jonathan's desires sully her reputation regardless?

Rosmanda tied off her last stitch and eyed the next line of stitching. This quilt had moved her through her grief, but as she worked tonight, she realized that it was moving her beyond Wayne and into the older griefs, too. Like leaving her family behind in Morinville, and losing her faith in a man's desire to protect her against the evils of the world.

She smoothed the fabric and tied a knot in the end of her thread once more. If there was anything she'd learned in her experience with men, it was to be incredibly careful with the kinds of feelings that could scramble up a woman's logical thought. Levi was just as dangerous as Jonathan, if not more so. The fumbled kisses she'd shared with Jonathan were nothing compared to the passion Levi sparked within her.

But Levi wasn't safe, either. He'd spent the last four years drinking, getting into bar fights and neglecting his spiritual life. And when his lips came down onto hers, she still melted. . . .

The door opened, and Rosmanda looked up, startled. She hadn't heard the buggy approach, or perhaps she'd just been too deep in her own thoughts. Levi came inside, and he kicked the door shut behind him. His movements

were slow and heavy, and she sat in the light of the
kerosene lamp, her needle poised above her work.

"What happened?" Rosmanda asked softly.

Levi pulled off his hat and rubbed a hand over his
forehead. "I dropped him off at the bus depot."

"Oh, good . . ." Rosmanda lowered her quilt to her lap,
relief flooding through her. "I'm so glad—"

"He said he isn't leaving, though," Levi added. "He
wanted me to drop him off at the hotel, and I didn't feel
like complying."

Rosmanda looked up at him, her breath bated. "He
won't leave?"

"No."

She licked her lips and dropped her gaze, her thoughts
spinning ahead.

"He said you've been writing to him for months," Levi
said. He pulled out a kitchen chair opposite her and sank
into it. "Is that true?"

This wasn't the same Levi from the chicken house . . .
or the same Levi sparring with her in the barn. This was a
different man in front of her—wiser, warier, and tired. His
dark gaze met hers. He saw her differently now—his eyes
didn't soften—and tears misted her vision as that fact
sank in.

Levi had just learned too much.

"He wrote me when Wayne died," she said, her voice
tight. "And I wrote back. It felt good to be able to talk to
someone about it. It was stupid on my part. I had thought
he was just being kind. We wrote back and forth a few
times, and then I didn't answer his letter because it seemed
a bit too familiar. I felt something . . . wrong . . . in it. Then
he wrote me another letter, saying he was coming out to
see me, and he had feelings for me . . . and all that."

She met Levi's gaze. "I admit that I wrote to him. I

admit I was probably too open with him. But I had no intention of starting up anything romantic!"

"But you did have a romantic history with him," Levi said.

"I was sixteen." She sighed. "And he treated me like I was much older. He opened up to me. He treated me like an actual friend. And I . . . fell in love with him. In a stupid moment, I asked him to kiss me, and he did. Yes, he was dating Mary at the time. And when I realized that they were engaged, I got competitive. I thought I could make him marry me, instead."

"So that was true?" Levi's tone was hesitant.

It seemed like Jonathan had told Levi everything, as she feared he would. But would he stop with Levi, or would he tell other people, too?

"I'm not proud of it," she whispered. "And I'm only telling you because after what you've done for me, you deserve some honesty. It ruined me in Morinville. I was young enough to be quite stupid, but old enough to play the game. It's not a great mix. I was branded the wrong kind of girl. That's why I came to stay with my aunt here in Abundance."

"Sixteen isn't very old," Levi said quietly.

"No, it isn't." A lump rose in her throat. "But it's old enough."

It had been old enough for the community to see her potential and to steer clear. Other girls got more distanced and stopped telling her about their boyfriends. Wives looked at her with pointed judgment. She'd crossed a line, and the women had turned on her.

Levi sighed. "You should get some sleep, Rosmanda."

He was dismissing her now. He was tired, and he'd have to get up before dawn to work. He'd just driven her ex-lover into town . . . He'd gone out of his way for her, but the old Levi she'd started to rely on had hardened and distanced himself.

"I'm not the same woman," she said softly.

"I hope not," he said with a nod.

"I was a good and true wife to Wayne," she went on. "I learned from my mistake."

Levi nodded, and for a moment that controlled mask of his cracked and the old, warm, tender Levi shone through. But mixed with the old familiarity was pain. She'd hurt him. "I'm not judging you, Rosie."

But he was judging her. There was no getting around it, and she wanted to shake him by his suspenders and make him react like his old self again. She couldn't do that, though.

"Will you keep my secret?" she asked earnestly, leaning forward. "I know it might get out anyway, but there's still some hope right now that it won't. For my daughters—will you keep my secret for them? If their mother has a stained reputation, you know it will make their lives that much more difficult."

"I won't tell anyone," Levi said. "It's your business."

Then he rose to his feet and headed toward the stairs.

"Levi?"

He turned back.

"I'm sorry," she whispered.

"Yah. I know," he said. "But you don't have to apologize to me. Best get some rest."

Then he turned again and headed up the stairs, leaving her in quiet. She sucked in a wavering breath as the reality of the situation sank onto her shoulders. Her secret was out. Her secret had arrived on a bus from Morinville . . . and her life was never going to be the same again. As she began to sew the next row of stitches, tears blurred her vision, and she let her work drop back down to her lap.

She never thought she'd care too much of Levi's opinion of her, but it turned out that she did. Whatever he used to think of her was soiled now, and he'd changed in the span of that one buggy ride. He'd closed off, and that realization stabbed deeper than she'd thought it could.

The stain from Morinville had finally reached her.

Chapter Ten

Rosmanda sat at the table, a bowl of applesauce in front of her and a small spoon held aloft. Hannah and Susanna both had applesauce on their chins, and Hannah opened her mouth for more. Rosmanda was tired, and while she'd cried last night, it hadn't emptied her out of tears, either, and she'd been struggling all morning to keep her emotions in check. She'd agreed to work with Ketura today, but she wasn't sure she had it in her to keep up appearances.

"Maybe I should just stay home today," Rosmanda said.

"Of course, you need to go," Miriam said. "You told Ketura you would, and if you're going to be helping her in her business, you should take this seriously. Ketura doesn't exaggerate things, and if she thinks you could make a good amount off your sewing, then you can. And Ketura won't work with just anyone. Bethany Yoder wanted to work with Ketura last year, and Ketura wouldn't do it. So this is . . . special."

Rosmanda had agreed to do this, and she would need the income from working with Ketura, too. And yet, she wasn't ready to face it all today.

"Why?" Miriam softened her tone. "What are you afraid of?"

"It's nothing." Rosmanda shook her head quickly.

"You're a good mother," Miriam said with a smile. "If you're worried about being away from your daughters, don't be. Doing something for you and letting me help out is normal. I promise you that."

Such warmth and support. Rosmanda had gotten used to this, but maybe she shouldn't. If news got out about her past in Morinville, this warm view of her as a mother and a widow would be well in the past, and she'd quickly find her experience with the women of Morinville repeating itself here in Abundance. Rosmanda had been married, yes, but her husband was gone. And not only did she need another husband, but she'd be seen as single and on the prowl. Even if finding a new man was the last thing on her mind.

Rosmanda scraped the bowl and gave a bite of apple-sauce to Hannah. Susanna didn't seem interested in it anymore, and Rosmanda leaned forward and wiped their mouths with a cloth.

"Was that yummy?" she asked, smiling into their faces. "Did you like that?"

It was amazing how quickly babies grew. It felt like only yesterday she'd been holding two downy-headed newborns in her arms, Wayne crouching next to her, looking at the infants with such awe on his face. . . .

But that was another lifetime ago.

Miriam glanced out the window. "Levi has the buggy ready. You'd best get moving. I'll clean the girls up. Don't worry about that."

Rosmanda and Levi were supposed to be moving on as if nothing had changed, but everything had changed between her and Levi. There was a distance there between them that hadn't been there before. Granted, they'd been fighting those feelings that kept tugging them together like magnets, but that didn't seem to be an issue anymore.

Levi now knew the worst.

After some kisses for her daughters and wrapping her shawl around her shoulders, Rosmanda gathered up the quilt she'd been working on, now carefully wrapped in a length of plastic and tied with twine. She headed out the side door and shut it firmly behind her. Levi had the buggy pulled up by the house, and he gave her a nod.

Rosmanda put her package in the back of the buggy and then pulled herself up to sit next to Levi. He gave the reins a flick and the horses started.

"I could have driven myself," Rosmanda said.

"Yah, but I've got some business with my aunt, anyway," he replied.

"Oh." He certainly wasn't here because he wanted to be. Hadn't that been her goal before—to lever some distance between the two of them? Whatever it was about Levi, he didn't leave her thinking straight. And that was dangerous. But this chilly gulf between them was more unsettling than she'd been prepared for.

"I thought we were going to at least pretend to be friends," Rosmanda said.

"Pretend?" He cast her a quick look.

"Obviously, you're upset," she said.

"Yah, I am." He leaned forward and looked both ways as they got to the road, and then flicked the reins for the horses to carry on onto the road.

"I was young," she said, her voice shaking. "I was, admittedly, very stupid. I didn't even know God very well back then. I thought I did, but it was all lip service. But I can assure you that I've gotten to know Him very well since. So if you think I'm that same girl now—"

"You think I'm angry because I'm judging you?" he demanded.

She'd seen the way his eyes had changed since he found

out her secret. The way he looked at her was different. The way he acted around her was more reserved, too. He didn't let his shoulder brush against her. He stood back and waited for her to pass in front of him lest his hand brush hers. His manners had become exhausting.

"Yah. What else would it be?" she said.

"I'm angry because—" He grit his teeth together. "It doesn't even matter."

"It matters to me," she countered. "You've changed toward me. You're different now, and you say you aren't judging my adolescent stupidity, but I think you are."

"I've changed, have I?" he shot back. "Maybe I have. I realized something, Rosmanda. You treated me like something under your boot for years. You acted like I was some kind of messed-up loser compared to you, the *bishop's daughter*." The words dripped with disdain. "You had expectations that men had to reach for."

"I didn't do that." Was that really how he saw her?

"You did," he said. "And then you tossed me aside for my brother."

"So, we come back to that?" Rosmanda shook her head. "I chose him. He was a good man, and he's the father of my children—"

"It's not about that anymore," Levi said, but another buggy was approaching, and he fell into silence. Rosmanda sat back in the seat, pasting what she hoped looked like a prim, appropriate look on her face. The approaching buggy was a neighbor, and he gave them a nod.

"Morning," the neighbor said.

"Good morning," Levi replied.

Rosmanda just nodded and gave a smile. The horses plodded on past them, and Rosmanda kept her stewing emotions silent for another couple of minutes, lest her words carry.

"So what is it about?" Rosmanda asked, turning toward him again.

Levi glanced over his shoulder at the retreating buggy. "Just tell me straight—how do you see me?"

"I don't even know how to answer that," she said with a shake of her head. "You're my brother-in-law."

"Who you kiss from time to time—"

"That was obviously a mistake!" Tears misted her eyes. "What are you saying, that I'm some kind of tramp?"

"No!" Levi turned toward her, his gaze filled with something she'd never seen before—a combination of anger and grief. "I don't think that of you. And don't say it again. My point is that *you* think I'm some kind of loser. I'm the one who wasn't safe enough to marry. I'm the one who messed everything up when you dumped me, and ended up drinking my nights away in the bar. I'm the one who's messed up, right?"

Rosmanda didn't answer, her gaze locked on him.

"Right, then," he said, as if that finalized it. "And all that time you had *this* hidden away?"

"You think I'd advertise it?" she asked with a bitter laugh.

"No. Of course not. I thought that if you had something of this magnitude hidden away in your past that you might have a little more empathy for people around you who have their own struggles. That's what I thought."

"I have empathy," she said, her voice shaking.

"All those years, you stayed away from me," he said. "You could have talked to me at service. You could have invited me for dinner. Anything—"

That wasn't a lack of empathy. That had been her own fears that whatever attraction had been there before would still be there . . . and everyone would see it.

"It wasn't my place to invite you—" she began.

"Was it your place to say hello?" he demanded. "Was it your place to treat me like a human being, or a part of the family?"

"I'm the daughter-in-law!" she shot back. "What power do I have? None! I do as I'm asked. I work hard. And I was a good wife to your brother. I was supposed to fix that rift between the two of you?"

"No, you were supposed to fix the rift between you and me!" His voice rose, and he shut his eyes for a moment, then softened his tone. "You made me feel like a walking failure, Rosie. Compared to you—compared to Wayne who'd been good enough for you—I was the black sheep."

Rosmanda fell silent. She'd been careful, yes. And Levi had proven himself just as unreliably dangerous as she'd feared he'd be. After all she'd been through in Morinville, she needed safety, security, even a little bit of boredom.

"You weren't a loser," Rosmanda whispered. "You were a risk."

"And I still am," he barked.

"Yah. You still are!" Was she supposed to lie to him? "You aren't a nice, stable farmer. You don't weigh your words before you speak. You don't find a nice girl who can cook and settle down like a rational man would. You're thirty years old, and you're still single!"

Rosmanda's hands were shaking and she met his gaze, refusing to look down. What did he want from her, for her to forgive all his shortcomings because she had a few of her own? She wasn't strong enough to make up for his! She had her own past chasing her down.

"Single. That's what makes me a problem?" he asked with a bitter laugh. "I'm single because I don't want to make a woman miserable. Would you rather I be like your friend Jonathan?" The name sounded bitter in his mouth.

"Be unfaithful?" she asked in disgust.

"I wouldn't ever do that, but I could marry a girl I don't love and let her find that out ever so slowly. It's not only physical unfaithfulness that can break a woman, you know. I could settle down with some nice girl and break her heart when I can't open mine. Does that sound better? Because from what Jonathan says, that's what he did."

"I didn't say that," she countered.

"Good, because I'm single. For good reason. I won't do that to a woman."

Rosmanda was silent for a moment, his words settling into her mind. He wouldn't put a woman through the misery that Mary was living right now. And that was commendable, but there was a solution that she could see rather plainly—one that would allow him to move on with his life, and would put him safely and solidly out of her reach.

"You *should* open your heart," she said. "You're right—holding yourself back would only hurt your wife. So why hold yourself back? Find a nice girl and marry her."

"The last time I opened my heart, she saw who I was in all my scarred and imperfect glory, and she married my brother."

His words were like a slap, and she blinked, settling back against the seat. She'd broken his heart when he'd opened up to her. He'd told her his fears and his hopes, his insecurities, and she'd recognized that he was more complicated than a stable, pious farmer would be. He thought more. He questioned more. He didn't accept simple platitudes to comfort him. And neither did she! She couldn't marry a man just like her. She saw the risk.

"So you're angry that I never told you this," she said.

"I understand you not telling me," he replied woodenly. "I'm angry you made me feel like the only one with issues."

Rosmanda had done that. It had been part of her carefully constructed new life. She had to be perfect, untouchable by gossip. She couldn't risk anything again.

"Well, now you know." Did he know how frightening this was for her? Did he recognize how vulnerable this made her?

"And I'd be glad if from now on you could recognize that I'm no more messed up than you are," he said.

She nodded, swallowing hard. "Yah."

His expression softened somewhat, and he sighed. "I get it. You had to find a safe farmer. My brother was just that. There were no layers with him. There were no complications. No risk."

"He was ideal," she agreed softly. "A genuinely good man without any guile."

"Well, a little bit of guile," Levi said humorlessly. "He did steal you away, after all."

Rosmanda sighed. Yah, a little bit of guile, it would seem, but it was nothing compared to what she'd done.

"You'll find another uncomplicated man," Levi went on. "And perhaps in the meantime, we could have a bit of mutual respect, you and I."

"I thought we had that," she whispered. "Lately, at least."

"Yah, but now it can be based on truth, not just a deal to avoid talking about the hard stuff."

Rosmanda smiled wanly. "You mean like real friends?"

"We might have earned it by this point," he said.

It looked like they had. But somehow, this real friendship felt harder to handle than their agreement to get along. Because before, she'd had the high ground to herself, whether she'd deserved it or not. And now, he knew the worst about her, too.

She didn't like this. It felt a little too much like the risk she'd been running from.

Levi drove up in front of Josiah and Anna's house and reined in the horses. He'd said too much—he hadn't meant to come out with all of that. He'd meant to keep it inside and let it inform how he went forward. That was the Amish way, at least. Arguing and confrontation didn't have a place in the Amish community. But then, he'd never been any Amish ideal, had he?

And neither had Rosmanda . . . underneath. He was still spinning from the revelations about her past. Rosmanda had been the image of Amish perfection here in Abundance. Had he made that up in his own head? He hadn't seen any indication that she was anything but. However, it was commonly known that a man could be blinded by a beautiful woman, and Rosmanda had always been the kind of girl that made his heart speed up at the very sight of her.

He looked over at Rosmanda sitting primly beside him. Could he really be blamed for believing the image she put out there?

"Go on in," Levi said. "I'll unhitch."

Rosmanda looked over at him hesitantly. "I can help."

Even that was the perfect Amish offer—a woman willing to pitch in where needed.

"I don't need help." He didn't mean for it to sound as harsh as it did, but he wasn't over his anger just yet, either.

"All right, then." She reached back for her package, and then slid down to the ground. Levi handed the quilt down to her, and she headed toward the house. He flicked the reins, getting the horses moving again.

He was angry still, he realized. And in times past, he would head out to the bar and drink it away. Or at least it had felt like his emotions were washed out with the alcohol, but it never worked. Not permanently. When he woke up the next morning with a brutal hangover, his problems would be right back where he left them. But he wasn't going to do that anymore, and it was taking more self-control to kick old habits than he liked. It wasn't the taste of alcohol that he missed, it was the temporary oblivion.

He reined the horses in next to another buggy, and when he hopped down, he saw Aaron leading some horses out to the corral. Aaron saw him and waved.

Levi had told himself that he'd face his problems from now on, but it seemed like he had more than his fair share right now.

"Good morning!" Aaron called, heading in his direction.

Levi nodded to him and started to unhitch. Aaron went to the other horse and began doing the same. They worked in silence for a few moments, until the horses were loose. They took off the saddles and Aaron patted the horse's neck, then looked over at Levi.

"Did you talk to your daet?" he asked.

"Yah." Levi nodded. "I did."

Levi took both horses by the bridles and led them toward the corral where they could have some oats and enjoy the relative freedom for a little while.

"And?" Aaron crossed his arms over his chest, staying where Levi left him.

Levi pulled the corral gate shut again. Why did Levi have to be in the middle of this? He had his own problems to deal with, and the way he saw it, Aaron had caused this one himself.

"And my daet's not keen on the idea of you marrying his sister," Levi replied. "I'm sorry."

Aaron frowned. "What was his reason, though? I make an adequate income to support her. She brings in a surprisingly good income from her quilts and crafts, too. So there would be no financial burden on your family. In fact, Ketura would be taken care of—"

"You know this isn't about money," Levi said with a sigh. "This is about your age."

"If she doesn't mind it, though—" Aaron started.

"Then it's up to her family and the community at large to protect her from making a choice she'll regret," Levi replied.

"Like Rosmanda's aunt Dina did?" Aaron snapped.

"What?" Levi hesitated.

"Was the community right when it came to you and Rosmanda?" Aaron demanded. "Because you never did stop loving her."

"No one said anything to Rosmanda," Levi said. "She would have told me."

"Then I guess you were wrong, because her aunt did tell her to marry Wayne instead," Aaron retorted. "Do you think the women aren't involved in every single match that's made? You're naïve if you think that."

"So, how do you know what the women are talking about?" Levi asked with a bitter laugh.

"The gossip was all over," Aaron said, and his expression turned slightly guarded. "I . . . I thought you knew, actually."

"No, I didn't."

Levi cast about inside of himself, looking for somewhere to put this new piece of information. She'd been warned off of him? So maybe she wasn't the only one who thought he was the wrong kind of man.

"This isn't about me and Rosmanda," Levi said after a moment of silence. "And from what she says, she made the right choice in my brother."

"Yah—but what about you? Was it right for you?"

Levi rubbed his hands over his face. "Can you let it drop?"

Aaron heaved a sigh. "Fine. Let's talk about me, then. You're trying to protect Ketura from a man who loves her, who will provide for her and take care of her. And if you warn her off of me, I'm not going to just get over her. I love that woman."

"Maybe they're concerned for you, too," Levi said. "My daet wasn't worried that you'd mistreat her. He was thinking about how people would treat you as a couple. You'd be talked about. You'd be outside the circle."

"For a while—" Aaron replied.

"She's going to age, Aaron!" Levi said, frustration rising. "She's not going to look like this for another ten years, even. She's almost fifty. She'll look like your mamm."

"I don't care."

"Does she care?" Levi demanded. "She loves you— I've seen that. But is this a temporary thing for her? Because they wouldn't only be making fun of you. They'll be saying that she looks like she's with her son. And that's going to hurt. She'll feel older than she really is married to you."

"Is that what she said?" Aaron asked, his expression clouding.

"No." Levi grimaced. "I'm not speaking for her. I'm just saying that this is more complicated than just your feelings for each other."

"And I know that," Aaron replied. "That's why I came to you before going to the elders."

The elders . . . they were the last stop when a couple wanted to marry and their families didn't approve.

"What about your mamm and daet?" Levi asked.

Aaron sighed. "They want me to have kinner."

So they weren't approving, either.

"Do *you* want kinner?" Levi asked.

Aaron sighed. "Yah. But I'll be willing to live without kinner of my own if God doesn't provide them. I love her. . . ."

"Have you really thought about this?" Levi pressed. "I mean, really . . . Have you considered what you'd be giving up, personally? It's a lot to ask of a man to face everything you'd have to—"

"Ketura and I have been seeing each other for three years now."

Levi sobered. This was no spur of the moment plan between them, it seemed. Not like him and Rosmanda. He'd fallen for her in a moment, and the romance that started up between them was hot and fast. He could argue that it had burned out just as quickly, except for him, it hadn't. She'd moved on easily enough, and he'd been left in his misery alone.

"I don't know what to tell you," Levi said. "I have no personal interest in blocking your marriage. I figure if the couple thinks they can face it, then they're the best judge. But you don't have my daet's support."

"All right, then." Aaron nodded.

"I'm sorry," Levi added.

"Yah." Aaron's expression was somber, and he fell into pace next to Levi as they headed toward the house.

"You said the women are involved in all the matches,"

Levi said, his boots crunching over the gravel drive. "What are they telling Ketura?"

"I don't know," Aaron replied. "We've kept our relationship a secret up until now. I don't think they know."

"She has no confidante?" Levi asked with a frown.

"All I know is what I tell her," Aaron replied. "And I tell her that I'd face anything to be called her husband. Anything at all."

They walked together up the steps, and Aaron opened the door first, stepping into the house. Anna and Josiah sat at the kitchen table, mugs of coffee in front of them. They looked up and gave Aaron a nod.

"The women are in the sitting room," Anna said. "My fingers aren't much help with the stitching anymore, I'm afraid. I can't see enough."

"But in her day, she made quilts for all of our children and grandchildren. They were so beautifully stitched that the bishop's own wife came to learn from her." Josiah gave a meaningful nod. "Come sit down, boys. Anna will get you a coffee—"

"And some pie. I made lemon meringue last night," Anna said, slowly rising to her feet. "Sit . . . sit . . ."

There wasn't anything else to be done, but to sit down and eat that pie. Normally, Levi would be joking with his hosts at the prospect of eating something delicious, but he wasn't here to visit, and he wasn't just a ride for Rosmanda, either. He'd come to see his aunt. He needed to know if her plans had changed at all.

But there wasn't much else he could do. He didn't belong in the sitting room with women at work, family or not. He looked in that direction, though, and he heard the sound of women's laughter—light, quiet.

"Yah, pie would be nice," Levi said.

Aaron sank into a chair next to him.

"So . . ." Josiah leaned forward. "Are we any closer to announcing a proposal this fall?"

Levi looked over at Josiah. On his last visit, the old man had been suggesting a match between Aaron and Rosmanda. Obviously, something had changed.

Levi looked over at Aaron, his eyebrows raised.

"I said we'd been keeping it a secret. But not anymore," Aaron said.

"Is that wise?" Levi lowered his voice. Putting this out there . . . People would have opinions—and strong ones at that. It was a brave stance, especially without family support to buoy a couple up. Marriages were held together by wedding vows, but also by community.

"I'm going to the elders, Levi," Aaron said. "I'm only telling you as a courtesy."

It looked like Aaron had the support of old Josiah. For what it was worth. Anna came back to the table and put a trembling plate of pie in front of both Levi and Aaron.

"When a man loves a woman," Anna said, slowly lowering herself back into her seat. "Sometimes it's better to just move out of the way."

Chapter Eleven

Rosmanda and Ketura worked hard for two hours. Together, they were able to finish much of the stitching. All spread out and with the backing nearly complete, Rosmanda's quilt did look rather fine, she had to admit. It wasn't finished, but it was closer to being complete now.

"It's breathtaking." Ketura smoothed her hand over the red and orange leaves.

Strange how work fueled by so much pain could be so lovely in the end. Rosmanda could remember every stitch, every piece, and the tears she'd blinked back as she worked. How many prayers had she said, the wordless kind where she didn't even know what to ask anymore . . .

"Was it the same for you when your husbands died?" Rosmanda asked. "Was it easier if you kept your hands busy?"

"I built a whole business on it," Ketura said.

"Do you want to marry again?" Rosmanda asked.

Ketura was silent. "I have good friends. I have family. I don't know if it's too much to ask. What about you?"

"I don't think I have the strength to do it again right now," Rosmanda said. "It's a lot of work getting to know a man's ways. I'd have to watch for his moods, his preferences, get to know his family . . . all while raising my babies. A woman shouldn't shy away from work, but I'd rather put my energy into my needle and thread right now. It's less complicated."

Ketura smiled wanly. "Husbands are a different sort of work, aren't they?"

"Wayne was a good man, but—" Rosmanda hesitated and looked over at Ketura. "It's just that life is harder than you think it will be."

"Yah, it is." Ketura smiled. "You don't have to talk carefully around me, you know. I understand."

"The question is, should I hold off and stay single?" Rosmanda said. "Or do I find another good man and put my back into it?"

"You're young," Ketura said softly. "Find another husband. I don't regret my second marriage for a minute."

"But who?" Rosmanda sighed. "They want me to look a little closer at Aaron, truth be told."

Ketura's smile dropped. "Do they."

Rosmanda froze—she'd hit a nerve there. "Ketura, I don't mean to step out of my kitchen, so to speak, but I think that Aaron has a bit of a crush on you."

Ketura's gaze flickered toward Rosmanda, but then she put her attention into folding the pieces of quilt together again, her hands working quickly and efficiently as if completely separate from the rest of her.

"Does he, now?"

"Well, he's here helping Josiah and Anna often enough, isn't he?" Rosmanda took the other side of the quilt to help fold it.

"Yah. He's very thoughtful that way," Ketura replied.

"But I've seen the way he watches you—" Rosmanda paused, eyed her for a moment. She knew that look. It was the same one she'd gotten from Levi time and again—the one that woke things up inside of her that should have stayed dormant. Ketura's cheeks pinked, and Rosmanda stopped. It suddenly made sense—but with Aaron? "Oh . . ."

"Oh, what?" Ketura snapped.

"Nothing." Rosmanda pressed her lips together.

No, it wasn't something to speak of. If Aaron was coming here for Ketura, then Ketura would have to be the one to set him straight. And maybe Ketura liked the attention. Maybe it gave her something different in her days.

"I'll finish up the quilt the rest of the way alone," Rosmanda said. "I'll tell you when it's done."

"Yah, that would be good." Ketura's composure was back and she smiled. "Don't feel pushed toward a man you don't want, Rosie. You're right about the work a husband takes."

Or was Ketura asking her not to be pushed toward Aaron? There seemed to be something there—something Ketura wasn't speaking of, but Rosmanda had had two boyfriends before she'd gotten married. So she did have *some* experience. . . .

Rosmanda laid her quilt in the center of the plastic and wrapped it up again. Then she hoisted it up and headed toward the kitchen.

Levi and Aaron sat at the table with Josiah and Anna, and when Rosmanda came in, Levi rose to his feet.

"Here—" Levi took the heavy quilt from her arms, hoisting it more easily than she had in one arm, his muscles flexed under the weight of it. He met her gaze, but his expression was granite.

"Thank you . . ." she murmured.

"You ready?" The words were casual, familiar, but his expression still didn't betray anything. He stood there with her plastic-covered quilt hanging over his arm, standing just a little bit closer to her than he needed to.

"Yah. We should get home," she said, then turned

toward Ketura. "Thank you for helping me today. I'll come by with the quilt as soon as I'm done. A few more days at most."

"Okay. See you then," Ketura said, and there was pink in her cheeks again.

There was tension in the room, and Rosmanda looked around. All she could see was Aaron, sitting at the table like he properly belonged, and Ketura refusing to look at him.

Levi led the way out, and Aaron came with them to help with hitching the horses to the buggy. It didn't take long with both men working, and after Rosmanda got up onto the seat, Aaron lowered his voice, but not low enough, because Rosmanda could still hear his words.

"Will you talk to your daet again?" Aaron asked Levi. The horses stamped their impatience, and Rosmanda leaned back in the seat.

"I can't promise that," Levi said. "If you're going to the elders, then do it. They'd have more influence over my daet than I would right now."

"Yah. All right then." Aaron stepped back, and Rosmanda dropped her gaze, pretending not to have heard. The elders? No one went to elders over an issue unless it was very serious, and her stomach clenched. What could be this important to bring it to the elders that involved their family? Had news about Jonathan gotten out? Did others know? He was in town somewhere, wasn't he? And maybe he'd been talking . . . The possibilities tumbled through her mind.

Did Stephen and Miriam know now? How many people would know about her humiliating mistake if this got out? Her mouth went dry and she looked over at Levi, trying to read that stony expression.

Levi flicked the reins and they started. Levi looked

back toward Aaron, who stood with his arms crossed, and it seemed as if Levi was going to say something, but he didn't. He just looked at his friend and then turned forward again, the buggy wheels crunching over the gravel drive. Rosmanda looked back at Aaron to find him staring morosely at the back of the buggy.

"Why is he going to the elders?" Rosmanda asked.

"I shouldn't say."

"Is it about Jonathan?" she asked, and her voice sounded tight in her own ears.

"No."

She wasn't sure she believed him. So far, he'd been hiding behind that stony expression of his—his real feelings locked away from her.

"Then what's it about?" she pressed. "What's happening?"

They reached the main road and Levi steered the horses onto it, and they picked up their pace.

"Levi, you're shutting me out. I know there's something going on, and if this has to do with Jonathan, I have the right to know."

"It isn't about Jonathan," he said, and he looked over at her. "You really want to know? It'll come out soon enough anyway."

"Yah! What is it?"

"Aaron wants to marry my aunt."

"He wants to . . ." Rosmanda's mind spun. This really didn't have anything to do with Jonathan, but— "Wait. He wants to *marry* her? It's gone that far?"

"What do you mean—you noticed?" Levi said, shooting her a cautious look.

"Yah, I noticed. He looks at her like—" She licked her lips. "Like a man who wants to pull her into his arms if only the rest of us weren't around."

"He's young enough to be her son," he said.

Rosmanda shrugged. "Doesn't seem to change the way he looks at her, does it?"

Whatever was happening between Aaron and Ketura didn't seem to require any permission from the rest of them. Aaron wasn't seeing a mother figure when he looked at Ketura—he was seeing the woman. But Rosmanda wasn't naïve enough to think it would stop there. The community's opinion mattered, too.

"He's going to the elders to see if they can get help getting family support then?" Rosmanda asked.

"Yah, that's his plan," Levi replied. "And don't get me wrong, I have no interest in stopping them if they're set on it, but people will talk."

"They always do," she agreed.

Was a romance between Aaron and Ketura smart? Not likely. It certainly wasn't the kind of risk that Rosmanda would take—especially not now. But Ketura had been married twice before, and she knew what she was getting into. She didn't need the sheltering protection of younger family members to get in her way. If anyone could appreciate the difficulties ahead, it was Ketura.

"Aaron told me something today," Levi said. The reins were tight in his hands, and his gaze stayed pinned to the road ahead of them.

"What's that?" she asked.

"That your aunt advised you not to get any more serious with me," he said.

Rosmanda paused, her mind going back to those days of freedom when no one knew her and she was the new, available girl in the community. Young men would stop and say hello, introduce themselves. There had been several young men who'd shown interest, but Levi had a way of turning her brain to mush. It wasn't just that smoldering look of his . . . it was the way he could catch her hand and make her think of nothing but his touch. Aunt Dina hadn't been quite so blind to the ways of young people as Rosmanda had believed, though. She'd sat Rosmanda down for a sober conversation about her future.

"Yah. She did," Rosmanda agreed.

"I didn't know that."

"People talk . . ." Rosmanda said feebly. "They'd have opinions. They always do."

"So I was the one not to be trusted?" he said.

"It wasn't that—" She paused. Actually, it was that. "My aunt thought you wouldn't have married me."

And that had been the goal, hadn't it? To find an Amish husband and settle down. She'd come to Abundance for that very reason. She wanted a wedding.

"You think she was right?" he countered.

"You're single still," she replied. If anything, Aunt Dina had been proven right over and over again. Levi had been trouble—too attractive for his own good and with a tendency toward drink.

Levi smiled slightly and glanced toward her. "So what did your aunt say, exactly?"

"That—" She laughed breathily. "That you were the kind of boy to make a girl lose her clear thinking. And that a girl needed clear thinking more than she needed to be kissed."

"You were always pretty level-headed," he countered.

"Oh . . ." She smiled ruefully. "Not always. You had this way of—" She stopped, her cheeks heating as she recalled those early days. He'd been so full of masculine energy, all of it directed right at her. She could still remember the way his lips had felt on hers . . . a whole lot like that kiss they'd shared in the chicken house.

"I had a way of doing what?" His gaze darkened and caught hers.

"Of distracting me from my focus," she said. "I came to find a husband—you know that well enough now. I needed a solid, Amish man to take me. I wasn't looking for—" She swallowed. "You know . . ."

"Distraction." His lips curled up in a slow smile.

"Exactly . . ." Her reply was fainter than she'd hoped, and she swallowed again, looking out the other side of the buggy at the passing reeds that grew up out of the ditch.

Her hand was on the seat between them, and she felt his warm hand cover hers. He closed his fingers around hers, and then his thumb started to move slowly over the tips of her fingers. His movement was methodical and slow. Her breath caught—it was something he used to do back while she'd been wasting her time, as Aunt Dina had put it, but she didn't pull away. Her mind was following the motion of his thumb going from tip to tip of her fingers, the rough skin of his work-toughened thumb scraping lightly against her fingertips.

"I kind of resent being called a distraction," he said, his voice low, then he released her hand, and she pulled it back into her lap, a little embarrassed.

Was he teasing her? Reminding her of the old days?

But then Levi reined in the horses as they came under the low-hanging branches of a tree, and the buggy stopped. Rosmanda looked over at him, her breath shallow. Her fingers still tingled where he'd touched her, and she caught herself wishing he'd do it again—touch her like that. Levi dropped his gaze then.

"Why have we stopped?" she asked, and she closed her hands into fists in her lap. She couldn't let herself think like that.

"Because I need to hear this. From you—straight." Levi

lifted his gaze again, and he shrugged slightly. "What made you think I'd never marry you?"

This question mattered to Levi. Amish men married—eventually, at least. Why would she think he'd be any different? Rosmanda stared at him, her eyes wide and fixed on him.

"Do you really want to talk about this?" she asked.

"Yah. I do." He shook his head. "Why would you assume that I had no interest in marriage?"

"It wasn't that you wouldn't marry me," she said. "I think you would have, eventually. But it wasn't about the kind of man I was naturally attracted to. It was about the kind of man I *needed*."

"So our attraction—that meant nothing."

"It wasn't enough to build a marriage on," she said. "Look at Jonathan! He got his wife pregnant before they were even wed, and is he the kind of husband a woman needs?"

"You're comparing me to *him*?" Levi shook his head, her words sinking beneath his defenses. She thought he was that kind of man? It stung, and he felt his mouth turning down in distaste.

"My feelings for you were very similar to how I felt about Jonathan, so yes." She nodded. "I did compare you to him."

"Your feelings, how?" he demanded.

"My . . . attraction." Rosmanda licked her lips. "It was powerful, sweeping me away before I could even think about things properly. All I could think about was him. All I wanted was him. And if he so much as touched my hand, I'd do anything he wanted."

"You were young, though," he countered. "Teenagers

can feel things more strongly because it's all so new. Besides, you didn't do just anything *I* wanted."

"No, I wasn't quite so stupid anymore," she said with a small, humorless smile. "But it was the same with you. I could be around the side of my aunt's house, and thinking nothing of the future, of my reputation, or anything else— just what it felt like to be in your arms."

"It was more than just physical between us, though," he countered. "We talked . . . a lot, actually."

"Not as much as you seem to remember," she said softly.

Had it really been such a physical relationship? Because for him, it had sunk right down into his heart. He reached out and took her hand, turning it over so he could see her palm, and he ran his fingers over her soft skin.

"Like that . . ." She tugged her hand back.

"What?" he asked.

"That's . . . the kind of thing you did. It made all my logical thought drain from my head." Rosmanda tugged her shawl a little closer around her shoulders. It was chilly here in the shade. He was tempted to move closer to her, but he didn't.

"Just touching your hand?" He felt a smile tug at his lips, and he reached for her hand again. "Just that?"

Was such a simple touch really that electrifying for her? It was a rather exciting thought, actually. Levi had no idea he still had that effect on her. He ran his finger down her palm, and this time, she didn't pull away. He'd always loved her hands . . . her beautiful, tapered fingers . . . and he liked to run his fingers over hers, feeling the softness of her skin, memorizing the shape of her palm and the faint lines that crisscrossed over it.

Rosmanda tipped her head to the side, her dark gaze following his fingers. It felt like a challenge, almost. She'd just told him that he'd woken her up in a very physical way—and maybe that had scared her. But she was right that it had been something very powerful between them.

"Contrary to what you seem to think about me," Levi said quietly, "I didn't feel like that with any other girls. It was only you."

"You'd had other girlfriends, though," Rosmanda said.

"Yah. But not like us . . . And not at the same time." How could he even explain that? With a few other girls, there had been some fumbling, some kissing, some awkward physical expressions, but it had never been like him and Rosmanda. He'd been looking for that kind of passion, and not even sure what to do with it once he found it. He and Rosmanda had shared an attraction that scared him, too. Wanting a woman that badly set up a man for heartbreak. And he'd been right about that.

"I don't think I believe that," she whispered.

So she thought he was lying? He wasn't quite sure how to prove himself to her.

"You think I was some guy working his way through the available women?" he asked with a low laugh.

"Maybe . . ."

"I wasn't." She seemed to give him credit for a prowess he didn't possess. It was *she* who woke it up inside of him.

"You seemed to know what you were doing," she countered.

Yah, maybe he had. But it had just connected with them, made them both into experts. Turned out she hadn't been quite so innocent either, but there was something about the way she fit in his arms, about the way she collapsed against him that made him feel like twice the man he was.

"I'm telling you, Rosie," he murmured. "We had something I'd never had before. That was new to me, too."

Levi moved closer on the buggy seat, and she looked up at him, her dark eyes filled with sadness. He hated that—the way life had changed her. She'd been through too much. They were both a little scarred now, and cracked. But whatever used to simmer between them hadn't died out, either.

Rosmanda didn't answer him, but when he moved closer, she didn't retreat, either. He ran a finger down her cheek. What was it about this woman that made him feel so much more alive, just by breathing her in?

"You're doing it again," she whispered.

"Doing what?" His voice was low and husky.

"That thing you do . . ."

Guilty. Maybe he was. He lowered his lips over hers, and she exhaled a sigh as she leaned into him. She was warm and soft, and he wanted to pull her closer than was even physically possible in a buggy seat. He wanted all of her, to feel the full length of her against him.

It was probably better that he couldn't, because with his heart hammering this hard, if she didn't stop him, he wouldn't rein himself in, either. It had been a very long time since he'd had a woman in his arms who made him feel like this—

He broke off the kiss with a ragged sigh, and Rosmanda's eyes slowly fluttered open.

"What's so wrong with feeling like that?" he whispered.

"I don't remember . . ." She laughed softly.

Yah. Neither did he. Not right now with her so close.

He'd missed her. After putting years of emotional energy into resenting his brother, he could finally admit the truth—he'd missed Rosmanda most of all. He missed her laughter, the sparkle in her eyes, the way she could make him chuckle with her dry humor . . . He'd missed the way her hair smelled, the way her fingers felt in his hands. She wasn't quite so easy to forget.

Knowing what he did about her past, he could see that it hadn't been just about finding a husband for her . . . it had been about re-creating herself. Well, Levi didn't have that luxury. He'd messed up in full sight of his community, and they'd never forget it. So she might have scraped up her new start, but he was still the same old Levi Lapp everyone had started to distrust.

Levi pulled back, putting some physical distance between them.

Rosmanda could never say he lied to her, because he hadn't. But what he had to offer—an honest heart and a passion for her that couldn't be stamped out—hadn't been enough, even when she was most desperate.

"You just remembered why we can't do this, didn't you?" she said softly.

"Yah."

"It wasn't Aunt Dina, you know," she said, "who scared me off."

"Then who?" He looked over at her, catching her eye.

"It was you." She looked away, but her soft voice still tugged at him. "You told me all the things you questioned, like whether the community really knew best for people, like if having a bit more space from everyone might make life easier, or if we should do what the bishop and elders told us, or just take it as advice. . . ."

Yah, he'd said all that, and more. And he'd meant it. He still did. He wasn't so certain that the community knew better about his heart than he did.

"Isn't that the same thing Aaron is struggling with right now?" he asked.

She looked back. "I suppose. But this community—it's

what protects us. It keeps us separate from the world, it provides for us when life gets hard."

"Like when your husband dies," he said.

"Yah," she agreed. "And when I need work to make some extra money, and when I need help with my daughters. The community will protect them. The Amish will wrap them close when they grow up and marry and have children of their own. What are we without our community?"

But Abundance hadn't done so well for him when he'd been heartbroken and trying to find some comfort when his brother stole his girl. Where had the community been then? They'd told him to get over it. A couple of married men from the community had tried to talk to him.

These things happen, they said. *There will be other women. A good girl from a good mother—she'll make you happy. Just move on. Get married, too. Have some kinner. You'll see.*

It hadn't been half enough, and the liquor had been a far sight more comforting. Levi flicked the reins and the horses started forward again. He was frustrated with himself because he kept doing this—messing with his own emotions, and hers. She'd known what she wanted back then—and it wasn't him. Well, now he knew what he wanted, and it wasn't a woman so easily scared off by his honest self.

"Maybe it's best to listen to the community," he said. Get married. Find someone else. Have some kinner of his own to help him forget . . .

"Yah. It tends to be best," she agreed earnestly.

Aaron and Ketura were in the midst of their own hopes and heartbreak, but Levi could see the wisdom of listening to the community in their situation. The couple couldn't see past their noses right now, but others could see a good ways in the future. The life Aaron wanted wouldn't be an easy one for either him or Ketura.

Rosmanda was right, it seemed—their attraction, no matter how passionate and strong, couldn't make for a future together. And he had a heart worth protecting, too.

Chapter Twelve

That night, Levi dreamed of his brother again. In his dream, they'd been young enough to be climbing the hay bales in the barn, and Levi was climbing ahead of Wayne. It was exhilarating—speeding up to the top, the energy of youth. The smell of hay had been so pungent and real, the tickle of straw poking through his pants against his knees as he scrambled upward. He could hear his brother's puffing breath behind him, but when he looked back, Wayne was slipping farther and farther down the pile of bales.

"Wayne? Hurry up!" He'd been annoyed. What was taking Wayne so long? His brother was trying, but he couldn't seem to get a hold, and he looked up at Levi with panic on his face.

"Levi, don't leave me!"

"Hurry up!"

The pile of bales seemed to go down forever, and Wayne struggled forward again, only to slip farther down. Levi's heart had been hammering in his chest, as he was unsure of what to do. He wanted to help his brother, but he didn't know how.

"Wayne! Climb!" He'd woken up in a sweat, the words on his lips. Had he said it aloud, or had it just been a mumble? He didn't know, but he'd pushed back the covers and sat in the predawn chill, his legs over the edge of the bed while he sucked in deep lungsful of air and tried to get himself centered again.

He wasn't a kid. And Wayne was gone. He wasn't sure that stark reality helped.

Levi and his brother had had a strangely competitive, yet protective relationship. Levi had been the louder, rougher brother, and Wayne had been quiet. It took a few years for Wayne to hit his growth spurt, and for a long while Levi was the same size as his older brother. When some of the other boys picked on him, Levi would stand up for him. He'd never been afraid of a fight, and Levi had been the kind of kid who fought dirty. Wayne was more noble—wanting to do the right thing. Levi had just wanted to pound the other kid and get him to shut his mouth.

When they became teenagers, Wayne finally started to grow, and he turned into a big, beefy teen. He didn't need Levi's fists anymore, and Wayne seemed to resent his little brother's protection then. Embarrassment, maybe? Or just frustration? Regardless, he started competing more with Levi, trying to prove himself. That competition never really stopped after that, but stepping in with Rosmanda—that level of betrayal had been a first.

Except now, Wayne was dead, and Levi couldn't fight with him anymore. He couldn't tell him off—Levi always was the more eloquent of the two of them. He couldn't make up with him, either. And now that Wayne was gone, Levi couldn't even stand up for him and go fight dirty with whatever was threatening his big brother, because in spite of it all, there was still that protective streak inside of him deep down. . . .

Levi finished up his chores with his daet earlier than usual. After the chores were finished, Stephen and Miriam got into the buggy and drove off to see Ketura and hear her out. Whether Ketura was serious about marrying the young man or not, this was no longer a private matter that had hope of fizzling out on its own. It was about to be very, very public.

The morning was a chilly one—frost sugaring the grass and the fence posts. Levi headed into the horse barn with some carrots from the cellar. The barn was warm and the hay-scented air tickled his nose. He'd already mucked out the stalls that morning, so it was clean and fresh inside. The other horses were outside already, but he'd left Donkey in his stall so that he could work with him alone. Levi laid a folded saddle blanket over the top rail, then leaned against the rails and looked at the massive stallion with appreciation.

"How are you doing, Donkey?" he asked in a low voice. "I want to get you in some plow tack today."

He wasn't sure if he'd manage it, but he'd try at least. He was glad to have some horse training to focus on today. Levi had done his best to keep to himself since he and Rosmanda had gotten back from Ketura's home. He couldn't play with whatever was brewing between them. Rosmanda might spark some fiery passion inside of him, and up until now, he'd been more concerned about what was good for her. But it was about more than that—this halfway romance wasn't enough for him, either. He used to silently pity men who claimed to marry their "best friends," because those friendly relationships with girls hadn't held a candle to the roaring blaze he felt with Rosmanda.

His female friends had been girls who might laugh and joke with him, who might have known him and Wayne since they were kinner climbing hay bales together. . . . They might be decent girls who would make decent wives one day, but to settle for a candle's light when he knew what a blaze felt like? It seemed sad somehow.

Now, however, he wondered if those young men hadn't been wiser after all. A female friend might see the best in a man, when a lover could be a harsh judge. Those men were married now, with kinner and homes of their own. They had the comfort of a warm stove, a wife's embrace, and kinner to play at their feet. And Levi . . . didn't. So, who had been the fool all this time? Maybe him.

Levi opened the stall door and eased inside. Donkey backed off, his ears going down, and Levi stopped. He held out a carrot.

"You want one?" he murmured.

He was getting Donkey used to his voice, too—associating it with safety, treats, and good things. Donkey leaned forward and gobbled up the carrot with large, snapping teeth. He crunched on the mouthful, then leaned forward for the second carrot. Levi gave it to him, watching him eat his treat.

Levi poured some oats into his feed bucket, then laid a hand on the huge horse's shoulder. The muscles trembled under his touch, but Donkey stepped forward to reach the oats. Levi pulled the saddle blanket off the rail, movements slow—no surprises. He reached forward and put his free hand on Donkey's muscular shoulder, but the horse didn't even look up from the oats.

Levi tossed the saddle blanket over Donkey's back. The horse raised his head and took a step back, looking over his meaty shoulder toward the saddle blanket. Levi had gone as far as getting a saddle blanket onto the horse before, but today, he wanted to add a plow saddle on top of that. The saddle was a part of the hitching equipment. So Donkey would never have to worry about carrying a man on his back. But if he could be hitched up, he'd be a beautiful source of horsepower.

With a deep breath and a silent prayer, Levi tossed the saddle on top of the blanket. Donkey shook himself restlessly and the saddle slipped off into the hay. Levi sighed, and he bent to retrieve the saddle, but as he did, the door to the barn opened with a creak, Donkey startled. Levi wasn't sure what happened next, but he felt a hoof connect with his chest, throwing him up against the stall rails.

The pain radiated around his rib cage, and everything spun as he clambered to hold on to something. He couldn't breathe—everything seemed to be clenched tight around his rib cage, and he crawled a couple of feet before he coughed out a breath. Sucking air into his lungs was excruciating.

"Levi?"

He didn't look up—all of his attention on trying to breathe, but he felt Rosmanda's hands under one armpit as she hauled him forward and out of the stall. He collapsed onto the cement floor, and he heard the stall being shut and locked behind him.

"Levi!" She bent down, her face hovering over his. "Are you hurt? How bad is it?"

He was still trying to breathe, and he feebly pushed her prying fingers away from his shirt.

"Stop it . . ." he huffed. "Stop . . ."

Rosmanda stopped, and he grimaced, pulling in a shallow breath. It was easier now—his breath coming back.

"Bad timing . . ." he whispered. "Thanks a lot."

She seemed to take his words as legitimate thanks, but he'd meant them in sarcasm. His voice just wouldn't give him enough flexibility to relay that.

"Let's get you inside," Rosmanda said. "Come on. Hurry up. The babies are sleeping and I can't leave them long."

Right. He staggered to his feet, and she slipped an arm around his waist. Rosmanda was stronger than he'd thought. And she felt good there—soft and warm. He leaned on her as much as he dared, and let her lead the way back to the door. He glanced back once and saw Donkey staring after him. He'd almost swear he saw a mocking smile in those liquid eyes.

That blasted horse. He'd hitch him up or die trying.

Rosmanda let Levi rest against the side of the house while she went ahead and pushed the door open. She'd heard the solid thunk of a hoof hitting flesh, and heard Levi's grunt. Her heart had felt like it stopped, and it was still catching up. She'd get him inside—that was her first goal—and then see how bad it was.

She pushed open the door and then hurried back to help Levi up the steps. He was heavy, and she had to move in closer to help him, her hip pressed hard against his. He pulled himself forward up the rail, his arm heavy around her shoulders.

"Almost there—" She let him lean against the door-jamb for a moment before he headed inside, his boots leaving a dirty track into the kitchen. When she pulled out a chair from the table, he sank into it with a grimace. He held his chest, breathing in a shallow whisper.

"What happened?" she asked, and this time when she pulled at his shirt, he didn't stop her. His hand dropped to his lap, and she undid his buttons as quickly as her fumbling fingers would allow. Then she pulled the shirt aside to reveal his broad chest. On the lower right, a large pink and purple bruise had started to spread along his ribs. She ran her fingers over the spot and he sucked in a hissing breath.

"Sorry . . ." she said. "That's a good kick, Levi."

"Yah."

"Do you think your ribs are broken?" she asked, and she ran her fingers along the other side of his chest. His flesh tightened into goose bumps under her touch. She found herself enthralled by the smoothness of his skin and the way his chest hair swirled.

"I don't know," he said. "It still hurts, but not quite as much. I'm going to say not broken."

It was about his injury, and she'd better keep that in mind. But there was something about this man leaning back in the chair, his shirt hanging open, allowing her to run her fingers over his skin—

"But badly bruised . . ." she murmured.

"Yah . . ." He held his breath and shifted his position slightly.

"What were you doing?" she asked, her heart finally slowing down again. If those ribs weren't broken, then they certainly needed some ice. She stood up and went to the icebox. It was run on a gas engine, but it stayed nice and cold for most of the day without having to start the motor. She pulled out a freezer bag of frozen corn from last fall's harvest and a tea towel, then went back to where he sat. She pulled a chair up facing him, and wrapping the bag in the towel, she placed it gently over the spot. He pulled back.

"You need cold," she said, shaking the towel off the bag and trying again. This time he allowed the bag to touch his skin. "Is that okay?"

Rosmanda looked up to find his dark gaze pinned on her. He licked his lips. "It's . . . not bad."

She smiled in spite of it all. "What *were* you doing?"

"I dropped the saddle." He smiled ruefully. "And like an idiot, I bent down to pick it up—"

"Oh." She shook her head. "Not smart."

"It would have been fine, but the door spooked him," he added, shooting her a slightly annoyed look.

"Sorry. I was coming to see if you'd want lunch today. I saw you in the horse barn when I went for eggs, and if you weren't coming for lunch, I'd"—she swallowed—"just make myself something small."

"Ah." His dark gaze met hers and they fell silent again. She held the corn against his body, and he slid his hand over hers. His fingers were rough and strong, but his touch was gentle. He touched the tip of her finger with his thumb and smiled slightly. He was teasing again.

"I should—" Rosmanda started to pull back, but he caught her hand.

"Stay," he murmured.

She could have pulled back—he certainly couldn't have stopped her if he tried, but there was something in his voice. His parents were out and weren't due back for a few hours yet. There were no other workers on the farm right now, and no one to interrupt. Her cheeks heated at the thought.

His bare chest drew her gaze, and she looked at those swirls of chest hair for a moment or two, and then before she could think better of it, she reached up and touched it with the tips of her fingers. Levi caught her wrist, running his fingers over her pulse, and when she lifted her gaze, he smiled slightly.

"We're alone," he murmured.

"Yes, I'd noticed that . . ." She smiled back, then shook her head. "We were supposed to be careful, Levi."

"Yah, I know." He tugged her closer and laid her hand against his chest, then slid his fingers down her side. "Come here."

"I'm already here . . ." she breathed, but she knew what he wanted. Those dark eyes stayed locked on hers.

"Closer." His voice was deep and commanding, and she licked her lips, leaning a little closer. He caught her dress in a handful of fabric and tugged her against him. She fell into his chest, and she went to pull back, but he held her firm.

"I'm going to hurt you," she said.

"I'm fine. It's the other side." Levi's lips turned up in a smile, and his fingers moved in small, encouraging circles over her side through the fabric. "Come closer."

"I don't think I can—" She laughed softly, but she knew exactly what he wanted. She could see the stubble on his face, the small lines around his eyes, one eyelash that lay on his cheek. She pursed her lips and blew it off. His skin was smooth against her fingers, and she found her breath had become a little shallow. She wanted to touch him, feel him underneath her hands.

"I've always loved your lips," he murmured.

She suddenly felt self-conscious of them as his eyes moved down to her mouth. She wasn't sure what to say to him, and he lifted his hand and ran a finger down her cheek, across her jaw and down her neck. He stopped at her collarbone, tracing a line along the neck of her dress with the tip of his finger.

"I'd kiss you myself, but it's going to hurt like hell if I sit up any more than this," he said with a slow smile.

"Oh—" She was about to pull back when his hand came up to her cheek again and his thumb moved down to her lips.

"Kiss me, then," he said.

She should say no. She should pull away and tell him it was inappropriate and— She swallowed, looking down at his own strong mouth, and she wondered if it would be so terrible if she did just that. . . . She leaned closer and just barely touched his lips with hers.

Levi's eyes shut and he laughed softly. "Kiss me properly."

Rosmanda leaned in again, and this time, she let her lips linger on his. He took it from there, his fingers moving up to her face, pushing deep into her hair, under her kapp as he pulled her closer. She could feel her hairpins come free as her kapp fell away. His kiss was hard and urgent, and he pulled his fingers through her hair, holding her close. His mouth moved over hers, and when she felt his tongue touch her lips, she sucked in a little breath of surprise and he deepened the kiss. It was a kiss that made her wish she could abandon all her principles and give herself over to him . . . because she ached for this, to be kissed like this, to be wanted the way he was wanting her right now.

This was the kind of kiss she'd never had in her marriage—not even once. And she'd been fine with it. She'd put it aside. She didn't need it—until moments like this when she felt like she'd tear into pieces if she didn't get more. . . .

Levi started to sit up, then he stopped and let out a low moan, breaking off the kiss with a ragged breath.

"That hurt you . . ." she said with a soft laugh. He'd have taken this further if the pain hadn't stopped him, and she felt the heat rise in her face.

"Yah . . . Never mind. Come here—"

"Levi, we shouldn't," she whispered.

"There's no one to come home," he murmured. "No one to interrupt. If not now, then when?"

She felt the urgency of his words, and she knew what he wanted—to think about it all later and to use this time to its best advantage. She longed for the same thing, but she'd only feel terrible about it later, even if they didn't cross any ultimate lines and sleep together.

Her hair hung loose around her shoulders, and she put her hands up, suddenly embarrassed. A woman didn't let her hair down in front of a man.

"Leave it," he breathed.

She paused, his dark gaze moved over her slowly, methodically, as if he were undressing more than her hair. He reached up and took one of her loose waves between his fingers, let it run through.

"I've never seen your hair loose before," he said, and he frowned slightly. "How is that possible?"

"I was careful to keep it pinned," she said.

She'd been careful lest her aunt come by or call for her. She needed to make sure her hair was neatly back inside her kapp so that no one could question what she'd been up to around the side of the house by the string bean stakes.

"I want to see you like this more often. . . ."

"It's not right—" She bent to pick up her kapp and the scattered pins. She couldn't exactly stop him from looking at her as she rewound her bun and covered it with her white kapp.

"I know," he said. "But I still want it."

"That's for a husband." Her voice shook when she said it, and she tucked the last pins into her hair, securing the kapp into place.

"I'm not asking for . . . all of you," he said. His voice dropped a little at the last words, and she felt the heat rise in her cheeks again.

"I know. But my hair is for a husband, you know that."

"You're beautiful," he said quietly.

"And you're badly hurt," she said with a breathy laugh. And it was just as well that he was, because if he'd simply sat up and pulled her into his arms, she wouldn't have stopped him. Levi reached up and tugged at a stray tendril playfully. She unwound it from his fingers and tucked it away where it belonged.

"Stop that," she said with a low laugh.

"Kiss me again," he said.

"No. You'll mess up my hair."

"I won't this time. I'll be good."

"Kissing me isn't being good." But she couldn't help the smile that came to her lips. What was with Levi, asking for more and more from her? It was like he used to be, drowning in her eyes, his fingers slipping closer and closer to forbidden territory.

Levi grimaced sitting himself up taller, and he shot her a rueful smile. "Okay. I'll survive."

But looking at him on that chair, his shirt open and those dark eyes moving over her, slow and warm, she'd never been more tempted in her life.

Chapter Thirteen

Levi touched his bruised ribs cautiously, his gaze on Rosmanda's retreating form. She adjusted her apron, her fingers moving back up to the pins that held her kapp in place. How wrong was it to enjoy that? He wasn't meaning to toy with her, but get him alone with this woman and all the logic seeped out of his head. He couldn't seem to stop himself, and the memory of her lips made him want to stand up and go make that happen again.

If she let him.

What was he thinking, though? Obviously, he'd have to cut this out. He put the bag of corn onto the table and pulled his shirt closed. Holding his arm out to button his shirt only made it hurt more, but he grimaced through the first three buttons, and then stopped.

"You need lunch," Rosmanda said. "I'll make some sandwiches. It's something."

She was trying to make it normal between them again, but when he looked at her, all he could think about was how her lips tasted, and how he wanted to do that again.

"Thanks," he said.

Rosmanda's gaze flickered toward him as she pulled out the bread. "The Englishers call it chemistry. This—the desire between us. They say it's called chemistry, and you either have it or you don't."

"Yah, I could agree with that. You either feel it or you don't. There's no forcing this."

Had she had a fraction of this with his brother? He wasn't sure he wanted to know. But he could be sure that it wouldn't have been the same. He'd been with other women when he'd been spending his time in the bars— Englisher women, mostly. So he knew what attraction felt like, but with Rosmanda there had always been something purer about it, somehow. Maybe it was that he'd always seen her as a girl he could have married.

"Well, see what happens to them?" She eyed him meaningfully.

"The Englishers?"

"They don't have the stability we do. They—" Color suffused her cheeks, and he wondered if she'd just realized what he had, that they weren't so different from the Englishers in this desire for each other. They weren't engaged. They weren't even courting.

"I can't help the way I feel for you," he said, and he felt like he owed her an apology for that, somehow.

"It doesn't make it good for us," she replied.

"You feel it, too," he said.

"I know . . . but I've also nearly ruined my life by following feelings like ours. And I don't blame you. I'm the same—I keep stumbling into this."

"I'm not the same as Jonathan," he said. "I'm not married. I'm not courting. I'm completely free, and I'm not trying to lure you into anything that's going to ruin you."

"If we were caught—" she said, then hesitated.

Levi eyed her for a moment. She might be slim and

petite, but she was strong, and he didn't hold any power over her. "You could tell me off. You know I'd stop."

"Because—" She sucked in a breath. "There is something about being desired like this . . . And it isn't just you wanting me . . . I don't know. Maybe chemistry is a good way to describe it."

"You don't find it every day," he said. He knew. He'd looked. It seemed like the best way to purge her from his system—find another woman who could wake up those feelings for him. It hadn't worked. "I'm not even convinced it's in every marriage," he added.

Rosmanda dropped her gaze and didn't answer that. Levi could see how easily Aaron had fallen into his relationship with Ketura, even if the whole community would be against it. Sometimes people didn't want to think about the future when the present was so intoxicating. Like alcohol with a tortured soul.

"Rosie, I don't know what this is, but it's real," he said. "It's . . . nothing I've felt before, not with any other woman. So I know it's messy, but we aren't hurting anyone. We're both single—"

"Someone *will* get hurt," she interrupted him, and she met his gaze with a look of longing so deep that it made him catch his breath.

"You've had no problem tossing me aside before," he said.

"Who said it was easy?" Rosmanda sighed.

"I don't know what to say, Rosie."

"Neither do I . . ." She looked at the clock. "Your parents should be home within an hour or two."

"Yah, about that," he agreed. Then there would be people around again—a human buffer between them and their feelings for each other.

Rosmanda pulled an envelope out of her apron pocket and put it on the counter. "My daet wrote me back. I got it this morning."

"What did he say?"

"He went to see Jonathan and Mary as soon as he got the letter, but he was too late. As we know already. And he said that Mary was a wreck. She was certain something was wrong and she was worried sick."

As she would be. Her husband had just up and left her with five kinner to care for.

"Did Jonathan tell her why he'd left?" Levi asked.

"Apparently, he told her that he had some business to attend to, and didn't know how long it would take."

A lie to keep his wife from suspecting too much . . . and for what? To keep the furor down until he'd convinced Rosmanda to run off with him? The thought was infuriating—and not only on his wife's behalf, but because this slug wanted to lure Rosmanda off with him.

"If Jonathan comes near you, I'll deal with him," Levi said curtly.

"In your condition?" She raised an eyebrow.

Levi didn't answer that. He'd heal. He wouldn't be quite this helpless for long, and his friendliness toward the other man had officially been spent.

"But Daet asked me to . . . send Jonathan home." Rosmanda sighed and pulled out the sauerkraut and cheese, her attention now on the food in front of her.

"Is that your responsibility?" Levi asked. "You didn't ask him to come out here."

"Whose responsibility is it, then?" she asked with a shrug.

"We don't even know if he's in town still," Levi said. "He might be on his way already."

Rosmanda raised her gaze to meet his. "Do you think so?"

"Why would he stay?" Levi shook his head. "He has no one here but you, and he hasn't been in contact again . . . has he?"

"No, he hasn't," she said.

"It doesn't make sense to just hang out here," he replied. "Letters take a bit of time, and for all you know, he's already back at home with Mary, lying about where he's been."

Rosmanda nodded. She added a layer of roast beef, then added the top piece of bread, her fingers working quickly.

"Rosie . . ." he said softly, and she looked up. "Do you need my help with this?"

"With Jonathan?" she said, then shook her head slowly. "I don't even know what he's doing."

"Do you want me to check around town tomorrow, see if he's around?" he asked.

"If you ask people, you'll only cause interest where there might not have been any before," she replied. "I'm not sure that's a good idea."

"Maybe not," he agreed. "But I'll help you if I can. You only need to ask."

Rosmanda carried the plate to the table, then set it down in front of him. He glanced at the clock—it was nearly noon. He grimaced and leaned forward to stand up, but pain shot through his side at the effort.

"Where are you going?" she asked.

"To feed the calf." It had to be done. There was a calf waiting on milk, and there was no other man to do it.

"You stay." Her gaze moved toward the stairs. "I'm going to check on the babies, and then I'll go feed the calf. Would you watch my daughters?"

"What if they wake up?" he asked.

"They shouldn't. If they do . . . I'll hurry."

Rosmanda didn't wait for him to argue, and her shoes tapped up the staircase. Levi sank back into his chair. The sandwich smelled good, but it felt wrong staying here while she went out. Was she running away from him? Maybe . . . and she was also just doing what needed to be done, like any of them. And one of these days, they'd have to face reality, like Aaron and Ketura were doing now.

Would Aaron marry the woman he loved? It was hard to tell. But Aaron and Ketura's was a cautionary tale—but not because the community would be against Levi marrying his sister-in-law. They would likely encourage it. The caution came because starting something like this was dangerous, because feelings this deep didn't always dissipate . . . Sometimes, three years later, as both he and Aaron had found out, a man found himself still helplessly in love with a woman who was still utterly wrong for him.

Rosmanda put the bucket of milk down in front of the calf and watched as it hungrily drank. The calf was grown enough to drink on its own, but she still needed to wait to make sure it didn't knock the bucket over in its exuberance.

That kiss was still seared into her mind. She could still feel the sensation of his fingers pushing into her hair, his lips moving over hers with such intensity—and she didn't regret it. She should—that much was certain—but she didn't. There was something about being caught alone with Levi that made all the perfectly good reasons for her to keep away from him evaporate.

And she'd missed those passionate feelings that sparked so easily between them.

When her sister married an older man she hadn't been terribly attracted to, Rosmanda had sworn she'd never do the same. But she had. She'd chosen the more stable brother—the strong, single-minded, pious man who asked her to marry him before he even courted her. And she had found a warm, safe place in his arms. They'd had a very affectionate marriage after dark, just not a terribly exciting one.

But this draw between her and Levi—this was different. Was it simply that Levi was wrong for her, that he was forbidden, that made his touch so powerful? This attraction was supposed to change! He wasn't supposed to awaken her like he used to. They'd been young back then, foolish. And now they were wiser. At the very least, she should feel some proper remorse for allowing herself to kiss him like that today, but she felt none.

Nor was fooling herself into thinking she should marry him. She'd marry another sensible man, and she'd find that warm, safe spot with him, too. She was confident that she could. She knew how these things worked between a husband and a wife now . . . But these stolen moments with a man she should be keeping clear of—

Lord, forgive me . . . for not being sorry!

It was a strange kind of prayer. It had been nothing more than a kiss—no other lines had been crossed. Well, except for her kapp. But that had been an accident. Still, that kiss had reached deep inside of her to a place that hadn't been touched in a very long time. And that was dangerous, because it might make her forget what her little girls needed.

Rosmanda rubbed her hands over her face, watching the calf drink the last of its bucket of milk. It stopped drinking, lifted its head, and looked around with those big, baby eyes.

"You done?" Rosmanda asked quietly. She reached down and collected the pail. There wasn't much milk left in the bottom, so the calf had a full stomach. She dumped the dregs down a drain, and then headed over to the sink to rinse the bucket.

Babies needed attention, care, guidance, reassurance . . . Even babies of the bovine variety. And her daughters were no different. She had to be thinking of them, not of her own carnal desires. Her daughters' future mattered more than whatever might fill her heart in the short term. When Rosmanda got back to the house, her daughters would be ready for their bottles, too, when they woke from their nap.

Rosmanda put the bucket back where it belonged and headed back out of the barn.

She saw her in-laws returning when she got back to the house—Stephen drove the buggy under the shelter to un-hitch. When she approached the house, she could hear her daughters' cries from outside, and she hurried inside, slamming the door shut behind her.

Levi wasn't in the kitchen where she'd left him, so she headed up the stairs toward her room. The bedroom door was open, and when she stepped inside, she saw Levi sitting on the end of her bed, his arm tight against his side. His face, or his profile that was visible, was ashen, but he sat there facing the babies who were on their knees, pulling themselves up in their cribs, his attention fixed on them.

"Your mamm will be back," Levi was saying. "Just hold on a little bit. You've got me . . . whatever that's worth . . ."

"I'm back," she said.

He turned and heaved out a sigh. "Oh, good . . . They started a couple of minutes after you left."

Rosmanda went over to the cribs and scooped the girls up, one at a time. Once in her arms, their tears stopped.

"What did you do?" she asked.

"I . . . watched them." He shrugged sheepishly. "Took me a bit to get up here. I didn't want them to think they were alone."

There was a kindness deep down in Levi's heart—one that not all men shared. She smiled, but then the side door opened downstairs, and Rosmanda could hear the sound of boots on the floor, the bang of the door, the murmur of voices.

"Your parents are back," she said, and she waited while Levi rose to his feet.

"Yah. I'd best head down—"

Levi paused as he reached her, and for a moment, she saw that tender glimmer in his eyes again, but then he continued past, and out the door. He went ahead of her, walking carefully, his arm pinched against his side. As he came down the stairs, his parents' voices halted.

"Levi, what happened?" Miriam exclaimed.

Rosmanda followed Levi down, the babies in her arms. Levi allowed his mother to pull up his shirt, looking at the damage.

"Levi! This is bad!" Miriam's voice went up in pitch. "What happened to you?"

"Donkey kicked me," he said.

"That animal should have been sold long ago," Miriam muttered.

"No. He's going to pull our plow—"

"Levi—"

"Mamm, I'll break him. Just let me work him."

"He's unmanageable! You could have been killed. You might need a doctor as it is—"

"I'm fine. I'm bruised. This isn't broken."

"A doctor could tell you that, Son."

"Mamm—"

Levi and his mother argued back and forth, but when Rosmanda looked up, she found her father-in-law's gaze locked on her. His expression was grim and she froze, her heart speeding up in her chest. Why was he looking at her like that? Had he seen something? Had they returned earlier than she'd thought? The possibility made her cheeks heat—but she'd seen them come in with plenty of time to spare.

Hadn't she?

Susanna started to fuss, and Stephen held out his arms for his granddaughter.

"I'll take her, Rosmanda," Stephen said, and she passed her daughter over, who reached immediately for a fistful of his beard.

The older man still looked grim, but he slowly turned toward Miriam and Levi with a sigh.

"Miriam, he's got breath enough to argue with you," Stephen said. "He'll be fine, I'm sure. If those ribs were broken, he'd barely be breathing."

Miriam pinched her mouth shut, but she eased up Levi's shirt again and winced as she surveyed the bruising.

"We have other matters to discuss," Stephen added.

Miriam looked back at her husband, and they exchanged a look.

"Yah, we do," she agreed. "Rosmanda, would you sit down?"

Rosmanda pulled out a high chair and put Hannah into it. Then she reached for Susanna and placed her next to her sister. Her breath was coming low and fast, and she felt lightheaded as she tried to hide her panic. What had happened?

"Sit down, Rosmanda," her father-in-law said sternly,

and she sank down into the chair next to her daughters. Levi looked at his parents questioningly, but the glance in her direction was a worried one.

"What's the matter?" Rosmanda asked.

"We were speaking with Aaron and Ketura today," Stephen began. "And while we were there, we heard that Jonathan Yoder is still in town."

Rosmanda didn't answer, and when Hannah whimpered and turned toward her, she simply put her hand out to let Hannah hold on to her fingers.

"Do you care to tell us anything?" Miriam asked quietly.

How much did they know? This must not be about the kiss she'd shared with Levi if their news had come from Aaron and Ketura.

"No," she said simply.

"He's been asking about you. A lot," Stephen said. "Why?"

Rosmanda looked over at Levi. Was she responsible for explaining this man?

"He should go home to his wife," Rosmanda said after a beat of silence.

"And yet, he hasn't," Miriam said. "He's been staying at the Abundance Hotel."

"He's married," Rosmanda said firmly. "He belongs with his wife. Not here. That isn't my responsibility."

"Rosmanda," Miriam said gently. "Something happened here at the house that upset you, and you sent him away. But he won't leave town, it seems. And people are starting to talk."

Rosmanda felt the blood drain from her face. "What are they saying?"

"They are suggesting that there is more between you than is . . . proper," Miriam said. "And it certainly looks that way to an outsider, doesn't it? This married man comes to town and asks after you for days and days. This isn't good."

"And there is more to this story," Stephen added. "Rosmanda, I know you deserve your privacy, but if we don't know what we're dealing with here, we can't help you."

How much should she say? The whole story wouldn't be good for her . . . but if the story got out and she hadn't told them . . . Her head was spinning.

"Are there any specific rumors that Aaron and Ketura heard?" Levi interjected.

"Well . . ." Miriam blushed slightly.

"We need to know the worst," Levi said. "What is it?"

"Some people are saying that in Morinville, Rosmanda tried to break up an engagement. Some are saying that this Jonathan Yoder was the man in question."

Rosmanda's mouth was dry and she stared at them. The rumor had made it this far? Someone must have a relative back in Morinville . . . or a friend. A pen pal?

"Obviously, it's not true," Miriam said with an uncomfortable laugh, but Stephen's gaze was locked on Rosmanda.

"*Is* this true?" Stephen asked.

She could lie. She could hide it a little longer . . . And she wanted to, but something inside of her wouldn't utter the lie.

"Yah," Rosmanda whispered.

"Not exactly," Levi cut in. "First of all, Jonathan was significantly older than Rosmanda at the time. She was only sixteen, and he was baptized and courting. So he was . . . what . . ."

"Twenty-one," Rosmanda said.

"There is a significant age difference, there," Levi said. "From what I understand, he was playing both girls for a while and ended up getting his fiancée pregnant. Not Rosmanda."

"I didn't sleep with him," Rosmanda confirmed. "But it's true that I wanted him to marry me instead of Mary. I'm ashamed of it now, but it's true."

"And what of his wife now?" Miriam asked.

"I don't know," Rosmanda said weakly. "I haven't spoken to her since their wedding. She hates me—for obvious reasons. But I didn't encourage him to come out here. I didn't encourage *this*—"

"So when you came to Abundance to stay with your aunt, it was to escape an unmarriageable situation in your hometown . . ." Miriam rubbed her hands over her eyes. "You weren't just passed over, were you?"

"I came to Abundance to start over," Rosmanda said softly. "I was deeply sorry for what I'd done back when I was a foolish girl. I paid the price. And when I came here, it was to start fresh. And I did that. I married your son and I was a devoted wife to him. I am not the same girl that I was before. I promise you that."

And it was true—on a heart level. She didn't want to be that foolish girl . . . except an hour ago, she'd been kissing their son rather passionately in this very kitchen. So she wasn't quite the pillar of virtue that she was still pretending to be. But she wouldn't confess that.

"So why is Jonathan here?" Levi interjected. "What is he hoping to gain?"

"We don't know," Stephen said gruffly.

How much should she tell? Rosmanda looked at the tired, sad faces of her father- and mother-in-law in front of her. When she looked over at Levi, his expression was granite, but his gaze glittered with a strange intensity. He seemed to be on her side, at least . . . Would he stay there?

"I asked Levi to make Jonathan leave this house when he came to see me," Rosmanda said. "He did that for me."

"So perhaps this is revenge?" Miriam shook her head.

"Jonathan wanted me to—" Rosmanda licked her lips. "He wanted to pick up our relationship where it left off nine years ago."

"To have an affair?" Stephen looked down at his hands instead of at Rosmanda.

"Yah . . ." she breathed. "He wasn't very clear, but it seemed he wanted an affair while he's married to Mary."

"And that was why you wouldn't let him stay." Miriam softened. "You told me at the time it was worthy of sending him off, and I questioned that."

"He'll deny all of this, I'm sure." Rosmanda looked between her mother- and father-in-law. "But I couldn't let him stay here. He'd sent a letter that I destroyed—one saying he wanted to know if I still had feelings for him and that he wanted more from me." She felt the crinkle of her daet's most recent letter in her apron pocket. "And my daet sent me this letter just today."

She pulled it out and pushed it across the table toward Stephen. He picked it up uncertainly.

"I'm sure your father wouldn't appreciate me reading his correspondence with you," Stephen said slowly.

"I'm asking you to read it," she said. "He went to see Jonathan's wife, Mary, and she's in a bad way. They have five kinner, and he told her he had come away for business, but she knows something is very wrong. My daet wants me to send Jonathan home to her. But if what I've done so far hasn't sent him back, I don't know what else I can do!"

Stephen and Miriam exchanged a look, and Rosmanda looked between them, then over at Levi. They all knew the worst now—and she was their responsibility to deal with.

And she felt their disappointment. She'd been the sweet daughter of a bishop up until now . . . and now she'd become . . . tarnished.

Stephen slowly picked up the letter, unfolded it, and read it over. He nodded, returned it to the envelope, and sighed.

"If you need to send me and the girls away, I understand," Rosmanda said, her voice trembling at first, but growing firmer as she continued speaking. "But I'm a much wiser, better woman now. Was I stupid? Yes. Was I brazen and wicked? Absolutely. But I am no longer any of those things. I know the position I've put all of you in, and I'm deeply sorry for that. I've begged God for forgiveness, and I ask it of you, too. But pulling apart my adolescent sin will not give you a clear insight into the woman I am today."

Miriam blinked at her and she thought she saw a smile at the corners of Levi's lips.

"And who are you today?" Stephen asked, his voice low.

"You know me," she replied. "I'm a mother to my girls. I'm your daughter-in-law, and I work hard to be of use to you in any way I can. And I will marry again so as not to be a burden to you—if I can."

"And if this gets around, what man will take you?" Miriam murmured. The question, though harsh, sounded only forlorn.

"An older man, perhaps," Rosmanda said, and an image rose in her mind of the old husband her sister had married—face lined, hair gray, skin already sagging . . . "A pious man, I hope. A man who is firm but fair. Who will help me raise my daughters and will forgive my wayward past."

"There is time enough for that," Stephen said with a sigh. "What will we do about Jonathan? That's the question right now."

"I'll deal with him," Levi growled.

"You will not go fight with an Amish brother," Miriam snapped, and then she sighed. "No matter how very satisfying it might feel right now . . ."

Was Miriam siding with her, just a little? Rosmanda felt her gaze mist again, this time in hope. Were they willing to protect her from this tumble from grace? Would they be the family shelter that she so desperately needed? If so, she dare not jeopardize this.

"And with your injury, you aren't much use in manhandling anyone," Stephen said curtly. "No, you'll have to speak to him yourself, Rosmanda."

Her heart sped up, and she licked her lips nervously. "I've been very clear with him so far. I've told him I don't return his feelings and that what he wants is wicked. I have not led him on in any way—"

"But he's still here." Stephen turned a steely gaze onto her. "The biggest threat to your reputation right now is his very presence in Abundance. I think we're past placing blame. If anyone is going to convince him to leave, Rosmanda, it will be you."

And her father-in-law was right. She knew it. But by confronting him again, she'd be putting herself into the public view. There would be curious stares. There would be stories passed along. And she'd confirm the wild things he'd been saying just by being seen to take them seriously.

But what else could she do?

"It would appear that this Mary needs any help she can get." Stephen pushed the envelope toward her again.

"I'll go with her," Levi said. "She'll need a man from our family to be present for this, just in case a witness is necessary later."

"What about an elder?" Miriam said, turning toward her husband.

"Bishop Graber hasn't asked her to include elders," Stephen replied. "He's asked her to send him home. I'll trust her father's wisdom on that. He knows both this Jonathan and the wife."

Rosmanda looked over at Levi, and his warm gaze enveloped her for a moment. She would be expected to fix this—and she wasn't sure that she could. Jonathan's preoccupation with her was more about his own unhappiness than it was about her, and she knew it.

"We'll go in the morning after chores," Levi said. "The sooner this is dealt with, the better."

Chapter Fourteen

Rosmanda clutched her hands in front of her as Levi flicked the reins and the buggy started. Apparently, Jonathan had been eating his meals at a local diner and sleeping at the hotel. Where he got the money for this extravagance, Rosmanda had no idea. If he was getting into debt, it would only hurt his family when they were forced to pay it off. The Amish avoided debt, but then, they also avoided extramarital affairs, so maybe she shouldn't be looking to Jonathan for typical behavior right now.

"You all right?" Levi asked.

They turned onto the main road and Rosmanda looked back toward the house. She couldn't see anyone, and likely no one was at the window watching her leave. She missed the days when she could count on her mamm and daet to be her support. Her in-laws loved her—she knew that—but it wasn't the same. She missed home.

"Rosie?" Levi said.

"Yah," she said, turning toward him with a forced smile. "I'm fine."

Rosmanda kept her hands firmly in her lap, and a good eight inches between them on the seat. He'd hold her hand if she put it down between them, but she didn't want that. Her mother- and father-in-law were supporting her right now both financially and through this scandal, and she wouldn't toy with that. She'd promised that she'd find a good, honest, Amish man, and she'd do just that.

It was time to marry again, whether she was ready or not. She needed the stability for herself and her daughters. She couldn't have them growing up in the shadow of her mistakes, and a marriage to a sober and good man would help to make up for that.

"We'll find Jonathan and set him straight," Levi said curtly.

"I hope so . . ." she said.

Because she wasn't sure what she'd do if he didn't leave. What if he decided to stay in Abundance? What if he spread more rumors? What if he got vengeful? The elders could help, of course, but she'd be tarnished for life in both communities. She'd tried to break up Jonathan and Mary once, and it would be incredibly ironic if she actually succeeded nearly a decade later when she wanted nothing to do with the man.

The ride into town felt long, and when they finally parked the buggy and set the horses with their feed bags, Rosmanda's heart was fluttering with anxiety. Every person they passed seemed to be staring at her—although they probably weren't. Just a look, a nod, a hello. It all felt invasive right now. How much did people know? How much did they believe?

Rosmanda stood by the buggy until Levi was finished, and then she joined him at his side as they headed toward the small diner.

"Would it have been better to bring him back to the house?" Rosmanda asked.

"To keep you out of sight?" Levi asked, then shook his head. "Stand straight. Look people in the face. Smile. You're not the one at fault here."

Yah, she understood that, and maybe he was right. Let people see her looking happy and confident. Let them question if Jonathan could even be right when they looked at her. But that was easier said than done.

Levi nodded to a woman in passing. "Good morning."

It was Merideth Lapp—a distant cousin of her in-laws. Her gaze skimmed past Levi and landed with open curiosity and a hint of judgment on Rosmanda.

"Good morning," Rosmanda said, shooting Merideth a smile and carrying on.

"Just like that . . ." Levi murmured. "Keep that up."

She felt a little better. Maybe she could do this. Maybe she could pass a few rumors of her own about that strange man from Morinville who had developed an unhealthy obsession with her. This story didn't have to be Jonathan's. She could tell it herself.

But it seemed obvious that the story about her had spread if Merideth Lapp was staring like that. And bringing Jonathan quietly to the farm wasn't going to fix the damage he'd already done to her reputation.

"After you," Levi said, pulling open the door to the diner, and Rosmanda stepped inside first, glancing around the establishment until her gaze stopped at a table in a far corner. Jonathan sat there with a cup of coffee in front of him and a *Budget* newspaper in front of him. He looked smaller, somehow. Older. He was in his mid-thirties, and she'd always associated some amount of wisdom and respect to men who were older than she was, but Jonathan seemed to be lacking in both. His body had aged, but his reputation and esteem had not.

Rosmanda hesitated, and she felt Levi's warm hand at her back, nudging her forward. She'd rather lean into his touch, but she wouldn't. It was up to her to do this. So she headed through the tables and stopped at Jonathan's. He slowly looked up, and when he saw her, some of the blood drained from his face.

"Rosie—"

"Don't call me that," she said curtly, then pulled the chair out opposite him and sat down. Levi did the same, and as he sat next to her, she felt the warmth of his knee touch hers. "I brought my brother-in-law with me today to act as a witness to this conversation."

Jonathan glanced over at Levi uncertainly and Levi met his gaze with a granite stare.

"What have you been telling people?" she demanded, lowering her voice.

"Nothing that wasn't true." Jonathan licked his lips. "I think I want more coffee—" He began to raise his hand to summon the waitress.

"No, you don't," Levi growled, and Levi's hand froze, then lowered. "You're just fine, and you want to hear her out."

"I'm here now," Rosmanda said. "What do you want, exactly?"

Jonathan sighed. "To talk to you. Alone. But you wouldn't even give me that."

"We did talk alone," she said.

"That was . . . unfair. It was short, and you ended our conversation angry. I wanted a real discussion"—his gaze flickered toward Levi—"alone."

"About what, though?" she pressed. "What do we have to talk about?"

"Everything." Levi shrugged. "I have your letters still. You wrote to me very openly about your feelings, about your hardships. You wanted to talk to me—I didn't imagine that."

"I was grieving," she said.

"Maybe I am, too."

Rosmanda sighed.

"Let me order you coffee," Jonathan said quietly. "At least."

"No—" Levi started, but Rosmanda put a hand on his arm. Levi caught her gaze but didn't say anything. Now was not the time to make a point—she'd done that already. Now was the time to send this man home. And she wouldn't get him there without hearing him out.

"Thank you, Jonathan. We'll both take a cup," Rosmanda said quietly.

After the waitress poured two more cups of coffee and left them, Rosmanda leaned forward.

"What's happening, Jonathan?" she asked. "What went wrong?"

Jonathan's gaze dropped down to his cup, and he turned it on the tabletop slowly. "She knows the worst."

"What's that?" Rosmanda asked.

"That I loved you more." He pressed his lips together. "I was drinking, and we were arguing over something stupid, and I—" He sighed. "I said more than I should. I told her that I'd wanted to marry you, and that I'd been forced to marry her, and—"

He didn't finish the story, simply let it hang there. Rosmanda's heart thudded to a stop. Poor Mary . . . to have a husband who had openly told her that he'd loved another woman more than her.

"But you were drinking," she said.

"Yah, but she believed me." Jonathan looked up at her. "I've been sleeping on a cot in the boys' room ever since."

"How long ago was that?" she asked.

"She was five months pregnant with our youngest when I said those things," Jonathan replied. "And our daughter is three weeks old now."

"And you've been gone for one full week," Rosmanda

said, shaking her head. "She's been on her own with those kinner."

"Her mother came to help. Mary's fine."

"She's not fine with her husband gone," Rosmanda said. "Trust me on that."

"Then she shouldn't have kicked me out of our bedroom!" Anger glinted in Jonathan's eyes. "To have me sleep with the kinner? What am I, a child? I came out here to see you. To . . . hopefully see more of you. But I see that won't happen."

"No, it won't," Rosmanda breathed.

"All the same . . ." Jonathan drew in a shaking breath. "She's told her parents about all of this—about the fight, about what I said. Her mamm and daet know, and they see me differently now. There's no respect there anymore."

"Oh, Jonathan," she sighed. "I'm sorry."

"So you can see why I can't just go back," Jonathan said with a weak shrug. "How?"

"How much do you drink?" Levi asked, interjecting for the first time.

Jonathan looked over at him in mild surprise. "What?"

"Were you drinking a lot?" he asked. "Daily?"

"Yah, a bit here and there." Jonathan shrugged. "More than I should."

"And stopping—you couldn't, right?" Levi pressed.

"I could stop," Jonathan said with a short laugh. "If I'd wanted to."

But he hadn't stopped—not even to save his marriage. Rosmanda could see where Levi was coming from on this, but how he'd seen it, she had no idea. Levi reached into his pocket and pulled out what looked like a coin—but it was blue, and attached to a leather cord. He put it down in front of Jonathan, who picked it up and looked at it.

"What's this?"

"A sobriety coin," Levi said. "It's for an Englisher group called Alcoholics Anonymous. That's my six-month coin."

"You were drinking, too—" Jonathan said.

"I spent every night in the bar. And it was because of my drinking that my brother is dead." His voice shook slightly. "I go to the meeting Monday nights. They help you to take these steps that keep you away from the booze when you can't do it on your own."

Rosmanda looked over at him, stunned. He was in an Englisher group for alcoholics? She had no idea . . . but he did seem to be staying away from the booze—at least she'd never seen him drink after the funeral. Or heard of him drunk at the bar again.

"To thy own self be true—" Jonathan read on the coin.

"It's their saying," Levi said. "Part of the recovery."

"What do you think I'm trying to do right now?" Jonathan asked bitterly, handing the coin back. "I'm being true to myself. I don't need your Englisher group."

"If you stay here, you'll lose everything," Rosmanda said. "Your wife does love you."

"My wife knows the worst of me, and she's put me out of her bed," Jonathan retorted. "If she loved me once, she doesn't anymore. My own sons see me crawl into a cot at night, the door shut on all of us."

"What will you do, then?" Levi asked. "If you don't go back, your kinner will grow up knowing that their daet left them."

"My kinner have no respect for their daet this way," Jonathan replied quietly. "I speak, and they look to their mother to see if they should listen."

"Will you go English, then?" Levi asked. "Because you know your choice here. Go back to your wife, or be shunned. There won't be any middle ground."

Jonathan didn't answer, and Rosmanda took a sip of the

lukewarm coffee in front of her. It was bitter, much like her heart right now. She looked over at Levi, who was staring grimly at the table.

"Please don't ruin me, Jonathan," she whispered, her voice tight with emotion. "I'm sorry that your marriage has gone so terribly. I am. I'd really thought you'd be happy with Mary. But if you stay here, I'll be utterly ruined. And I have children to worry about."

"You want me to go home," Jonathan said woodenly.

What she wanted was for him to go away. She hadn't cared where he went, but looking at him now, she did pity him. Back in Morinville, Mary was a wreck. And she'd need her husband's financial support to raise those kinner. Jonathan and Mary had taken vows, for better or for worse, and they *were* joined. Marriage before God was for life.

Marriage wasn't always sweet. It could be bitter and difficult, too. That was why Rosmanda was so deeply grateful that she'd missed marrying Jonathan Yoder, after all. A good, solid, emotionally distant husband would be better than the likes of Jonathan. God had put His protective hand over her . . . A renewed sense of gratefulness for that undeserved protection rose up inside of her.

"Your wife needs you, Jonathan," she said quietly. "Even if she doesn't want you right now. Life is long. Marriage is long. There is more ahead than is behind. Go back home to her. See if you can start over."

Jonathan was silent for a moment, but she saw something change in his expression . . . He was softening. Or perhaps he saw there was no other choice.

"I won't sleep in the boys' room again. If I go back, I'm going to sleep in my own bed, whether she joins me or not."

"Do you have enough money to get a ticket?" Levi asked quietly.

Jonathan glanced over, then slowly shook his head. Levi dug in his pocket again and pulled out a wad of bills.

"Come on, then," Levi said. "We'll get your bag and I'll buy your bus ticket."

Jonathan cast Rosmanda a sad smile. "I really did love you, Rosie . . ."

Had he? He'd been "loving" two women at once back when Rosmanda was too young to have any perspective. And now that his wife was giving him trouble, he was back. It wasn't quite the definition of love that would be tempting for her. It was an escape. It was panic.

Levi stood up, and when she started to rise, he shook his head.

"We men will take care of the rest," Levi said softly. "Drink your coffee. I'll come back and get you in a few minutes."

And Rosmanda was suddenly deeply grateful for Levi right now, too. He was a man to take care of the men's domain, to protect her reputation, to help her clean up this mess and get Jonathan out of town. She nodded and watched the men leave, then she leaned back in her seat, her mind spinning.

Take care of Jonathan, Lord, she prayed in her heart. *Take care of Mary, too. . . .*

Rosmanda didn't even know what to ask for her old friends. But she did know what to ask for herself. She needed a solid, pious man to marry her. And she'd be grateful for him. She'd cook his meals and mend his clothes. She'd scrub his house to a shine and lovingly tend to his family. And if she lay in bed at night next to a snoring old man who smelled of bad breath and ill health, she'd remind herself that it could be infinitely worse. She'd be grateful for a redeemed reputation, and for a chance to prove herself good once more. And she'd be grateful for her daughters' second chance.

Safety and security were key. She had to attain them for her daughters' sakes.

And the kinds of kisses that seared through her veins would simply have to be put aside.

Poor, poor Mary.

When Levi and Jonathan arrived at the bus station, Levi went to the ticket booth and inquired about tickets to Morinville. There was a bus leaving for Morinville arriving in a few minutes. Levi looked over his shoulder at the other man. He stood there, his suitcase beside him, his arms crossed over his chest. Was that defiance? It was hard to tell.

"One ticket for Morinville, please," Levi said. "I'll pay cash."

When he had the ticket in hand, he jutted his chin toward the plastic seat, and Jonathan followed him in that direction. They sat down together, Jonathan's suitcase in front of him.

"You don't have to watch me like this," Jonathan said quietly.

"It'll make us all feel a bit better," Levi replied. He'd be able to report back to his parents and to Rosmanda that the man had been shuttled out of town.

"To see the back of me?" Jonathan laughed bitterly.

Yah, but it was rude to say.

"What had you thought would happen coming here?" Levi asked instead.

"I don't know. I just wanted to see her."

"You're married, though. What could you offer her?" Levi pressed.

"You don't know what it was like with Rosmanda . . ." Jonathan sighed. "I know it was a long time ago . . ." Jonathan shrugged. "Sometimes it isn't about a logically thought-out plan. Sometimes a man just hurts so much he wants a little comfort."

Yah, Levi did know what it was like with Rosmanda, but when Jonathan had known her, she'd been little more than a girl. She'd had a woman's body perhaps, but she'd been a sixteen-year-old girl nevertheless. Whatever Jonathan had felt for her, whatever he'd awoken in her, it hadn't been that of equal adults.

But Levi could understand that search for comfort. It was the reason he'd turned to booze—the liquid comfort. He'd known it was ruining him. He'd known how people looked at him. He'd known he was an embarrassment to his family and his community, but it was the last thing that *could* comfort him.

Even now, he felt that pull toward the bar. He'd skipped the last couple of meetings, and that was a mistake. He could hold himself back from the drink now, but there were days that he clung to that medallion in his pocket, reminding himself that he could go one more hour, one more day. Sometimes a man could ruin himself for a little comfort.

"You could have gone to the elders, the bishop, gotten some help with your marriage," Levi said.

"No."

"Why not?" Levi demanded, the words tasting bitter. "It's what the Amish do. You're married for life. You knew that when you took the vows."

"Mary knows the worst of me, you know?" Jonathan glanced over. "Do you know what that's like to have a woman look at you with disgust in her eyes when she's figured you out?"

It wasn't disgust, exactly . . . but he'd seen Rosmanda change in the way she looked at him. She'd gone cold, and he hadn't been able to figure out why . . . She'd simply stepped back, and the gulf between them had hurt more than anything had hurt before.

"Yah, I think I do," Levi admitted.

"My wife used to look at me like the one who filled her whole heart," Jonathan said. "She'd wait by the window for me to come home from work, and my meal would be warm in the oven, she'd ask if I'd missed her . . ."

"Had you?" Levi asked.

Jonathan shrugged. "A little. I guess. I couldn't tell her what she wanted to hear though—that she filled my thoughts. Because she didn't. I knew what it felt like to be head over heels for a girl. And I'd never felt that for my wife."

The bus pulled up then, the hiss of the breaks cutting through the air. The front doors opened and the driver came out, followed by the first of the passengers. There was no more time, and Levi felt a wave of relief to get this man out of here—away from Rosmanda.

"Consider stopping the drinking," Levi said. "It changes more than you think."

"It won't change what's past," Jonathan replied woodenly, and he stood up, picking up his suitcase.

"I hope you find what you're looking for," Levi said. "I hope you get your wife's love back again."

Jonathan shook his head. "Not likely now. Not after this."

There were some things that a man could regret, but he could never undo. Being the reason his brother died topped that list for Levi. But attempting to abandon his family was equally unforgiveable . . . Levi could understand

Jonathan's plight, even if he deeply disagreed with every choice the man had made.

"Regardless, don't come back here," Levi said, meeting his gaze meaningfully. "If you do, I'll handle you myself. No elders. No bishop. And Rosmanda will never know about it."

Jonathan's eyes widened slightly at the threat, and he didn't answer. Instead, he headed toward the glass door where new passengers were waiting to board the bus. An older Amish couple was waiting with several Englishers, and when the last of the arriving passengers had vacated the bus, the others started to get on board. Jonathan didn't look back. He stepped up into the bus behind a couple of Englisher girls, his head down, his hat firmly in place.

Levi had meant it—he'd pummel this man if he returned and tried to meddle in Rosmanda's life again. He'd learned a lot in his drinking days, and a few of those lessons had been in fighting dirty. It wouldn't be Christianly or Amish, but it would get the job done.

The bus doors closed, and the brakes hissed again as the big vehicle started to move. Good. Job done. He pressed his arm against his aching side. Now Levi would go back to the diner and pick up Rosmanda. He'd take her home. She deserved some rest.

But as for Levi, he had a horse to break, bruises or not. Call it competition with the brother he'd never have the chance to compete with again . . . Call it evening the score with the brother who'd taken everything from him . . . Call it trying to prove himself to a woman who'd never see him as good enough . . . but that horse *would* pull a plow.

Chapter Fifteen

Rosmanda sat at the table, her newly finished quilt spread out over the tabletop, over the backs of the chairs and hung suspended before her. It was a beautiful quilt, even if she did say it herself. The rich reds, maroons, oranges, and yellows all blended together in a mosaic that truly did resemble the leaves of a tree in the fall.

She ran her fingers over a stray thread and tugged it free. This quilt had been the recipient of so many emotions, so many evenings and quiet moments stolen away from other chores in order to add a few more patches. She'd promised Ketura that she'd bring it by when it was done, and now it was.

Miriam stood at the sink washing breakfast dishes, and she looked over her shoulder.

"It's a gorgeous quilt. It should sell for a lot, Ketura says."

"I hope."

The money would be useful, but the quilt would be very difficult to part with it. Wayne was in these stitches, her daughters, even Levi now. So much of herself had gone into this quilt that simply selling it and banking on the Englisher sentimentality when it came to a story behind a craft felt cheap, somehow.

She turned over an edge, looking at her neat stitches

and when Susanna crawled over from the blanket and grabbed a handful, Rosmanda pried those chubby fingers free.

"Don't touch, sweetie," Rosmanda said, scooping her daughter up and planting her on her hip.

"Let me help," Miriam said, pulling her hands from the water and drying them on a towel. "Come to Mammi, Susanna—"

Rosmanda handed her daughter to Miriam with a smile. "Thank you."

"You'll bring it to Ketura today, then?" Miriam asked.

"I suppose I should." It was what she'd promised, wasn't it? "Or maybe tomorrow."

"Are you changing your mind?" Miriam paused.

Tears misted Rosmanda's eyes. Today, it all seemed so muddled—all the grief rather close to the surface. "I don't know . . ."

"We have to carry on," Miriam said. "It's all we can do. You'll make another quilt to replace this one. There will be more."

More husbands. More quilts. More heartbreak. More trials. There was always more waiting around the bend. For some girls who started out right, they could look for more blessings, but Rosmanda feared she'd always be looking over one shoulder, waiting for someone to find out her secrets.

Footsteps sounded on the steps outside, and the side door pushed open, a swirl of chilly air rushing inside. Rosmanda looked up to see Levi come in. His dark gaze met hers and he held up a bundle of mail—some flyers and a white envelope.

"There's some mail," he said.

"Would you grab it, Rosmanda?" Miriam asked. "I've got to get back to the dishes."

Miriam put Susanna back on the blanket next to her sister, and Rosmanda crossed the room. She took the mail, but Levi didn't let go right away, and she looked up at him, startled.

"So the quilt is done?" he asked quietly.

"Yah." She glanced over her shoulder at the quilt that lay over the table.

"It looks good," he said.

"I think so, too . . ." She sighed, then tried to shake it off. There would be more of everything, as her mother-in-law had said. "I'll have to bring it to Ketura later."

"Do you want me to drive you?"

There was something in Levi's gaze—something warm, soft, and inviting. She knew what he was asking—if they could be alone for a little while on that ride to Josiah and Anna's house. It was tempting, but she had to stop this. Her in-laws were sheltering her, and she was not only repaying them badly by fooling around with their son, but she was proving some very ugly rumors to be not so unfounded, after all.

Whatever she felt for Levi had no future, and honest or not, it wasn't right. This had to stop.

"No, I'll drive myself if your parents can spare the buggy for a couple of hours," Rosmanda said, and she gave a tight smile.

Levi nodded. He released the mail and she pulled it against her stomach.

"Did I offend you earlier?" he asked softly.

"No," she said. "I'm just doing my best to behave better."

Levi nodded, then sighed. "I should probably do that, too."

"You should. If nothing else, Jonathan is an excellent reality check, wouldn't you say?"

"Jonathan is an idiot, a liar and a cheat," Levi retorted. "And he's also a desperately unhappy man."

But something in Levi's gaze has cooled, too. He saw it—the excuses that Jonathan used to defend bad behavior. Feelings didn't matter half so much as propriety, and everyone thought their emotional turmoil was so much more deserving of bad behavior than anyone else's.

"Yah . . . Okay, well. I'll hitch you up if you need," he said.

"Thank you, Levi." She wanted to say more—longed to say more—but she wouldn't. Levi was not the proper, pious husband for her, and she had to stop caving in to her desires.

Levi pressed his lips together and turned and headed back outside, looking over his shoulder only once before she shut the door behind him. What was it about Levi that tugged at her heart like that? He was dangerous—and she'd known that from the start. But the chemistry that sparked between them was almost addictive.

She looked down at the mail in her hand and saw that the only letter in the bundle that lay on top was addressed to her. Rosmanda tossed the flyers onto the table and noted the Indiana return address before she tore open the envelope, but before she could pull out the letter, she spotted Hannah crawling toward the kitchen stove.

"Hannah," Rosmanda said, hurrying across the kitchen and scooping up her daughter before she got to the stove. "No. Hot."

Miriam looked back and shook her head. "They're getting more active, aren't they? It isn't too early for a slap on the fingers, you know."

Rosmanda smiled wanly. It felt too early for that. What these girls needed was a present mother—not a woman rushing about to finish quilts, dashing off to chase away men who wanted too much from her . . .

Susanna crawled in the other direction, stopping at a kitchen chair and pulling herself up to standing next to it. Rosmanda kept Hannah on her hip as she shook out the page from inside the envelope, but she walked in Susanna's direction, just to keep her corralled. The letter was written in her mother's neat hand:

> *Dearest Rosie,*
> *Your daet and I have been talking, and we think*
> *you should come home.*

Rosmanda stilled, her attention sharpening and clatter from the dishes seeming to melt away behind her. The letter went on to outline Mamm's reasons for this invitation, but as Rosmanda's gaze flowed over the words, she felt like she could hear her mamm talking next to her again, and a homesickness so strong that it brought tears to her eyes rose up inside of her.

"Are you all right?" Miriam asked, her voice piercing through the fog.

"It's a letter from my mamm," Rosmanda said.

"Has something happened at home?" Miriam pulled her hands out of the water and dried them off.

"No, nothing's happened," Rosmanda said, shaking her head, and she put a foot out to stop Susanna from reaching for the quilt that hung down from the sides of the table. "But my parents want me to come home again."

"All the way to Indiana? Why?"

"Because . . . of everything that's been happening. Jonathan still wasn't back when Mamm wrote this, and she worried that people would think he was with me and it would ruin my reputation beyond any repair. But if I lived with my parents, there would be no question of where I was, and my father's word, as the bishop, would end the gossip."

"But Jonathan's on his way back now to Morinville—" Miriam said. "He's probably there already. Levi saw him onto the bus yesterday, didn't he?"

Rosmanda didn't answer. Her mother's invitation, a hopeful, heartbroken one, had wrapped its way around her heart. *Rosie, dear girl, come home. I miss you. We all do. We can help you with your baby girls—you'd be home with us. It would be more comfortable with your daet and me, wouldn't it? I think having some babies in the house would be good for your daet these days. His health hasn't been good. . . .*

And Rosmanda did miss home so much these days that it almost hurt. She missed her daet's eyes when he smiled. She missed her mamm's shoofly pie—even Miriam couldn't match it. She missed her sister Sadie and her nieces and nephews . . . She missed her old bedroom, the dresser that once belonged to her grandmother, the old clock on the mantel in the sitting room that kept stopping and having to be reset by Daet's wristwatch, and that one broken floorboard in the mudroom . . . It was funny the details that melted together and grew bittersweet with distance.

"They're afraid for your reputation, then?" Miriam asked.

"A little," Rosmanda replied, looking up. "But they're my parents. If I should be a burden on anyone, it should be them."

"Do they have a potential husband for you there?" Miriam asked.

"Not that they've mentioned."

Miriam shrugged sadly. "You miss your family, don't you?"

"Desperately." Rosmanda blinked back tears. "If the rumors have reached me here, staying won't help me."

"Sometimes it's better to face it," Miriam said. "If you're away, you're in their imaginations. If you're there—they have to look you in the face."

Perhaps her mother-in-law was right. Maybe enough time had passed, and Rosmanda's presence could start to heal the rumors and ugliness again. Jonathan had obviously proven himself lacking, and if she could be a good widow—honest, hardworking, and proper—maybe public opinion would start to shift again.

"Is there hope for finding me a marriage here?" Rosmanda asked.

"I don't know . . ." Miriam shook her head. "People have started to talk . . ."

Rosmanda nodded quickly.

"You are not being chased out of our home, Rosmanda," Miriam added.

"I don't think that for a minute," Rosmanda said quickly. "You've been nothing but good to me. And two babies do cost a lot to raise . . . You've done more than your duty by me."

"It isn't about money, Rosmanda." Miriam's voice sounded choked. "You have to think about your own future, and what we can reasonably do for you here."

She had to think about whose problem she should be if she didn't marry again, either. She wasn't Stephen and Miriam's problem for the long term. They'd done well by her after Wayne's death, but she wasn't their daughter, and her mistakes predated her time with them. Hannah squirmed in Rosmanda's arms, and she looked down at her baby girl.

On the ground, Susanna reached for the quilt and managed to grab a handful, tugging it down on top of herself on the floor before Rosmanda could catch it.

"Oh, Susanna—" Rosmanda said, grabbing the quilt in one hand to lift it off the baby, and Miriam hurried forward to scoop Susanna up, whose little mouth had opened in a wail. They stood there facing each other, a baby in each of their arms. Miriam was jiggling Susanna as her cries subsided, and Hannah reached up to tug at a loose tendril of Rosmanda's hair.

Was this it, then? Would she leave the Lapp farm and go back to her family with her little girls?

"It's a beautiful quilt," Miriam said, reaching out to finger the edge. "You're very skilled, Rosmanda. You'll find a way."

"Yah . . ." Was that a good-bye? Rosmanda wasn't sure. "I really should bring this quilt to Ketura, though. I can drive myself, if you'd watch the girls."

Miriam nodded. "I'm always happy to watch my granddaughters. We'll be fine together. You go ahead and take the buggy. And give Ketura our love."

It was like everything had gone back to normal again, but it hadn't. A watershed moment had happened in this kitchen . . . something had changed. Whatever Rosmanda chose, her past regrets were going to haunt her. Was it even possible to go back to Morinville again as her parents hoped? Was it possible to find a good, sober man now that the rumors had reached her here in Abundance? She had no idea. All she knew was that she no longer felt safe. Her cautious new beginning hadn't protected her, after all.

* * *

Levi adjusted the bridle on Donkey—he'd had to extend some of the straps to fit the large horse, but it was worth the extra work. Donkey, for the first time in his life, was hitched to a hay wagon. Not a plow yet. He only meant to get the horse used to some rigging. Levi stood back, surveying his work in satisfaction.

"You did good, Donkey," Levi said, running a hand down the horse's huge shoulder.

Hitched up! Levi wasn't sure that he'd attempt to drive him today, but hitching up was a huge feat, considering that no one had been able to get near this beast in the past.

The stallion was too big to work as a pair—none of the other horses could match him for size and strength. But he didn't need the help. He could pull this wagon alone—even piled high with hay. He was all muscle, sinew, and bad attitude. He could do a whole lot more than he thought. Sometimes a horse just had to be shown what he was capable of.

Levi heard a rustle behind him, and he turned. Rosmanda stood in empty space next to the sliding barn door. A shawl was pulled around her shoulders, a plastic-covered bundle in her arms, but her gaze was fixed on Donkey in open shock. Her mouth opened slightly, and she blinked.

"Hi," Levi said, turning back to Donkey again. At least she'd come in quietly this time.

"He's hitched," she breathed.

"Yah. I think he felt bad for kicking me." At least it seemed that way to him. Donkey had been gentle and accommodating this time. Not so much as a nip.

"I don't believe it . . ." She shook her head. "That horse was impossible."

Obviously not, though, if Levi had managed to get him hitched, and he sensed the compliment in her tone. Wayne hadn't been able to break this horse. Neither had the previous owners. Maybe it took a fellow rogue to gain this beast's trust. And maybe it took being kicked in the ribs to bond with the stallion. There were stranger ways to go about things.

"I said I could do it," Levi said.

"You say a lot of things." She cast him a rueful smile, and he couldn't help but chuckle. She was relaxing around him again, and he liked it.

"Are you heading out to see Ketura?" Levi asked.

She nodded. "I can hitch up the horses myself—"

"Just let me get Donkey unhitched and give him a treat," Levi said. "Then I'll take care of you."

"You aren't going to drive him a little bit?" Rosmanda asked.

"Nope. One step at a time. It's about trust. He's got to know I'm as good as my word."

"Hey, buddy . . ." Levi murmured as he reached for the buckles and began loosening the straps. "You did really good today. I appreciate it. I've got carrots for you, too."

It didn't take him too long to get the horse unhitched, and he left the wagon where it was—he'd deal with it after he finished hitching up the buggy for Rosmanda. She was standing by the open door again, but the plastic-covered package was gone now. In the buggy already, probably. He gave Donkey a few carrots, praised him a bit more, and then headed back into the buggy barn, feeling satisfied with himself.

"Wayne tried with him," Rosmanda said.

"Yah. I know. He gave up, too."

His brother had told him about this horse—his hopes for it, and then his disappointment in it. This horse—the one creature his brother hadn't managed to charm.

"So . . . what was this, then? Competition?"

Levi met her gaze for a moment, then shrugged. "It might have started out that way, but it turned into something more."

"Like what?"

"Like proving to myself that I was more than the loser everyone thought I was."

She dropped her gaze.

"Proving it to you . . ." he added after a beat of silence.

"I wasn't being fair to you, though," she said quietly. "It wasn't quite so simple."

"Nothing ever is," he agreed, and he took the bridles down from their hooks on the wall, then headed toward the stalls where two quarter horses waited, munching on oats.

He worked in silence for a few minutes, putting the bridles on the horses, then the saddles and other hitching gear.

"I got a letter from my mother," Rosmanda said after a few moments of watching him work.

"Yah?" He looked up, and those dark eyes of hers were pinned on him. He straightened. "Something about Jonathan?"

She shook her head. "Not directly. They want me to go home."

"A visit?"

"They want me to go home to stay," she said.

Levi froze, her words sinking in. "To stay?"

She didn't answer—she didn't have to. He came out of the stall and walked up to her so close that she had to tip her head back to keep looking him in the face, and he tweaked her chin between his fingers and thumb. Her lips were so close, and he wanted to dip his head down and kiss them, but he wouldn't. She was trying to behave, wasn't she? And he knew he should do the same.

"That's crazy," he murmured. "Your home is here."

"My home *was* here," she countered, and she turned her face. He dropped his hand. "Wayne is dead."

"Your girls—my parents—I don't see my mamm giving up on having them around."

"I think your mamm wants me to go," she said.

"I don't believe that." The words came out sharper than he intended.

"Then don't believe it," she retorted. "I don't care! But I'm the daughter-in-law, Levi. It's different. I'm not a blood relative—"

"Yeah, I know that," he said. "I know it real well. But you can't seriously be considering going back there. I mean, what about Jonathan and Mary?"

"What about them?" she asked. "They have a family of their own, and I won't have the Yoders dictating where I can and can't live with my little girls. I miss my mamm and daet. I miss my sister and brothers and nieces and nephews . . . and the next time Jonathan goes missing from his family, at least no one will suspect he's with me!"

So she *was* considering it. He felt like his breath had been knocked out of his body. Somehow, he hadn't thought of her returning home. She belonged here . . . with him . . . with them . . .

"Won't that be worse?" he asked. "Being there?"

"I don't know." She shook her head slowly. "But my secret is out, regardless. Here, there . . . there isn't much difference once that story spreads."

Tears misted her eyes, and she started to turn away, but he caught her hand, squeezing it tightly.

"It's not so terrible," he said.

"It is." She turned back. "To everyone else, I'm . . . the wrong kind of woman. I'm not to be trusted."

"I trust you," he said.

Levi tugged her hand, easing her closer. She followed

his coaxing touch, sliding closer and closer until it took all of his self-control not to pull her all the way against him.

"You aren't the quilting circle," she said. "You aren't the other mamms with babies my daughters' age. You aren't the other women in the kitchen, going silent when I walk in."

"I'm not a woman at all," he said, his voice low.

"I'm a scandal now," she said.

"You aren't a scandal," he breathed. "You're a real woman. You aren't perfection—"

"What every woman wants to hear!" she said bitterly.

He leaned down and caught her lips with his. He ran his fingers behind her neck, and when he broke off the kiss, he said huskily, "Who says you have to be perfect?"

"Everyone . . ."

"Not me!"

She pulled back again, and he released her, the space between them feeling cold and harsh.

"I thought you were going to work with Ketura," he said. "I thought you had a plan."

"That plan didn't involve all of Abundance knowing my secrets," she said. "Things have changed."

As easy as that. But *he* hadn't changed. He was the same guy, stuck here in the community that would never completely forgive him, either. And she'd leave.

"What am I supposed to do, Levi?" Her gaze was filled with conflicting emotions. "Stay here and keep doing this with you?"

"And why not?" he demanded. "I'm the one person who isn't demanding perfection!"

"You're the reason I have to go!" she shot back. "Don't you see that? I don't want to be this woman who can't behave like a proper Amish widow. I don't want to be sneaking around, longing for your touch, dreaming of it—" She blinked back tears.

"You long for me?" he breathed. He hadn't dared hope that she'd even think of him when they were apart . . . but longing? He had experience enough in longing for her, too.

"I don't want to be this woman!" She sucked in a wavering breath.

Her words stung like a slap across his face, and he licked his lips, then looked away.

"I want to be better than this!" she went on. "I want to be able to control myself, to know what's right, what's wrong, and what I need to do. I hate being this way— kissing you while I know there is no future . . . while I know that I'm only proving the gossips right about me!"

"Right," he said gruffly. "I'll get you hitched up, then."

"Levi—" she started.

"No, it's fine," he said curtly. "You've made your point. You don't want to do this."

He led the horses to the buggy and spent the next couple of minutes hitching them up. Rosmanda stood to the side, watching him. She was right, of course. What were they toying with? There was no future between them. Jonathan had married a woman who looked down on him, and while Jonathan's wife's scorn might have been entirely warranted, the feeling would be the same for Levi if he married a woman who saw his bruised heart and thought it was too big of a risk.

Rosmanda knew what she needed, what she wanted. And it wasn't a guy on her level—an imperfect man with a few emotional scars. No, she wanted better than him, and she'd find a way to get it, he had no doubt. Rosmanda Lapp knew how to act the part. He'd never been such a great actor himself.

Levi fed the reins up to the seat, and Rosmanda pulled herself up, and arranged herself on the seat.

"You think I'm a hypocrite," she said softly, meeting his gaze.

Not the word to enter his mind, but he'd take it. He didn't answer her.

"But you forget, I have little girls to raise who need to look up to their mother as an example of all the virtues she teaches them about. I have little girls whose eventual suitors will look to their mother as an example of the kind of woman these girls will grow into. Everyone is looking to me to be perfect, Levi. Everyone. It's kind of you to accept me like this—in all my broken glory. But it isn't helpful. And it isn't realistic."

She flicked the reins and horses started. She didn't say anything else, and he stood there watching her drive away.

She didn't want what he could offer, even if it came from the purest corner of his tattered heart.

Chapter Sixteen

Rosmanda's gaze slid over Ketura's kitchen—a pile of dirty dishes sat next to the sink, and there were pots still on the stove. Rosmanda had arrived before Ketura had managed to get to it. Ketura slid a mug of tea in front of her, then sank down opposite her. Her eyes were red-rimmed, and she looked wan and pale.

"I can help clean," Rosmanda said for the third time. The disarray was bothering her.

"It's okay . . ." Ketura sighed. "I'll do it myself. I find it soothing to do dishes alone."

"Josiah and Anna are out?" Rosmanda asked hesitantly, leaning forward to look toward the sitting room.

"Their daughter and son-in-law picked them up to take them to town," Ketura said. "So I'm on my own." She forced a smile, then it dropped from her face. "I'm sorry if I caused trouble for you, Rosmanda. The rumors— Aaron told me about them, and he didn't want to say anything to Stephen and Miriam. He said it was only passing along untruths. I was the one who thought it was better they know. Well, I thought that *you* needed to know—"

"I did need to know," Rosmanda said quickly. "It's okay."

Ketura nodded. "I'm glad. I was worried I hurt you— or made it worse."

"It was much better to know," Rosmanda reassured her. "By far."

"What happened?" Ketura stirred her tea, the spoon *tink*ing against the side of the mug, but she didn't lift it to drink. She fixed her gaze on Rosmanda's face. "I know it couldn't have been as bad as the gossip made it out to be—"

No, it was worse. Rosmanda licked her lips. "Levi and I went to town, met up with Jonathan, and convinced him to go home to his wife. They'd had a fight, I think." Rosmanda was making it sound so much simpler than it was—as if all Jonathan had needed was a little chat and some Scripture to set him back to right.

"Why was he asking around about you, then?" Ketura asked.

Was it right to pass along ugly truths about Jonathan? He was gone home now. Although, it wasn't Jonathan she pitied right now, but Mary.

"I'm not sure he knew how bad that would look," Rosmanda said with a wince. "But he's gone home now, so . . ."

"Marriage can be complicated," Ketura said softly.

"Yah, it can."

"And some men can be . . . not as thoughtful as others," Ketura added with a small smile.

It was as close to a criticism of men as would come from Ketura, and Rosmanda laughed softly. Englisher women made fun of their men—or so Rosmanda had heard from women who'd heard the Englisher women in more relaxed settings. Amish women didn't do that. They respected their men, but there were times that a woman had to bite her tongue, like with Jonathan.

"But like I said, he's gone now," Rosmanda said.

The smile slid from Ketura's lips, and she took a sip of

her tea. She looked older this morning, sadder. Something was definitely wrong, and while Rosmanda had hoped Ketura would open up on her own, she seemed more inclined to slide in morose silence.

"Ketura, are you all right?" Rosmanda asked softly.

Ketura's chin trembled and she put her mug back down. "I will be."

"I know that Aaron was going to talk to the elders about smoothing the way for you to get married," Rosmanda said. "I don't mind saying that I was happy for you."

"There won't be a wedding," Ketura said quickly.

"The elders wouldn't agree?" Rosmanda asked weakly.

"I have no idea," she said with a shake of her head. "Aaron never asked. I told him not to."

"But *why*?"

"Isn't it obvious?" Ketura wiped an errant tear from her cheek. "It wouldn't work, Rosmanda. You've been married. You know what it's like."

"I know what loneliness is like, too," she countered. She'd experienced enough of that, lying in her bed at night, the space next to her empty. Those were the hours when she remembered Wayne's tenderness, the way he used to sit in that rocking chair with the babies on his chest, softly humming a hymn while they fell asleep . . . Yes, she knew what it was like to lie in that bed alone now.

"I had gotten used to the loneliness," Ketura said. "And then Aaron came along."

"Wouldn't you rather be with him, than without him?" Rosmanda asked. "Because it isn't like he's chosen someone else. He's chosen you."

Ketura was silent for a moment. "This is no longer about a romance. It's now about marriage, and marriage isn't only about your life with the man, it's about your life in the community. Isn't that our Amish way? It's about all of us, banding together, taking care of each other. The Englishers might run off together and set up some little love shack where no one else can bother them. But that isn't God's will. It's too easy. He didn't give us community because it's the easy path—it's the much harder way. But it makes us better."

"That is noble and very likely true," Rosmanda said. "But I can't help but point out that the community won't keep you warm at night, either."

"It isn't only about that . . ." Ketura dropped her gaze.

Was she imagining strong arms and passionate embraces? Rosmanda was imagining a few of those herself.

"Rosmanda, I might not have kinner of my own, but if I'd been able to have them, my oldest would be Aaron's age."

"He's no child."

"No, he isn't. But marrying me—he'd never have kinner of his own. He lost that baby when his wife died, but that doesn't mean he should never have more. He wanted a big family, you know, and he's still holding out hope that God will work a miracle inside my womb and give us kinner. At my age."

"God might," Rosmanda said feebly.

"But He likely won't," Ketura replied. "I've prayed for thirty years for kinner. God hasn't changed my body yet. Is that fair to Aaron to ask him to give up little ones of his own?"

"That's for Aaron to choose."

"And maybe that's for the community to foresee." Ketura cast Rosmanda a miserable look. "I'm not the only one who knows and loves him."

"Will you be able to . . . stop?" Rosmanda asked. "Loving him, I mean. If he came over, would you be able to serve him pie and send him on his way without letting him hold you again?"

Ketura's eyes welled with tears. "I could if he were married to someone else. He should be with a younger woman. In fact, more than one person has pointed out that you're actually the perfect match for him. I might hate that, but it's true. He needs a woman young enough to have more children, and maybe someone else who understands all that he's lost."

Rosmanda could hear the bitterness on the edges of those words. Ketura said she wanted Aaron to marry, but she didn't. Not really.

"I'd be foolish indeed to marry a man who's in love with another woman," Rosmanda said with a short laugh. "You're right—I've been married before. I know what it's like, and that is where I draw the line."

Ketura smiled sadly. "He does love me."

"And you love him," Rosmanda said.

"I love him enough to let him go. A marriage is about the community, too," Ketura said with a shake of her head. "And they care. They might seem callous sometimes, even heartless. But they see things we can't. They look into the future and they see the things we're too afraid to face. What interest does the community have in ruining the happiness of two decent people? None. But they have a great deal of interest in protecting us."

Like her aunt had done with Levi. She'd sat Rosmanda down and talked to her straight. Rosmanda did understand—all too well.

"So that's it, then?"

"Yah." Ketura shrugged weakly. "It will have to be."

"What will you do, though?" Rosmanda asked, and tears rose in her own eyes.

"I think there is wisdom in your mourning quilt. I'll make a quilt of my own," Ketura said. "And that quilt will hold my grief. And while I stitch out my loneliness and heartbreak, I will allow God to provide for me." Ketura's gaze moved toward the plastic-wrapped quilt on the chair next to Rosmanda. Rosmanda looked toward it, too.

"I think you're very smart when it comes to business," Rosmanda said. "But I can't sell it. I brought it here to let you sell it, but I can't."

Ketura nodded slowly. "I understand."

"Do you?"

"It takes time to let go. I was rushing you."

"I'm thinking of going home," Rosmanda said, and when Ketura cast her a confused look, she added, "to my parents in Morinville."

"Really?" Ketura reached out and put her hand over Rosmanda's. "You'd leave us?"

"I have to find a way to carry on," Rosmanda said. "And I miss home."

Outside the window, snowflakes started to dance by, and Rosmanda looked over at them with a sigh. It was supposed to be spring. But it wasn't only the weather that was fooling with her. She was supposed to be a wife, not a widow. She was supposed to be strong and moral, not this passionate woman who kept falling into the wrong man's arms.

"Will you marry again?" Ketura asked softly.

Would she? She didn't want to. She was so very tired, so very sad. She didn't want to pretend to be okay when she wasn't. What she wanted was to go home, curl up in her mamm's kitchen, and cry out her tears.

"I don't want to," she confessed.

"We women are shuttled around a lot," Ketura said quietly. "From father to husband, to husband, to husband . . . But there is a way to do it on your own, and it doesn't only lie in making some money to support yourself. You need more than money. You need other women."

Rosmanda knew that. Even if she married again, she needed other women. The women held each other up, kept each other sane. They encouraged, laughed, cried, sympathized.

"I've found," Ketura went on, "that my female friends have lasted longer than my husbands have."

Rosmanda smiled sadly. "Something has to last, doesn't it?"

What Rosmanda wouldn't give for some friends she could count on, women to see the best in her and to rally around her when times were hard. She'd had that in Morinville as a girl, but her adult life had been different. Was it even realistic to hope for friends like that again . . . after all that had happened?

Ketura's gaze moved toward the window again, and Rosmanda looked out, too, watching the swirling flakes come dancing by the glass. From inside the house, it was cozy and warm, and the snow was pretty. But she was far from home, and far from her little girls. That spring snow would only make her drive home more perilous.

"We'll get through. God will provide for us," Rosmanda said.

"He will." Ketura nodded, straightened her spine.

"Thank you for the visit," Rosmanda said. "But I have to get back to my girls. That snow . . . I didn't expect it."

Ketura pushed herself to her feet. "I'm glad you came, Rosmanda. I'm glad for your friendship, too."

Rosmanda met her gaze and smiled. Yes, they had become friends, and she would miss Ketura when she left Abundance.

"I'll help you hitch up," Ketura said. "Best get ahead of that storm."

* * *

Levi stood by the window, looking out at the falling snow. It was coming down thicker now, and a gust of wind whipped it sideways. He'd been watching for Rosmanda's return with the buggy, his anxiety ratcheting up with each howl of the wind.

His parents were both in the kitchen—Mamm kneading a bowl of bread dough, and Daet sat at the kitchen table with a sandwich. The babies were in their high chairs—a way to contain them at this point—hammering on the table with spoons to occupy themselves.

"Rosmanda said that you wanted her to leave," Levi said, turning from the window.

"I didn't say that!" Mamm said. "It wasn't like that, Son. She's your brother's wife and the mother of our grandbabies. Do you really think I'd throw her out?"

No, he didn't. But maybe she didn't need to be thrown. Maybe she just needed to have the door opened for her. . . .

"Then what happened?" he demanded.

"Watch how you talk to your mamm," his father said past a bite of sandwich.

"Mamm, what happened?" Levi asked, adjusting his tone.

"Her parents wrote to her . . ." Mamm poured some oil onto her hands and then smoothed them over the roll of dough. "And I'm a mother, too, so I understand how much they miss her, and how much she misses them."

"She'll take Susanna and Hannah with her, you realize," Levi pointed out.

"Yah." Mamm looked up. "Of course. But we'll still see them. She'll come visit, and we can go see her in Indiana and bring the girls some treats—"

"Is this because of that business with Jonathan?" he asked. "Because I took care of it. He's gone."

"It isn't about that," Mamm said. Her hands moved over the dough, flattening it, rolling it, then pausing while it pulled back together again.

"People are talking," Levi said. "Won't they talk more if she suddenly up and leaves?"

"I'm not concerned with gossip," Mamm replied tightly. "A good Amish Christian will keep her mouth closed when it comes to that kind of thing."

"And yet, they're talking anyway," Levi said bitterly.

Susanna reached forward and grabbed a block from the tabletop, then pushed a corner into her mouth, gnawing on it for a moment before she looked down at the soggy wood. Stephen handed another block to Hannah, but Hannah was less interested in it. She reached for her grandfather instead, and Stephen scooped her out of her seat and settled her onto his lap.

Watching his daet with his granddaughters, Levi had to wonder why this was suddenly so easy to do, if it weren't about people talking, their family reputation being tainted along with Rosmanda's. Because everyone was attached to these baby girls, including Levi. But his heart wasn't aching because of the babies. . . .

"Is it that easy for you?" Levi shook his head. "This is her home. Here, with us!"

"Her husband is dead!" Mamm said, her voice rising. "Dead!"

Levi hadn't expected that explosion, and silence descended in the kitchen. Even Susanna stopped her banging. Levi looked over at his father, and Daet put down his sandwich, eyeing Mamm uncertainly.

"And you blame me for that—" Levi said, his voice tight.

"No!" Mamm pressed her lips together. "This isn't about placing blame for his death, it's about accepting it.

Rosmanda's husband is gone, Levi. You don't seem to understand the implication of that. She isn't ours. She was *Wayne's*. And now her parents are asking her to go home."

Yah, she'd been Wayne's in name and in marriage, but she belonged here, too, in a different way. Rosmanda belonged with him. They meant something to each other. This was no formal, polite arrangement anymore. It wasn't about sending her off to find a respectable husband to help support her. She'd become a part of the fabric here, and tearing her out wouldn't be so easy. Not to him.

"You'll miss her, too," Levi said.

"Of course I'll miss her!" Mamm said with a sigh. "I've spent every day with her in the kitchen, hung laundry with her, canned vegetables . . . I've helped raise these girls. We've been a family, but I also know how much we have a right to. And she's got to live her life."

"In Morinville?" Levi said.

"Sometimes you have to face your past," Daet said, and he looked up at Levi pointedly. "There's no moving forward until you do, Son."

Had this just become about him? He glanced out the window again, and the snow was coming down much harder. Maybe Rosmanda decided to stay with Ketura until the storm had passed . . . or maybe she hadn't. Was she out on those roads in this mess?

"Is this about me now?" Levi asked. "Because I'm no longer drinking. You know that."

"Yah, and I'm proud of you for that," Daet replied. "But I'm talking about your brother."

"My issues with him are buried with him," Levi said with a sigh.

"No, they aren't." Daet stood up and came to the window to look outside. "You're still competing with him. You're still fighting him, even now."

And maybe Levi was, but what was he supposed to do about that? His competition with Wayne had fueled most of his choices in life . . . and maybe it was the same for Wayne, too. They'd played off each other, competed, jostled. But now that brother was gone, and he had no one else who cared enough to fight with him.

"You backed him up," Levi said, turning toward his father. "You knew what it would do to us, and you backed him in going after Rosmanda."

"Your brother didn't ask our permission," Daet replied.

"Yah, but when he came home and said he'd asked her to marry him, you told me to celebrate with my brother." Levi shook his head in disgust. "Celebrate!"

"Actually, first of all I told you to forgive your brother," Daet replied.

"I loved her, Daet!" Levi exploded. "I loved her!"

"And we didn't know it—" His father brought the baby to Miriam and handed her over. "Levi, how many girls did you play around with?"

"I wasn't playing around . . ."

"They were all rather hopeful that you'd start courting them. That hope came from somewhere!" his father snapped.

"Rosmanda was different," he said. "And if you'd asked me, you'd have known that."

"Did your brother know it?" Daet asked. "Because from what he told us, he thought you were toying around with Rosmanda, too, and he figured he was doing her a favor—giving her an honest to goodness proposal."

"Trying to win," Levi said. "Always trying to beat me."

"No." His daet shook his head. "Not competing. Not that time. Wayne loved her. From afar, granted. But he loved her. And he thought you didn't." His father glanced toward Miriam, then sighed. "By the time he figured out that whatever had been between you and Rosmanda had been genuine, it was too late."

This new information swirled through his mind like the snow outside the window. He'd never heard this part of the story.

"What do you mean?" he asked.

"They were already married," Daet replied with a weak shrug. "And he realized that she'd loved you, too."

"It broke his heart," Mamm added. "So you weren't the only one hurting after that wedding. Your brother spent every single day after that trying to win her love. Not her respect. Not her admiration. Not her affection. But her love."

"But she married him—" Levi frowned.

"Yah. She did." Mamm sighed. "And I don't think she ever saw what Wayne was doing. She just thought he was considerate, and she appreciated it. He was a good husband. But he'd wanted more than appreciation. It was why he wanted to keep you away from her, and why I didn't step in to stop it."

His brother had been trying to win over his wife . . . and had been failing? The thought brought a lump to his throat. He'd spent so much time simmering with fury over his brother's betrayal, that he'd never stopped to consider the fallout of his brother's hasty marriage.

"Why didn't you tell me this before?" Levi asked.

"It was your brother's burden," Daet said. "It was his private pain. It wasn't our place to pass it around. Besides, what would you have done? Come around more often? Wayne would have seen something between you—even if you never acted on it—that he couldn't compete with. It was better to leave it."

So Wayne had still been competing . . . still feeling inferior . . . still worried that Levi had something he'd never have. It explained why his brother would come to see him at the farm he worked and never invited him home. It explained why Wayne went out of his way to keep Rosmanda as far from him as possible. It explained why Wayne hadn't wanted Levi in the lives of his newborn twin girls. . . .

And yet, it didn't explain why when Rosmanda was able to see Levi's heart laid bare, why she'd willingly married a man she didn't love. As a way of escape, maybe? It didn't change things with Rosmanda, but it might change his memory of his brother.

He looked out the window, his thoughts in a jumble, and he finally focused on that swirling snow. She was out there.

"The snow is getting bad," Levi said.

"She should have been home by now," Mamm said.

"She probably stayed when she saw the snow," Daet said, adjusting Hannah in his arms.

"No, she'd have tried to make it back," Mamm said. "You know how she is with her daughters—she never leaves them for long."

His mamm was right—Rosmanda would come back for her girls, and the storm had arisen out of nothing, it seemed. She'd be on her way.

"I'm going to check the road for Rosmanda," Levi said, turning toward the door. "She should be back."

"Levi," his mother said, and there were tears in her voice. "We couldn't tell you your brother's secrets. You understand that, don't you?"

He looked back at his mother and saw her anxious gaze locked on him.

"Yah, Mamm," he said past the lump in his throat. "I understand that."

Levi headed into the mudroom, plunged his feet into his boots, and grabbed his coat off a hook. He didn't want to deal with his feelings right now, or his memories. He wanted to get out there, find her, bring her home, and fix something in this miserable day. Because the way it seemed to him, life was a jumble of broken people, broken promises, and dashed hopes . . . Sometimes, a man had to have one win.

And maybe Wayne had wanted the same thing—and gotten so much more than he'd bargained for.

Chapter Seventeen

Rosmanda pulled her shawl closer—the biting wind whipping through the wool. The snow swirled over the asphalt ahead and wind drove snow into her face, clinging to her hair, freezing her ears. She pulled her shawl up over her head, and she dug out some gloves from under the seat, pulling them on as her cold aching fingers got a bit of relief. She already had the lap rug over her legs to keep her protected from the elements . . . it just wasn't warm enough. Some spring snow wasn't unusual, but this was a little late for a blizzard.

Rosmanda leaned forward, squinting to get a glimpse of some familiar landmark. She was trusting the horses to know their way home, at this point, because if it were left up to her, she'd probably drive them straight past the farm.

The horses plodded on, and another gust of wind blocked her view. She held the reins tightly, trying to see the edges of the road. She didn't dare put the buggy in the center, because there were cars who were equally blinded, but the ditch was deep, too.

God, guide me. . . .

She'd been praying ever since she'd started out. At first, she was praying for wisdom in her upcoming choices. Was going back to Morinville really the best path? Could

she find a way to support herself here if she stayed?
Maybe she and Ketura could start making more money
and she could rent a room in town, or something. Maybe
an older couple like Josiah and Anna would make a
similar arrangement with her—a roof over her head and
a place to raise her girls in exchange for cooking, cleaning, and basic chores. Maybe there were options that could
allow her girls to be raised with dignity in the community,
but didn't require her to marry right away . . . She was
willing to do what she must, but marriage wasn't easy, and
she doubted a second marriage would be any easier than
her first.

But then the falling snow had started to whip into a
proper storm, and her prayer became a whole lot more
immediate.

Father, guide me . . . Get me home to my girls.

Anything else could wait.

The wind let up, and a pair of headlights pierced the
veil of snow down the road. The car slowed as it approached, and the driver cranked down the window. It was
a young man.

"Hey, you okay?" he shouted out the window.

"Yah! Thank you!" she shouted back in English, and
the horses carried her past the vehicle. She looked behind
and the taillights glowed red for another few seconds
before the car started off again.

The Englishers were well-meaning, but she didn't know
what they expected to do for her . . . give her a ride and
leave the horses in a storm? Unless that Englisher was a
skilled buggy driver, he wasn't much use to her.

The Englisher car had disappeared before she realized she wouldn't have turned down a coat . . . but it
wasn't likely anyone would have an extra coat kicking

around, either. What she needed was to get home as soon as possible.

Another blinding swirl of snow circled the buggy, and this time, she felt the wheel slip . . . not just a small slip on icy pavement, but an actual sideways slide. Her stomach flew up into her throat, and she put a hand up, catching herself before she slid down the seat, too. The horses' hooves scrambled against the asphalt, and they squealed in fear.

"Oh, God!" Rosmanda said, and the buggy tipped sideways, throwing Rosmanda with it. She landed heavily in snow, but nothing landed on top of her. She'd fallen outside of the buggy, and when she looked around, she saw that the buggy had landed on its side against the snowy bank on the other side of the ditch. The horses had been pulled with it, one on its side, too, and the other already scrambling to its feet.

The horses! Rosmanda pushed herself up. She wasn't hurt—at least not badly. There was a muscle along her leg that throbbed warningly, but she was in one piece. Her shoes slipped against the wet snow on the ground, and she slid down the bank into ankle-deep slush. She let out a gasp of shock, then scrambled up the other side, water seeping out of her shoes as she clambered up. Her wet feet would have to wait. The horses were in trouble. One was pinned—held down by the hitching tack. She had to undo it, and she pulled off her gloves to free up her fingers, started at the first buckle she could reach, pulling hard against the leather to loosen it enough to undo the hold.

"It's okay," she said aloud. "I'm helping you. Just stay calm, and I'll get you out."

The last thing she needed was to collide with the hoof of a frightened horse. Levi might have gotten away with nothing more than bruised ribs, but people had died from kicks like that, and she wasn't taking chances.

The horse's eyes rolled around as it tried to heave itself up again. Rosmanda pulled her hands back, and the horse collapsed back on the ground. She reached for the buckle again, this time getting it loose, and she started on the next one.

This would take her forever, and tears of frustration welled in her eyes. Her hands were cold, even through the gloves, and her muscles weren't responding with strength or dexterity. She looked back at the buggy—the axle looked broken, from what she could tell. It would be an expensive fix for her father-in-law . . . She couldn't pay for this—and if the horses were injured, too, because she'd stupidly started out when she should have waited—what could she tell them?

She was their dead son's wife, not their daughter. They'd been kind, but this would be too much.

"Rosie!" The voice came through the howl of the wind, and she squinted through a swirl of snow. The wind drove the pellets straight into her face and she shut her eyes against it. "Rosmanda!"

"Levi?" she called, but her voice was whipped away in the wind. Was Levi out there, or had she imagined it? When the blast of snow cleared, she saw the dark outline of another buggy parked facing her, and Levi's familiar form leapt down from the driver's seat. She felt a rush of warm relief.

"Help me!" she called. "I have to unhitch them!"

Levi ran, slipping toward her. The ground was slick, and when he reached her side, he grabbed her hand and looked her over, his gaze going up and down her in a quick examination.

"Are you okay?" he demanded, almost angrily.

"I'm—I think so—" She blinked up at him, trying to curb the tears that threatened to spill down her cheeks. The buggy wasn't. The horses weren't. . . .

Levi looked past her toward the wreck behind, and then dragged his gaze back to meet hers. "You could have been killed!"

There had been a similar night that winter, and she sucked in a ragged breath. Would it have been appropriate somehow if she'd died in a buggy accident like her husband had?

"It threw me clear," she said, her voice shaking.

Levi turned his attention to the horses, leaving her free of that scalding gaze filled with complicated emotions. Whatever they were feeling, whatever trauma was coming back at the memory of that other buggy accident that had killed Wayne, it would have to wait until they had the luxury to feel it.

Levi was stronger than she was, and he worked through the buckles faster than she'd been able to, grabbing the straps, hauling them upward and undoing buckles with fierce effort. He finally released the first horse from the rigging that had held it down. It scrambled to its feet, and Levi turned to the other horse.

"Catch him!" Levi barked.

Rosmanda caught the first horse's bridle and led it a few feet off, then put a reassuring hand on its nose. It settled down, dropping its head as another wave of wind and snow swept around them. Her feet were more than cold now, they were numb, a dull ache moving where she thought her toes were. She didn't trust her feet to hold her up if she stamped them, so she stood still, praying in her heart for Levi to hurry.

The second horse bounded to its feet, although a little

more slowly and less gracefully than the first. It limped as it came toward them, and Rosmanda felt a torrent of guilt.

"It's hurt," she said woodenly when Levi got to her side.

"Hey, you could have been worse, and so could the horse," Levi said gruffly. "Come on. We'll tie the horses up behind and lead them home. We aren't far. We'll take it slow."

"The buggy—" she started.

"—will still be here tomorrow. We'll haul it out," Levi replied. "Come on. I'll tie up the horses."

Levi led the horses around the back of the buggy, and Rosmanda tried to hoist herself up into the seat. She put her foot on the runner and stepped, but her foot slipped and she fell heavily against the side, the air rushing out of her lungs. She sucked in a choking gulp of air.

"You okay?" Levi asked, coming up behind her.

"My feet—they got wet—" She tried to lift her leg up again, and this time Levi's strong hands clamped down on her waist, and he lifted her upward. She grabbed at the handle and pulled herself up onto the seat with the last of her strength. Levi came up after her, taking the reins and settling himself next to her. He put his arm around her, pulling her solidly against him.

"Hold on to me," he ordered, and he grabbed a lap rug from the seat next to him and dropped it over her, then flicked the reins.

She'd done enough here, damaged enough and put her in-laws through plenty with Jonathan's scandalous visit. She wasn't their problem, and things with Levi had gone too far already.

"Woman, you're wet and cold. Hold on to me!" he barked.

Rosmanda slid her arm under his, the warmth from his body emanating against her. She shivered, and locked her arm down over his, shutting her eyes against that drilling snow.

For the moment, she was safe, and never before had she been quite so grateful to see a man arrive to her rescue. What had she been thinking about doing this on her own? She could raise her daughters by herself, given an adequate income, but it was about more than money. It was about all those things that men did in an Amish home—like this. A woman could be many things, but not everything.

She couldn't do it alone. If there was no husband, then she at least needed her family—her daet, her brothers, her sister, her mamm and the other women, because community was there for a reason. They needed one another, whether they wanted to or not. Pride stood tall and unique. But community—the kind God ordained—was about accepting your own limitations, accepting help. She was no better than any other woman, no more deserving of taking her own path than any of the others were.

The horses plodded on and Rosmanda leaned into Levi's strong, warm shoulder.

God, guide me. . . .

The storm had whipped into a fury by the time Levi turned the horses into the drive. He stopped the buggy in front of the house, then got down first so that he could help Rosmanda. She nearly fell into his arms as she came down from the fender, and he grabbed her tight around the waist and all but carried her to the side door. It flung open before he got to the steps, and the sound of crying babies came out toward them. Miriam came out to help, and between them they carried her inside.

Mamm pulled a chair in front of the stove, and Levi

helped Rosmanda sit. Her lips were white and she was trembling with cold. The babies' cries rose in a desperate wail, and Levi felt a pang. Those cries—he wanted to fix whatever was the problem, and he looked to his mother, looking for guidance, or an order, maybe.

"What happened to her?" Mamm gasped. She started running hands over Rosmanda's limbs. "She's drenched!"

"The buggy flipped. She was in the ditch," he said. "Her feet are so cold she could barely stand—"

Mamm's fingers moved quickly down Rosmanda's calves and she pulled stockings off of her feet, and reached over to a nearby drawer and pulled out clean dishtowels.

"These will do—" She gently covered one of Rosmanda's feet and looked back at Levi. "Go! Take care of the horses. We'll be fine."

"Are they okay?" He looked toward the sound of the crying—coming from upstairs.

"They want their mamm. And she's here now."

"Where's Daet?" he asked.

"At the cow barn. You can help him when you're done there. We're fine. Go!"

Rosmanda met his gaze, but he couldn't read what she was feeling. And he headed for the door. There were horses to bed down, an injured leg to see to, and the cattle that would need tending as well. . . .

He shot Rosmanda an apologetic look, and then turned for the door. They'd eat—and talk—when the work was done.

When Levi finally stumbled back into the house that night, all was quiet once more. The noise and confusion from when they'd first arrived was gone, and the house smelled of food. Levi pulled off his boots, then his coat, and headed into the kitchen. Rosmanda stood there, a shawl still around her shoulders, and she wore thick socks and no shoes, but she looked more like herself. There was pink in her cheeks, which he was grateful to see. He looked around the kitchen. There was no sign of his parents.

"Are we alone?" he asked.

"Your daet needed your mamm to help with another cow giving birth. Something about twins and the mother wouldn't accept, either. They don't want any more bottle babies, so they're trying to get things going." Her voice was low, and she pulled a plate off the stove and put it onto the table next to a fork and knife. "So they're at the barn . . ."

The plate was filled with cheddar mashed potatoes, fried sausage, and a pile of peas. His stomach rumbled. It had been a long time since he'd eaten last. She sat down kitty-corner to him at the table and leaned her elbow on the tabletop.

"The babies are down for the night, I take it?" he asked. The memory of their cries still tugged at an uncomfortable part of him.

"Sleeping like babies." She smiled at her little joke.

So they were alone . . . He put the fork into the potatoes—it smelled amazing—but he couldn't take a bite. He'd been thinking about her, worrying about her, ever since he dropped her off at the house, shivering, shaken, and worn. Even when he was staying clear of the family farm, giving her space with his brother, she'd been a part of this place. To have her leave . . .

"The quilt—it's in the back of the buggy still."

He'd seen it when he brought the horses in, and he'd

meant to take it inside for Rosmanda when he came back from chores.

"I don't think I can sell it," she said softly.

"Rosmanda, are you really thinking of going?" he asked, putting down his fork.

She looked up at him, her eyes like dark wells. "Yah. I am."

"Was Ketura encouraging you to go, too?" he asked bitterly.

"No. Well . . . not encouraging, exactly. But she understands."

Even Ketura . . . Why were they so eager to push Rosmanda away?

"Am I the only one who wants you to stay?" Levi demanded. He pushed back his chair and stood up, walking over to the kitchen window and staring out at the falling snow, illuminated with golden inside light.

"Levi, it's time!" she said, rising to her feet. "I'm not a daughter here! I'm a daughter-in-law . . . and not even that anymore. I'm the mamm to their granddaughters. And yes, that matters. Yes, I'm still a part of the family, but I'm not their responsibility for the rest of my life!"

"So you think you're a burden then?" he demanded.

"It isn't about wanting me to leave," Rosmanda said. "Ketura has been married before. Twice. She knows my situation."

"I know your situation, too," he said bitterly. "And I still say this is your home."

"I ruined your parents' buggy," she said. "It will cost a good amount to fix it. And the horse might be lame now—"

He'd set the horse up in a stall with fresh hay. He'd

bound the leg himself. A sprain, nothing more. He was certain of that.

"It's not lame," he said.

"Good. I'm so glad . . ." She smiled weakly. "I was afraid I'd hurt it, and it would suffer because of me, too."

Levi shook his head. "Are you really thinking that we're counting pennies around here? It could have happened to anyone! Accidents happen. Hell—accidents *kill* people!"

The smile slipped from her face, and she winced at those last words. He didn't mean to be so crass—he hadn't meant to swear, either. But he'd been through one too many buggy accidents—and the last one had taken Wayne.

"I should have stayed with Ketura—" she said.

"Yah, you should have!" He was angry now, and he couldn't seem to rein it in. He felt his eyes mist, and he blinked it back. The image of that buggy—a shadow through the snow—rose up in his mind and his heart sped up at the memory. "Do you know what I thought when I saw that buggy turned over in the ditch?"

"I know—I'm sorry."

"I thought I'd—" Emotion choked off his voice, but he forced the rest of the words out. "I thought I'd lost you, Rosie . . . I thought I'd have to find your body, and—"

"Oh, Levi—" She took a step toward him.

"And if I had to lose you, too . . ." He sucked in a breath, trying to find some sort of foundation, some resolute calm, but there was none. "If I had to lose the woman I love—"

The words were out before he could think better of them, and Rosmanda stared up at him, stunned. She opened her mouth to say something, then closed it, her dark eyes fixed on his face. He hadn't said it aloud until now, but he was in love with her—still, or maybe again.

"And I'm not taking that back," he said, closing the distance between them. He put his hand on her cheek, and she leaned into his touch. "I love you, Rosie. I have for years—when it would have been better to move on. But I loved you. And I couldn't help it."

Neither could his brother, it would seem. They'd had that in common.

"Levi, don't—" she started.

"Don't what?" he cut her off. "Don't tell you the truth? Don't allow myself to feel more than I should? Do you think I have a choice?"

Tears welled in her eyes. "It won't help us."

"I don't care!" He dropped his hand, the inches between them feeling like a mile. "It never mattered anyway, did it? You married a man you didn't love!"

"Levi . . ."

"Are you going to deny it?" he asked. "Did you fall in love with him? At any point, even after the wedding—did you?"

Rosmanda licked her lips. "Wayne was a good man. A strong, pious, moral man. I trusted him with my life, with my children. He was a good husband—"

"Were you in love with him?" Levi met her gaze, daring her to lie to him.

"I learned to love him," she whispered. "That was enough."

"No, it wasn't." He turned back toward the window again, his heart hammering so hard that he could feel it in his throat. "He knew it, you know."

"He was kind and generous!" she said, her voice rising.

"He was the kind of Amish man a woman could trust to never change!"

"But were you in love with him?" He turned, the anger pulsing through him. "Answer me! It should be simple, shouldn't it? Did you love my brother?"

"I—" A tear slipped down her cheek. "Not in the way you're asking. No."

"But he did love you," Levi said, shaking his head. "You knew that, didn't you? He loved you, and he worked and worked to get you to love him back—"

Levi turned back toward her, his anger under control again. She needed to know this. If she was going to go off and do the same thing all over again to another man, she needed to understand exactly how to break an unloved man.

"I was a good wife!" Rosmanda said, anger snapping in her eyes. "I worked hard! I cleaned, I cooked, I ironed his clothes. I gave birth to his babies, and I would have stood by him for life!"

"But you loved *me*—" Levi said quietly.

Silence stretched between them, and she shrugged weakly.

"Yah, I loved you." Her voice shook. "But he didn't know it."

"You think?" Levi met her gaze. "He knew it. That's why he wouldn't let me near you. Because he knew how you felt, and he knew he couldn't compete with that. You loved me, but you chose him."

"You know why," she said.

"Because I was a risk," he said gruffly. "Because I opened my heart to you and showed you everything—my weaknesses as well as my strengths. And you *loved* me."

"Stop saying that!" Tears slipped down her cheeks. "I

had to let my head lead! I had to make the wise choice! I'd already trusted the wrong man—it didn't matter if I loved you. What good was that? It doesn't matter if I still do!"

She pulled her shawl tighter around her, and she looked so slender and frail standing there. He pulled her into his arms and looked down into her face. Then he lowered his lips over hers, kissing her with all the pent-up longing of the years he'd spent loving his brother's wife. She sank against him, and his hands moved up her sides, up to cradle her face. He loved her so much that it ached within him, and he'd somehow gotten used to this constant pain.

He broke off the kiss with a ragged breath.

"Stay, Rosie," he pleaded. "Don't leave. Just . . . stay . . ."

She blinked her eyes open and looked up into his face. "For what?"

"For this." He shrugged. "You belong here. You can't deny that."

"There was a time when Aaron and Ketura did the same thing, Levi," she whispered. "They knew there was no future, but they kept going anyway. It didn't change anything. And the heartbreak was there waiting for them—"

"Do we have to know everything up front?" he asked helplessly. "Can't this be enough for now—knowing that we love each other? Because this is real, and if you're afraid I'll just stop loving you one day—"

"I'm not a strong Amish woman," she whispered. "I'm weak in the ways that matter most—in faith, in self-control. I can't be with a man who is just like me, Levi! I need a man who is strong next to my personal weakness. I need a man who can stand by our faith like a pillar, who isn't shaken, who doesn't question—"

"Even if you don't love him?" he asked woodenly.

"I know what I need. I know what my daughters need! They'll pay for my weakness, Levi, unless I can make up for it!"

Levi sighed. He knew that—she was right there. Her mistakes would reflect on her little girls both here and in Morinville. And maybe they were just like Aaron and Ketura, continuing something that had no hope in the real world. He loved her, but to marry her? Dare he tie himself for life to the woman who'd never think he was enough? And maybe they hadn't had much choice in their feelings, but carrying on—it had only made it harder when they did have to face reality.

"Marriage isn't just about longing and love," Rosmanda said, tears welling in her eyes. "It's about the everyday things, too. The community, the work, the kinner . . ."

"I know," he said woodenly. "Jonathan told me that things changed when his wife saw him for what he really was. And you've already done that. It isn't your fault—but you know my weaknesses."

Boots sounded on the steps outside, and Rosmanda took a step away from him.

"I'm sorry, Levi," she whispered. "Let's not draw this out when we know how it ends—"

"So you're truly going back to Morinville, then?" Levi asked softly.

Rosmanda's chin quivered. "I think that's best."

The door opened and his parents came inside. Levi heard them stomp off their boots, and Rosmanda turned for the stairs, hurrying up and out of sight. When his father emerged into the kitchen, he looked over at Levi quizzically.

"Are you okay?" he asked.

"Yah." Levi swallowed hard. "Yah, I'm fine. I'm going to check the horses."

He might be a fool for loving her, but at least he'd told her how he felt. They'd both go on to marry others whom they'd never love half as much as they'd loved each other. And maybe it could be enough. Maybe the others wouldn't know that it could have been deeper.

But right now, he just needed to get out, so he left the food on the table, plunged his feet into his boots, and pressed out into the night.

Chapter Eighteen

Rosmanda sat on the edge of her bed, tears trickling down her cheeks. She sucked in a shuddering breath, trying to keep her sobs silent. She loved him . . . She'd been holding that back for too long because it didn't matter. She wasn't looking for love. One day when her girls were grown, they were going to need husbands of their own, and she couldn't allow her own selfishness now to stand in the way of their future.

What would have happened if Jonathan hadn't gotten Mary pregnant before their wedding? What if he'd married her instead? Would she be happy now with a man of such low character? Of course not. She'd be miserable, all because she followed her stubborn heart after the wrong man.

And Levi was the wrong man, too. He might love her, and she might love him. He might make her heart race and she might long for his touch like she'd never longed before . . . but he was too much like her. He wouldn't hold her firmly to the faith, to the community. He wouldn't make up for her failures, and she already had plenty. Her mistake with Jonathan would not go away, and she'd have to be proving herself with every step she took from now on.

Especially when she went home.

Rosmanda looked over at her sleeping daughters in the light of the little oil lamp on her dresser. It flickered, and Hannah sighed deeply in her sleep. They were so very small, and yet she could imagine them as older girls playing with neighbors and gossiping with other girls on Service Sunday. Ketura was right—marriage wasn't just about how a woman saw herself, but how the community saw her, too. And that bled onto her daughters. They wouldn't be this small for long. . . .

Tomorrow was supposed to be church at the Peachy farm, but with this snowfall, it would be cancelled. Everyone would be digging out. Rosmanda stood and looked out the window. The snow was falling more gently now, the wind having died down. Out there in the buggy barn, Levi was avoiding her. She'd seen him leave the house from her window, heard the slam of the door. What was he thinking now? And what did it say about her that she wanted nothing more than to run outside and go to him?

She knew he was wrong for her. She knew her feelings were betraying her. She knew it! And yet, all she wanted was to feel Levi's arms close around her once more.

"Stop being weak," she murmured to herself.

Rosmanda owed Wayne's memory better than this. She owed his daughters better than this . . . If she could just go home to her own family, maybe she could get her balance back at long last.

Her gaze moved away from the buggy barn and toward the drive that led to the main road. She couldn't see far through the snowfall, but she didn't have to. She'd stared out this window so often . . . Somewhere, along the road, the buggy lay in a fractured heap, and it felt like a crack in her own heart. She'd caused enough trouble for her in-laws, and when they finally dug out here at the farm, the men would go get that buggy and drag it home.

That was life—one job after another, one obligation after another. And she'd officially become the family obligation, the problem to be fixed. Ironically, she understood how Levi felt around here a little bit. He'd been the family problem for far too long, and now she'd supplanted him in that.

Rosmanda closed the curtain and pulled off her dress and slipped into a soft, warm nightgown. She unwound her hair from the bun, and let it fall over her shoulders. Tomorrow morning, she would ask Stephen to buy her the bus tickets to take her and her daughters back to Indiana.

One last expense, and she would be off of her father-in-law's conscience.

The next day, Levi stayed busy as he and his father dug them out from the snowstorm. Temperature had already risen overnight, and the snow started to melt, making each shovelful of snow that much heavier. Paths needed to be forged from the barn to the house and to the chicken coop, too. The cattle needed hay to be delivered to the feeders, water troughs to be filled . . . And after all of that was done, they took a team of horses to pull the buggy out of the ditch. Service Sunday would be postponed.

"Rosmanda has asked that I pay for her to go back to Indiana," Stephen said as they hitched up a chain to the buggy.

"When?" Levi asked hollowly.

"Obviously not today," Stephen replied. "Tomorrow, maybe."

Levi sighed.

"Is there something still there, Son?" Stephen asked. He waded through the deep snow toward the horses, then looked back at Levi.

"I don't know what you mean."

"Ah. So that's the tack you're taking."

"Daet, she was Wayne's."

Wasn't that the point Mamm had hammered home so well yesterday? Wayne was dead and they had no right to hold on to Rosmanda. *He* had no right to hold on to her.

Stephen didn't answer, and he took the horses by the bridle. "Hya. Forward. Hya!"

The horses started to pull and the buggy creaked as it tipped upward, great avalanches of snow falling off the smooth side as it slowly rose higher and higher. When it finally came down onto its wheels, it rocked a couple of times, and Daet stopped the horses.

"I want you to bring her to the bus depot for me," Daet said.

Levi eyed his father warily. Did he even want to do that? It wouldn't make things any easier, but at least he'd get a good-bye. He nodded.

"Yah, I can do that."

"Good." Stephen nodded to the buggy. "Watch to see if it'll roll properly, will you?"

The rest of the day was filled with sweat and hard work. They brought the buggy back home, parked it in the buggy barn, and proceeded with all their regular chores with knee-deep, melting snow to slow them down. When they got back for meals, he ate hungrily, but Rosmanda didn't give him much opportunity to talk to her. She stayed at the sink washing dishes while he ate lunch, and after dinner, when Stephen told her that Levi would take her to the bus depot the next day, she smiled gratefully.

"Thank you," she said, and her gaze swung toward Levi. "I appreciate it."

And then she'd taken her daughters upstairs to change their diapers, and to pack. Levi stood in the kitchen, staring at the empty staircase.

"We'll all miss her, Levi," Miriam said softly.

"Yah."

Rosmanda was avoiding him. She had been ever since they'd said everything there was to say. They loved each other, and there was no future there. She was right that it was better to break it off and quit torturing themselves, but her distance from him still hurt.

"It won't be the same around here without a young woman," Miriam said. "Maybe you'll start going to the youth meetings, find a girl to drive home from singing."

A wife—that was his mother's solution here? Yah, he understood it from her point of view. Rosmanda, the woman who'd caused so much strife in their family, would be sent off to Indiana again, and they could get back into a regular routine. And why wouldn't a young man marry? He was eligible, and while Rosmanda might not want to take a chance on him, there were plenty of young women who would love nothing more.

But he wasn't interested in finding some sweet girl to let down. He knew what real love was, and tying himself down to a woman he didn't feel that kind of passion for seemed cruel. It couldn't be faked.

"I don't know about that, Mamm," he said.

"A home isn't a home without a wife, Son," she said. "And you're a grown man now. Being here with your daet and me is going to only frustrate you. You need a wife. It's time."

It's time—wasn't that what Rosmanda had said about

her returning to Indiana? It was time. Things needed to change. Everyone else seemed pretty convinced about that.

"I'll take Rosmanda to the bus after chores in the morning," he said.

He wasn't talking about the future, pretending that Rosmanda's departure could be good for him. Because it wasn't.

The next morning, after chores, Rosmanda's suitcase and a couple of boxes sat by the door, the plastic-wrapped quilt on top of them. Levi looked at them morosely—was that all that was left of her life here with them? She had a baby bag packed to bulging. Her bedroom had been left clean—he'd looked inside her room, and found the bed and cribs all stripped, the floor swept and mopped, the surfaces dusted. It was like she was wiping out the last trace that she'd ever been here.

Stephen and Miriam both gave her a hug and each of the babies a kiss, and then it was time to leave. Levi felt conflicted. He didn't want this moment to come, and yet he wanted to get it over with, too.

"Let's pray together," Stephen said.

Levi stood next to Rosmanda as his father prayed for traveling mercies, for protection, for a fresh start in her hometown. He could feel the warmth of her hand close to his, but he didn't touch her. When they lifted their heads, Rosmanda hugged Stephen and Miriam once more, and then followed Levi out the door.

Levi carried out the boxes first and put them in the back of the buggy. Stephen carried her suitcase and that quilt, and put them in front of the boxes. Then Levi helped Rosmanda up into the buggy seat, Susanna and Hannah were handed up to her, and they were ready to leave.

Levi flicked the reins and the horses started out. The day shone warm, the snow from the blizzard steadily melting away, and the sound of dripping coming from the trees. It would be empty here without her. He looked over at Rosmanda, both babies cuddled close on her lap. Her eyes were filled with misgiving, and her gaze flickered in his direction as she noticed his scrutiny.

"You can change your mind, you know," he said with a small smile.

"No." She looked down at her daughters on her lap. "This is good for us. My parents will be so happy to have these two to dote on—"

"Yah," he agreed.

"You know I have to do something, Levi," she said. "You know that. Even if I stayed, I'd have to find an appropriate husband. Things would have to change."

"I know." He hated it, but he knew it.

"Levi, this is good for you, too," she said quietly.

Was she imagining him marrying some girl and settling down the way everyone hoped he would? Would that actually comfort her?

"I'm going to miss you," he said.

"Me too." She cast him a misty smile.

"Just promise me that you'll tell me before you get married," he said. "Tell me who he is."

"So you can hate him a little bit?" she asked with a low laugh.

"Yah. I think it's only fair."

"All right. I'll write you and tell you then."

"You could write about other things, too. . . ." He hesitated. "I want to know that you're okay—no ulterior motives."

"I know," she said. "You're not Jonathan. Trust me, I know that."

"So, you'll write?" he said.

"Yah, I'll write. To all of you—your mamm and daet, too."

Not quite the fulfilment of his hopes, but he understood. Their earlier intimacy couldn't just change forms. It had to be over.

His heart was heavy, and a couple of times after that they tried to start up some small talk, but it felt empty and they let it drop, opting for silence instead. Silence seemed more honest, anyway.

When they got to the bus depot, Levi tied the horses up at the hitching post outside, and then carried her boxes and bags into the depot. There weren't many people inside—a young couple at one end of the station who seemed quite preoccupied with each other, and an older woman reading a book. There were no Amish there today, and he was glad for that. This wouldn't be an easy goodbye, and he didn't want to do it in front of people he knew.

When he went back to the buggy, Rosmanda handed the babies down to him one at a time, and he looked down into those little faces with a wistful smile. The next time he saw them, they'd be little girls, running around. They wouldn't remember him. . . .

Rosmanda got down from the buggy and took Hannah in her arms, leaving Susanna with him.

"Thank you for buying my ticket," she said. "I appreciate all you and your parents have done for me. I know I've caused some damage recently, and—"

"Rosie, stop that," he said with a shake of his head. "If you need anything, I want you to tell me. If Jonathan gives you any trouble, I'll come down myself and deal with him personally."

She smiled. "That's sweet."

"I mean it," he said. "Just write to me. I'll drop everything."

"We can't do that, Levi," she said, sobering. "You know it. We have to just . . . part ways. Move on. There is only misery waiting if we drag this out."

Levi sighed. "Let's go get your ticket, then."

Inside the depot, Levi paid for two tickets, since Rosmanda would need both seats. The trip from Pennsylvania to Indiana would take ten hours including their rest stops. He handed her the tickets, and her fingers lingered on his for a moment.

"Who will pick you up?" he asked.

"My daet. Your father called the Englisher neighbor and left a message for him last night. They'd bring him the message right away. He'll be there."

Levi nodded. She'd be fine. Her family would be glad to take care of her from here on in, but he hated letting go. She wasn't just his nieces' mother, or his late brother's wife. She was Rosie, the girl who had held him by the heartstrings ever since he first met her. Falling in love with her had been a terrible idea, but it had happened years ago, and there was no undoing it, just living with it.

He longed to pull her into his arms and kiss her the way she should be kissed . . . but he wouldn't. They already knew where they stood.

"Levi, this *has* to be good-bye," Rosmanda said, tears welling in her eyes.

"I know," he said. "The next time I see you, you'll be married, I'm sure."

"God willing." She dropped her gaze. "For my girls' sake, at least."

"Do you want me to stay until the bus comes?" he asked, glancing in the direction of the glass doors where the buses arrived.

"No," she said with a shake of her head. "I'll be fine. I'll sit next to that older lady, and I can guarantee you that she'll help me with the girls."

Community—even the Englisher kind—was going to take over now. She wasn't his to hold on to, and she'd find her way without him.

"Okay, well . . . I guess this is good-bye, then," he said, and a lump rose in his throat.

She hesitated, then nodded quickly. "Yah. I think that's best. Good-bye, Levi."

Staying any longer wouldn't make this any easier, so he leaned down and kissed her cheek one last time, then touched the heads of each of his nieces.

"God go with you," he said gruffly, and he turned and forced himself to walk away.

Every step was a deliberate choice going against his heart, and it took all of his personal strength to do it. When he got outside, he turned and looked back. He could see her through the window, her pale face turned toward him, her eyes filled with grief. He wanted to march back in and drag her back home with him, but that was foolish. Rosmanda had made her choice—even if it tore out her heart. She'd always been strong like that.

He untied his horses and got back up into the buggy. His throat was thick with emotion, and he flicked the reins. The buggy started forward, and he wouldn't look back again. It was taking everything inside of him to hold his emotions in check.

So he guided the horses through town, and when he got out onto open road at last, tears leaked past his defenses and trickled down his cheek. He tried to blink them back and dashed them away with the back of his hand, but they wouldn't stop.

He was crying for Rosmanda—the only woman he'd

ever truly loved. And he was crying for his brother, who had loved her, too. He was crying for all he'd lost, and all he'd hoped for, and the life he knew he didn't deserve.

God, take away this love . . . make this easier!

And he truly hoped God would answer his prayer, because he didn't know how he was going to get through this without a drink. The thirst was rising up inside of him, a desperate longing for that comforting distance that alcohol brought.

He wiped his face and cleared his throat. He wouldn't let himself cry. Not anymore. He looked at his watch. Yah. There was time, and he wouldn't be missed.

There was an AA meeting starting in a few minutes in the Elk Hall in town. He'd head in there and get past the temptation. Then he'd go home.

He wasn't much use to anyone if he lost this sobriety token, anyway.

Chapter Nineteen

Rosmanda's daet, Benjamin Graber, sat at the kitchen table the next morning, both of his granddaughters on his lap. He was a solidly built man who ordinarily faced the world with a solemn expression, but with the babies on his lap, he smiled tenderly. Susanna reached up and took a handful of his gray beard, giving it a tug.

"You'll pull it off," Benjamin said. "Oops! See? It'll come right off!"

He dipped his head down and Susanna broke into a smile. She tugged again.

"You sure are big," he said. "Aren't you? Aren't you?"

He made a face and Susanna giggled, but Hannah continued to stare up at him seriously.

"This one doesn't think I'm funny," Benjamin said, looking mildly disappointed.

"That's Hannah, and she takes a bit longer to win over," Rosmanda said, and she chuckled. This was good for her girls . . . and good for her daet, too. He'd retired from farmwork because of his heart condition, but he did make one supervisory trip around the farm a day, checking on the work of his employees. And he was still bishop, too, even though he had the elders do most of the preaching now.

"So, we told Sadie that you were coming—" her mamm, Sarah, began.

"Your mamm got into the buggy and went straight to their house to tell them," Benjamin said. "Sadie's excited, and the kids all want to see their aunt again. You haven't met her youngest, Benjie—he's almost walking now."

"He sat up," Mamm said, casting Daet a flat look. "That's a far sight from walking, Daet."

Benjamin chuckled, and Rosmanda couldn't help but smile. Her daet had never been quite this playful—not in her childhood, at least. Coming home felt a little foreign— a lot had changed. Bishop Graber had taken everything very seriously back when she was young. But he'd softened over the years, it seemed.

Sadie, Rosmanda's older sister, had married Elijah Fisher, and Elijah now ran his father's fencing business. They'd been married nearly ten years and had six children. Rosmanda had kept up with her sister through letters, but the busier Sadie got, the more sparse her time for letter writing. The last letter had been a picture drawn by one of the kids showing a Bible story, and a quick note saying that they were thinking of her in her time of grief and that her oldest son, Samuel, had written a Christmas poem that he read in front of the class at school. The letter had arrived in January.

"Anyway," Mamm said. "Sadie is hosting the quilting night at their place tonight, and I said we'd come."

"Quilting night—for all the women?" Rosmanda asked hesitantly.

"Yah, but I think it's best you walk in with your head held high. You're a widow. You've been married. And you're a mamm, too. Don't give them an inch, Rosmanda."

She'd come back to make Morinville her home again, and she knew it was probably best to start out strong. If she went to the quilting night, she could prove that there was nothing to be ashamed of. She wouldn't hide.

Besides, she missed Sadie.

That evening, Rosmanda and her mother, Sarah Graber, piled into the buggy with the babies and headed down the road toward the acreage where Sadie and Elijah Fisher lived. The night was warm—spring being much more advanced in Indiana than it was in Pennsylvania—and Rosmanda inhaled the scent of new growth. The sun was setting, and Rosmanda looked toward the pink sky.

"Rosie, it will be all right," Mamm said, giving the reins a flick. "I know it will."

"Hmm?" She looked over toward her mother, then sighed.

"You've been so sad ever since you got home," her mother added. "I know that losing Wayne was a big blow. But God will still take care of you, my girl. I promise you that. Life isn't over."

"I know . . ." She sighed. "It's worse than that, though. It's Levi."

"Wayne's brother?" Her mother eyed her uncertainly. "I thought he was drinking."

"He stopped." Rosmanda tipped her cheek onto the top of Susanna's crisp bonnet. "But we were spending more time together. He came back to the family farm to help Stephen, and—"

This made her look worse—so much worse, and tears welled in her eyes.

"Did he hurt you?" her mother asked, her voice hushed.

"Mamm, I fell in love with him," she said, trying to blink back the tears. "And it's stupid. I know that! It's so stupid. He's not the kind of man I need, and knowing how we are when we're together, I should have just avoided him."

"How you are—" Mamm looked over at her. "I know he was a beau once upon a time . . ."

"It sparked back up," Rosmanda said, and she felt her cheeks heat. "And that's a big reason why I came home. I had to get away from him. I don't want to be *that woman*!"

"He isn't married or courting, is he?" Mamm asked hesitantly.

"No!" Rosmanda shot her mother an annoyed look.

"Then you aren't that woman!" Sarah said more firmly. "He's free. So are you. If he's not the right man for you, then fine. But that doesn't make you a bad woman."

But there were things that Rosmanda wouldn't confess to even her mother—like those searing kisses, the way her thoughts drained from her head once she got into his arms, and all the things he made her feel . . . Falling in love with him had been her own foolish fault. She'd known better!

"You're home," her mother added, reaching over to touch Rosmanda's arm. "And I know it will be better. I just feel like you coming home is an answer to prayer."

"Yah." Rosmanda nodded quickly. "Me too."

If only getting over this heartbreak could happen a little faster, because while she was home in body, her heart was still back in Pennsylvania.

When they arrived at Sadie and Elijah's house, Elijah came out to help them with the horses. They all said hello, shook hands, said how good it was to see each other again. But Rosmanda's gaze kept moving toward the house. The windows glowed with kerosene light, and Rosmanda felt a rush of hope at seeing her sister again.

They headed up the side stairs and the door flung open to reveal a group of kinner.

"Aunt Rosie?" said a little girl who looked about four.

"Yah! Is that Tabitha?"

"Yah, it's me!" Tabitha said with a grin. "Oh, my baby cousins are so cute!"

Sadie stood behind all of the children, and Rosmanda took her time, handing the babies over to the older girls, and hugging each of the children one at a time. An older boy stood to the side. He was with the other kids, just as eager to see her, but he stood awkwardly, looking uncomfortable.

"Sammie?" Rosmanda said, straightening up.

"Hi, Aunt Rosie," the boy said, but his voice was deep, and she looked at him in surprise. He didn't look quite old enough for a voice like that, but he must be.

"My little Sammie is grown up!" Rosmanda said, shooting her sister a look of shock.

Sadie laughed softly, and after Rosmanda had given the boy a hug, she went to hug her sister, too.

"I'm glad you're back," Sadie whispered, holding her close. "How are you?"

"I'm doing well." Rosmanda watched as Sadie's daughters doted over Susanna and Hannah. Hannah was so surprised by the overflowing attention that she didn't even try to reach for Rosmanda.

The kitchen was comfortably warm—a teapot hissing on the stove, and plates of cookies and pie covering the tabletop. It was good to be back with her family again, and she looked around her sister's home with a wistful smile. She'd imagined what it would be like to come see her sister, sit in her kitchen . . . But the warmth of this home only reminded her of what she was missing in her own life. She was going back to live with her parents again, and she didn't have a kitchen of her own—not really. She didn't have a husband to spend her evenings with, to crawl into bed with and put her cold feet against under the quilts. . . .

"We're working on a big quilt for out in the sitting

room," Sadie said. "Everyone's here—" She hesitated, though. "Um, Mary Yoder is here, too."

Mary . . . Rosmanda swallowed, her gaze moving toward the doorway that led into the sitting room. Dare she go in? She looked over at Mamm, who gave her a firm nod. Starting strong—that was the plan, right?

"Did she know I was coming?" Rosmanda asked her sister, keeping her voice low.

"No . . . I didn't tell her." Sadie winced. "Some things are better as a surprise, I think . . . At least I hope."

"Come on, then," Mamm said, pulling a pincushion out of a cloth bag. She'd have all different colors of thread in there, too. Mamm was always prepared on quilting nights. "Let's go find a place and get to work."

Sarah went first into the sitting room, and Rosmanda sent up a quick prayer, then followed. When she walked into the room, at first no one noticed her. The women were bent over their work, chatting quietly with the women sitting next to them. But then one looked up, smiled at Sarah, and then froze at the sight of Rosmanda.

"My sister is back!" Sadie said, perhaps a little too cheerily. "And we couldn't be happier to have her home."

The group of women seemed to be a shade less happy about Rosmanda's arrival, because they stared at her in open shock. A couple looked secretly delighted—there were always a few who didn't mind something more interesting to gossip about. But one pair of gray eyes stared at her with such disgust that Rosmanda nearly took a step back. That was Mary Yoder—sitting beside the quilt, but nursing a baby instead of sewing.

"Rosmanda—" One of the older women was the first to find her voice. "You look well. Where are the babies?"

"With their cousins—getting acquainted," Rosmanda said, but her voice sounded thin in her own ears.

"My girls have been anxious to get their hands on the twins," Sadie said, and she put a hand on Rosmanda's back and thrust her toward the empty chair next to Mary. "Go on, have a seat. We need all the hands we can get, if we're going to finish this quilt tonight. We're adding the backing."

Mary held a small baby in her arms that she was feeding beneath a white blanket tossed over her shoulder. Rosmanda looked back at her sister, but Sadie wouldn't make eye contact.

"Mary," Rosmanda said with a weak smile. "So good to see you."

"What are you doing here?" Mary demanded.

"Visiting my sister at present," Rosmanda replied, just in case Mary needed a little reminder of whose home this was. Mary was well within her right to never invite Rosmanda into her own home, but she couldn't dictate who else Rosmanda visited.

Mary looked down at the infant in her arms, and the little one made a little grunt as it fed, and Rosmanda sat down at the empty spot.

"Here, Rosie, a needle," Mamm said, handing Rosmanda a needle and a spool of white thread.

"Thanks, Mamm," she murmured, and set to work threading it, wishing against all hope that she could just sink into the floor. The other women were all looking at her now, and her cheeks blazed with heat. Should she have come? Not that it was much use worrying over that now. She was here—and if she ran off to another room to avoid the women, she'd only make things worse.

"Ladies, let's get to work," Sadie said, her tone sounding like the mother she was. "We can't do a quilt sale in town without quilts, now can we?"

The other women dropped their gazes again, and the

quiet conversation they'd started up was now a little more eager. They were likely talking about her, Rosmanda realized, and if nothing else, she was providing the group with some gossip tonight.

"Why are you here?" Mary snapped. She patted the baby's diapered bottom gently, a strange contrast to the suppressed fury in her gaze.

"I've moved back home to Morinville," Rosmanda said. "My husband is dead, and—"

"Yah, I know that. *My husband* talked about nothing else for months."

The implication was clear, and Rosmanda swallowed hard. Jonathan had been telling his wife about Rosmanda's situation? She turned her lips down in distaste. "Mary, I sent him home."

He'd gone home . . . hadn't he? She eyed Mary uncertainly.

"Yah. He's home. But after how long?"

Was it to be Rosmanda's fault that Jonathan had stayed in Pennsylvania so long? Was Mary going to take no responsibility for her own marriage? Anger rose up inside of her, but Rosmanda pushed it back.

"My brother-in-law was the one who talked to him most," Rosmanda said. "I was busy with my children."

"And I was plenty busy with mine." Mary's tone dripped disdain. "But Jonathan felt so badly for you— how lonely you were without your man."

"Mary, I—"

"I read your letters," Mary said tersely. "So before you deny anything, you shouldn't have been that open with a married man!"

"Yah, I realize that now . . ." Rosmanda sighed. "But if you read those letters, you also know that I was expressing no interest in your husband. At all. In fact, I didn't answer the last three letters he sent to me, because I felt that it wouldn't be right. So I'm not the woman you think."

"You're the woman my husband went to Pennsylvania to check on," Mary said bitterly. "Leaving me at home with four kinner and a brand-new baby."

"I don't know what to say," Rosmanda said feebly.

"How about an apology?" Mary said. "It might be a start!"

And apology for what, though? Rosmanda hadn't asked him to come! She'd tried to stop him, and she'd not encouraged any of his advances. She'd sent him home to his wife.

"I have no desire to talk to your husband, or even see him across a room," Rosmanda hissed, lowering her voice. "He caused enough trouble for me in Pennsylvania! I don't want to steal him, or flirt with him, or distract him from you in any way, I can assure you. So stop glaring daggers at me. I'm no more responsible for his bad behavior than you are!"

Mary looked startled at that, and tears welled up in her eyes. She adjusted her dress, put the baby up on her shoulder, and rose to her feet.

"I'm going to get some tea," Mary said. Her lips trembled, and she edged around the working women, heading toward the kitchen doorway. Rosmanda watched her go, and she felt a wave of regret.

No, she hadn't meant to cause any trouble in the Yoder home, but Mary had been cut deeply by her husband's emotional desertion. Mary had been the one to have her heart torn out. She'd been the one embarrassed in front of her whole community when her husband didn't lie about his reason for going to Abundance quite so well as he thought, and Mary was now faced with the woman her husband had been pining for. If Mary had been a bad wife, as Jonathan claimed, then she had certainly paid for that in full.

Rosmanda was home in Morinville again, and it would take more than a confident reentry to change the community's mind about her.

And even with all of this regret stewing inside of her, her heart was aching, too. She and Mary had some heartbreak in common, and maybe they both deserved what they got. Maybe they didn't. Sometimes a woman paid for her sins for the rest of her life.

Levi put a plate of cold chicken, some cheese, and some crackers down in the center of the table. It was a light lunch—but the best he could scrounge up on his own. Ketura sat at the table, and she looked thin to him. Much like Rosmanda, he realized with a squeeze in his heart. Ketura probably hadn't been eating well since her break with Aaron, and he nudged the plate toward her.

"No, I'm not really hungry," she said.

"Well, you still have to eat," Levi replied. "Put some effort into this, or I'm reporting to my mother that you're losing weight, and she'll bring the whole community in to feed you."

Ketura smiled wanly. "You're cruel."

"I am," he agreed, but he was gratified to see her take a cracker and a piece of chicken.

"Your mamm asked me to come today—" Ketura looked around the kitchen.

"It was a favor for me," Levi said. "She was going to

see you anyway, and . . ." He sighed. "Aunt Ketura, are you all right?"

"I will be," she said quietly. Her eyes had rings underneath them, and she looked paler than usual. "But how are *you* doing, Levi?"

"I'm—" He hadn't quite expected his aunt's direct stare. "I'm fine."

"You're lying," she said. "You just said good-bye to the woman you love, and it's killing you."

Levi swallowed a lump in his throat. He hadn't been eating much either the last few days, and when Aaron pleaded with him to speak to his aunt on his behalf, he'd said no at first. He was so tired, so achingly sad . . . But even if he couldn't have the woman he loved, it didn't mean that Ketura shouldn't have her happiness. So he'd agreed.

Maybe God would look down on this small, well-intentioned deed and reward him by reducing his own pain.

"Yah," he agreed. "But there isn't much else I can do about that. She knows what she needs, and it's a far sight better than I can give."

"No," Ketura said with a shake of her head. "Rosmanda knows what scares her. That's what she's very certain of. She doesn't know what she needs."

"And what does she need?" Levi asked woodenly.

"The man she loves." Ketura shrugged weakly.

"We're on the same mission, Ketura," he said with a small smile. "I invited you here to convince you to take Aaron back."

There was a rustle by the sitting room door, and he and Ketura both looked over at the same time. Aaron took off his hat, rubbed his hand through his hair, and then replaced it. His gaze was locked on Ketura with a look of agony.

"I invited Aaron," Levi said feebly. "I thought you two could talk."

"Levi—" Ketura sighed, but Aaron came into the kitchen and pulled up a chair next to Ketura. He put his hand over hers. The words seemed to evaporate, and she stared at him in mute sadness.

"Don't blame Levi," Aaron said. "I begged him to do it. I had to see you. And I was hoping he'd convince you that I was worth seeing."

"You came in a little soon for that," Levi said, and he started to rise to his feet, but his friend waved him back down. Levi eyed them hesitantly. He'd thought they might want some privacy for this, but Aaron seemed to have other plans.

"I couldn't wait . . ." Aaron swallowed. "And what I have to say is short. I won't belabor this too much. Ketura, I love you."

"And I love you," she whispered. "But—"

"No, I have to say this," Aaron said, cutting her off. "You said Rosmanda knows very well what she fears, but so do you. You're afraid I'll stop loving you as you grow older. You're afraid I'll regret some hasty decision to marry you while you're young enough to look like this—"

"Yah, I am," Ketura said with a teary nod.

"But love and marriage is about trust," Aaron said. "Because I'm scared, too. I'm scared that when people tease you about your young husband, you'll lose respect for *me*."

"You're the best man I know," she breathed.

"And I will love you for the whole of our lives. I'll love you as you age, and I'll be proud to grow older at your side. But you have to trust me, Ketura. Has my love for you wavered these last three years?"

She shook her head mutely.

"Then trust me!" he pleaded. "Trust me to keep on loving you! And I'll trust you to keep on respecting me."

"It's a risk," Ketura said, but a smile had come to her face—a different kind of smile, and Aaron seemed to sense his victory.

"Ketura, let me go to the elders. Let me tell that that we're engaged and we want to get married. Please."

Ketura nodded, and Aaron pulled her into his arms and kissed her. Levi shot his aunt a smile when she looked blearily in his direction.

"Congratulations," Levi said. "Now you can eat again, Auntie."

Ketura wiped her eyes and reached for Aaron's hand. "Am I crazy, Levi? Talk me out of this now, if I am."

"The best things in life are a risk," Levi said. "If you're looking for my blessing, you both have it."

Aaron shot him a grin. "Thank you, Levi. I don't know how I'll repay you, but I'll sure try."

"Then make my aunt eat," he said with a low laugh. "She's getting too thin."

Ketura put a piece of chicken into her mouth, and Aaron picked up a piece of cheese and handed it to her, his gaze locked on her lovingly. Levi watched them, Ketura and Aaron suddenly so rosy in their happiness. Levi had seen what being apart was doing to both of them. They were in love, and while the community meant well, sometimes they were wrong. Life would be hard, but love was surprisingly tough.

"And what about Rosmanda?" Ketura asked, turning toward him.

"She's back home with her mamm and daet," he said.

"And you still can't be with her?" Ketura asked. "You, the believer in love?"

"She saw me at my most vulnerable, and she decided I wasn't worth the risk, Ketura," he said. "I'm not perfect, and I know that. But you need your wife to see the best in you, not the risk."

Ketura licked her lips and was silent for a moment. "She's afraid, Levi."

"Me too."

"She's been through a lot," Ketura said. "She's trying to keep things safe for her daughters."

"I know that, too," he said. "It's okay, Ketura. I'll be fine. Eventually."

"Levi, my sweet, stubborn nephew," Ketura said, her tone firming. "I'm going to be as clear as I possibly can. You meddled in my love life, and now I intend to meddle in yours."

"Okay . . ." Levi looked at her hesitantly.

"Are you ready?" she asked.

"Yah. Go ahead."

"You have to forgive her for being afraid. And you have to forgive her for playing it safe. It's ever so easy to do when you have so much to lose. Yah, she's scared, but that doesn't mean she doesn't see the best in you. It means she's already seen the worst in the world around her. So forgive her, Levi."

"Forgiving her isn't the hard part," he said. "But she saw all of me, and she chose my brother. She knows the worst—"

"She's afraid," Ketura said. "But she won't be afraid forever."

Ketura was looking at him, waiting for an answer, but his heart was thrumming and his head was spinning. She'd made a good point—Rosmanda had seen the worst in the world, and he knew that better now than he had all those years ago when she'd cast him aside. Jonathan had played games with her that continued into the present. But Levi wasn't the same man he used to be, either.

Levi had been so certain that even if she'd have him, he couldn't marry the woman who couldn't see past his weaknesses to love him as he was. But he wasn't the same man he used to be . . . Back then, he'd had his heart broken and turned to drink. Now, he'd faced the worst heartbreak of his life, and he hadn't had a drop to drink, despite the fact that he was a recovering alcoholic. He'd proven something to himself, too—he *was* man enough. And it wasn't about breaking a horse or winning a woman. It was about his own ability to face the worst that life could hand him, and to stay on his feet. Rosmanda might be scared, but he could be absolutely certain that he'd never give her reason to doubt him again.

"Aaron," Levi said, turning to his friend. "Is there any chance I can get that favor from you?"

"Anything," Aaron said.

"Help my daet with the farm for a couple of days. I have something I have to do—"

Aaron and Ketura exchanged a look, and there was a twinkle in Ketura's eyes.

"Is it in Indiana?" Ketura asked.

"Yes, Auntie!" he said, irritated. "It's in Indiana. And Aaron, I also need a ride to the bus station. If I remember right, there should be an overnight bus to Morinville."

Levi knew what he had to do—and it might not change a thing for her, but he had to let Rosmanda know what had changed for him. He'd never be able to live with himself if he didn't. But he wouldn't stay and pester her. He'd say his piece, and then he'd leave, if that was what she wanted.

He loved her, but he wouldn't push himself on her, either.

Maybe, just maybe, she'd see the man in him that he'd longed for her to see all this time—the one who'd stand by her, protect her, and love her for the rest of his life, if only she'd let him.

Chapter Twenty

The next morning, Rosmanda stood at the Yoder door, her shawl wrapped tight around her. The morning was chilly, but Rosmanda could feel some latent warmth in the air. The sun shone warm, and a couple of magpies squabbled from a tree. She wouldn't stay long. She'd come to do the right thing—to make up with Mary, if she could—and she'd been assured that this time of day was safe to make sure that Jonathan wouldn't be home.

Rosmanda hadn't slept well the night before because she felt guilty. No, she hadn't meant to cause trouble in this home—at least not this time—but she did regret the misery Mary had gone through. Mary had deserved better—for her entire marriage, she'd deserved better.

Rosmanda knocked hard, and she could hear the chatter of kinner from inside, and the wail of the baby. It took a moment, but the door opened and Mary stood there, the infant in her arms and three little girls standing behind her to see who this unexpected visitor was.

"Hello," Rosmanda said.

Mary gave her an unfriendly look, then turned toward the children behind her. "Girls, go outside and fetch the eggs."

The girls left, but slowly because they still wanted to see who this visitor was. Mary didn't ask her to come in, and Rosmanda remained on the step, her shawl clutched together in one fist. Her heart sped up just a little bit. She wasn't welcome here, that much was plain—not that she'd expected anything different.

"Why are you here?" Mary asked when the girls had clattered out the side door.

"I need to talk to you," Rosmanda said.

"Then, talk." Mary adjusted the baby in her arms—the infant was fast asleep.

"Mary, I don't want to be your enemy," Rosmanda said.

A boy appeared around the side of the house, and he stopped short, staring at her.

"Come inside," Mary said with a sigh, and when Rosmanda stepped in, Mary shut the door with a firmer hand than necessary. "So you've come to make peace?"

"Yah." Rosmanda shrugged weakly. "Mary, we're in the same community. We can't avoid each other, and we can't go on like this, either."

Mary sighed, but tears misted her eyes, and she pressed her lips together in an attempt to control her emotions.

"Then go back," Mary said. "And leave me and my husband alone."

"I *can't* go back." Rosmanda's voice shook. "My husband is dead, Mary. I was living with his parents, but they can't afford to just keep me like that. And . . . Mary, I had to come home. Where would you go if you lost Jonathan?"

"*If* I lost him?" Mary retorted. "I lost him nine years ago, before our wedding! Yes, we're married. Yes, we have kinner—but he's been mooning after you ever since! But I think you know that, or you wouldn't be here."

"You think I'm here to try and take him," Rosmanda said. "You really think that of me? And what would I do with him, exactly? Run off and go English?"

Mary dropped her gaze, and then shrugged. "I don't know what to think."

Rosmanda felt anger rising up inside of her, but not at Mary. This was rage directed at the man who had made them both miserable.

"If he's been mooning after me—Mary, I was sixteen. Sixteen! I know I felt so very grown up, but I was a girl still. And yes, I acted horribly. I'm so embarrassed about that, even now. I'm sorry for what I did back then. But whatever he felt for me, he was feeling it for a sixteen-year-old."

Mary blinked, and she absently stroked the baby's head with one hand.

"So if he carried that around, he was stupid to do it. I'm sorry to be so blunt or to talk badly about a man, but you have to see that. I'm no longer that sixteen-year-old girl. I'm a grown woman. I've been married, I've buried a husband, and I have kinner of my own to worry about. I'm not the same at all, and I can guarantee you that he saw that when he came out to Abundance."

Mary sucked in a wavering breath. "He did?"

"Look at me!" Rosmanda lifted her hands. "Am I some unspoiled girl? I've given birth to twins! And I'm not quite so easy to sweep off my feet anymore."

"Did he try?"

Rosmanda paused, unsure of what to say. "I'm not sure. Maybe. It didn't go well. I had my brother-in-law to help me with him, so . . ."

Levi . . . dear, sweet Levi with those dark eyes and the boyish grin. She might not be easy to sweep away, but Levi sure managed it. Or maybe she'd swept him. Regardless, thoughts of him still tugged at her heart without any rest. She couldn't just put him aside.

Mary walked into the sitting room and sat down. Rosmanda followed her, accepting it as a grudging invitation to sit, too.

"If I hadn't been pregnant, and I knew about you, I would have called off the wedding," Mary said. "Because he's never been mine."

"That isn't true," Rosmanda retorted. "You'd have given up the man *you* loved because of some teenaged girl? I wasn't old enough to marry, and Jonathan wasn't interested in a lengthy and respectful courtship. So you'd have simply walked away from all those wedding plans?"

"It would have been smart."

"And what woman in love is thinking things through so thoroughly?" Rosmanda shook her head. "Even if you hadn't been pregnant, we'd still be here. And Jonathan would still be yours. The elders would have stepped in regardless, and Jonathan would have seen sense. He had no interest in a chaste and lengthy wait for me. I was . . . young and convenient. He's your husband. He married you before God and the community. He is most certainly yours."

"Is he mine still?" Mary asked curtly. "Running off to check on another woman?"

Rosmanda was silent for a moment, and then she said, "I've been told that marriage is long, and that no season lasts forever. Right now, it might not feel that way, but you have five kinner together. He might be disappointing, but I think—" She swallowed, hoping she wasn't overstepping. "I think he needs you to love him."

"And I haven't?" Mary demanded.

"I think . . . he needs you to forgive him."

"He hasn't said that."

"He mooned after me, you said," Rosmanda said. "And I must have been a disappointment when he found out the woman I grew into. He was lonely. He didn't want me . . . he wanted"—Rosmanda shrugged—"maybe he wants the same thing you want. To be loved. To be understood. To be cherished. Maybe. I don't know."

"Marriage is certainly long," Mary said, her voice tight. "I was a good girl, you know. I did everything right. I was quiet, I worked hard, I did as I was told. And the one mistake I made—with Jonathan—resulted in my eldest."

"It happens," Rosmanda said weakly.

"And I was a good wife," Mary went on. "I continued to work hard, I was supportive, I was loving, I made him look good. I did it all right! And then . . . one day . . . I just had enough. And I'm not such a good wife anymore."

Rosmanda sighed. "You're a woman, Mary."

"What?" Mary blinked at her.

"You're more than a wife, you're a woman. Wives have a job to do, and a woman . . . well, a woman has a breaking point."

Mary smiled faintly. "That is strangely wise."

"Don't be so hard on yourself," Rosmanda said. "Your husband is acting like a fool right now, and fools are hard to suffer."

"Yah, he is," Mary agreed, and she shook her head. "I shouldn't speak of him that way."

"You didn't, I did," Rosmanda said, and then she sobered. "You love him, Mary."

Mary didn't answer. The baby in her arms stretched in her sleep, flinging an arm up over her head.

"I know you do," Rosmanda went on. "Or you wouldn't fight for him like this. He might not deserve it, but you do love him. And you're a good woman, no matter what you say. It will sort out. This won't last forever. With a new baby, things are always a bit hard, aren't they?"

"Seems to be," Mary agreed.

"I won't be any trouble to you," Rosmanda said quietly. "I promise that I will never contact your husband or speak to him. If he comes to me, I will coldly send him away. There will be no friendliness."

"Thank you."

"And Mary, I know you might not forgive me yet, but I am deeply, truly sorry for my adolescent stupidity." Rosmanda swallowed hard. "If I could take it back, I would. And I am not that girl anymore. I will never act that way again as long as I live. And I am so very sorry for what I did to you."

Mary looked over at Rosmanda with tears in her eyes. "I have to forgive you, Rosmanda. I'm a Christian."

Rosmanda nodded quickly. "Thank you." She rose to her feet. "I won't keep you any longer. I'd best get back to my daughters."

Mary stood up, too, and she followed her to the door. The girls returned then, the side door banging open, and Mary looked over her shoulder. The girls were chattering about something—teasing the older one, it sounded like. The baby squirmed again in Mary's arms and let out a hungry-sounding cry.

Any possibility of quiet was past.

"Good-bye," Rosmanda said, and she stepped back outside.

The boy stood in the front yard, and he waved shyly. She smiled back and headed for her buggy. She'd done the right thing, and she felt a little bit better. At least she'd be able to see Mary in church service, or at a sewing circle, and they could be respectful. And she'd stand by her word—she'd have no contact with Jonathan again. He belonged at home, fixing his marriage.

As Rosmanda drove the buggy back toward her parents' farm, her mind was chewing over that conversation with Mary. Mary had done it all right—or nearly all of it. She'd been careful and cautious. She'd worked hard and raised good children. She'd devoted herself to her home and her husband, only to have everything go disastrously wrong.

Had Mary made a mistake in marrying Jonathan? Possibly. Maybe she should have found a man she felt more of a mutual connection with—a man who adored her as much as she adored him. But it wasn't like an Amish community had so many men to choose from. Young people had to travel, sometimes, to find a marriage partner. There weren't always a lot of options.

Rosmanda felt a wave of pity for Mary Yoder. It was possible for a woman to live so cautiously and carefully that she lost everything she longed for. Maybe Jonathan hadn't wanted a perfect housekeeper and mother for his children—maybe he'd just wanted to be understood. It didn't excuse him, but it might explain him. Mary had worked so hard on being good, and she'd lost out on the romance with her husband.

Being good—it was the safe road. It kept a woman from judgment in the community and it was supposed to give her a happy and rewarding life. A good woman could avoid the risks. But what if she never got what she wanted most because she was so carefully avoiding any risk at all?

Rosmanda sucked in a breath of crisp, spring air, her mind spinning. Maybe she wasn't so different from

Mary Yoder, after all. She'd done the same thing—being so careful to be good to make up for her adolescent mistake that she'd given up Levi, the one man she'd loved heart and soul. Would she end up any happier than Mary?

Her daughters needed a strong, Amish father, but they also needed to see their mother loved and cherished. Were the Yoder kids any better off with their parents at odds like this?

"I've made a mistake . . ." she breathed. There was no one to hear her confession, but somehow she needed to say it aloud.

She'd made a horrible mistake, and right now, all she wanted was to feel Levi's strong arms around her, feel his breath against her hair, smell the hay that clung to his clothes . . . Because she loved him. She loved him so much that she ached without him. And while he might be a risk, living without him was going to be agony.

Levi stood by the side kitchen window of the Graber farmhouse, watching for Rosmanda's buggy. She had an errand to run, her mamm had said, and she wouldn't be long. He looked over to see Sarah Graber watching him curiously.

"You love her," Sarah said.

Levi cleared his throat. "I . . . uh—" He wasn't used to confessing his feelings to a woman's mother. "Yah. I do."

"Good." She nodded. "My girl deserves that. But what are you going to do about it? Because if you're here to scramble up her head and then leave again, you'll only make her angry at this point."

And her family would be angry, too, no doubt. "I'm not going to pester her, Sarah. I promise you that."

"Hmm." Sarah didn't look convinced, but she did dish up a piece of apple pie and hand it to him on a plate. "You might as well eat something."

Levi took the plate from her gratefully and took a big bite. He hadn't eaten since dinner last night, and he'd hired an Englisher taxi to drive him out this way without pausing to get breakfast at a diner or something in town. He'd been eager to get here, and he hadn't exactly factored in a wait for Rosmanda to return. He'd had his speech all prepared, and now it seemed to be disintegrating in his head.

"Are you going to propose, then?" Sarah asked after a moment of silence.

He looked over at her, unsure if he could put off the bishop's wife or not.

"Yah," he said at last. "I do intend to propose."

"Hmm." Sarah nodded and her expression betrayed nothing of what she thought of this bit of information.

"I don't know if it will make any difference to her," he added. "And I don't intend to do what Jonathan did and pester her. But, I've realized a couple of things, and I wanted to tell her. Face-to-face."

"What things?" Sarah asked, and she poured a glass of milk and handed it over. "You might as well drink that, too."

He took the milk and drank half of it, eyeing Sarah cautiously. She was watching him expectantly.

"I . . . uh . . ." He smiled uncomfortably. "I realized how much I love her, and that she's got good reason to be careful and cautious. And . . . maybe I shouldn't take that so personally."

Saying it out loud, it didn't sound quite so earthshaking

as it felt inside of him, but it certainly did change things. For him, at least.

"Hmm." Sarah nodded. "You looked down the barrel of a life without her, did you?"

"Yah." He smiled ruefully. "That about sums it up."

Levi heard the clop of hooves and he looked out the window to see the buggy coming down the drive.

"Sarah, if you don't mind, I think I'll go tell that bit to Rosmanda," he said, putting the cup and plate down on the table.

"A good idea," Sarah said, and he thought he saw some humor glimmer in her gaze. "Go on, then."

Levi headed out the side door, his jacket forgotten. He didn't care—he had to say this to the right woman, not her mother. He glanced over his shoulder and saw Sarah in the window. She was smiling this time—a little personal smile that turned up the corners of her lips. Perhaps he'd have her family's blessing, after all.

Rosmanda paled when she saw him, and she reined in the horses. Levi headed over to where she'd stopped and looked up at Rosmanda with the reins in her hands.

"I thought I'd lend a hand," he said. "Help you un-hitch."

"That's why you've come?" she asked breathily.

"No, I came to . . . to see you," he said. "I—" He couldn't do it like this. He held his hand out. "Come down here, would you? A man can't propose from down here."

"Propose?" she whispered.

"Come down here," he repeated. "I'm kissing you first."

Rosmanda took his hand and as soon as her feet were on solid ground, he gathered her up in his arms and covered her lips with his. It felt like coming home—warm and sweet and slow. She melted against him, and when he pulled back, she blinked blearily up into his eyes.

"I love you," he whispered.

"I love you, too, Levi."

"And I know you want to be careful, Rosie. I know I've had a rocky few years, and that probably proves I'm not the kind of guy you can trust, but, you've got to know that even with my heart in tatters and thinking I'd never see you again, I didn't take a drink."

"Levi, that's wonderful," she said.

"I'm not perfect, but I love you more than you know. And I'll be good to you. I'll come home to you. I'll open up to you and be the man you need me to be. I just . . . I was scared, too. You didn't want me when you saw me at my most vulnerable, but that doesn't mean I shouldn't try this again. You know me now as a man—and you've seen me now. So . . . what do you think?"

It hadn't come out exactly right, and she looked up at him in silence for a moment. He tried to remember what he'd just said. It hadn't quite been a proposal, had it?

"I've been thinking, too," she said, her voice low. "I've been so careful after my big scandal at sixteen. I've done everything I could to avoid any more risk. And now with my girls, I wanted to keep them safe, to keep them as far from my bad choices as possible . . . but it's also possible to be so good and to avoid so much risk that you miss out on the one thing you want most—"

"And what do you want?" he whispered.

"You . . ."

"Yah?" He put a hand on her cheek and looked down at her hopefully. "I don't think I actually said the words yet. Rosie, marry me. Please."

Rosmanda nodded, tears welling in her eyes. "Yah."

Had she really just agreed? Levi kissed her again, and this time the feeling of her in his arms felt like the greatest blessing of his life. The thought of marrying Rosmanda, raising the twins with her, having more kinner together, and being the man who got to slide into bed next to her at night made him feel like life couldn't get more beautiful than this.

When he finally broke off the kiss, the side door to the house opened and he turned to see Sarah Graber standing in the doorway, a smile wreathing her face. From inside, he could hear the cry of babies—woken from their nap, perhaps?

"Come inside, then!" Sarah called. "The babies are awake, and if there's an engagement, we have planning to do!"

So it would start—his life with Rosmanda. Rosie hurried ahead of him, and he went into the kitchen to wait on her. When she came downstairs with the babies in her arms, his heart flooded with love. They'd be his . . . and he'd do right by all three of them.

Sarah put a hand on his arm, and he looked over at his soon-to-be mother-in-law.

"You might want to start calling me Mamm," she said. "In private, of course, until we announce your engagement in church."

"Thanks, Mamm," he said, and she pressed him down into a kitchen chair and nudged the plate and cup in front of him again.

"Eat up," she said.

Rosmanda tipped Susanna into his arms, and then sat in the chair next to him. Here in her mamm's kitchen, he couldn't exactly kiss her again like he wanted to, but there would be plenty of time for the leisurely things he wanted to do with her. A whole lifetime.

"I love you," he whispered.

And Sarah pretended not to see, but Rosmanda leaned over and kissed him briefly anyway. He couldn't wait to marry her.

Epilogue

Normally, an engagement was kept secret until the very end of the summer when the banns would be announced in church. But it was hard to keep this secret. Between the four whole rows of celery the Grabers were growing that summer, and all the visits from Levi Lapp, who came a full four times before the actual banns were read, the whole community was unsurprised when they were formally invited to the wedding. But as Sarah Graber said, some weddings required a little more fanfare to keep down the gossip, and every single last stalk of celery was going to be needed for wedding soup that fall, seeing as they were inviting so many people.

When the harvest was done, Levi and Rosmanda were married on a Thursday. The day was sunny and bright, and they were married outside in a field to accommodate all the guests. Stephen and Miriam traveled out for the wedding, and Miriam and Sarah kept the wedding trailer bustling as the women cooked up a feast to feed three sittings of guests.

The party went on late into the evening, and when Rosmanda and Levi retired to Rosmanda's old bedroom in her parents' house, the toddlers were snuggled into the bedroom with their grandparents to give the new couple some privacy. Susanna and Hannah were both walking now, and both slept through the night without any trouble. So much changed in a matter of six months.

Rosmanda sat on the edge of her bed feeling bashful as she looked up at Levi. She knew what to expect from a marriage now, but facing this particular man in her bedroom started butterflies in her stomach. They were married . . . and all that she'd been longing for could finally be hers.

Levi took off his black hat and tossed it onto the dresser, then eased his suspenders off his broad shoulders. He sank onto the bed next to her and leaned back onto one elbow.

"I love you," he said.

"I love you, too . . ." She smiled hesitantly, then licked her lips. She felt nervous now, for some reason. A little anxious.

Levi pushed himself back up and leaned over to cover her lips with his. She let her eyes slide shut, enjoying his kiss. When he pulled back, he reached behind her head and took the pins out of her hair that held her kapp and her bun in place. He removed them one by one, dropping them onto the quilt next to them until her hair fell down around her shoulders. She smiled, then.

"Your hair is for your husband," he said quietly. "Well, now it's for me. Finally."

"It's only proper," she said.

The room was chilly at this time of year, and the cold air from outside crept toward them from the window.

"I'm going to take care of you," Levi said quietly. "I'm going to provide for you and our kinner, and I'm going to be coming to bed with you every single night for the rest of our lives. That's a promise."

"I know, Levi," she said.

"But I need you to hear it," he said. "These are promises on top of those vows we took today, but I want them to count just as much. I'm not going to drink another drop of alcohol, and I'm going to be the man you need, Rosie. Not just the one you want."

"You're the man I love," she said, and she leaned forward to kiss him. His lips were warm and supple in response.

"Come to bed with me," he said, and he stood up, tugging her to her feet, too. He peeled off his shirt, and then whipped back the wedding quilt that she'd been working on so long that summer. It was a tree—but this one was in full summer glory. There were birds in the branches, and different colors of green melding together for the leaves. It represented a fresh start, a new beginning . . . a new marriage.

Levi tugged her down to the bed, and as they pulled that quilt over them on their first night as husband and wife, Rosmanda knew she was safe in Levi's arms and in his heart. But more than safe, she felt the immense blessing of having married the man who filled her heart to overflowing, too.

A happy life wasn't about being a "good wife," it was about being a truly satisfied wife, and her happiness overflowing to her home around her.

"Levi, the lamp," she whispered, and Levi moaned, and she laughed at his frustration. He flung the quilt back again and got up to snuff it out. Darkness descended on the room, and he crawled back into bed next to her once more.

"Good enough?" he asked quietly.

"Yah," she said with a soft laugh. "Perfect."

"Good," he said, pulling her close once more. "Now, where were we?"

This day was the beginning of the biggest risk she'd ever take, but the most satisfying, too. He wasn't the perfect Amish man any more than she was the perfect Amish woman, but he was perfect for her. Maybe he wouldn't be strong in all the ways she was weak. Maybe she'd have to strengthen herself, too. But it was worth it—to belong to each other.

Rosmanda was Levi's wife, and as she melted into his embrace, she knew she was well and truly home in his arms.

Please turn the page for an exciting sneak peek of
Patricia Johns's next Amish romance,

JEB'S WIFE,

coming soon wherever print and eBooks are sold!

"Rebecca's far enough along in her pregnancy that she's showing," Rosmanda said, nudging the plate of shortbread cookies toward Leah. "I'm sorry to be the one to tell you, but you'd notice it on Service Sunday. She's not exactly being modest about it. It's as if she refuses to let her dresses out until the last minute. I'd tell her that it's not proper, but it isn't my place. She'd got a mamm of her own. All I can say is, I'm much further along than she is, and I'm perfectly capable of letting a dress out. And as for my girls, I'll make sure they act with more propriety than that."

Leah forced a weak smile, but she didn't touch the plate of cookies. It wasn't right to be talking behind someone's back—but sometimes an update was necessary so she could smother her natural reaction to seeing her ex-fiancé's new wife. Leah had been gone for eight months while she taught school in another community, and a lot had changed.

"You have a few years yet before you have to worry about your girls," Leah said with a short laugh. "They're only four."

"I'm thinking ahead," Rosmanda replied, but humor didn't glimmer in her eyes. She was serious.

"The thing is, Matthew wanted children," Leah said. "At least he's getting them."

It was the kindest thing Leah could think of to say. Matthew had broken her heart and tossed her aside, then immediately began courting a girl just off her Rumspringa.

"That isn't your fault," Rosmanda said, lowering her voice. "Leah, I don't know why God allowed you to be born with a malformed uterus, but it isn't fair to cast aside a woman because she can't give birth."

"Maybe it is fair." Leah shrugged. "Matthew wanted children—what Amish man doesn't? And I can't give that! So, if he knew what he wanted, and we weren't married yet, he wasn't in the wrong. Technically."

"So he's married himself an eighteen-year-old wife," Rosmanda said, and she shook her head. "I don't mean to degrade her. She's family, after all. Rebecca is beautiful, sweet, and from what my husband says, she's a good cook. But she's *young,* and Matthew is—how old is he now?"

"Twenty-five," Leah replied, her voice tight.

Leah was thirty, and dating a boy five years younger than her had already been a stretch. She'd prayed for a husband since she was a young teenager. And now that she was advancing into her old maid status, she'd thought that Matthew was her answer to prayer—her reward for patient waiting. God rewarded the good girls, didn't He? He worked miracles. He made a way. But her wedding had never happened. He'd dumped her, and she'd accepted a teaching position that would allow her to get out of town and try to heal from the breakup.

"Rebecca's only eighteen . . ." Rosmanda grimaced.

"When you're eighteen you think you're ready to take on marriage and children, but you're not quite so grown-up as you think. She married a man who'd been dating another woman for *three years*. And no one warned her that there would be complicated feelings left between you and Matthew."

"I don't want to hold him back," Leah said. "She has nothing to worry about me."

"I might have wanted to hold *her* back!" Rosmanda retorted. "I've told you about Mary Yoder, haven't I? Many a girl plows ahead with a marriage and lives to regret it. I didn't want that for Rebecca. But she's related to my husband, and I'm just an in-law there."

"Matthew made his choice," Leah replied.

"Did you know that Matthew's been asking about you?" Rosmanda replied. "And spending a whole lot of time with your brother."

"They're good friends," she replied. "They have been for years. And if he still cares what becomes of me, maybe I should be glad that some of his feelings might have been genuine."

Rosmanda sighed. "And I also know you, Leah. I'm not saying Rebecca has anything to worry about you . . . You're a good woman, and he's officially off-limits. But that doesn't mean this will be easy on Rebecca."

And maybe it wouldn't be, but Rebecca had won. She had Matthew as her husband, and she was pregnant with his child. Uncomfortable or not, Rebecca would survive just fine.

The side door opened and four-year-old Hannah came into the kitchen, followed by her twin sister, Susanna. They weren't quite identical twins, but it was close. Hannah had always been just a little bit blonder than her sister, and right now, their dresses were covered in dirt from the garden and their bare feet were brown with soil. Rosmanda heaved a sigh.

"Little girls need to stay clean," Rosmanda said, rising to her feet, her own pregnant belly doming out in front of her as she rose. "We'll have to wash your dresses now, and that's even more work for your mamm!"

"Sorry, Mamm . . ." Hannah wiped her dirty hands down the sides of her dress, and Leah couldn't help but smile. The girls started toward their mother.

"No, no!" Rosmanda said. "Stay right there. I don't need dirty footprints all over the house."

Those girls were a handful, and in a matter of months, Rosmanda would have a new baby to add to the mix.

"I should get back home," Leah said, standing, too. "Thank you for the chat."

Rosmanda grabbed a cloth from the sink and shot Leah an apologetic smile. "So soon? You've hardly eaten a thing."

Leah didn't have much appetite anyway.

"I've got to start dinner for my brother, and I can't be holding you up, either," Leah said. "I'll see you again soon, I'm sure."

Leah smoothed her hand over Hannah's hair as she passed the girl on her way to the door. Kinner . . . she'd never have any babies of her own, and there was a part of her heart that ached when she saw her friends' little girls. This was the goal for an Amish woman—to marry and have a family of her own. Leah hadn't managed to do either of those things, and at the age of thirty, her chance at those domestic joys were past. It was best to admit it and face the truth.

Outside in the warm June sunlight, Rosmanda's husband, Levi, helped Leah hitch up the buggy. Rosmanda and Levi Lapp lived on two acres of land near the town of Abundance and a short buggy ride from the Amish schoolhouse. That would be convenient for them when the girls were old enough to start school. They had family concerns . . . and they were fortunate. Other women were married, having babies, raising kids. And Rebecca was already round with her pregnancy. That mental image was an uncomfortable one, and Rosmanda's warning had been well-meant.

No one had written to tell Leah. That was how pity worked, though. People smiled sadly and kept their mouths shut. Was that the point she was at now—being pitied?

Maybe she was grateful to not have had that thought of Matthew's impending fatherhood the last few months. And maybe she wasn't, because it meant that she was beyond hope in the community's eyes.

When the buggy was hitched and Leah had hoisted herself up onto the seat, Levi gave Leah a friendly wave.

"Thank you, Levi," she said. "It's much appreciated."

"Take care now," he said, giving her a nod, and she flicked the reins and the horse set out for home.

The sun was high and bees droned around the wild-flowers that grew up out of the ditch beside the road. Coming back to Abundance for the summer was more work than teaching in Rimstone. She'd have canning to do to refill their pantry, herbs to dry, a thorough cleaning of their little house to accomplish, too. Her brother, Simon, had been working at an RV manufacturer in town, but he'd been laid off, so his money had dried up. Besides, he was a man, and he only did as much women's work as would keep him fed and clothed in her absence. Finding a wife might be prudent for her brother, except he'd made a name for himself already and the daughters in Abundance stayed clear of him.

Leah felt more responsible for Simon than most. Their parents died in a buggy accident when Leah was sixteen, so she'd skipped her Rumspringa and raised her eight-year-old brother the best she knew how.

Her mind was moving ahead to dinner, though. Simon liked her fried chicken, and this being her second day back in the community after returning from her teaching position in Rimstone, she wanted to make something special they could enjoy together. They'd stopped by the grocery store when her brother picked her up from the bus station, so the cupboards were stocked once more, and she was looking forward to cooking in her own kitchen again. A woman of thirty needed some counter space to call her own.

The horse knew the way home and plodded steadily down the road toward the little house she'd rented on an Amish farm. The horse turned into the drive without any need for her guidance, plodding past the main farmhouse. She looked over at the house, silent and empty at this time of day. But then, the most they ever saw from that house was a kerosene light in the kitchen after dark. Two widowers used to run this farm together—Peter and Jebadiah King. Uncle and nephew. They acted as landlords for the cottage, too, but the older of them had passed away, and now it was just Jebadiah, a scarred and mysterious man, running the farm alone.

Jeb made her uneasy—he always had. He was tall, muscular, and badly scarred from a barn fire. His halting gait was recognizable from a distance, and it always gave her a shudder.

As Leah approached their rented one-story cottage, she

saw a buggy pulled up next to the house. And there was Jeb, reaching up and steadying her brother as he climbed down from the seat.

Simon moved slowly, and he wasn't wearing his hat. Simon looked toward her, and she saw smears of blood under his nose and mashed, bruised skin around one eye. Her heart skipped a beat and then hammered hard to catch up.

"Simon?" she called, and she pulled her buggy up short, tied off the reins, then jumped down. She lifted her skirt to keep it from tangling with her legs as she ran toward him.

"Hey, Sis . . ." Simon grimaced as he took a step toward the house. "It's not as bad as it looks—"

"I find that hard to believe," she said, but her voice didn't sound as firm as she would have liked. "Simon, what happened to you?"

Simon leaned on the larger man, and she turned her attention to her brother's rescuer. Jeb was about forty, and he stood head and shoulders taller than Simon. Burn scars went down one side of his face, then disappeared under his beard. His neck and left arm were scarred, too, and his limp suggested the burns hadn't stopped there. Jeb adjusted his grip on Simon's shoulder.

"Nothing, nothing . . ." Simon murmured. "Don't worry about it. Just a misunderstanding."

"Yah?" Leah looked toward Jeb. "What happened to him? I want the truth."

"I found him like this, walking by the side of the road on my way home from town," Jeb replied, but when he looked down at Simon, his gaze lacked proper sympathy.

"Simon!" Her voice was rising and she couldn't help it. "Who did this?"

"What are you going to do, drag them off by their ears?" her brother muttered. It was a jab at her job as a schoolmistress, but she wasn't amused. She was about to retort when Jeb cut in.

"Who do you owe money to?" Jeb interjected, pinning Simon with a hard stare.

"Some men . . . it's nothing—"

"It's enough to have yourself beaten like a tough steak," Jeb retorted. "So I'm thinking this isn't legal. That leaves gambling and booze, and you don't smell like alcohol."

Leah's gaze whipped between them. Jeb was only voicing what she was already thinking.

Simon grimaced. "It was a sure thing. I thought I'd beat him. I had the perfect hand, and I was so sure he was bluffing. . . ."

Leah took her brother under the other arm and as she and Jeb both helped him into the cottage, she could feel Jeb's wrist brushing against her waist. When they got him inside, he hobbled to a kitchen chair and Leah stepped back. Jeb seemed to fill up more of the small kitchen than both she and Simon combined. Simon winced as he lifted his shirt to inspect his bruised ribs, and Leah went straight for the sink.

"How much do you owe this time?" Leah asked, turning on the water and putting a fresh cloth under the flow.

"How much did you make for teaching?" Simon asked instead.

"Enough to pay my room and board in Rimstone, and keep our rent paid. Not a penny more than that," she retorted. "How much have you got saved?"

Simon didn't answer, and maybe she should have expected that much. Simon didn't save, he spent. Besides, they weren't alone.

"How much do you owe?" she asked instead. This was a more important question, and she wrung out the cloth and came over to where her brother sat. She dabbed at the blood beneath his battered nose. Whoever had done this to him was a monster, and she had to hold back tears as she dabbed at his swollen flesh.

"Fifty thousand," her brother said.

The breath whooshed out of her lungs, and for a moment, the room felt like it was spinning. A strong hand caught her elbow and lowered her into a kitchen chair. She looked up to see Jeb standing over her, his expression granite. But there was something close to sympathy shining in his dark eyes. He pulled his hand away and she sucked in a wavering breath.

"Fifty thousand dollars?" Leah breathed. "Simon, where on earth are we going to get that kind of money?"

Jeb should leave—he knew that. He wanted to leave, in fact. Everything inside of him wanted to bolt for the door and get some space again, but when Leah had blanched like that and just about fainted, he didn't have a whole lot of choice.

He went to the sink and opened two cupboards before he found the glasses. There were a few dishes inside, but not many. Jeb couldn't boast much more in his own cupboards. He and Katie had started out with some proper dishes, but after her death, he and his uncle had broken them one by one through their own clumsiness and he was down to an assorted few.

Jeb grabbed a water glass and filled it from the tap, then returned to the table. Leah was ashen, her lips almost as white as her cheeks, and when he handed her the glass, her gaze fell to his scarred hand with the puckered, stretched skin. She licked her lips uncomfortably. He still wasn't used to this reaction—the revulsion. He placed it on the table next to her and pulled his hand behind his back and out of sight.

He knew what he looked like now—his face was worse than his arm and hand were, and his left leg was probably the worst of all. Kinner stared if they saw him on the road, clinging to their mamms' aprons, and they burst into tears if they were faced with him in an aisle in the farm supply store and didn't have an easy escape.

"Thank you," Leah said, a beat too late.

Jeb didn't answer.

His hip ached, and the skin on his arm was so tight that he couldn't fully extend it. He'd worked on that alone in his room, pushing past the point of comfort, grunting with pain—but something had happened to the tendons in that fire and they'd shrunk. He wasn't going to be the man he was before ever again.

Simon sat at the table and wiped blood from his nose on the back of one hand. He might be beaten up, but he'd heal up all right. Jeb's damage was more permanent . . . and he dared to say, it went deeper. He'd lost his wife and his naïve optimism all in one tragic accident. He'd gained both these scars and his freedom from a marriage to a woman who loathed him. . . .

And he hated that he was relieved.

"We'll figure out the money," Simon said to his sister. "We always do."

"You mean *I* always do!" Leah's voice shook, and Jeb looked over at Leah. Her color hadn't come back yet, and she looked exhausted.

Jeb took the cloth from her fingers and he turned to

Simon. The younger man's gaze jerked up in surprise, but Jeb put a solid hand on his shoulder to keep him put, and carefully wiped the blood and dust from his face.

When Jeb had seen Simon stumbling down the road, his hat missing and blood dribbling from his face, he'd felt about how Leah looked right now. This was bad—and if whoever he owed was willing to give this kind of message, it wouldn't stop, either. But what could he do? He'd pulled his buggy to a stop and helped Simon up onto the seat. There would be blood splats Jeb would have to hose off his buggy floorboards before the day was out.

But there was no confusion as to what had happened . . . and fifty thousand dollars wouldn't be easy to come by.

Jeb finished wiping off Simon's face, then he crossed his arms, looking the young man up and down. "Your leg—what happened there?"

"It's my knee," Simon said. "It'll be okay—"

It very likely required a hospital visit, but that cost money, too. Jeb sighed, then crouched down in front of Simon and gently felt the joint in question. There was a fair amount of swelling, but nothing felt broken or dislocated.

"Who did this?" Jeb asked, his voice low.

Simon didn't answer, and Jeb's anger started to rise. This was no game, and the idiot might end up dead in a ditch next time if he kept trying to play with whatever Englisher crooks he was associating with.

"This was no random attack, Simon," Jeb said, and he rose to his feet. "So who did this? And who do you owe?"

"Just some people. I'll get them the money—"

"How?" Jeb demanded. "You're going to make your sister come up with it?"

Leah cleared her throat. "It's okay, Jeb. My brother and I will discuss it."

He doubted that she had it. A man leaning on a woman like that—it put a bad taste in his mouth.

"You should go talk to the bishop," Jeb said. "Maybe the community can step in—"

"They've already threatened to shun me," Simon said, his words slurring past his swollen mouth. "We're not going to the bishop."

Leah looked away, and her expression was grim. She was a woman very much on her own—single, and trying to fix problems too big for any solitary person. He might like his privacy, but there were times when a community could be of help. He wasn't blind to that.

"You just inherited this farm, didn't you?" Simon asked after a beat of silence. "Your uncle Peter just passed, and you were named heir. I know that."

Leah looked over at Jeb in surprise, and he felt the heat hit his face. That was private business, and he preferred to keep it that way. But apparently word was out. He had his own problems at the moment—namely, finding a new home.

"Yah, I was named heir, but there are a few complications there," Jeb replied. "Peter stipulated that I had to be married within four weeks of his passing in order for me to inherit, so my cousin Menno will get this land."

It had been a cruel stipulation, because Peter knew exactly why Jeb wouldn't remarry after his wife's death, free or not.

"Do you have any savings?" Simon pressed.

"Simon, stop that!" Leah seemed to be getting her color back. "I'm sorry about your uncle, Jeb. And I'm sorry for how callous Simon is being. My brother isn't himself right now—"

"Yah, I know," Jeb said.

"I did hear about the funeral," Leah added. "And I was going to send a letter of condolences, but—"

No, she hadn't been. That was a lie that he was willing to forgive.

"It's fine," he said, and he headed to the sink to rinse out the cloth. "The funeral was very nice. The community did well by him."

"God rest his soul," she murmured.

"God rest his soul," he echoed, then wrung out the cloth and tossed it toward Simon. "Put that under your nose." Then he turned to Leah. "If I were you, I'd bandage up his knee nice and tight. I got kicked hard by a horse once, and that's what helped most. Do you have any steak in the house?"

Leah shrugged weakly. "I've got an old sheet to use for bandages, but no steak at the moment."

"I have one in the icebox at home. It was going to be my supper, but you can have it for his face."

It was something. Someone had to help her. Simon had some of Jeb's sympathy for the pain he was in right now, but he'd brought that punishment on himself, the young fool. But Leah was caught in the middle, and she was doing her best to provide for herself without a husband.

"I'll bring you some dinner," Leah said. "And then you won't go hungry. If that's okay with you."

"Yah. A fair trade," he agreed. "Thank you."

A woman's cooking . . . it had been a very long time since he'd had some.

Simon adjusted himself in his chair, leaning forward as he nursed his nose. Leah looked uncomfortable, her gaze flickering toward Jeb uncertainly. Right. He wasn't exactly welcome here.

"I should go," Jeb said and he turned toward the door. Leah stood up and followed him.

"Jeb—" she started, and he glanced back. She closed the distance between them, tipping her face up to look him in the eye. He saw her slight recoil as her gaze moved over those scars. "What do you know about what my brother has been up to?"

Jeb glanced back at the young man. He wasn't about to keep his secrets, and if Simon hated him for it, so be it.

"He's been gambling with some dangerous Englishers," Jeb said. "They do this kind of thing when a man hasn't paid up. I can only imagine how long that debt has been growing." Jeb rubbed his good hand over his beard. "I saw him with a black eye and a sprained wrist once, and another time with a bloody nose. So this isn't the first time he's been beaten up."

"And no one thought to tell me," she breathed.

"He's an adult."

"He's my brother!" she snapped, but her chin quivered. Was she angry at him for not writing to tell her? As if staying in communication with his late uncle's renters was his responsibility.

Jeb had bigger problems.

"Really?" was all he said.

She licked her lips. "If you could maybe keep me informed of what he's up to—" she started, but the words evaporated on her lips when she saw his face. Were his feelings about her brother that obvious? Or was it just the scarring that stopped her like that?

"I won't be here," he reminded her. "Menno will inherit this land, remember? I'm sure my cousin will be happy to keep you on as renters. It's income, right? So if you want someone to keep an eye on him, you'd have to talk to Menno."

Leah nodded, and tears misted her eyes. Blast. It wasn't just a beautiful woman crying that softened him like this, it was this particular woman. Life hadn't been easy for her, either. There were some people who got left out when it came to marriage, and he could sympathize. Although it might be a blessing in disguise.

"I'm sorry," he added feebly. "If there was something I could do, I would."

Jeb pulled open the door and stepped outside. He couldn't stay here. He had work to do, a farm to run on his own for the time being, and getting emotionally involved in other people's problems wasn't good for him. The community might be a great support for others, but it hadn't ever been for him.

"If I came by at six, would you be at the house?" Leah asked.

"Yah. I can do that."

"I'll bring some fried chicken, in exchange for that steak."

Jeb nodded his agreement, then headed toward his buggy, the horse waiting patiently. Chicken in exchange for steak . . . Except an idea had started to form that just might be the solution to both of their problems. She needed money, and he needed a legal wife in order to collect on that inheritance.

He glanced back and saw her standing at the door, her dark eyes fixed on him with a worried expression.

Leah was beautiful, and he was scarred. She was ten years younger than him, and far less emotionally damaged than he was. But she'd been left over in the marriage market, and she needed money.

He could get that money, if he inherited the land under his boots.

Was this as crazy as it sounded?

Books by Bestselling Author
Fern Michaels